MORE MISCHIEF

*Also by Kate Thompson and published by
Bantam Books*

IT MEANS MISCHIEF

MORE MISCHIEF

Kate Thompson

BANTAM BOOKS

LONDON · NEW YORK · TORONTO · SYDNEY · AUCKLAND

MORE MISCHIEF
A BANTAM BOOK: 0 553 81246 7

First publication in Great Britain

PRINTING HISTORY
Bantam Books edition published 2000

Copyright © Kate Thompson 1999

1 3 5 7 9 10 8 6 4 2

Set in 11/13pt Baskerville by
Phoenix Typesetting, Ilkley, West Yorkshire

Bantam Books are published by Transworld Publishers,
61–63 Uxbridge Road, London W5 5SA,
a division of The Random House Group Ltd,
in Australia by Random House Australia (Pty) Ltd,
20 Alfred Street, Milsons Point, Sydney, NSW 2061, Australia,
in New Zealand by Random House New Zealand Ltd,
18 Poland Road, Glenfield, Auckland 10, New Zealand
and in South Africa by Random House (Pty) Ltd,
Endulini, 5a Jubilee Road, Parktown 2193, South Africa.

Printed and bound in Great Britain by
Mackays of Chatham plc, Chatham, Kent

Acknowledgements

Enormous thank yous are due to (in alphabetical order or as near as dammit): Ashford Castle, the Clarence Hotel, the Great Southern Hotel in Galway and Quay Cottage for the gorgeous locations; Lucy Bennett for finding Deirdre; Castlebar General Hospital for reassuring me that I'd got it right; Tommy Cleary and Declan Collier for the phone calls, and Eileen Cleary for keeping me sane; Siobhan Collins for the dates; Hazel Douglas for the view; Enya Egan for letting me see round her office; James Hickey for allowing me to pick his brains; Edwin Higel for the encouragement; Pauline Hutton for not wanting to put it down; Marian Keyes for sharing her savvy; Romilly Larken for the cottage; Francesca Liversidge for being so clever; Felicity Rubinstein, Susannah Godman and especially Sarah Lutyens for handling all the real life stuff; Sadie Mayne for the detective work; Fiona O'Brien for the girly stuff; Monica Frawley, Maureen McGlynn and Frances O'Rourke for their positivity after seeing sneak previews; Padraig Murray and my father, Desmond Thompson, for the architectural advice; Deirdre Purcell for showing me how to do it; Vincent Woods for his extraordinarily generous contribution to the Dantë cantos; and my husband Malcolm and my daughter Clara for being the real stars of the show.

Acknowledgements

Enormous thank yous are due to (in alphabetical order or as near as dammit): Ashford Castle, the Clarence Hotel, the Great Southern Hotel in Galway and Quay Cottage for the gorgeous locations; Lucy Bennett for finding Deirdre; Castlebar General Hospital for reassuring me that I'd got it right; Tommy Cleary and Declan Collier for the phone calls, and Eileen Cleary for keeping me sane; Siobhan Collins for the dates; Hazel Douglas for the view; Enya Egan for letting me see round her office; James Hickey for allowing me to pick his brains; Edwin Higel for the encouragement; Pauline Hutton for not wanting to put it down; Marian Keyes for sharing her savvy; Romilly Larken for the cottage; Francesca Liversidge for being so clever; Felicity Rubinstein, Susannah Godman and especially Sarah Lutyens for handling all the real life stuff; Sadie Mayne for the detective work; Fiona O'Brien for the girly stuff; Monica Frawley, Maureen McGlynn and Frances O'Rourke for their positivity after seeing sneak previews; Padraig Murray and my father, Desmond Thompson, for the architectural advice; Deirdre Purcell for showing me how to do it; Vincent Woods for his extraordinarily generous contribution to the Dantë cantos; and my husband Malcolm and my daughter Clara for being the real stars of the show.

Chapter One

On the morning of her twenty-fifth birthday, Deirdre O'Dare received nine birthday cards, a small parcel, and a postcard from Montana, USA. The cards were from friends; the parcel – which contained a wisp of hand-painted silk chiffon and a book on the history of soap opera – was from her parents, and the postcard was from her on-off boyfriend, Rory McDonagh. There was no mention of her birthday on the postcard, which had a picture on the front of a horse racing through a desert. All it said on the back – in block capitals – was, WILD WEST . . . Love R. XXX. It was the first communication she'd had from him in weeks. Bastard. Deirdre arranged the birthday cards on her mantelpiece, tied the chiffon in her hair, and dumped the postcard in the bin. Then she made coffee, did her face, went down to the front entrance of the Georgian building where she had her flat, and pumped up her bicycle tyres.

When she opened the front door to wheel her bicycle through, she found herself face to face with a spectacular arrangement of white roses. Behind the roses was a delivery man, and behind the delivery man was an Interflora van with its engine still running.

'Howrya, love,' he said. 'Answer me this. Does someone by the name of Deirdre O'Dare live here?'

'Yes,' she said. 'That's me.'

'Well,' said the delivery man. 'These are for you, so.' He winked at her. 'You must be someone's brown-eyed girl, to quote Van the Man. I'd say there's near forty there altogether.'

She gathered the flowers in her arms. He had sent her favourite Vendella roses. 'Wow,' she said. 'Thanks. I suppose I'd better put them in water right away. They're beautiful.' The word was inadequate, she realized, as she ran back upstairs with the bouquet, tearing off the attached note. It read: *Happy birthday. I find I'm obliged to take some time off from this epic. Brace yourself for a flying visit and look out that Agent Provocateur underwear. R.*

She put the roses in a vase, tweaked at them rather ineffectually and then stood back to admire them. They floated on their long, elegant stems like ethereal meringues. Bastard, bastard, bastard, she thought. Bloody beautiful bastard. Bloody beautiful, generous, incorrigible *bastard.* Then she went back into the kitchen, took the postcard out of the bin, wiped coffee dregs off it, and slid it carefully between the pages of her diary. As she left her flat she found herself wondering when his time off was due to happen. She was a little mortified by the flutter of anticipation the thought produced in her.

Deirdre had allowed herself plenty of time to get to work for a change. It was going to be a busy morning for her. She had a voice-over assignment to get out of the way before getting back on her bike to cycle to the television studio where she worked almost full-time. Three years ago she had landed a plum role in RTE's weekly soap opera, *Ardmore Grove.* It was a seasonal soap which put out forty episodes a year, and Deirdre had notched up at least twenty each season, which wasn't a bad quota for a freelance actress. Amber, the character she played, had been involved in most of the more sensational storylines, and had inspired copy for numerous tabloid hacks. 'Sizzling' was the most common adjective used to describe her on-screen exploits, closely followed by 'steamy' and, in third place, 'troubled'. Poor Amber was constantly confronting disaster in her life. Sometimes Deirdre wondered if she hadn't been typecast.

It was raining now as she cycled through central Dublin gridlock, but she didn't mind getting wet. It was better than being stuck in a car listening to *Time-saver Traffic* and fuming over the fact that you should have taken the South Circular instead of going via the canal. She wove in and out of the traffic, pedalling fast. She was determined to reach the recording studio in Herbert Street as quickly as possible – not just to get out of the rain, but because she knew it was important to be punctual. Studio time cost the client money, and she was anxious to please this client. When she had first recorded a commercial for Heeney Holidays last autumn, the producer of the ad had professed himself so taken with her voice that he'd suggested an exclusivity deal to the client. Her agent had negotiated a deal which guaranteed her voice-over work with Heeney Holidays for a year, providing she did the honourable thing and turned down commercial work for any other holiday companies that might approach her. However, since that first session the style of the ads had changed dramatically. The new ones were a much harder sell – full of stresses and exclamation marks and over-the-top adjectives. She'd been hired originally to do a soft sell, and she knew her voice wasn't really right for these brasher commercials.

The previous day, when she'd been approached about the nine a.m. recording session, she'd hesitated. It was going to mean that getting to RTE for the usual nine-thirty rehearsal call would be impossible. But the advertising agency had told her that they needed the recordings by lunchtime today, and it was incumbent on her to be as accommodating as possible. Exclusivity meant a lot. The *Ardmore Grove* stage manager had been a sweetheart when she'd asked him about fitting in with her timing. 'You sneak in as near to ten as you can,' he'd said. 'Your scenes aren't scheduled to be rehearsed until around a quarter-past. Promise me you won't be any later, or you'll banjax the running order.'

She'd promised.

She arrived at the recording studio with five minutes to spare. She padlocked her bike to the railings outside, ostentatiously ignoring an appreciative comment from a passing courier as she bent over the front wheel. Then she raced up the steps to the front door of the studio and rang the bell, shaking droplets of water from her hair. When the buzzer sounded she pushed open the door and dived in, out of the rain.

'Hi,' she said to the receptionist, who was scanning a desk diary with sleepy eyes.

'Oh – hi, Deirdre.' The girl got to her feet, yawning. 'Coffee?'

'It's made already? You're on the ball this morning, Emer.'

'Not really. Just thought I should have everything organized well in advance for the client from hell.'

Deirdre looked aghast. 'Oh no, Emer! The *client's* not going to be here?'

' 'Fraid so. We're talking too many cooks, this morning.'

Deirdre bit her lip. She knew that when the client sat in on a recording session, the gig took twice as long. Janine Heeney always came up with what she considered to be much better ideas than the experts from the agency whom she'd hired to make the commercial, and would insist not only on rewriting the script, but also on making Deirdre try hundreds of alternative ways of reading it. When the studio door finally shut on her, the 'creatives' would be tearing their hair out and screaming for a shot of whiskey.

'Hell,' said Deirdre. 'I've to be in RTE at ten-fifteen.'

'Can't you ring them and say you're running a bit late?'

'I've already called in a favour. I'll be toast if I'm any later. How long is the studio booked for?'

Emer checked the diary. 'Two hours.'

'Two hours? Shit! It shouldn't take anywhere *near* two hours. Ben faxed me the scripts yesterday evening. It's dead straightforward, Emer.'

'Yeah, but as soon as they knew Janine was showing up they booked an extra hour's studio time.'

Deirdre sat down on the big velour-upholstered couch in an attitude of despair. She looked at her watch. It was precisely nine o'clock. The doorbell sounded, and she and Emer exchanged looks of stoical resignation.

*   *   *

'Get her to do it again with more stress on the word "amazing".'

It was nearly ten o'clock. Deirdre was starting to sweat.

'Deirdre?' came a voice in her headphones. 'Janine would like you to try another read with a little more stress on the word "amazing".'

'Sure.' Deirdre tried to sound bright and obliging. Her sense of rising panic made it very difficult. She had spent the past half-hour tearing paper tissues to shreds, keeping her hands hidden under the table so

14

that the client wouldn't notice her obvious distress. She knew if she didn't do something with her hands, the distress would start to show in her voice, and that would be disastrous.

The sound engineer and the people from the agency had been models of diplomacy. They'd taken on board the least outrageous of the client's ideas for 'improvements' to the script, toned down her more OTT suggestions, and experimented with at least half a dozen backing tracks before they came up with one that met with Janine Heeney's approval.

Deirdre cleared her throat for the umpteenth time that morning and waited for her cue from the sound engineer. She caught his look of sympathy as their eyes met, and the lush strains of the Hawaiian backing track swept into her ears.

'Tired of the treadmill?' she began. 'Weary of the weather? Sick of your schedule and ready for a rest? Don't let that dream holiday slip through your fingers! We at *Heeney*'s guarantee *amazing* savings on our summer holiday deals – but don't delay! Take advantage of these *staggering* summer savings now – it's *never* too early to book your place in the sun! Check out our fabulous full-colour brochure. You'll be *amazed* at our deals – they're not just incredible – they're *unbelievable*! Whether it's night-life, shopping and *craic* you're after, adventure or sporting activities, or simply sun, sea and sand – whatever you want, you'll find it – between the covers of a *Heeney Holidays* brochure!'

She sat back in her chair and drew breath. There

were so many words to get through that she'd had to take the read at a bit of a lick. 'How was that for time?' she asked.

'Bang on thirty seconds,' said the sound engineer.

Deirdre shot a look of polite enquiry in Janine Heeney's direction. The mastermind behind the Heeney Holidays advertising campaign was sitting on the big black couch in the control room with her legs crossed and her arms stretched out along the leather back. One smartly court-shod foot was jerking rhythmically to and fro, and the high-gloss Lycra tights stretched around her calves made Deirdre think of shiny, uncooked sausages. She transferred her attention to Janine's face. Glinting basilisk eyes looked out from the carefully applied mask of her make-up: her mouth was a thin red trap, and her earrings were the kind of clip-on flying saucers Deirdre despised.

'It sounded a bit rushed to me.' Janine's voice came through her cans. 'Get her to do it again, only in a more *languorous* kind of way. Can she hear me?'

'Yes, I can.' Deirdre snuck another peek at her watch, and then looked up again to meet Janine's supercilious gaze through the glass panel of the recording booth.

'You see, Deirdre – we're talking about *holidays* here. We're talking about escaping from the stresses and strains of ordinary life and *relaxing* – do you know what I mean?'

Deirdre could relate to that. 'Yes, I do,' she said.

'So could you take it a bit easier, please? We're

not going on our holidays on an *express* train, you know.'

Deirdre gritted her teeth and forced a laugh. 'I've gottcha, Janine,' she said. 'But it's difficult to get through the script without sounding a little pacy. There are a lot of words to get through. Do you think we might cut some of the copy? Then I could manage a more laid-back delivery.'

'What do you think, Janine?' The agency copywriter looked from Deirdre to the client. 'Deirdre has a point, you know. There's a lot to get through in thirty seconds – it can't help sounding a bit rushed. I know you're keen on keeping the superlatives, but are they all strictly necessary? Those two adjectives you suggested – unbelievable and incredible – are – um – well, they're actually tautological, you know. Maybe we could lose that particular line? Then we'd have plenty of time.'

Deirdre could tell by Janine's face that she didn't have a clue what the word 'tautological' meant.

'No,' Janine said dogmatically. 'Every word is important. It just needs an *air* of relaxation. Can't you make your voice sound more relaxed? It's your job, after all.'

'Sure.' Deirdre would agree to anything at this stage just to get out of there. 'I'll give it a go.'

* * *

'I think Deirdre's a bit pressed for time, Janine,' said the sound engineer after ten more takes.

Deirdre was nearly crying. It was now half past ten. She was in deep shit.

'She's *paid* to be here, isn't she?' came the terse response. 'We'll just have to carry on until she gets it right. Let me hear that last one again.'

The Hawaiian music started again. 'Tired of the treadmill?' Deirdre heard herself say for the hundredth time that morning. 'Weary of the weather? Sick of your schedule and ready for a rest?' *Yes, yes, yes!* screamed a voice in her head. *The answer's yes to all those questions!*

The Hawaiian music came to its pingy end and a silence fell. The faces of all the participants of this charade looked grey, apart from Janine's. She was wearing a thoughtful expression. 'You know, Ben – maybe you're right about that line. Maybe "unbelievable" and "incredible" is just a *teeny* bit tautological – although I don't think most people would have enough cop-on to notice it, really. But maybe it's a good idea to have a listen back to one of the earlier reads.'

'How far back are you talking, Janine?'

'Oh – back to a read which didn't include that tautological line.'

'But you put that line in at the third read, Janine – right back at the beginning of the session,' said Ben. Deirdre could tell that he was trying hard to keep the edge out of his voice.

'Yes – I know I did.' There wasn't a trace of apology in her tone. 'We'll go back to the first two, shall we? And see if they're a bit more relaxed-sounding?'

18

It was obvious from Ben's demeanour that he wanted to turn round to Janine Heeney and bash her skull in. 'OK, Simon,' he said to the sound engineer. 'Let's listen back to takes one and two.'

Simon complied. The secret language of looks between him, Deirdre, Ben and the producer was becoming more meaningful with malevolence towards Ms Janine Heeney by the second.

'Tired of the treadmill?' they heard again. 'Weary of the weather? Sick of your schedule and ready for a rest? Don't let that dream holiday slip through your fingers! We at *Heeney*'s . . . blah blah blah . . .' Deirdre couldn't listen any more. She could have been talking ancient Egyptian as far as she was concerned.

'Mm,' said Janine, after a beat. 'That's not bad. It's certainly more relaxed, isn't it? Let's have a listen to number two.'

The second take was played back. 'That's the one!' said Janine brightly. 'Good work, everybody! It's a wrap. Isn't that how they put it in television parlance, Deirdre?' She contorted her face into what was presumably an attempt at a sunny smile.

Deirdre wondered how Janine Heeney could be so apparently oblivious to the fact that every single person in that studio wanted to see her dead. She tore the cans off her head, grabbed her backpack, and swung through the door of the recording booth, resisting the impulse to aim a sharp kick at Janine's shiny shin.

'Gotta dash,' she muttered. There was no time for pleasantries.

'Deirdre – you need to fill out your paperwork!' The agency producer waved a form at her.

'Oh, hell, Matthew – could you just stick it in the post for me?'

He sensed her urgency. 'Sure. Good luck. And Deirdre?'

She turned to him as she went to open the studio door. 'Yes?'

'Thanks.' She knew it came from the heart.

*　　*　　*

Outside it was raining even harder. It was at least a three-mile cycle to RTE – she was going to be unforgivably late. She leapt onto her bike and cycled in the direction of the dual carriageway like someone in the *Tour de France*, cursing a coach that lumbered round a corner and stymied her progress for a good quarter of a mile. The tourists were peering out through rain-spattered windows at a grey Dublin, looking as glum as Deirdre felt.

She wondered how advanced the technical rehearsal would be. Technical rehearsals were more for the benefit of the crew than the actors, and were therefore deemed to be considerably more important. The scenes to be rehearsed today were all exteriors scheduled to be recorded tomorrow. It would more than likely be raining again, and Deirdre hated the raincoat that had been allocated to her by wardrobe. Amber was not just 'troubled', she was also seriously challenged in the sartorial department.

It had been a miserable winter weather-wise, which had done nothing to improve the spirits of cast and crew who had to hang around locations on grey days, getting soaked through. Deirdre had been nursing a cold since the beginning of January. *Weary of the weather?* she intoned as she cycled through Donnybrook. *Sick of your schedule and ready for a rest?* Oh yes, indeed. But the end of the current series was more than two months away. She still had eight more episodes to get in the can before the end of March. And she wouldn't be able to think about taking a holiday – not even a Heeney one – until she knew what sort of involvement she'd have in the next season. If they decided to cut back on her episodes she'd be financially stymied.

It was nearly eleven o'clock when Deirdre cycled past the main studio block of the television station. She padlocked her bike outside the sound stage and headed straight for the Ladies. She desperately needed to go to the loo before the confrontation that was waiting for her. She was so late already that another few minutes wouldn't make any difference.

As she sat on the loo, she heard the door to the Ladies open and someone come in. Two people.

'Anyway, that's what my agent told me.'

'I thought it had been cast already?'

Actresses.

'No. It's a shame I'm not available.'

'I might give them a ring.' There was the sound of a zipper, and then Deirdre heard fishing-in-handbag noises. 'Nice lipstick, Sophie.'

'Mac.'

Sophie Burke. The most temperamental actress on the soap since Ann Fitzroy's departure after a nervous breakdown three years ago. She had been cast as a kind of replacement for Ann Fitz – albeit a much younger one. The character she played – Fran, the hard-nosed rich bitch – was one the soap opera audience loved to hate. It had crossed Deirdre's mind on more than one occasion that Sophie was perfectly typecast.

There was a beat. Then Sophie's voice came again.

'Oh, Cressida! I nearly forgot a wonderful piece of gossip. You know I was in LA a couple of weeks ago?'

Everyone knew that Sophie had spent time in LA recently. She'd talked about nothing else all last week. But Cressida McCormack hadn't been in last week's episode. 'No, I didn't,' she said. 'Business or pleasure?'

'A bit of both,' came the urbane response. 'Anyway. Guess who I ran into?'

'Who?'

'Deirdre O'Dare's significant other.'

'Rory! How is he?'

Deirdre had finished on the loo, but she remained sitting there. She wasn't going to let an opportunity of eavesdropping on Sophie slip her by, especially when the topic of conversation happened to be the man who'd sent her forty Vendella roses that morning.

'Having a ball. Working on the new Cameron movie—'

'Wow!'

'Yeah. Nice cameo. A couple of months' commitment with lots of time out. He was heading off to Montana when I ran into him. I've some interesting photographs. Have a look.' More rummaging-in-handbag noises.

After a minute Cressida said, 'Great photographs, Sophie.'

'Pentax Espio.'

'Sorry?'

'Top of the range camera.'

'Christ, McDonagh looks so *sexy*, doesn't he?' Cressida gave a little laugh.

Sophie made an unimpressed noise. 'He's never done anything for me.' Deirdre was having difficulty in containing the extremely obvious bitchy comment which sprang to mind.

Then Cressida's voice came again: 'Uh-oh. Who's the babe?'

Her intake of breath was almost audible.

'Some chick who's working on the flick with him. She couldn't keep her hands off. Followed him to Montana.'

'Don't blame her. Shit. You caught McDonagh off guard there, Sophie. If he'd known you were wielding a camera he'd have demanded the film back, sure as hell. You'd better not let Deirdre see these.'

'Might wise her up a bit.' Deirdre dug the nails of her right hand hard into the palm of her left. 'Where the hell has she got to this morning, anyway? I'd have been finished ages ago if it hadn't been for her. I've been hanging around for the past hour waiting to rehearse our street scenes.'

'She said something about a voice-over. It must have run overtime. Here – take your photographs, Sophie. Might be best not to show them around.'

Deirdre heard the hiss of a perfume spray and then a click as the lid was replaced. Gucci's Envy came wafting over the cubicle door. 'Right,' said Sophie. 'I'm not hanging about in studio any more. Frank can bloody well come and get me in the canteen when Ms O'Dare finally deigns to roll up.'

There came the noise of the door opening and closing behind the pair of actresses. Their voices faded as they disappeared down the corridor.

Deirdre remained sitting on the loo, stiff with shock. So Rory was shagging some babe in LA, and she had to find out second-hand from a first-class gossip. This was it. She'd eat his fucking Vendella roses before she'd take him back this time, thorns and all.

Thorns and all. That wasn't a bad way of describing their relationship, she thought with bitter irony. They'd gone through a few thorny patches in the three and a half years they'd been together. In fact, the very first one had occurred during the first

24

theatre production they'd ever worked on together, *A Midsummer Night's Dream.* They'd been cast as warring lovers in that, but like the lovers in the play they always managed to sort things out. The cold wars they sometimes waged just didn't suit their temperaments; their blood was too hot to maintain duellists' sang-froid for long, and they'd suddenly find themselves back in bed together without really knowing how they'd got there. Their physical rapport was so powerful that Deirdre still experienced a sexual *frisson* whenever she cast her mind back to the first time they'd come together – in the best possible sense of the word.

So, until now, getting back together had been axiomatic. Rory had used that adjective to describe their predicament once. It had been on an afternoon when they'd accidentally bumped into each other at the Octagon bar in the Clarence Hotel, and had found themselves booking into a room within the hour. When she'd asked him what it meant he'd just breathed the word into her ear over and over again as he made her come, and afterwards he'd told her to use her loaf and look it up in the dictionary. 'According to established principle' was what it meant, according to the *Concise Oxford.* But the situation in which she now found herself wasn't axiomatic – it was intolerable. This had to be the straw that would finally break their beautiful beast with two backs.

Deirdre finally hauled herself to her feet and slid back the bolt on the cubicle door, numbly assessing the situation. She couldn't go out onto the studio floor now, knowing what she did. She couldn't bear the thought that every single actress in the building would know that Rory had treated her like a piece of shit. Cressida had obviously been the last to be told. Everyone else would have been in the know since last week.

She turned on the tap and, cupping her hands, bent over the basin and splashed cold water onto her face, over and over again. She didn't care if she smudged her mascara. She needed something to wake her out of her shocked state. Straightening up, she regarded her reflection in the mirror above the basin. She looked awful – pallid and pathetic, like some kind of freakish cartoon character. This person looking out at her was nothing like the description she'd read of herself in a recent interview she'd given to a women's magazine: *Troubled and beleaguered Amber bears little resemblance to her off-screen persona. In real life Deirdre O'Dare has wicked hazel eyes, a smiling, very kissable mouth and a tumbling* coiffure *so glossy any red-blooded heterosexual crimper would ache to lay his hands on it* . . . What a load of crap. In real life Deirdre O'Dare had eyes like a panda, chapped lips and a *coiffure* so straggly any red-blooded heterosexual crimper would ache to cut it off. She splashed her face again and waited for the cold water to have some impact on her brain. Slowly it started to function again.

There was nothing to do except pretend that nothing had happened. She'd never heard that conversation between Cressida McCormack and

Sophie Burke. Hell's bells – people who didn't have better things to talk about than other people's private lives had to be pretty sad individuals. What a prime example of ethical lowlife Sophie was! What a snake. What a sneaky, slimy, gossipy little underhand hell-hag. Deirdre O'Dare couldn't let a reptile like Sophie bring her down. She'd rise above it. Who was it who had said, 'There is only one thing in the world worse than being talked about, and that is not being talked about'? Oscar Wilde. The ultimate sophisticate. She could do it: she could do sophistication. She'd swan into studio looking carefree and unconcerned . . .

No, she wouldn't. She had to go and eat crow. She had to go and beg forgiveness from Frank the stage manager for being late and messing up the technical rehearsal. She'd have to apologize to the director and the entire crew and all the cast members who had scenes scheduled with her. She looked at herself in the mirror and made a face at the bedraggled creature looking back at her. Scrunching her hair with her fingers in a vain attempt to put some life back into it, she took a shuddery breath and went out into the corridor.

As chance would have it, she ran into Frank in the scene dock. At least there was no-one else around to see her grovel.

'Frank, I'm so sorry! It was the recording session from hell and it went on far longer than I'd imagined it would and I know people are totally pissed off with me and–' Oh, God. She was going to start boo-hooing any minute.

'Calm down, Deirdre! Calm yourself. There's no problem, I cleared it with Keith and shunted all your scenes to the end of the schedule.' He laid a reassuring hand on her shoulder. 'Hey, look at you – you're soaked to the skin. How could I give out to a poor little drowned rat? Especially considering the day that's in it. Now, why don't you nip down to the canteen and get yourself a takeaway coffee?'

'Are you sure, Frank?' This was odd. She'd been convinced she was in for a severe bollocking.

'Sure. But be quick.' He smiled at her and shooed her off in the direction of the canteen before disappearing through the door that led into the studio.

She ran to the canteen and helped herself to coffee in a polystyrene cup, glad that there wasn't a queue. Jamming the lid ineffectually on the cup, she scooted back to the studio block, slooshing coffee as she went. As she slid through the lobby door into Studio 2A and emerged onto the pub set, the strains of 'Happy Birthday To You' started their familiar swell. Deirdre stopped in her tracks. There was a pile of doughnuts on a plate with a candle stuck into the top-most one. They'd found out it was her birthday! She walked towards the doughnut mountain as the last 'Happy Birthday To You' rose to a tuneless crescendo, and then she blew out the candle.

'Thanks, thanks, thanks so much . . .' she repeated as colleagues came up to give her hugs and kisses. When Keith the director plonked a kiss on her cheek she gave him a rueful look. 'I'm dead sorry I was late this morning, Keith. Did I foul up the schedule big-time? I was expecting the bollocking from hell.'

'You would have got it, too, if Maeve hadn't told us it was your birthday. We decided that an entente cordiale was the best present you could have got. Nobody likes to be bawled out on their birthday.'

'It's been such a shite day up till now that I'd actually forgotten all about it,' she said. 'Things can only improve from now on in.'

'I wouldn't count on it,' said Keith. 'There've been some major script changes. You've two new scenes tomorrow. Sorry, Deirdre, but it looks like you're going to spend the rest of your birthday learning fresh-off-the-page dialogue.' He raised his eyebrows at her and headed in the direction of the doughnuts.

'Frank?' Deirdre grabbed the stage manager's sleeve as he walked past. 'Frank – Keith's just told me that I'm involved in some brand-new scenes tomorrow!'

'Oh, yeah – that's right.' Frank leafed through a bundle of stapled sheaves of paper. 'Here we are. You've got your work cut out for you today, girl. We'll be rehearsing till the cows come home.'

'Is my call for tomorrow morning changed?' Deirdre had been delighted when she'd been told that her call for the morning after her birthday was a civilized eleven o'clock.

'Let's see.' Frank ran his finger down the revised call sheet. 'It's been changed, all right. Seven-thirty at base, eight-thirty on location.'

What a bummer. There was no way she could go out tonight and celebrate as she'd planned. She'd have to spend the entire evening learning her new dialogue. She turned away, scanning the pages. There were at least a dozen of them.

'Hi, Deirdre. Happy birthday.'

A gift-wrapped present was slipped into her hands. She looked up from the script to find her old friend, Maeve Kirwan, smiling at her. Maeve's calm countenance was the most reassuring sight Deirdre could have wished for. She threw her arms around her and held on tight, trying not to gibber with pent-up rage and frustration. Then she released her friend from her clingy embrace.

'Sorry for the display of mawkishness,' she said. 'I'm so wound up I feel like kicking something. I nearly kicked the client's leg at that session this morning.'

'Kick this,' said Maeve, holding up a velour prop Barney which had been plonked incongruously on the pub counter.

'No,' said Deirdre, after a moment's consideration. 'I'd have to be in a seriously bad way before I could kick Barney. He's an even sadder bastard than I am. I'll open my present. That'll cheer me up.' She tore off the wrapping to reveal the latest Roddy Doyle novel. 'Oh, brilliant – thanks! I've been dying to read this.'

'Well?' said Maeve, raising her eyebrows at her. 'Are you going to tell me about why you wanted to kick the client?'

'The client,' pronounced Deirdre in a voice that dripped venom, 'was Janine Heeney.'

'Then there's no need to elaborate.' Maeve took a chair and swung a leg effortlessly over it, sitting astride it and leaning her arms on the back.

'D'you know something, Maeve? This birthday sucks,' said Deirdre, sitting up on a bar stool and positioning Barney so that it looked as if he was clinging drunkenly onto an empty gin bottle. 'And do you know something else? We're going to have to cancel the restaurant this evening. I've just heard I've two new scenes to do first thing in the morning. And both of them are with Sophie.'

'Scenes with Sophie and no birthday party?' Maeve winced. 'Ouch! That's grim, Deirdre.'

Deirdre sighed and shook her head. 'It doesn't really surprise me, the way things have been going today. You're a sneak, by the way,' she added. 'I begged you not to let on to anyone that it was my birthday. Having people sing "Happy Birthday" to me always makes me feel stupid.'

'When I saw the way things were shaping up this morning I thought it was the best thing to do. Frank hates giving out, really, and he'd hate himself even more if he discovered he'd given out to a forlorn birthday girl.'

'Do I really look forlorn?'

'You really do look really forlorn. What's happened?'

Deirdre considered, twisting a damp strand of hair around her finger. She badly wanted to confide in Maeve, but Maeve was Rory's friend as well as hers, and she couldn't ask her to take sides. 'Oh, just a bad hair day, I suppose. I should have been warned by my horoscope when you read it out to me the other day.'

'What did it say? Something about bad news from abroad, wasn't it?'

'You're amazing, you know. I can't usually remember my own horoscope, let alone other people's.'

Maeve had gathered up her curtain of ash-blonde hair and twisted it into a chignon on the nape of her elegant neck. 'Well? Has it happened?'

'The bad news? Yeah.'

'Something to do with Rory?'

Deirdre bit her lip. Maybe Maeve could help – advise her what to do. She'd helped in the past. The temptation to spill everything out in a great turbulent stream-of-consciousness was suddenly too strong to resist. 'Well–' she began.

'Maeve?' Frank poked his head round the door of the snug. 'We need you now. Episode thirty-two, scene nine.' The head disappeared. 'Cressida, Jean-Claude?' They could hear him calling across the studio floor. 'You're involved in this.'

'Sorry, Deirdre. Bad timing,' said Maeve, getting to her feet. 'I'll talk to you later, OK?'

Deirdre watched the actress stroll over to the fake newsagent's door, admiring her poise. She knew there was no way that Maeve would be clued-in on Rory's misdemeanour. Maeve was the one actress that Sophie would emphatically not have gossiped to. Aside from being a close friend of Deirdre's,

Maeve had no truck with dressing room gossip. She would lacerate Sophie if she knew what rumours she'd been spreading round about Rory.

'Happy birthday, Deirdre!' Suddenly Sophie was there, aiming air-kisses at her cheeks. The scent of Envy was in the air again. Deirdre stiffened. Sophie and she never, ever communicated on a social level. They were obliged to work together on a regular basis, but they were always careful to put distance between each other after their scenes were in the can. There was mean history between them. The fact that Sophie was actually instigating conversation with her now was a serious danger signal. The actress took a step backwards and stretched her slickly MAC-ed mouth in a smile, and Deirdre prepared herself for the body-blow. 'Do you know, I completely forgot to tell you? I can't imagine how it slipped my mind! Had you heard that I ran into Rory when I was in LA?' Sophie's kittenish green eyes looked disingenuously at her.

'Really?' said Deirdre, with studied nonchalance. 'He didn't mention it in his letter. I got a birthday card from him today.' She couldn't resist it. 'And forty Vendella roses.'

'Forty?' Sophie managed to convey by her tone that she thought forty roses was pretty cheapskate. 'Well. Rory seemed to be getting along great. It's an amazing break for him, isn't it? He told me he's going to be out there for another month or so.'

'Yup.'

'You must miss him a lot, do you?' A look of sham

33

concern spread itself across Sophie's neat features.

'Oh, no, not really. I'm too busy to miss him.'

'Still – he's been gone for over a month already, hasn't he? It's a long time to be apart.'

'Yeah, well – Rory and I have a very loose arrangement, you know? We're not into tying each other down.' Actually, they were – with silk scarves occasionally, after a bottle or two of good claret – but she wasn't going to fill Sophie in on *that*. 'We just go with the flow, you know?'

'Oh, Ben and I are totally the opposite. We're completely committed to each other. Any time we're apart I feel absolutely secure in the knowledge that he's not going to even *look* at another woman. We thrive on an atmosphere of mutual trust.'

'Yeah?' Deirdre raised a cynical eyebrow, as if she found the notion of mutual trust not only inconceivable, but also about as appealing as middle-aged spread.

Just then Sophie's mobile phone shrilled as if on cue. 'Oh! Pardon me, Deirdre!' The actress prinked, and hummed irritatingly along with the electronic melody as she retrieved the tiny phone from her Mulberry shoulderbag. Deirdre noticed that the colour of the keypad cover matched not only the leather of the bag, but also the leather on Sophie's Mary-Jane shoes.

'Ben!' she exclaimed when she picked up, giving Deirdre a smirky look that contrived to say, *Oops! Told you so*! She put her hand over the receiver momentarily. 'He may be a drop-dead gorgeous

34

ultra-cool dude, but he's just a pussy-cat at heart!' she said. Then she cooed into her phone. 'It's a bit public in the studio, darling,' she said. 'Let me take you outside.'

* * *

When Deirdre got home later on that day there were only two messages on her answering machine. One was from her mother to wish her a happy birthday, and the other was from her dentist's receptionist to let her know there'd been a cancellation and they could fit her in next week. She picked up her diary from where she habitually left it, lying beside the phone. As she flicked through the pages to check on next week's schedule, something slipped out onto the floor. It was the postcard that had arrived from Rory that morning. She stood for a while, looking through the window at the neat Georgian square below without really seeing it. Then she picked up the postcard, took it into the kitchen and dropped it back into the bin.

The Vendellas next: she marched straight back into the sitting room to fetch the flowers. She'd bloody well trash those, too. How dare he think she'd be won over by an ostentatiously expensive bouquet of roses? She picked up the vase she'd stuck them in. The mass of luminous blooms shuddered. Deirdre put the vase down again and lifted a hand to touch a satin-smooth petal. She just couldn't do it.

She remembered the first time he'd bought her

Vendellas, on her twenty-second birthday. Three years ago to the day. She'd had Vendellas every birthday since, and much, much more. Once he'd given her a tiny bikini and a course of scuba-diving lessons so that they could dive together on a forthcoming trip to Australia. Another time he'd bought her a stunning full-length black leather coat and suggested that she walk down Grafton Street with nothing else on except black Wolford stay-ups and her black leather boots. That January had been a particularly mild one, and she'd agreed without batting an eyelid. The expression on Rory's face as they'd strolled through town with his arm slung proprietorially around her shoulder had been one of blissed-out gratification. Last year he'd come back from London – where he'd been working on a television play – with masses of Agent Provocateur lingerie for her. She'd literally bounced up and down when she'd clocked the logo on the carrier bags he'd chucked onto the bed. 'Get back in there,' Rory had said, as she jumped out from under the duvet to fling her arms around his neck. 'We're spending your birthday in bed.'

As she turned away from the roses and picked up her script with a heavy sigh, Deirdre realized that this was categorically the worst birthday she'd ever had.

Chapter Two

The next day Deirdre got up at half past six, had a quick shower, ran her eyes over the dialogue she'd stayed up half the night learning, and then cycled out to RTE. She could have taken a cab on the station's account, but it wasn't raining and she knew the exercise would clear her head. She was the only passenger in the minibus that picked her up at base to take her to location. Sophie's name was on the transport list, but Sophie always drove herself in the smart little Clio that her father had given her for her twenty-fifth birthday, probably imagining she was just like the latest Renault girl in the television ad.

She was going to need her wits about her today. Scenes with Sophie were always painful. Sophie liked to get up to little tricks, like subtly shifting the blocking in their two-shots so that Deirdre's face would be angled away from the camera, or suddenly launching into a vocal warm-up just before a take so that Deirdre's concentration would be thrown, or handing over the wrong prop in the middle of a scene. The camera couldn't discern that Sophie was handing Deirdre a nailfile instead of the loose change specified in the script, but Deirdre could. The last time she'd played that particular trick, Deirdre had had to stop the scene. 'Sorry,' she'd said. 'Can we do that again with the correct prop this time?'

'Oops – sorry! My fault!' Sophie had said brightly. 'I couldn't locate the coins in my bag, so I just grabbed the first thing that came to hand.'

Deirdre had sent her a hard look.

Today make-up and wardrobe facilities had been set up in a hotel conveniently situated close to location. Deirdre fetched her costume and took it to the hotel room that had been allocated to the actresses as a dressing room. Sophie was already there, sorting through a bag of costume jewellery.

She looked up when Deirdre came through the door. 'Hi, Deirdre,' she said in her usual effervescent tone. 'Which do you think? The silver or the enamel?' She held a pair of earrings up to her earlobes.

'The silver.' Deirdre didn't bother to examine either pair too closely. She threw her costume over the back of a chair and started to unbutton her shirt.

'Mm. Do you really think so? They're a bit too vulgar for my character. I think I'll go for the enamel.' She hooked the earrings onto her ears and held her head to one side. 'Yes,' she said with satisfaction. 'These are perfect.'

She turned to Deirdre and smiled, and then she let the smile fade as her eyes travelled down Deirdre's body. 'Oh . . .' she said.

'Oh, what?' Deirdre didn't much like the way she was being scrutinized.

'Oh, nothing,' said Sophie airily. 'It's just that – oh,

no. Never mind!' She looked back at her reflection and hummed a little tune, and then she turned to Deirdre with concern in her eyes. Warning bells immediately started to go off in Deirdre's head. 'Deirdre?' Sophie said. 'I hope you don't mind me saying this, but have you put on a teensy bit of weight recently?'

'I don't have a clue, Sophie. And I don't really care, either.'

'Pardon me, Deirdre. But I think you might have put on a little. Just a teensy bit. It would only take about – oh – a month's dieting to lose it. I hope you don't mind me telling you? I always prefer it when people are honest with me about these things, then I can do something about it before I let myself go completely, d'you know what I mean?'

'Actually, Sophie, this is none of your damn business, but Rory prefers me with a bit of a belly. He doesn't go for the stick-insect or the obsessive exerciser look, and neither do I.' Deirdre started to pull a jersey in an unattractive shade of puce over her head.

'Oh? He'll be glad to get back from LA, then. All the women over there are incredibly slender and well-toned. Of course, they all watch their diets – lots of fruit and fresh vegetables, no alcohol–'

'Sophie.' Deirdre's head emerged through the neck of the jersey. 'Would you shut the fuck up?'

Sophie threw her an injured look. 'Oh! I *do* beg your pardon, Deirdre. I was just offering some friendly advice.' She got to her feet and flounced across the room. 'If I were you I'd take it, too,' she said ominously, before disappearing through the door.

Deirdre shut her eyes, sighed, and sank down on the hotel bed. It was going to be a tough day.

* * *

Much, much later, she sat down beside Maeve in a pub in Donnybrook. She'd been through the mill. It had rained, Sophie had sniggered when Deirdre's radio mike had come adrift in the middle of a take, and she'd had to hang about all day after she'd finished her first two scenes so that she could deliver one line of dialogue to the actor who was the soap's oldest living resident.

'I'm jaded,' she said, as she put down her pint. 'I'm jacked. I'm knackered and I'm fed up.'

'In that case you'll be glad to know that I've reserved the Troc for Sunday night,' Maeve said. 'We'll celebrate your birthday a few days late. You'll be in better form after a weekend off.'

Some cast members were on their second or third pint, others were just beginning to trickle into the pub. Some of the actors were in exuberant form, others looked as tired as Deirdre felt. It was the end of a long week.

'Eight more episodes to go,' said Deirdre ruminatively. 'Has Sally been on to you about next season's contract yet?' Sally Ruane was the agent they both shared.

40

'I'm not coming back next season, Deirdre,' said Maeve.

'What?' Deirdre turned to her friend in disbelief. 'Why?'

'I've only just found out for sure. I didn't want to say anything about it until it was in the bag. I've been offered a year's contract with the RSC.'

'Oh, Maeve! That's brilliant news! Plum parts?'

'Pretty plum, yeah. Olivia, Charmian, Nora Clitheroe.'

'No shit. You must be wildly excited.'

Maeve smiled. 'You know me, Deirdre. I don't get wildly excited over anything.'

'When are you off?'

'Next month. RTE's been really decent about it. My storyline was kind of dragging to a close, so they've telescoped it into four episodes and let me go. I want a decent holiday before I hit Stratford.'

'Hell.' Deirdre was morose suddenly. 'I'll really miss you, Maeve.'

'I'll miss you too, Deirdre.' The pair of actresses smiled at each other, and Deirdre leant across and gave Maeve a kiss on the cheek.

'Congratulations,' she said.

'Thanks,' said Maeve. She took a sip from her glass. Then: 'What's the word on next season, anyway?' she asked.

'I don't really have a clue,' replied Deirdre. 'I'm not sure they'll be able to get much more mileage out of my character.'

'Amber's kind of wrung out, isn't she?' said Maeve.

41

'Yeah.' Deirdre started fraying a beer mat. 'I suppose negotiations will be underway soon. I must give Sally a ring next week. For all I know my job's on the line.'

'Mine's not.' Sophie Burke sat down beside them. 'One of the script-writers just tipped me the wink. I'm going to change my mind at the last minute about the abortion. They're giving me a baby next season, so I'm definitely back.' Sophie dropped a sweetener into her cup of coffee. She had a sick-makingly dreamy expression on her face. 'I can just see Fran as a mother. I think her innate maternal instinct has been sublimated by her dedication to her career. You know they did some audience research recently?' she added. 'The character of Fran came in among the five most popular in the series.' She looked at Deirdre and smiled. 'I wonder where yours came in?' she asked sweetly.

Deirdre was spared the necessity of responding to Sophie's barbed enquiry by the arrival of Jean-Claude Valentin. He was a French actor who had been brought into the soap two seasons ago to add a dollop of sophisticated sex appeal. He was universally perceived to be one of the sexiest men on Irish television. He had come-to-bed eyes, an amazing physique, and he wore Paul Smith. The fact that he was somewhere in his late thirties only enhanced his appeal because it lent him an air of irresistible savoir-faire. On top of all that he had a wonderful, smoky French accent.

Jean-Claude sat down on a chair between Deirdre

42

and Sophie, and smiled all round. 'There is no better way to end the day,' he said, 'than in the company of beautiful women.' Sophie dimpled and Maeve smiled and raised her eyes to heaven. Deirdre looked at him speculatively. Jean-Claude Valentin had a reputation for being a bit of a flirt. He was also emphatically married. Deirdre had had one disastrous experience with a married man early on in her career, and had vowed that she'd never make the same mistake again.

'You came first, Jean-Claude,' gushed Sophie.

He looked puzzled. 'I came first? First in what?' he asked.

'First in the market-research poll to find out who were the most popular characters in *Ardmore Grove*.'

'Goodness gracious. What an unexpected compliment.' The Frenchman smiled a self-deprecatory smile.

'I came in fifth. Not bad going, really. And I'm almost certain that Fran's popularity will soar even higher next season, because they're going to give me a—'

'Sophie,' said Dierdre. 'There's Ben.'

Sophie's boyfriend was beckoning to her from the door of the pub.

'Oh! Pardon me, Jean-Claude – I must fly. We're off to—'

'Can I get you a drink, Jean-Claude?' interjected Deirdre. She didn't want to hear where Sophie and Ben were off to. It was bound to be somewhere hip and expensive.

'No, no, no – allow me. A pint of Guinness, Deirdre?'

'Well – yes. Thanks very much.'

'And another Ballygowan for you, Maeve?' Jean-Claude Valentin rose to his feet.

'No thanks,' said Maeve. 'I'll have to make tracks soon. I've a show to do this evening, remember?' Maeve was currently double-jobbing, working on the soap by day and in a production of *The Caucasian Chalk Circle* in the Abbey theatre at night.

'Are you sure I can't persuade you and Ben to join us?' said Jean-Claude as he gestured with a slight bow for Sophie to precede him through the crowd.

'Quite sure, thank you. We're running late already. You see, we're off to—'

Thankfully Sophie's voice was drowned out in the surrounding din before Deirdre or Maeve could hear any more. The two actresses watched her retreating back, and then they exchanged looks.

'Agh,' said Deirdre. 'D'you know something? I just can't imagine Sophie's character with a baby. *She's* obviously delighted with the idea, though. She's probably envisaging some kind of Madonna and Lourdes Ciccone scenario, with her wafting all over the place kitted out by Voyage.'

'A more interesting angle might be the stress of single parenthood,' said Maeve ruminatively. 'Maybe poor Fran won't be able to cope with the demands of juggling her high-profile career and looking after a new baby. Maybe she'll let herself go, start to hit the bottle. Maybe her baby won't be like Lourdes Ciccone at all. Maybe it'll be a whingey pain-in-the-arse monkey lookalike.' She looked at Deirdre and smiled, and then she drained her glass and stood up. 'You never can tell in soap opera.'

Deirdre pulled a rueful face and heaved a great sigh.

'Why so forlorn-looking, suddenly?' asked Maeve, pulling on her coat.

'Am I looking forlorn *again*? That's the second time in two days you've told me that.'

'It's the right word to describe you these days.'

'It's just that now I'm going to be left on my own with Jean-Claude, and I never know what to say to ridiculously handsome men. The kind of guff I come out with is even more banal than usual.'

'You could always practise your French on him.'

'My French is crap. I'd sound even more banal than I do when I'm talking English. *Bonsoir, Jean-Claude. Comment-allez-vous ce soir? Il fait beau temps, n'est ce pas?*'

'It's not *beau temps*, Deirdre. The weather's bloody awful out there. Anyway, there's the crowd from the sit-com over there if you get bored. You can always join them.'

Deirdre looked over to where a bunch of actors were sitting morosely by the door. 'Yeah. Although I get the feeling that they're as forlorn as me. Must have been a hard day on the sound stage for them as well. Hey – don't forget your sandwich.' She indicated the cling-filmed pub sandwich that Maeve had ordered earlier.

'The glamour, the glamour. Tuna sandwiches in

the dressing room knocked back by tepid tap water.'
Maeve stuffed the sandwiches into her backpack. 'I'll
look forward to red meat on Sunday.'

'Sunday?'

'The Troc. Eight o'clock. Your birthday dinner,
remember?'

'Oh. Of course, thanks. See you then. Enjoy the
show.'

'Enjoy brushing up your French. Take it easy,
Deirdre.' Maeve slung her backpack over her
shoulder and negotiated her way through the crowd,
pausing to give Jean-Claude Valentin a kiss on the
cheek as she passed him.

'Thanks, Jean-Claude.' Deirdre lobbed a big smile
at the actor as he settled into the chair beside her and
set a pint of Guinness in front of her. She took a sip
and then wiped away the little moustache of foam it
had left on her upper lip.

'You missed a bit. Just there.' Jean-Claude Valentin
indicated an area just to the left of her mouth.

'Thanks.' She took a second swipe at her face.

'Missed again. Here, allow me.' He produced a
big, immaculate linen handkerchief from his pocket
and gently swatted away the foam. Then he sat back.
'That was a tough week, was it not?'

'Yeah. But at least we've the evenings free to recuperate. Could you imagine if you had to get into
the theatre now and do a show? Poor Maeve must
be doubly knackered.'

He gave her a look of enquiry. 'You used to do a
lot of theatre work, didn't you? Do you miss it?'

She found herself thinking about it for the first time in ages. She considered herself more of a television than a stage actress now. Her agent still put her up for the occasional stage play or film, but her involvement in the soap meant that potential employers lost interest when they realized they'd have to work around her availability. She'd actually turned down a terrific role in a play by an up-and-coming new playwright a couple of months ago. Although she'd have loved to do it, she simply couldn't afford to. The actors were being paid on a shares basis from the box-office receipts, and as the theatre was tiny, she knew she'd end up with minus nothing at the end of the week.

'I don't miss the insecurity. But yeah, I'd love to have a crack at it again some time. Maybe I'll put out feelers for work once the season's finished.'

'There's a big movie happening later on in the year – filming in the west, around Galway. A film about Grace O'Malley – you know, the pirate queen?'

'Oh?'

'Yeah. It was to have been shot a few years ago, but there was a big problem with finance.'

Deirdre started to smile. She remembered how Sophie had crowed about landing the role of the young Grace O'Malley before the plug had been pulled on the project first time round.

'You should get your agent to put you up for it,' said Jean-Claude.

'Who's casting?'

'Juliet Rathbone-Lyon.'

Now she laughed out loud. 'Then I don't stand a chance. I had a fierce run-in with her once.'

'Oh? What happened?'

'I walked out of a casting session my agent had set up with her.'

'Why did you do that?'

'She was treating me like shit.'

'That was a courageous thing to do.' He pronounced the word 'courageous' with the stress on the 'rag' and a soft 'g', making it sound incredibly sexy.

Deirdre stretched in her seat. 'I dunno. It was actually a pretty stupid thing to do, but I was never any good at toadying for work. The only time I ever did it I ended up in the job from hell, working for a cowboy from Texas.'

'Maybe you should write a screenplay,' he suggested. 'Lots of actors are trying their hand at that these days. There is big money to be made there if you have success.'

'It's funny you should say that!' Deirdre leant forward, lighting up with sudden enthusiasm. 'I have an idea for a screenplay! As a matter of fact, I've been working on it in my spare time. It's my pet project.' She took another sip of her pint and looked away, feeling a bit shy suddenly. She hadn't talked to anyone about her screenplay idea, apart from Rory.

'Oh?' He leant back in his chair, looking at her with interest. 'Tell me about it.'

'Well. It's – um–' She didn't want to give too much away. She might be hexing herself if she did. 'It's a

48

bit inchoate at the moment.' 'Inchoate' was her current favourite word.

'"Inchoate"?' Jean-Claude looked at her in amusement. 'My English isn't that good, Deirdre. What do you mean by "inchoate"?'

'Um. It means "embryonic", I suppose. You know – something that's only just begun. All I really know about my film is that it's set in the West of Ireland and it's a love story.'

'Then you are on to a winner,' said Jean-Claude. 'All the best love stories are set in the West of Ireland.' He gave her a sideways smile. 'You will have fun doing your research.'

'Yes, I will. I'd love to beat a retreat to my gran's old cottage with my laptop for a while.'

'You have a laptop? I am impressed. You must be serious about this screenplay idea.'

'Oh, I am. Except the laptop's not really mine, yet. I'm paying it off on the never-never.'

'So your grandmother lives in the west?'

'Well, no. She died a couple of years ago, but my mum and dad kept the cottage as a bolt-hole. I get down there as much as I can.'

'Where is it?'

'On a very remote peninsula called Carrowcross on Clew Bay.'

'Paradise.' He smiled at her.

'Yes, it is.' Deirdre smiled back at him. He was a really nice man, she thought. She'd never really had a proper conversation with him in the three years she'd worked on the soap – they'd hardly ever had any scenes together. Most of her scenes were with the more delinquent-type characters. A silence fell between them and she looked away. When she looked back at him she could tell that he was studying her with new interest.

'What do they have in store for you next season, Deirdre?'

'God knows. I've only been on the show for three years, but I seem to have been there, done it all, worn the T-shirt. Let's see.' Deirdre started counting on her fingers. 'Amber's done drugs, she's done adultery, she's done shoplifting, she's done black-mail, she's suspected of having had an abortion – though it *may* have been a miscarriage – she's done computer fraud. Maybe the only way for her to go is out. How about suicide? Splat! Over the Powerscourt waterfall. I'd love to write the dialogue.'

'Try a sample out on me.'

'Um. Let's see – how about this? "Oh, God, help me please. I am so fed up having to wear this horrible raincoat that I can't go on, and if I have to do another scene looking meaningfully at someone over a plate of biscuits in the kitchen I may do something rash like take my own life".'

'"No, Amber, do not do it,"' said Jean-Claude, entering into the spirit of things. '"Life is wonderful – it is a great gift."'

'"It's too late. Here I am at the top of the water-fall, poised to jump. Oh no, what is happening? I think I'm having a sudden change of heart. Give me your hand, quick – help me to – aaaaagh . . ."

50

There she goes,' said Deirdre with satisfaction.

'Very good,' said Jean-Claude. There was another pause while they smiled at each other, pleasantly aware of the rapport they'd established. 'I too got drugs, adultery, and blackmail,' he added equably. 'But I am not yet ready for the suicide and I am the wrong sex for the miscarriage.'

Deirdre laughed. 'Maybe I should get out while the going's good,' she said. 'I'm getting a bit sick of the tabloid stuff.'

'How do they describe you?'

'They use all the "S" words. You know – sizzling, sexy, steamy, seductive, smouldering, sultry, scorching, blah blah blah.' They exchanged grimaces. 'You must get a lot of that, too, Jean-Claude. What's their favourite moniker for you?' she asked. 'No, don't tell me – let me guess. "Latin lover"?'

'You are right first time. "Lecherous Lothario" is another.' He took a swig of his Guinness. 'It can be undignified sometimes,' he said. 'But it sure as hell beats being on the dole.'

'What was your most undignified moment?'

'Let me see. It had to be that scene in the bath with Cressida. It was most embarrassing for both of us at the time, but we managed to laugh about it later. You?'

'Well, remember when Amber collapsed after the abortion/miscarriage and the family dog was supposed to discover her lying on the beach?'

'Yeah?'

'Rex – or whatever his name is – wouldn't co-operate, so they had to smear dog food on my face. I spent nearly an entire afternoon lying there in the freezing cold with Rex snorting dog-breath in my ear and slobbering all over my cheek.'

Jean-Claude laughed. 'Consider yourself lucky. Some actresses have to lie back and have middle-aged actors like me slobbering all over them.'

'You're not being fair on yourself, Jean-Claude. You screen-kiss beautifully, and you're too much of a gentleman to slobber.'

He gave her one of his rather sexy, amused smiles, and she took a slug of Guinness to cover her embarrassment. 'Let me get you another drink,' he said, starting to get to his feet.

'No, no – it's my round,' she said hastily, laying a hand on his sleeve. 'Please, let me.'

He gave a little Gallic shrug of resignation as she jumped up and started to navigate the crowd. She was a bit unsteady on her pins, she realized. Two pints of Guinness on an empty stomach wasn't a good idea, and it had been rash of her to offer to buy another round. Still, she was having fun chatting with Jean-Claude. She was having more fun than she'd had in ages.

She ordered two pints and then leant against a bar stool while she waited. Catching sight of her reflection in the mirror behind the bar, she automatically lifted a hand to fluff out her hair. She certainly wasn't looking forlorn any more, she decided. She was actually looking quite animated. It was amazing what the company of an amusing man could do to a girl. Her mind ricocheted back to Rory. She wondered who he was amusing right now. Hell. Why had he intruded on her thoughts at this particular juncture? He had no right to be annoying her like this. But she had to admit that he was always there somewhere in the back of her mind, ready to make his presence felt at the most unwelcome moments, like a rash. She wondered idly when his mysterious 'time off' was likely to occur. What was all that about? He'd hardly come all the way back from LA just to visit her if he was involved with some looker over there.

She paid the barman for the pints he set in front of her and made her way back to Jean-Claude, saying, 'Hi,' to the sit-com actors as she passed them by. Maybe Sophie had made a mistake about Rory and the chick from the flick. She was feeling so mellow that she was almost prepared to turn a blind eye to her erstwhile lover's philandering. After all, he'd sent her Vendellas. And he'd never made an actual promise to be faithful. Nor, come to think of it, had she.

* * *

An hour and a bit later she decided it was time to go home.

'You're not driving, I hope?' asked Jean-Claude.

'No, no. I don't have a car. I'm on my bike,' she responded breezily. Then she remembered something. 'Shit. Someone stole my lights.'

'Then you had better not think of bicycling,' said Jean-Claude, getting to his feet. 'Share a cab with me. I'm going into town.'

'But that means my bike'll be stuck out in Donnybrook,' she protested. 'I'll *have* to cycle home, otherwise I'll have to get a bus all the way out here tomorrow to pick it up.' She started rummaging around in her backpack for bicycle keys. 'Don't worry. I'll be fine. I'll stick to the pavement.'

'No you will not,' said Jean-Claude with decision. 'I cannot allow you to knock down the upright citizens of Dublin 6 as you weave your way along their footpaths. For their own protection, you will do as I say. I will instruct the taxi-driver to put your bicycle in his boot.'

'But—'

'No buts, Deirdre.'

'OK,' she replied meekly, shrugging into her jacket. She was feeling warm and dozy, and was actually very grateful to Jean-Claude for his offer. She'd been dreading the prospect of cycling home in the cold and dark.

As she followed him towards the door she passed the table where the sit-com actors were congregated. 'Sophie Burke was telling me she saw Warren Beatty on Rodeo Drive,' one of them was saying. 'And you'll *never* guess who she saw – oh.' On catching sight of Deirdre, the actress broke off and started to ad lib unconvincingly. 'Um – I mean, you'll never guess who was with him. Annette Bening!'

'What's so unusual about that?' said another of the actors, plainly unimpressed by Sophie's LA gossip. 'They're married, after all.'

'Yes. Well. She was just saying what a stunning couple they make.' As Deirdre turned away she saw the actress shoot a warning look across the table to her perplexed colleague. She knew what that look meant. It meant: *Let's-change-the-subject-I'll-fill-you-in-later.* Word was obviously around the entire acting fraternity of Dublin that Rory McDonagh was having a fine time shagging bodacious bimbos in LA, and wasn't it awful that poor Deirdre O'Dare knew nothing about it.

She pulled the pub door shut behind her with such vehemence that Jean-Claude gave her a curious look. 'Something wrong?' he asked.

'No. Yes. Oh, shit.' To her horror, Deirdre started to cry.

'What is it?' asked Jean-Claude in a concerned voice. 'Come here.' He held out an arm in invitation. Deirdre teetered towards him and allowed herself to be hugged. 'There, there,' he said. 'What is this? You have become a little – *qu'est ce que c'est le mot juste?* What is the word? When people go weepy after one drink too many?'

'Maudlin,' she sobbed. 'Sorry. It's stupid. It's just that I overheard someone talking about my boyfriend on my way out of the pub. It seems he's having it off with some bimbo in LA.'

'Ah,' said Jean-Claude. There was a pause. 'There are two ways of dealing with that, you know, Deirdre,' he said, looking down at her with interested eyes.

'Yeah?' She wiped away a stupid tear, and was glad to find that it wasn't followed by another. The tears had stopped almost as soon as they had started. They'd been spurty, angry tears like a flash flood – quick to start and quick to stop.

'Yes. Get rid of him. Or get back at him.' He raised an eyebrow at her, a half-smile playing around his lips. 'Think about it,' he said. Then he turned away from her and raised his right hand in the air. 'Taxi!' he called in an authoritative voice.

Her bike was stowed in the boot after a fiver from Jean-Claude stopped the cab-driver's grumbling. He opened the rear door for her and Deirdre slid into the back seat with a mild dilemma simmering in her mind. Had she imagined it, or had Jean-Claude issued an oblique invitation? She darted a sideways look at him as he instructed the driver where to go. He really was ridiculously attractive, with his crinkly, humorous blue eyes, collar-length wavy black hair and strong jaw. And that accent! Deirdre knew that women found the accent irresistible – she'd heard enough of his female fans mooning about him in queues for the supermarket check-outs, or in hair salons. She felt vaguely smug that such a sexy, mature, intelligent man was showing an interest in her. She wished Rory could see her now – sailing along in a sleek Merc at the side of one of the most desirable men in the country. But something told her that Rory wouldn't be impressed. Bastard.

She turned to Jean-Claude. 'I've thought about it,' she said on an impulse.

He raised an eyebrow at her.

'About what you just said,' she continued. Then she took a deep breath. 'I'm going to get back at him.'

'I rather hoped you would say that,' said Jean-Claude Valentin. He looked deep into her eyes and then he put out a hand and very lightly traced the contour of her ear with his index finger. 'And who is to help you perpetrate your revenge?'

'You,' she said. 'That is, if you don't mind.'

'I couldn't think of anything that would give me more pleasure,' he said, before leaning down and touching her mouth with his. Deirdre parted her lips, shut her eyes, and drank him in.

When they broke the kiss they had almost reached the Georgian square where she lived. She looked at him meaningfully.

'I won't come in,' he replied in answer to her unspoken question. 'I have to meet someone in town. Give me your phone number.' She dictated it to him, and he noted it down on a card. 'I'll telephone you,' he said. She nodded, and leant over for a last kiss before getting out of the car. 'I'll telephone you soon,' he repeated. 'And Deirdre?'

She turned back to him. 'Yes?'

'*Tais-toi.*' He placed a finger first on his lips, then on hers. Then he pulled the car door shut and the Merc glided away from the pavement.

'Oh shit!' exclaimed Deirdre, jumping up and

down and waving her arms about wildly. Her bike was still sticking out of the boot.

*   *   *

The phone was ringing as she opened the door to her flat. She picked it up before the answering machine could kick in.

'Deirdre.' It was Jean-Claude's voice.

'Oh, hi! Jean-Claude, I—'

'You left your bicycle in the taxi.'

'Yes. What—'

'Don't worry. I will send the driver back with it.'

'Oh, thanks, Jean-Claude. I'm an eejit.'

'You are not an eejit.' The word sounded odd in his sexy accent, and she found herself smiling. 'You just got distracted, that's all. We both did.' She could tell by his voice that he was smiling, too. 'I'll talk to you very soon, OK?'

'OK. Bye, Jean-Claude.' She put down the phone and bit her lip. What was she doing, encouraging overtures from a married man? It could only end in tears. Getting back at Rory, that's what she was doing. It was very, very childish of her. But there was something about Jean-Claude Valentin that was difficult to resist. He was so . . . in control. Unflappable – that was the right word to describe him. It was a nice feeling to know that there was someone out there who handled things with easy aplomb, instead of flailing through life the way she did.

The doorbell rang. Grabbing her purse, she ran

down two flights of stairs to open the door to the taxi-driver. He was hauling her bicycle out of the boot. 'Thanks a lot,' she said breathlessly, pulling out a fiver. 'What's the damage?'

'It's already paid for,' came the brusque response.

Deirdre tucked the money back into her purse and bumped her bike up the front steps of the tall Georgian building, thinking about Jean-Claude Valentin. What she was thinking was that he thought of everything.

* * *

Back in her flat she made hot chocolate and took it to bed with her book. Too much Guinness meant that she couldn't concentrate properly, and when she found herself reading the same paragraph over and over again, she realized it was time to go to sleep. She shambled into the bathroom to clean her teeth, noticing as she sat on the loo that there was evidence of Rory everywhere. His toothbrush was still in the toothbrush holder, his shaving gear sat beside her body lotion on the rickety Victorian commode, there was an issue of *Esquire* poking out from under her pile of *Marie-Claires*. She'd trash his stuff tomorrow. She had every right. After all, Rory didn't live here. They'd tried living together once, and re-alized that because they both liked to have space to themselves it wasn't going to work out. So although Rory stayed over most nights, they didn't get in each other's hair. Deirdre didn't sleep at his place very often because his dog, Bastard, was jealous of her.

She rinsed and flossed, and then she got a pair of fluffy white slouch socks out of the airing cupboard and put them on. She didn't bother with pyjamas – she always slept naked – but the last few nights had been very cold. Her feet had been so freezing that she hadn't been able to get to sleep. Bed socks were the only answer.

She slid between the sheets, set her alarm – turning it off again when she remembered that she didn't have to get up tomorrow – and fell asleep instantly.

She dreamt about Rory, as usual. It was a blissfully erotic dream involving ice-cream, except the ice-cream was warm. Rory was saying something in her ear in a voice that was so low and husky it almost tickled. What was he saying? She was feeling so delicious that she couldn't concentrate. *Don't panic, darling,* murmured Rory's voice. *Wake up nice and easy. It's me. I'm back again – you're not dreaming.* Then he was pulling the sheets away and trailing a hand down her ribcage and over her belly. The voice trickled on in her ear. *God – you're glorious. I missed you like crazy.* A pause. Then: *Wow. White socks. You can keep them on.*

'Rory?' She half-opened her eyes and smiled at him. He was looking at her with that half-interested, half-lazy expression she loved so much. Then she closed her eyes again and stretched luxuriously. He was between her legs, now, and she was aware that he was fully clothed as he slid a finger into her. 'What were you dreaming about, you naughty girl?' he asked, unzipping himself. 'You're ready for me already.' Deirdre orgasmed as soon as he entered her. She just couldn't help it.

* * *

The next morning she woke to find their limbs still intertwined. She disengaged herself carefully and sat up, looking down at his sleeping face. His skin was lightly tanned, and his hair – which had been dark blond the last time she'd seen him – had been streaked the colour of corn by the West Coast sun. It was longer, too: he had let it grow down almost as far as his shoulderblades. There was a smattering of golden stubble on his jaw. She reached out and ran her palm over it, careful to keep her touch feather-light. Then she traced the curve of his lips with an index finger, hoping he might take her finger into the warmth of his mouth. He smiled in his sleep. Bastard, she thought, smiling back at him. She wanted to wake him so that they could make love again, but he looked dead to the world. Jetlagged, probably.

Deirdre slid out of bed and padded through to the kitchen, pulling on a robe as she went. She was still wearing her white socks. Trying to make as little noise as possible so that she wouldn't wake her sleeping partner, she put on the kettle and stuck some tomato bread in the toaster. She could hear music pulsing from the flat next door. Bart, her neighbour, was a freelance actor who was currently unemployed. This meant that she was subjected to a barragement of Radiohead at all hours of the day and night. Rory had left his hold-all on the kitchen table, alongside a duty-free carrier bag. She snuck a look inside. A couple of bottles of good St Emilion and a spray refill for her Diorissimo. Sweet of him, she thought as she spooned coffee into the cafetière.

She gave a little shudder of pleasure as she remembered the way dream and reality had merged so seamlessly last night, and when she took a slug of pink grapefruit juice she realized that her mouth was satisfyingly swollen from the hundreds of voracious kisses they'd exchanged. She had to admit to herself that she was actually slightly relieved that Rory had taken her unawares. If he hadn't seduced her as she slept there was no way that she'd have let him near her – not after the way he'd betrayed her. But what was she to do now?

Plonking her toast and coffee on the pitted pine surface of the kitchen table, she sat down to think. She had landed herself in an extremely awkward situation. She supposed she'd just have to confront him and let him know that she was aware of his liaison in LA. She suspected it probably didn't mean much to him. There had been a couple of indiscretions in the past that he had confessed to – and more than likely some he hadn't confessed to – and she had forgiven him before. It wasn't always a barrel of laughs being involved with a dude deluxe like Rory. The unfortunate fact was that he adored women, and this made him sexually irresistible.

Women of all ages flirted blatantly with him – even in front of her – and he usually found it impossible not to respond. This didn't excuse his behaviour, of course, but it did make it easier to understand.

As she plunged the cafetière she heard the bedroom door open, and her demon lover wandered into the hall, pulling up the zip on his jeans. He wasn't wearing anything else, and she suddenly remembered Cressida's reaction to the photos Sophie had shown her: *Christ – McDonagh looks so sexy, doesn't he?* She couldn't return the smile he sent her.

'Morning, sourpuss,' he said, dropping a kiss on her head. 'What's with the pout? I stay up half the night with the cat who got the cream, and wake up to this.' He gave her a quizzical look. 'No sunny smile for your returning knight errant?'

She couldn't bring up the subject of his indiscretion now. It wasn't the right time. She'd do it later – over dinner or something. She lifted her feet onto the seat of her chair, hugging her shins and resting her chin on her knees. The smile she managed felt crooked. 'Welcome home, Rory,' she said. 'What brings you back so unexpectedly?'

'Your charms, of course, you irresistible siren.' He slung a smile over his shoulder at her as he shambled, yawning, towards the fridge and opened it. 'And Juliet Rathbone-Lyon.'

'Juliet Rathbone-Lyon? You've come all the way back to Dublin for an interview for the Grace O'Malley flick? That's bananas, Rory.'

'I have not come over for an interview. I'm here to screen-test some actresses. I have been offered and have graciously accepted the role of Dónal O'Flaherty – Grace's first husband – and Juliet needs to try out some potential young Graces with me.'

'But that's one of the leads!'

'Yeah. I'm hot and happening, Deirdre. An interview with *GQ* can't be too far away. The pinnacle of my ambition. Apart from shagging Uma Thurman. Joke, darling.' He yawned again, and stretched, and Deirdre tried not to admire him too obviously. 'You've been looking after your nutrition as assiduously as ever since I've been away, I see,' he remarked, scanning the contents of the fridge. 'White wine, Miller Lite, ice-cream, dodgy cheese, hummous that passed its best-before date a week ago.' He took the carton of grapefruit juice from the fridge door, drained it and dropped it in the bin. Then he narrowed his eyes and looked her up and down. 'How do you contrive to look sexy in bedsocks, O'Dare? D'you fancy going back to the scratcher?'

She did quite, but she wasn't going to let him know that. 'No. I'm sore,' she said. 'Have some coffee instead.' He helped himself to a mug from the cupboard and sat down opposite her. 'When did you get the news about the film?' she asked.

'Last week.'

'That all happened very fast.'

'Sally warned them that Columbia was sniffing around. There wasn't time for the usual game-playing.'

'Good money?'

'Sally's happy, so I'm happy.'

'Who else has been cast?'

'It's pretty stellar. Eva Lavery's playing the older Grace. Stephen Rea's playing her second husband. Liam Neeson's been approached about Dubhdara O'Malley, young Grace's da. That's all I know so far.'

'Class acts. Shit, Rory. Are you heading for the stratosphere?'

'My feet are on the ground, baby.' He kissed his forefinger and then leant across the table and rubbed her mouth with it. 'How've you been?'

'OK. Busy.' She filled him in on recent events, taking care that neither Sophie's nor Jean-Claude's name featured in the narrative.

'But you'll be free from around April as usual, won't you?' he said when she'd finished. 'Why don't you ask Sally to put you up for something in the movie?'

'You know there's no way Juliet Rathbone-Lyon would consider casting me, Rory. Not after the last débâcle.'

Rory shrugged. 'That would be water under the bridge by now. Juliet's too sharp to allow personal feelings to get in the way of getting her casting right.' He took a swig of coffee and stretched again. 'I can't say I'm looking forward to testing the unfortunate candidates. There's nothing worse than snogging recalcitrant actresses.'

Deirdre suspected that few of the candidates would be recalcitrant.

'D'you know who's up for it?'

'A dozen or so wannabes. The only one I know is Sophie.'

'Sophie *Burke*?'

'Yeah. I'm dreading that. The last time I had to snog Sophie on stage she was about as pliant as Barbie.'

'She's too old for the part now.' Deirdre knew she sounded pettish. 'And she wouldn't match up well with Eva. The only thing they have in common physically is the fact that they're both blonde.'

Rory shrugged. 'They've both got great tits,' he observed.

Deirdre gave him a withering look. Then: 'I believe Sophie ran into you in LA?' she said nonchalantly, helping herself to more coffee. She knew she shouldn't have broached the subject, but she couldn't help it. It was like trying not to scratch an insect bite.

'Yeah. There's no getting away from some people.' Rory's tone was as casual as hers, but she noticed that he avoided her eyes. He pushed the duty-free bag across the table. 'Got you some perfume,' he said, deftly changing tack.

'Diorissimo! Thanks,' she replied, glad that she'd been diverted from the subject of Sophie, even though she knew she couldn't avoid it for ever. 'Oh – scrummy. St Emilion, too. Will we have it with dinner tonight?'

'Not if you're cooking,' said Rory. 'Let's eat out.'

*　　*　　*

He took her to the Clarence, U2's hotel in Temple
Bar. They decided to eat early because Rory was
jetlagged and knackered – although he wasn't too
knackered to make her come again before they left
the flat. They wandered into the restaurant around
seven, Deirdre feeling sloe-eyed and syrupy from a
surfeit of sex.

She loved the Clarence. It was the classiest joint in
the world as far as she was concerned. Any time she
walked through the door she felt as if some of its glamour rubbed off on her – it made her feel ultra-special.

They were led to a table between elegant, ceiling-
high windows by a softly spoken Italian. After
scrolling through the menu, Deirdre sat back to
enjoy the ambience. Uniformed staff were gliding
from table to table with effortless-looking efficiency,
taking and delivering orders. Louis Armstrong
played low on the sound-system. There were
massive, Zen arrangements of birds-of-paradise
flowers positioned at intervals along the oak-
panelled partition that divided the long room.

Suddenly Deirdre stiffened. She could not believe
what she was seeing. Bono was sauntering through
the restaurant with proprietorial panache. He was
wearing black jeans and a tight black T-shirt, and
he looked even sexier in real life. Deirdre gave an
involuntary little squeak of excitement.

'What's wrong with you?' asked Rory, glancing up
from the menu.

'It's Bono!' she said in a stage whisper. 'There – by the bar. Don't you *dare* look!' she hissed, sneaking looks at Bono from behind her menu.

'I wasn't going to,' he said, looking irritatingly unimpressed by the rock star's proximity. 'And neither should you. You know how *you* hate it when *Ardmore Grove* fans gawk at you.'

He was right, of course. Deirdre put down the menu and concentrated hard on not looking at Bono.

Rory looked at his watch and gave a jetlagged yawn. 'It's time to order, Deirdre,' he said.

She had the soufflé of cheeses to start, followed by grilled corn-fed chicken. Rory had saucisson foie gras and roast cannon of lamb, and ordered an excellent bottle of claret. Deirdre's eyebrows shot up when she got a load of the price, but Rory just said, 'Why not? I've just signed a sweet contract. We're celebrating.'

In fact, they felt so celebratory that a second bottle was ordered halfway through the main course. As the evening wore on, Deirdre felt less and less inclined to bring up the subject of his fling in LA. She was having too much fun with him, and felt too relaxed to bring up unpleasant matters like infidelity. Hell – she loved the bastard who was sitting opposite her, smiling as he spooned warm papillotte of banana and vanilla into her mouth. But Sophie's words still niggled away in the back of her brain like the buzzing of an insect, and as the level of the wine in the second bottle got lower, the niggling progressed from rearward to forefront in her thoughts.

'Rory,' she said, after the waiter had set double espressos down in front of them. 'There's something I need to ask you.' She took a deep breath. 'Were you screwing someone while you were in LA?'

He stirred his coffee for a couple of seconds, and then he looked at her. 'Yes,' he said. The expression he wore was one of naked candour. 'I was screwing somebody. I suppose Sophie told you.'

She looked away. She couldn't speak for a minute. Then she said. 'No, actually. It was worse than that. Sophie didn't tell me, but she told everyone else in town. I overheard her spreading the news one day.'

'I'm sorry,' said Rory.

'For what? Screwing some *Baywatch* bimbo or sorry that I heard from Sophie fucking Burke?'

'Both,' said Rory in a level voice. 'She was an exceptionally lousy lay.'

'You bastard.'

'Yes,' said Rory. Then he said 'Sorry,' again.

They sat on in silence for a while. Finally: 'Is that it?' he asked.

Deirdre didn't know what to say. There was a grim inevitability about the situation now. She wished she could rewind the scenario. She wished she'd never brought the subject up. It really didn't matter that Sophie Burke knew that Rory had cheated on her – it really didn't matter if the whole world knew. She couldn't face the prospect of not having Rory McDonagh in her life. She looked at him and cleared her throat. She could hardly believe the words that emerged when she opened her mouth.

69

'That's it,' she heard herself saying. Then she stood up. 'Maybe you'd order me a cab. I'm going to the loo.'

She spent ten minutes in the Ladies. When she came back downstairs the bill had been paid and there was a taxi waiting out front. Rory held the cab door open for her. 'Deirdre,' he said. 'I think we should talk about this.'

'There's nothing to talk about,' came the automatic, time-honoured cliché.

'As you like. But I have to come home with you.'

'Don't think you're staying with me tonight.'

'I've no intention of staying with you in the mood you're in. I just need to pick up my bag.' Rory slid into the back seat beside her and she immediately shifted farther to the right, keeping her gaze fixed out of the passenger window. The taxi-driver slid the car into gear and joined the flow of traffic heading up the quayside.

After several minutes, Rory broke the silence. 'It's not the fact that I was unfaithful, Deirdre, is it? That's not the real issue here. It's the fact that Sophie Burke is part of the equation, isn't it?'

Deirdre said nothing.

'I know you, sweetheart,' continued Rory. 'I sometimes think I know you better than you know yourself. If I had come clean – which I had every intention of doing sooner or later – you wouldn't have taken it so badly, would you? You just can't hack the idea that Sophie has something over you. Are you going to let *that* wreck what we have going for us?'

Deirdre remained stubbornly silent, still staring out of the window.

'You know something? You're behaving like the Deirdre I first met three and a half years ago. The Deirdre who used to play silly-bugger relationship games. I haven't forgotten the little tricks you used to get up to, darling. The energy you put into refusing to acknowledge what was staring you in the face–'

'Such as?' she interrupted, hating herself for sounding childish.

'Such as the elaborate lengths you went to, to deny to yourself that you were smitten with me from the word go.'

'Your egotism is astounding, Rory McDonagh.'

'I'm not being egotistical. I'm just stating the truth, pure and simple. I never denied that I was equally smitten.'

'How adult of you,' she sneered.

'That's a good word, O'Dare. Adult. I thought you'd have made the transition from emotional adolescence by now. Why are you insisting on behaving like a spoilt brat?'

She turned on him. 'I won't have you screwing other women every time my back's turned–'

'I don't,' came the laconic interjection.

'And I won't be made a laughing stock.'

'So who's laughing? Sophie Burke? So what? What does it matter what other people think? You're giving yourself all this grief over an ill-advised fling I had in another country, for fuck's sake. I've admitted it. I've said I'm sorry, and I meant it.'

Deirdre looked down at her hands in her lap. Then she looked back at Rory. He was reclining with his right arm draped along the back of the seat – outwardly relaxed, but with a watchful air. She suddenly ached for his touch, but he made no move towards her. Then: 'We've arrived,' he said.

Rory paid off the cab while she struggled with the unwieldy lock on the front door. He joined her on the top step just as the door swung open, and she felt suffused with relief when he followed her through. As she climbed the stairs to the flat she was agonizingly aware of how close he was behind her, but still he didn't touch her.

When they made the hallway of her flat she automatically hit the replay button on her answering machine and then went on through into the sitting room to close the curtains, turn on the lamps and get some heat going. She was glad of the mundane tasks – they allowed her to buy time while her mind worked hard. What had possessed her to be so supremely intransigent? What idiotic impulse had compelled her to play hard to get with the man she loved? What stupid point had she been trying to make? He had apologized. What more could she wring out of him? He was right. She was behaving childishly, and the wine hadn't helped. She hovered for a moment, wondering what was the best way to work towards a *rapprochement*. All she knew was that she wanted him to take her to bed right now.

In the hall the muffled message on the answering machine had come to an end, and she heard the usual rewind noises. She shut her eyes and quickly rehearsed the only speech she knew she could make. 'Let's forget about this, Rory. I love you and I forgive you. Again.' Deirdre took a deep breath and headed towards the hall. Rory was standing with his hand on the doorhandle, his bag slung over his shoulder.

'Where are you going?' she asked uncertainly, as he opened the door to the flat.

'I told you I just wanted to pick up my bag,' he said. Then he paused. 'I always knew you had a vengeful streak in you, Deirdre. But I never, ever took you for a hypocrite.'

'What are you talking about?'

'Have a listen to the message on your machine. Bye, sweetheart.'

The door swung shut behind him.

She stood there looking at where he'd been a moment before, too shocked to move. How had this happened? How had she *allowed* this to happen? She should have reached out to him in the taxi, she should have confessed outright to him that yes, she'd been stung by the fact that she'd heard the news from Sophie and not him. Instead she'd sat there doling out the silent treatment, trying out pathetic, snotty little one-liners on him, waiting for – waiting for what, exactly? Waiting for Rory McDonagh to beg? She almost laughed at the absurdity of the notion. Rory could be patient. He could allow her plenty of time to forgive him, and he'd woo her so masterfully in the interim that she'd know in the end that she had no choice *but* to forgive him – but he would never beg. She knew that much about him.

As for how well he knew her? *I know you better than you know yourself* . . . he'd said in the taxi. And then, just now: *I always knew you had a vengeful streak in you . . . But I never, ever took you for a hypocrite . . .*

What did he mean by that? Her eyes were drawn to the red light on the answering machine, and as she stared at it she was overcome with a sudden, awful premonition. Stretching out a hesitant hand she pressed the playback button, and then wrapped her arms tightly around herself while she waited for the message to replay.

Jean-Claude Valentin's smooth voice slid over the speaker: 'Deirdre. I have been invited to open an exhibition of paintings by a friend of mine in Belfast on Saturday. I thought it might be an ideal opportunity for us to slip out of town together. Discreetly. I will book a hotel room immediately I hear from you. My telephone number is—' There was a sudden hiatus, and then a light laugh. 'How careless of me. I will of course telephone you. *À bientôt.*'

Then the line went dead.

Chapter Three

For the next few days she couldn't get Rory out of her head. She couldn't even enjoy her birthday dinner in the Trocadero. When she came home in the evenings she would trawl through the messages on her answering machine praying that one of them would be from him. She dropped into Meagher's, the pub he frequented, on a couple of occasions, convinced that she'd see him there. She even went out of her way to walk past his flat on the off-chance of running into him. Again and again she picked up the phone and punched in his number, letting it drop like a hot coal when she heard his recorded voice pick up. What would she say to him? Should she apologize? Apologize for *what*? She had nothing to apologize for.

As time wore on she found herself becoming more indignant. She had given him absolutely no reason to cold-shoulder her like this. She hadn't betrayed him by shagging someone else, the way he had betrayed her. But a small voice inside her head reminded her that in a way she was as much to blame as he was. She had agreed to Jean-Claude Valentin's suggestion that she get back at Rory through him, she had gone so far as to snog the actor in a taxi – and she knew she would have invited him in that night if he hadn't had to be elsewhere. The thought that Rory would have caught them *in flagrante delicto* if Jean-Claude *had* come to bed with her made her catch her breath in horror.

She didn't see Jean-Claude all week. He was involved in interior scenes while hers were all exterior, so their schedules didn't dove-tail at all. She didn't hear from him either, and she was rather relieved by this. She wasn't sure that she wanted to spend a night in a hotel in Belfast with a married man – even one as sexy and grown-up as Jean-Claude Valentin. Anyway, his suggestion that it would be a way of getting even with her boyfriend was no longer valid. There was currently no boyfriend to get even with.

On the following Tuesday morning she was sitting at the kitchen table, wrestling with dialogue for episode thirty-three, when the phone rang. She knocked over her coffee cup in her haste to reach it, but, realizing that she was going to sound terminally uncool if she picked up the phone in such a state, she allowed it to ring a couple more times before she picked up. 'Hello?' she breathed, in as languid a voice as she could manage, trusting that she sounded impressively uninterested. But it wasn't Rory. It was their agent's voice on the other end of the line.

'Deirdre? Are you all right? Your voice sounds very strange.'

'Oh, hi, Sally. Yeah – I'm fine.' She made an

attempt at a little cough. 'I've a tickle in my throat, that's all.'

'Listen to me. Are you interested in being seen for a film?'

A film? Oh, yes. Yes, she was.

'Yes. Yes, I am.' she said.

'OK. This is starting mid-March, but you wouldn't be required much before April. We could ask RTE to be flexible if one or two dates clash.'

'What's the gig, Sally?'

'You heard that the Grace O'Malley picture is back on line?'

'Yes.' Deirdre felt a faint twinge of disquiet.

'Will you test?'

Her disquiet increased. 'But Juliet Rathbone-Lyon is casting. There's no way she'd consider me!'

'Her assistant is setting up the tests. She knows nothing about the run-in you had with Juliet. Anyway, Deirdre, that was over three years ago. Juliet's shrewd enough not to bear grudges. It's not in her interests to be so intransigent.'

'What role?'

'Young Grace.'

Deirdre's heart plummeted to the pit of her stomach. She'd be testing with Rory. There was no way she could do it. What to say to Sally, though? She tried to dream up an excuse, but couldn't do it quickly enough. She'd just have to be straight with her agent. 'Sally? There's a bit of a problem there. I'll have to screen-test with Rory.'

'Deirdre – I'd have thought that might be to

your advantage. Think of the chemistry.'

'Unfortunately not. We've split.' Now that she heard herself say the words for the first time, she knew with awful clarity that it was the truth.

'Not *again*,' came Sally's incredulous response.

'Yeah.' Suddenly she felt like crying. Up until this moment she had somehow successfully persuaded herself that she and Rory would get it together before he had to head back to LA.

Down the phone her agent sighed. 'You really get your timing right, don't you, Deirdre?' Deirdre's muffled acknowledgement must have made Sally decide to soften her tone, because her manner when she continued was a lot more sympathetic. 'Shit. I really am sorry to hear about this. No chance of a reconciliation?'

Deirdre had thought about this long and hard. She knew that Rory was unlikely to make the first move. The only way she'd get him back now would be by crawling to him, and she was no better at begging than he was. 'No. It's final this time.'

'I've heard that before,' said Sally with a touch of scepticism.

'I know,' said Deirdre, labouring to inject a note of apology into her voice. It just succeeded in making her sound defeated.

'Oh, poor Deirdre,' said Sally. 'What a grisly position to be in. I'd love to be able to say take twenty-four hours to think about this, but I need to let Juliet's assistant know ASAP so that she can draw up a schedule. They're under pressure to get all the tests in the can this week – McDonagh's been called back to LA sooner than he thought.'

'Oh?' Deirdre felt as if she'd been knifed. 'When's he off?'

'Thursday afternoon. If you're prepared to test you'll be called tomorrow or Thursday morning at the latest.'

'I can't do it, Sally.'

Sally sounded resigned. 'OK, I'll give them a ring and say you're not available. Shame.'

The spectre of the young Grace O'Malley rose before Deirdre's mind's eye. It was a part to die for, and she'd lost out first time round. Now she was being handed another opportunity to go for it. She couldn't let her bastard ex-boyfriend stand in the way. How could she even entertain the idea that she might not test?

'Shit – no. What am I saying? I'll do it,' she said.

'Excellent. I'll get on to them right away.'

'Hang on a sec, though, Sally. If Eva Lavery's playing the older Grace, why do they want to see me? We bear absolutely no resemblance to each other physically. I'm dark, she's fair. She's petite and curvaceous, I'm lanky. She's gorgeous, I'm just–' What was the right word for what she was? 'I'm just *ordinary*.'

'Mine is not to reason why, Deirdre. The thought had struck me too, that you're far from an ideal physical match. All I know is that they asked for you. And by the way, you're neither lanky nor ordinary. You're svelte–' Ow. Rory had used that word about

79

her the first time he'd ever made love to her. 'And you're far too unconventional to be ordinary.'

'Really?' said Deirdre. 'Then it must be fun to be conventional. My life's been shite lately.'

*　　*　　*

Her test was arranged for eleven-thirty on Thursday morning. She made damn sure she was looking her best. These were preliminary tests – there would be no wardrobe or make-up facilities – so Deirdre took care to ensure that her street make-up was faultless. After she had applied a layer of Lip-cote (she knew from experience that a fixative was necessary when screen-kisses were required) she sat back and surveyed herself in the mirror, wondering if she was going to all this trouble for Rory or for the casting people. Don't be stupid, she told herself, shrugging out of her robe and rummaging through her knicker drawer. Of course it was for the casting people. *Oh?* said that irritating small voice in the back of her head. *In that case, why are you rooting around for your Agent Provocateur underwear?*

At eleven-fifteen she walked into the makeshift studio where the tests were to be shot. There was an actress Deirdre didn't know waiting in the reception area. She regarded Deirdre with suspicion when she sat down beside her.

'Hi,' said Deirdre, trying to sound breezy. 'Are they on schedule?'

'No. Running late,' replied the other girl shortly,

returning her attention to the page of dialogue she was studying. Deirdre got her own pages out of her backpack. She was used to the slight hostility which existed between actresses in situations like this.

Sally had faxed her a couple of pages of dialogue after their phone conversation on Tuesday. The scene in question was to show Grace and her new husband meeting for the very first time on their wedding day. Their mutual attraction was to be obvious from the moment they set eyes on each other, and the scene culminated in a kiss. There was little dialogue, but it was well-written and easy to learn. Deirdre had studied it till she was dead-letter-perfect, trying hard not to visualize Rory feeding her the cue lines. She hoped that she wouldn't be thrown when she stepped in front of the camera with him.

The door to the studio opened and a PA stepped into the reception area, followed by a very young, very beautiful redheaded actress. Deirdre had seen her in a show at the Phoenix theatre recently, and had been impressed. She suddenly felt ridiculously old and decidedly unattractive. The little actress was talking in an undertone to the casting assistant, who was scribbling down details on a sheet of paper.

'Thanks,' said Juliet Rathbone-Lyon's assistant when she'd finished. 'Your agent should hear from us in a couple of weeks.' She turned her attention to the girl sitting beside Deirdre on the long couch. 'Are you next? I'll call you in a minute or two,' she said, before turning and going back into the studio.

'Hi, Lauren!' fluted the diminutive redhead,

dimpling at the girl on the couch. 'How's it going?'

'Hi, Iseult,' returned the actress called Lauren.

Lauren! Iseult! thought Deirdre despondently. Even her name put her at a disadvantage.

'I'm a bit nervous, actually,' continued Lauren. Deirdre noticed that the girl was actually shaking.

'Oh! there's no need to be,' Iseult reassured her. 'He's *divine*!'

'To look at or to work with?' asked Lauren.

'Both,' said Iseult, with a meaningful smile. 'I've never been kissed like *that* before. And certainly not on screen.'

Bastard. Fucking, fucking bastard.

Iseult started buttoning up her coat. 'D'you know something?' she said in a sick-makingly sexy voice. 'I'd play the role for nothing if it meant I could do bed scenes with a man like that. Wow!' Then she gave her head a little shake, as if trying to rouse herself from a reverie, and headed for the door. 'Break a leg, Lauren!' she added over her shoulder, sounding as if she meant it.

'Same to you, Iseult!' said Lauren with equal warmth, getting to her feet as the PA beckoned her through into the studio.

Deirdre sat there on her own, simmering inwardly. It wasn't right that other women should feel that way about her man! And how crass to broadcast it like that! Except he wasn't her man any more, she reminded herself. Hell! What a night-marish situation to be landed in! She wasn't going to be able to hack it – she knew she wasn't. She looked at her watch. It was half past eleven. Hers was the last test scheduled – Sally had told her that Rory needed to be out of there by midday if he was to make his flight to LA. Maybe she should just cut her losses and make herself scarce. Sally would understand if she backed out. But Juliet bloody Rathbone-Lyon wouldn't, and she couldn't land Sally in the shit again. Her agent had already taken enough stick for that last run-in with the casting director. Deirdre should have realized the minute she'd agreed to test that there could be no backing out.

'I'm sorry,' the casting assistant was saying as she came through the door. 'You're not on my list, and I'm under strict instructions not to test anyone who hasn't been put forward by an agent. You've wasted your own time by coming here today, and what's more, you've pissed me off by wasting my time as well. I suggest you do things by the book next time, instead of resorting to subversive tactics to get seen.'

The girl called Lauren was skulking in the casting assistant's wake, looking so mortified that Deirdre felt sorry for her. She slid through the door, directing a furtive, murderous backward glance at the world in general.

'Deirdre O'Dare?' Juliet Rathbone-Lyon's assistant was looking at her with one eyebrow raised. There was something peremptory about her manner. Deirdre didn't have to wonder who her role model was. 'I'm Katie, Juliet's assistant. Would you like to follow me through?'

She led the way, not waiting for an answer. Deirdre screwed her courage to the sticking place and walked through the door into the studio, trying to look elegant, casual, nonchalant and unconcerned. What a performance! she thought.

Rory was sitting on a table at the opposite end of the room, swinging his legs. He evinced no surprise at seeing her. 'Hi, Deirdre,' he said. 'I see you're last on the list.'

'Hi, Rory,' she said back. 'I hear you're off to LA again today.'

'Oh – you two know each other, do you?' said Katie. 'That makes things easier.'

No it doesn't, thought Deirdre. She had a suspicion that Rory was thinking exactly the same thought.

'Would you like a little rehearsal before we roll tape on you?' asked Katie.

'I don't think that'll be necessary,' said Rory, jumping down from the table. 'Unless you'd prefer a rehearsal, Deirdre?' he added, politely inclining his head in her direction.

'Let's not bother,' she replied, returning his urbane smile. The fewer times she had to go through this grotesque scenario, the better, as far as she was concerned.

Katie shot a look of enquiry at the video operator. 'Rolling,' he said.

'All right.' Katie took a seat on the demarcation line of the playing area. 'We'll be in close on you, Deirdre. Are you certain you wouldn't like to run the scene once or twice before we record? A little fore-play, if you know what I mean?'

Jesus! 'Certain, thanks.'

'Well. Whenever you're ready, then.'

Deirdre bowed her head and waited for Rory to initiate the dialogue.

'You're much more beautiful than your portrait.'

She raised her eyes to his. His expression was watchful, but there was a hint of amusement there too.

'And you look nothing like yours,' she responded. She was relieved to find that she could meet his eyes square on.

'I'm glad to hear it. It's an execrable portrait.' He moved in towards her. 'What shall we do now?' he asked.

'What's customary behaviour for newly weds after the ceremony?'

'They spend a lot of time fucking. Or so I'm told.' Rory hadn't once allowed his eyes to leave her face. He'd tweaked the dialogue. The line in the script read 'making love', not 'fucking'.

'We met for the first time today, Dónal.' She held his gaze. Grace O'Malley wouldn't flinch at the word, and neither would she. 'It's hardly customary to *fuck* someone you've barely been introduced to.'

'I agree that while it's not customary for mere *acquaintances* to know each other carnally, it's not unheard of between man and wife.'

'True. And it's not unheard of between people who feel lust for each other.'

85

'Do you feel lust for me, Grace?' He trailed a finger down the side of her face. Then he took her hand, raised it to his mouth and licked the palm.

Deirdre smiled at him. 'I have never yet desired to be intimate with a man, Dónal. I'm not sure that I know what lust is. Perhaps you could teach me to recognize it, if I ever should – *perchance* – have experience of it?'

'What do you feel now?' He moved her hair away from her neck and kissed her lingeringly on her collarbone. Deirdre caught her breath.

'I feel strange.'

'Warm?'

'Yes.'

'Ardent?'

'That, too.'

'Is there a better word to describe how you feel?'

'Yes.' Deirdre reached up, took Rory's face between her hands and kissed him on the mouth. 'I feel aflame.'

Rory laughed. 'You are as brazen as you look, Grace. I think I'm going to enjoy being married to you.' He looked at her with amused eyes for a moment, and then he bent his head down and kissed her.

Deirdre felt her lips part as their mouths fused. The kiss they exchanged was soft, almost tentative, as befitted the first kiss between lovers. Then Rory started to explore her mouth with a leisurely tongue, and things suddenly became more urgent. She found herself clinging to him, kissing him back with a passion that took her by surprise.

'Cut.'

Rory and Deirdre continued to kiss.

'Uh – cut.'

He broke the kiss for her, but continued to hold her wrapped in his arms, looking at her with a kind of enquiry in his eyes.

'Um. That was very nice.' The casting assistant was obviously stuck for words. 'You two have a terrific – er – rapport.'

Deirdre disengaged herself from Rory's residual embrace. She knew she was looking rather flushed.

'Thanks very much, Deirdre.' Katie had got to her feet and picked up her clipboard and pen. 'I'll need to take down a few details before you go. Come through to reception, will you?'

Deirdre followed the casting assistant, busily pretending to do up a button on her cuff.

'Bye, Deirdre.'

She turned. Rory was still standing where she'd left him. 'Good luck,' he said.

'Thanks, Rory. Enjoy LA.'

'I'll send you a postcard,' he said.

'You're with Sally Ruane, aren't you?' asked Katie. Deirdre returned her attention to the casting assistant, who was motioning her towards the door.

'That's right.'

'And you *are* available, aren't you? We're not considering any actresses who may have conflicts.'

Bloody hell, thought Deirdre, as she walked out of the studio. If Deirdre O'Dare was cast opposite Rory McDonagh, there'd be plenty of those.

* * *

That evening she got a call from Jean-Claude Valentin.

'Hello, darling. What are you up to?'

'Nothing much,' she replied miserably. 'I'm bogged down in dialogue.'

'I know how you feel. Marc has his speech to the dock next week, and I am having huge problems with it.'

'Marc? Who's Marc?'

'The character I play in *Ardmore Grove*, Deirdre.' Jean-Claude sounded amused.

'Oh – yes. Oh, God – how stupid of me! I really am not thinking straight.' In fact she'd spent the entire evening thinking about Rory. She hadn't been able to rid her mind of what Iseult, the little redheaded actress, had said about him that morning: *I've never been kissed like that before . . . I'd play the role for nothing if it meant I could do bed scenes with a man like that.* He'd obviously had a ball for the past couple of days, indulging in a vicarious sex life with some of the most nubile actresses in Dublin.

'It sounds to me like you need a break, Deirdre. Have you thought about coming to Belfast with me?'

'I – well, I'm not . . .'

'Please don't feel under any pressure. I simply thought it would be an ideal opportunity for us to get to know each other a little better.'

'You said something about opening an exhibition?'

'Yes. That will take a mere hour or so. I have been invited to join my friend for dinner later, but I will tell him I need to get back to Dublin. Then we can escape somewhere – go out for a lazy lunch. I know of a wonderful little restaurant just out of town. It is very discreet; the food is excellent. And as much champagne as you can drink. Cristal, I think, for you.'

Cristal. The champagne of the tsars. The picture he was painting sounded very inviting. Hell. She *could* do with a break. But she still wasn't sure about the sexual side of things. What if they decided that they didn't have much in common, after all?

'Jean-Claude – I – don't really know how to put this. What if . . .'

'What if you don't want to go to bed with me? That won't be a problem, Deirdre. I have a rule that I never sleep with a woman if I sense in any way that she is reluctant.'

'I wouldn't say that's been much of a problem for you. I'd say every woman in the country finds you irresistible.' She wasn't massaging his ego. Impressed by his directness, she was simply trying to match it.

'That's a kind thing to say. There is one notable exception, of course.'

'Oh?'

'My wife. Or should I say my soon-to-be-ex wife.'

'You're getting divorced?'

'Yes. We have been living a lie for too long. I've decided to move out.'

'Ah. Where to?'

'I'm looking for a place at the moment. I've been going through a pretty unpleasant time lately.'

'Poor Jean-Claude.'

'Yeah. That's why – *merde*. I hear the front door. She's back. Listen, Deirdre. Will you come with me or not? No strings. I'll organize separate rooms for the night if that will make you feel happier?'

'I'm not really–'

'I'm under pressure, Deirdre. Will I pick you up at your place at around nine o'clock on Saturday morning?' His voice was urgent.

'I – well, OK, Jean-Claude, but–'

'Very well. Thanks for sorting that out for me, Frank.' *Frank*? Oh, of course. His wife must be within earshot. 'See you soon,' he said in a breezy voice. 'Goodbye.'

'Bye, Jean-Claude,' she replied uncertainly. Then she put the phone down, feeling a bit fluttery. What was she doing? This was classic rebound behaviour. Rebuffed by Rory, she was lobbing herself straight into the arms of another man. And not just any man – a married man. It didn't matter that he claimed his marriage was on the rocks – it wasn't over yet.

She wandered to the fridge and helped herself to a can of Miller. Not bothering with a glass, she pulled the tab and held the can to her lips. Then she fetched a tube of Pringles from the cupboard and sat back down at the kitchen table. Miller and Pringles, she thought. It was a bit bloody sad, really. She pictured herself in the intimate ambience of some small restaurant in Belfast, sipping champagne and eating lobster with Jean-Claude Valentin. What the hell. She'd go. He himself had said there would be no strings; he was booking separate rooms. There was no pressure.

She got up to go to the loo, catching sight of her reflection in the mirror over the bathroom basin on her way through. She paused and studied herself, noticing that a little furrow of uncertainty had formed between her brows. Rory had always taken her head between his hands any time he spotted it, and smoothed her frowns away with a kiss. There was his toothbrush, still stuck in the holder by the basin.

She stalked into the kitchen and pulled a binbag out of a drawer. Then she walked through the flat, dropping his belongings into it, systematically getting rid of every trace of her ex. The only thing she didn't trash was a photograph that she'd had framed for him, which had somehow ended up living in her flat rather than his. It had been taken when they'd been holidaying in the West of Ireland, and while it wasn't a particularly good shot of Rory – his face was in partial shadow – *she* looked great. She left it where it had always stood – on her bedside table.

Chapter Four

Jean-Claude rang her bell punctually at nine o'clock on Saturday morning. She was packed and ready to go, and she was leaving last-minute instructions with Bart, the actor who lived next door, about feeding the cat. Betty Grable had put on a lot of weight recently, and she was on a special 'lite' cat food which she hated. Deirdre warned Bart not to give in to her pleas for more, no matter how heartfelt. She had to lower her tone when issuing this directive, because she could see Betty Grable eyeing her suspiciously.

Bart had let out a whistle when he'd answered his door to her. 'You're looking particularly elegant,' he'd said. 'Where are you off to? And with whom? And does McDonagh know?'

Deirdre had tapped her nose. 'I have a hot date in Belfast, nosy parker. And McDonagh and I are ancient history.'

'*Again*?' Bart raised a cynical eyebrow. She knew she was going to have to get used to this stock response to the latest update in the McDonagh–O'Dare affair. 'I heard you two going down the stairs last weekend sounding very lovey-dovey.'

That would have been the Saturday they'd gone to the Clarence.

'I *wasn't* eavesdropping,' Bart added, registering the look she gave him. 'You were both in such rollicking good form it was impossible not to hear. What's happened between you now?'

That's when the doorbell had rung. 'I don't have time to explain right now, Bart,' said Deirdre, swinging her overnight bag onto her shoulder. 'I'll invite you for supper some evening next week and tell all, OK?'

'OK. But let me do the cooking, will you?'

Deirdre smiled back at him as she hurried down the stairs. 'It's a deal. I'll provide the wine.'

Jean-Claude was standing at the bottom of the front steps, waiting for her. He raised a hand in warning when she stood on tiptoe to give him a kiss. 'Caution. Caution, Deirdre,' he said, holding the passenger door of his Porsche open for her. 'We don't want to be observed.'

'Cool car,' she remarked, as she slid into the passenger seat.

'I decided to be nice to myself. At my stage in life a man deserves a few treats. That series of after-shave commercials paid for it. It's not new, I need hardly add.'

'It doesn't matter. It's still stunning. Do you get a lot of admiring looks from beautiful women?'

'Yes, I do, as a matter of fact.'

'It doesn't surprise me.'

'Well. Not so much me as the car,' he said, with his charming, self-deprecatory smile.

As the Porsche slid away from in front of the house, Deirdre looked up and saw Bart saluting her from his sitting-room window. She stiffened a little. But Bart was a very good friend. If he had recognized Jean-Claude, she knew that she could trust him to keep schtum for her.

The journey north took just over two and a half hours. Jean-Claude was extremely good company. He made her laugh a lot, paid her extravagant compliments, and he had excellent taste in music. Deirdre found that as the journey wore on, any doubts she may have had as to whether she was doing the right thing became increasingly vestigial.

Jean-Claude filled her in on his failed marriage. He had married very young – while he and his wife were both in their teens. He had two children, one at college in France, one in her final year at school in Dublin. They were both old enough to understand that their parents' relationship was on the rocks; that it had been for some time. In return, Deirdre told him about Rory; about his compulsive flirting and how it had resulted in one infidelity too many.

Jean-Claude was philosophical. 'It is for the best, I'm sure,' he said. 'A man like that – a man who constantly betrays the woman he loves – is bad news, Deirdre. That is the right phrase, yes?'

She nodded.

'Sooner or later he will break your heart, and then you will be his prisoner – you will become a victim of love. No woman should allow herself to be treated with such indignity. A woman who is a victim is a sad, sad thing.'

'I don't think there's much fear of me ever becoming a victim, Jean-Claude. I've always had a stubborn streak.' The image of Rory as she had last seen him suddenly crossed her mind's eye. She saw again the look of enquiry that he'd directed at her as she'd extricated herself from his embrace after their passionate screen kiss. 'Sometimes I wonder if I'm not *too* stubborn. It's a very Capricorn thing. What star sign are you, by the way?'

'Scorpio,' he replied.

* * *

Once they got to Belfast, Deirdre was given the task of map-reading. They'd both visited the north before, but neither of them had ever negotiated Belfast city centre by car. Deirdre's sense of direction was dodgy at the best of times, but in an unfamiliar city she was worse than inept.

With a sigh, Jean-Claude pulled over in the nearest convenient parking place and consulted the map himself. Then he looked at his watch. '*Merde*,' he muttered. 'Midday. I'm running late. The gallery is just around the corner, but the one-way system means I'll have to go at least a kilometre out of my way. In traffic, too. That will make me later still.' He took a last look at the map, folded it and put it away in the glove compartment. Then he turned to

Deirdre. 'It's probably easier if I leave the car here and walk. I'll give you a call on your mobile when I'm finished and we can meet back here.'

'What do you mean?'

Jean-Claude looked at her quizzically. 'What do *you* mean?' he asked.

'Well, why do we have to meet back here? Why can't I come with you?'

'Oh, darling – I would have thought that was obvious!' Jean-Claude took her hand in his. 'I never dreamt that you would expect to come with me to the gallery this morning. I thought it would be more amusing for you to spend a couple of hours browsing around the shops. It would look very bad, don't you think, if I arrived to open an exhibition with a beautiful woman on my arm who was not my wife?'

'But we're work colleagues!'

'Deirdre. Deirdre! We may be colleagues, but you know how people love to gossip. For me to escort an actress to a social event is simply asking for trouble – especially when that actress has a reputation for being sizzling, sexy, sultry and seductive.'

He smiled down at her and she returned his smile with an effort.

Why did some people never accept that there could be such a thing as a *non*-sexual relationship between men and women? Why did everybody automatically jump to conclusions? Although in this instance they'd probably be jumping to the right conclusions, she admitted to herself, with niggling reluctance. Two and a half hours spent in the close confines of his car had only succeeded in heightening the sexual dynamic between them.

'You see, darling – things are at a critical stage between Chantal and me. If word got back to her that I'd been seen in public with an extremely desirable young woman – *phut*! Our divorce proceedings would become thoroughly unpleasant. You do understand, don't you?'

She made an ambiguous little *moue* and shrugged her shoulders. She simply hadn't anticipated this. 'So I'll just mooch around town until you're finished?'

'*Mooch* is not a good word, Deirdre. Shop. Belfast is full of wonderful shops.'

Belfast may be full of wonderful shops, she thought darkly, but her credit card would be of absolutely no use to her. She had maxed out again.

Jean-Claude unfastened his seatbelt and stretched. 'I will be as fleeting as I can,' he said, giving her an appreciative smile. 'I will warn them that I have a very important assignation, and that I sadly cannot stay long. What is your mobile number?'

'I don't have a mobile.'

'No mobile? That makes things a little more difficult.' His furrowed brow just succeeded in making him look even sexier. 'Let me think. An hour should suffice. Maybe one and a half to be on the safe side. I will meet you back here at half past one.' He leant over and gave her a light kiss on her mouth. Deirdre just resisted the impulse to reach out and draw him closer. 'Enjoy your shopping,' he added with another smile as he leant back and opened the passenger door for her.

She slid out of the car and pulled her coat collar up. It was cold and there was a faint drizzle falling.

'Have you money enough for shopping?' Jean-Claude asked her as he zapped the locks. 'If you have insufficient, I can let you have some.'

'I'm OK.' Deirdre had some sterling: not much, but she wasn't going to let Jean-Claude know that. From his tone she inferred that he was talking about a gift, not a loan, and she didn't know him well enough to be beholden to him.

'Well. Enjoy the rest of your morning, darling.' One last smile, and he was striding down the road away from her. She thrust her hands in her pockets and turned in the direction of the city centre, preparing herself to mooch.

*   *   *

At the appointed time she made her way back to where Jean-Claude had left the car. Her one and a half hours of mooching had resulted in two purchases: a slim volume of short stories by Anaïs Nin, and a Lion Bar. She'd spent some time sitting over a cappuccino in a hip little café reading three of the short stories, and had been taken aback by the intense eroticism of the writing. Anaïs Nin's latin lovers were seriously hot, and she found herself looking forward to this evening with more than a flutter of anticipation. What was it exactly that gave continental men that unmistakable, sexual edge?

Jean-Claude was waiting for her in the Porsche. Deirdre was impressed by his time-keeping. She'd half expected him to be late – she was aware how difficult it could be for a celebrity to get away from openings and launches. She'd emcee'd a charity fashion show once, and everybody had wanted a little piece of her. In the end, Rory had given her an ultimatum: he'd leant into her and murmured, 'I'm not going down on you for a week if we don't hit the pub in five minutes.' They'd hit it in four.

'Hello, darling,' said Jean-Claude as she opened the passenger door and got in. 'What? No carrier bags?'

'I couldn't see anything I liked,' she lied. The city centre shops had actually been full of desirable items, and she had cursed herself for her deficiency of credit card cop-on.

'Ah, well. I have a little something for you that I hope you will like.'

'A present?'

'Mm-hm. I saw it in a shop the day after you agreed to come to Belfast with me, and I was inspired to buy it. I just knew it was for you.'

'Jean-Claude, you shouldn't have!' she protested feebly. She loved getting presents. 'What is it?'

He tapped her on the nose with a finger and laughed. 'A surprise. I will let you have it later.' Then he started the car and took a left, heading away from the city centre.

'Aren't we going to the hotel?' Deirdre asked.

She'd assumed that they'd check in before lunch.

'I booked a table in the restaurant for two o'clock,' he said. 'If we are going to get there on time we'd better get started.' He stopped at a pedestrian crossing to let a young woman with a buggy cross, registering her grateful smile with a gallant little inclination of his head. Deirdre couldn't help but feel a bit smug to be sitting beside this gorgeous Frenchman in his Porsche. 'A stroll along the coast afterwards would be nice, don't you think? The restaurant is not far from Carrickfergus: there are some lovely places to walk. I came here with the children once.'

Deirdre didn't much like being reminded of Jean-Claude's children. His marital status still hit a circumspect nerve somewhere inside her. 'We're not really dressed for a walk in the country, Jean-Claude.' She looked dubiously down at her Russell and Bromley heels.

'Don't worry. We'll stick to the roads.'

* * *

The restaurant was perfect. The ambience was intimate, the staff were friendly but unobtrusive. There was champagne in crystal flutes, there were proper linen tablecloths and napkins on the table, and there were fresh flowers in a little silver vase. Nat King Cole was on the sound system. Jean-Claude had oysters, and Deirdre had lobster. Sexy food – and sexy conversation to go with it. Jean-Claude made

100

her laugh, and when Deirdre O'Dare laughed, she positively lit up.

They had a lot of fun devising nonsensical scenarios for their soap opera characters, and Jean-Claude's imperfect English made the dialogue he came up with sound even more absurd. They discovered that they both secretly despised Chekov – 'I don't know how any actress alive could come out with that "I am a seagull" line without corpsing,' observed Deirdre – and they agreed that Sam Beckett was the finest and funniest playwright of the century. They talked about the French Impressionists and they talked about how they hated the word 'zany' and they talked about what the smell of freshly baked bread reminded them of. At one point the actor took her hand to suck melted butter off her fingers and Deirdre nearly swooned.

When they finished, Jean-Claude helped himself to one of the blossoms in the little silver vase and tucked it behind her ear. 'Let's go for that walk,' he said.

The walk was an excellent idea. It gave them an opportunity to exchange their life-stories. Deirdre's was much shorter than his, of course, because she hadn't lived as long or had as eventful a life as he had. The more he told her about the tragedy of his loveless marriage, the more she found herself warming to him – and the more the notion of taking him as a lover appealed to her. They stopped at one point so that she could lean up against a five-barred gate and give him her undivided attention, and Jean-Claude kissed her properly for the first time since the night in the taxi. By the time the kiss had ended some ten minutes later, the notion of taking him as a lover was no longer appealing. It was quite irresistible.

On the drive back to Belfast, Jean-Claude outlined the agenda for their overnight stay. 'We'll have to keep a low – hm – how do you say it? A low silhouette while we are here, Deirdre. We can't run the risk of any unfortunate encounters.'

'You mean a low profile, Jean-Claude,' she said, smiling at him. She loved the way he handled the gears of the Porsche – with a kind of insouciant dexterity.

'A low profile,' he repeated. 'That's why I chose somewhere off the beaten trail for us to have lunch. I know I can trust them to be discreet in that restaurant.'

She wondered how he knew that.

'You are aware, aren't you, that if we go anywhere in the city together, people will be bound to notice?' he continued, giving her a wry smile. 'Someone might even think it newsworthy enough to let slip to the tabloids.'

She'd never really got used to being public property. Being in soap opera meant that people tended to notice you a lot. Sometimes she'd find herself wondering why people were staring at her before remembering that she was beamed into their sitting rooms nearly every week. So it was wise to be circumspect – but not always easy. One of the tabloids had stooped so low as to send an undercover hack to a restaurant where an actress friend was having her hen night, and the party – which had hardly been riotous – had been exaggerated out of all proportion in the Sunday edition. They had described Deirdre as looking 'sexy and sensational in a skimpy frock' when she had in fact been dressed head-to-toe in Ghost.

'Do you think we could manage to get by on room service for the duration of our stay?' he asked. 'I can have something sent up to our room later.'

Deirdre noticed his use of the singular. 'Room? I thought you were going to book two rooms, Jean-Claude, just in case we–'

'I'm sorry, darling. Didn't I mention it to you? There's a conference this weekend – the hotel's fully booked. I was fortunate to be able to get any kind of room at such short notice.'

'Oh.'

It was *fait accompli*, then.

*   *   *

Jean-Claude checked in solo while Deirdre mooched around the hotel shop. He had commandeered her bag, telling her it would look suspicious if she was seen getting into the lift with an overnight bag, and he had insisted that she allow a discreet five-minutes interval before following him up to the room. She spent the time pretending to be interested in the magazines on display. As she headed towards the lift, she noticed that the one she'd finally felt obliged to buy contained explicit advice on how to perform a blow-job. She scanned it on the way up. Why hadn't Rory *told* her she'd got it so wrong all these years? Well, hell – he certainly hadn't complained – and what kind of a sad individual had to make a living out of writing magazine articles about blow-jobs, for goodness' sake?

She slipped the magazine into her backpack and zipped it shut just as the lift deposited her on the sixth floor. Tapping lightly on the door of room 609, she cast a cautious look over her shoulder. There was no-one around to observe her, and if there had been they'd hardly have registered her presence, because Jean-Claude was at the door in a flash to usher her inside.

'Excuse me,' he said. 'I'm on the phone to room service. One minute, darling, all right?'

Deirdre dumped her backpack on the floor and looked around. The hotel brochure described its rooms as being 'luxurious'. In fact, the room was standard hotel. Comfortable, pristinely clean, with Regency striped wallpaper below the dado rail and subdued dove-grey above. Reproduction Renoirs hung above the king-sized bed, which was draped in a slate-blue quilt. Ambling over to the window, she drew back the net curtain that covered the plate glass and looked out at the grey cityscape.

'Veuve Cliquot will do then,' Jean-Claude was saying into the phone. 'Yes. Thank you.' He put the phone down and she turned to him. He had changed from the suit he'd been wearing earlier into jeans and a sweatshirt. He looked at her intently and in silence for a long minute. She found it extraordinarily sexy. Then he smiled. 'They don't keep Cristal, I'm afraid, my darling. Come here.'

Deirdre found herself doing as she was told. He took her in his arms and touched his lips to her ear. 'I've thought about this all week,' he breathed, and his accent sounded Frencher than ever. The tip of his tongue curled behind her earlobe, then trailed down the side of her neck to her collarbone. His hands were sliding down her back now, pulling her tight against him. She caught sight of her reflection in the dressing-table mirror quite unexpectedly, and for some reason she remembered how she'd told him what a beautiful screen kisser he was. He certainly looked the part now, with his dark head bent over her neck and his arms wound around her. Then he raised his head and looked at her searchingly, and she couldn't see herself any more. When his mouth met hers, she was ready.

The kisses they exchanged were increasing in passionate intensity when there was a knock at the door. Jean-Claude broke the embrace immediately.

'One moment, please,' he called in his authoritative voice. Then he moved quickly to the bathroom door and held it open, motioning Deirdre inside. 'Through here,' he hissed.

For a moment she was completely flummoxed, and then she recollected the clandestine nature of their tryst. She slid through the door, feeling rather foolish as she swung it shut behind her. To her dismay, the edge of the door didn't make contact with the doorjamb, and as Jean-Claude went to open the door she realized that the bathroom door was swinging open again. If she lunged for it the porter would be certain to notice. She backed further into the room, and then stopped dead as she saw that the bathroom mirror was positioned directly opposite the door. Jean-Claude's hand was on the doorknob. There was only one thing she could do. She stepped quickly into the bath and pulled the shower curtain across just as Jean-Claude said, 'Thank you. Please, put it over there.'

There was the sound of ice clinking and coins being handed over. Deirdre jumped as she felt a drip from the shower land on her head. Then she heard the porter murmur a discreet, 'Thank you, sir,' and at last came the gentle thud of the door as it closed. She could breathe again.

She drew back the shower curtain to find Jean-Claude standing in the bathroom.

'What are you doing in the bath?' he asked.

'Hiding,' she replied.

He laughed as another drip descended on her head, and she felt a bit pissed off. After all, she'd done it for him. *She* wasn't as up to ninety about being found out as he was. *He* was the one who was married.

'Come out,' he said, extending a hand to help her climb out of the bathtub. 'Before you catch cold from all that dripping. There's champagne,' he added, as he let her precede him into the bedroom, 'but only one glass. So I will make do with the toothmug.' He flashed her a gallant smile and reached for one of two glasses upended on the bathroom shelf.

He uncorked the champagne bottle. A plume of vapour rose from the neck like a will-o-the-wisp as he poured. He tilted the bottle to let the fizz settle, then continued to pour with manifest expertise. '*Santé*,' he said, handing her the champagne flute and raising his glass.

'*Santé*,' she echoed. There was a pause while Jean-Claude looked at her with meaning. She took a sip of champagne and set the flute down on the bureau, suddenly feeling a tiny prickle of apprehension. Affecting a nonchalance she did not feel, she picked up the hotel guide and started to leaf through it. 'Let's see what this place has to offer,' she said. 'I love seeing what services different hotels provide.' In fact, she hadn't stayed in that many hotels. Any of the ones she'd stayed in on the few theatrical tours she'd done around Ireland had been kips. The only time she'd ever been to a proper hotel had been when she'd done a telly-play for Granada, who had put her up in the Stakis in Manchester.

'Do they have a masseuse?' asked Jean-Claude.

'No,' she said, scanning the list. She had got to the room service menu. She was hungry suddenly. Her lunch had worn off, and the sea air that had buffeted them as they walked along the coast had sharpened her appetite. She craved the kind of sandwich that hotels did so well – soft white bread with the crusts cut off, and slivers of chicken breast inside, served with potato crisps and bits of frilly salad. 'Jean-Claude?' she said. 'D'you think we could order some sandwiches? I'm suddenly very hungry.'

He gave her an indulgent look. 'Of course, darling. What kind?'

'Chicken, please.'

'Chicken it is. I had better order only one round, though. If I send down for two the hotel staff will either suspect correctly that I am harbouring an illegal alien in my room, or they will think that I am a serious glutton. As it is, they probably think I am a chronic alcoholic for ordering a whole bottle of champagne for myself. I must order some Perrier too, in case we are thirsty later.' He sent her his sexy smile as he punched in the numbers.

Deirdre sat down on the reproduction Regency chair at the reproduction Regency desk and continued to go through the hotel brochure. A card displaying breakfast options fell out. How would they manage breakfast, she wondered? They'd blow their cover if they ordered breakfast for two, and one orange juice and a piffling 'Continental style' breakfast wouldn't go far between them. They'd have to order a big fry-up and share it. At one stage she'd pictured them sitting up in bed with coffee and bagels and smoked salmon and cream cheese, with a pale pink rose unfurling in a miniature vase on the tray in front of them. She'd even fancied that there might be mimosas on the menu, that they could sip between kisses. The reality looked like rashers and sausages, flaccid toast and marmalade. How easily the bubble of her idyll had been punctured. You'd think she should know by now that real life and her fantasy life were poor bed fellows. She turned to the next page, which listed all the television channels.

Jean-Claude put down the phone and moved across to her. He started to lightly kiss the nape of her neck while studying the brochure over her shoulder. 'Phew,' he whistled. 'That's a pretty stiff tariff for the adult channel, isn't it?'

'I wouldn't know. I've never accessed the adult channel.'

He raised an eyebrow at her. 'Oh? You surprise me. Perhaps I should introduce you to it later. I think that you will find it makes – interesting viewing.'

For some reason his sexy smile didn't work as well this time.

She turned the page again. 'Hm. Swimming pool, sauna, jacuzzi,' read Jean-Claude. 'Pity we did not bring bathing clothes. I would like to see you in a sexy little bikini. Which reminds me. You must be wondering about your present.'

Deirdre had actually forgotten all about it.

Jean-Claude rose to his feet and went over to the wardrobe on the opposite side of the room. She noticed the suit he'd been wearing earlier hanging on the rail. It was now zipped up in a plastic cover. Other sundry articles of clothing were so pristinely folded Benetton would be put to shame, and his highly polished shoes stood to attention on the wardrobe floor. He reached up to the top shelf and drew down a glossy, gift-wrapped box.

'Here,' he said, presenting the box to her with a formal little bow. 'I hope you like it. I've spent the last few days thinking about how you will look in it. I would like to think you might model it for me later.'

'Thank you, Jean-Claude.' Deirdre gave him a slightly uncertain smile as she tugged at the broad ribbon which held the gift-wrap in place. It gave immediately, and the paper rustled to the floor to reveal a red cardboard box with 'Scandalous Scanties' emblazoned in black on the lid. Deirdre let the ribbon drop. Ditto her heart. Inside, lying on a bed of black tissue paper, was a red satin boned basque with black lace suspenders attached, a matching red satin G-string with black lace trim, and a pair of glossy black lace-topped stockings. She took the items out and stared at them, open mouthed and utterly dumbfounded.

'Beautiful, isn't it?' he said, reaching out a hand to finger the black lace trim on the basque. 'I trust you don't mind the rather intimate nature of the gift? You know that we French men love to buy lingerie for women. Here. Have a look at this. I had a hard time choosing.' He delved under the tissue paper and produced a catalogue with 'Scandalous Scanties' in swirly print on the front, superimposed over a babe wearing a black PVC playsuit with zips and thigh-high boots. She was toying with the handle of a whip.

'Shit, Jean-Claude. Do you *like* this kind of stuff? I'm not . . .'

'It may not *all* be to your taste,' he interjected

smoothly. 'I'm not interested in that dominatrix stuff either, darling. Of course it's not the ensemble itself so much as the woman who wears it.' He gave her his meaningful smile and started to leaf through the catalogue. 'Some of the ensembles are rather charming, I'm sure you'll agree. This, for instance.'

He paused at a page which bore the legend 'Wedding Night.' A pouting broad with tumbling curls and come-to-bed eyes smouldered on a satin sheet, sucking a suggestive finger. She was wearing a flimsy nylon lace bodice, white lace-trimmed stay-ups, and a transparent lace thong. The *pièce de résistance*, however, was the 'bridal' skirt. It was also made of flimsy white nylon, of mid-thigh length, and it was split to the crotch. 'I think it somehow combines just the right hint of sexiness with a lovely *naïveté*, don't you agree? I was tempted to buy it for you, but the basque is a little more – what is *le mot juste*? *Sophisticated*, Deirdre. I suspect that you are a very sophisticated young lady. I've suspected it from the first time you kissed me.'

Deirdre tucked the items of lingerie back under the tissue paper, trying to breathe normally. Jean-Claude actually thought that slapper in the bridal outfit looked *naïve*? He considered that tacky satin basque *sophisticated*? How had he got her so wrong? How had she got *him* so wrong? She had made a big mistake. It was time to let him down.

Just then the phone rang.

'Excuse me.' Jean-Claude politely inclined his head and picked up the receiver. 'Ah.' There was a hiatus before he said anything else. Then: '*Hallo? Oui. Oui, ça va. Oui. Bon. J'étais sur le point de descendre pour dîner. Oui. Oui. Oui. Bon.*' There followed a long stream of French which Deirdre found difficult to understand. She could, however, make out that the person on the other end of the phone was most certainly Jean-Claude's wife. He was pitching his voice as low as he could, and she could tell that all those *ouis* and *bons* were so stilted and unnatural that they were being used as stalling tactics. He was obviously trying to give as little away as possible, and Deirdre suspected that it was for the benefit of not only his wife, but for the benefit of his putative mistress, also. He was playing them both on the same line, and she had a sudden shrewd notion that Jean-Claude Valentin's marriage wasn't that unhappy after all. He made an apologetic face at her, shrugging his shoulders and mouthing 'sorry'. Then he said, '*Oui, oui, moi aussi. Il faut que je te dis ces mots? Eh bien – oui, oui – je t'aime, moi aussi.*' This last sentence came out in such a rush that Jean-Claude sounded practically strangulated. Then he put down the phone sheepishly.

'Your wife.' She didn't bother to make it a query.

'Yes.' He didn't bother to lie.

'I'm out of here.' Deirdre reached for her backpack just as there was another knock at the door.

'*Merde*! Room service!' moaned Jean-Claude. Then he raised his voice for the benefit of the porter. 'One moment, please!' He turned to Deirdre. 'Listen to me, Deirdre, it is not what you think. I can explain

112

everything. Don't run out on me without giving me a chance to clear this up. Please.'

His performance as the abjured husband was no longer convincing.

'Give me a break, Jean-Claude,' said Deirdre in a pitying tone.

'Look. Listen.' He was flailing now. 'Stay in the bathroom again, will you please? I'll let the porter in and we can talk when he's gone.'

Deirdre almost said, 'There's nothing to talk about, Jean-Claude,' before realizing that if she came out with *that* stock response – the stock response she'd used on Rory that fateful night in the Clarence – she'd be talking in the kind of clichéd language he was using. *It's not what you think. I can explain everything.* What did he take her for? A totally dim-witted walkover?

However, she didn't particularly want to be subjected to the smirking glances that the hotel porter would be sure to send in her direction. She moved resignedly towards the bathroom, flinging Jean-Claude a contemptuous look over her shoulder.

'Wait!' Jean-Claude lunged towards where she'd left the box of lingerie lying on the bed and thrust it into her arms. 'I cannot leave this lying around.'

'I don't see why not,' responded Deirdre with equanimity. 'He'll just assume you're into dressing up in women's clothing as well as being a glutton and an alcoholic.' Then she turned on her heel and walked into the bathroom with as much dignity as she could muster, making sure this time that the door stayed firmly shut behind her.

She sat down on the loo seat and fumed silently. What a fiasco!

Beyond the door she could hear Jean-Claude's urbane tones as he instructed the hotel porter where to leave the tray.

Slimy git, she thought. Smarmy French sleazebag. She poked among the layers of tissue paper and re-examined the get-up he'd wanted her to wear for him. How could he have imagined that she was some pliant little girl who'd accommodate his sordid fantasies by dressing in whores' underwear? She rubbed the fabric of the basque between finger and thumb. At least it was real silk, not some tacky man-made fibre. That would have been even more of a blow to her self-respect. The thought of it made her shudder. Yeuch! What future scenarios might he have had in mind for her if she'd obliged him this time round? A French maid's outfit?

She suddenly recalled the occasion when Rory had surprised her with the Agent Provocateur lingerie. It was seriously beautiful, seriously expensive and *seriously* sexy. At least Rory had had taste.

As she listened to the clinking sounds of plates and cutlery being laid out in the bedroom next door an awful thought struck her. She shot a look at her watch. It was a quarter to eight. What time did the last train leave for Dublin? The prospect of being stranded in Belfast filled her with intense alarm. She got to her feet and put her ear to the door. Thank heaven. Jean-Claude was tipping the porter. She could be out of this sad hotel room within seconds.

The instant she heard the door close she burst out of the bathroom and grabbed her stuff.

Jean-Claude laid a restraining hand on her arm as she made for the door. 'Deirdre – please. I told you I could explain. I am not the type of man you are mistaking me for. I . . .'

Deirdre gave a hollow laugh. 'Oh, yes, you are, Jean-Claude. You're a walking fucking cliché of the type of man I *know* you are. Enjoy the sandwiches,' she added, flinging open the door. 'And try persuading your wife to wear the tart's outfit. If she agrees, your marriage is obviously not as moribund as you wanted me to believe. Bye.' Turning away, she raced down the hotel corridor and banged the call button for the lift with a fist.

She shifted from foot to foot with impatience as she waited for it to arrive, and as soon as she hit the lobby she made a beeline for the reception desk. 'Excuse me?' she queried rather breathlessly. 'Can you tell me what time the last train leaves for Dublin?'

'Certainly,' came the smooth response. 'It departs at ten past eight.'

She had twenty minutes. She knew it wasn't far to walk to the station, but she wasn't sure how to get there. She'd have to hail a cab. 'Thanks,' she said to the woman behind the desk, not waiting for the automatic, 'You're welcome.'

A taxi had just pulled up on the concourse outside

the main door of the hotel, but there was a man getting into it. Desperation strengthened her nerve. 'Excuse me?' she said, touching him lightly on the arm. 'I wonder would you mind terribly letting me have your cab? If I don't get one right now I won't get to the train station on time and I'll be completely stranded.'

The man looked down at her. 'Hop in,' he said. 'That's where I'm going. I'd be delighted to share a taxi with such a gorgeous creature.'

Oh *fuck*. Not another sleazebag. She'd just have to grin and bear it.

'Going to Dublin?' he asked too casually, as she swung her bags onto the back seat, between them.

'That's right.' She dimpled obligingly.

'So am I. Perhaps you'd like to join me for dinner in first class?'

She was so hungry that she was almost tempted. 'Sorry,' she said, injecting her voice with a regret that somehow contrived to sound genuine. 'I'd love to, but I'm afraid I'm meeting my boyfriend in standard.'

*   *   *

Her dinner consisted of a tuna sandwich made from bread that tasted like polystyrene.

At the other end of the line she joined the queue for taxis, trying to avoid the man she'd shared the cab with in Belfast. In fact, she soon surmised that there was no need to avoid him because he was obviously avoiding her, too. He was hovering on the opposite side of the concourse to where the taxis lined up and was refusing to look in her direction. The reason for his stand-offish behaviour was apparent as soon as a soft-top BMW swooped down and carried him off. The driver was an immaculately groomed, blonde, thirty-something woman.

Deirdre got into the next taxi that pulled up and sat back in the seat with a weary sigh of relief, hoping that Bart would be at home when she got there. She badly needed to talk to someone sane.

Chapter Five

As she let herself in through the front door she could
hear Radiohead pounding from the region of the
second floor. Bart was in, which was unusual for
him on a Saturday night. Bart was a party animal,
and most Saturday nights he would boogie down
to Meagher's, the actors' pub in the centre of town, to
suss out some action. If he was working nights in the
theatre he very often brought the party home with
him, which was bad news for Deirdre. She couldn't
resist going next door to join in, which meant
staying up till all hours – disastrous if she had an early
call the next morning. She'd skulk palely into make-
up with bags under her eyes, apologizing to the
make-up artist for the extra work she'd have to do on
her face.

Deirdre trailed up the stairs in time to the music,
hoping her friend wouldn't have anyone with him.
She wasn't in the mood for being sociable this
evening, and Bart's latest girlfriend was hard work.
She was a Norwegian student with limited English,
and Deirdre always had to explain any jokes she
made to her. By the time she'd finished explaining,
the joke wasn't funny any more.

She had to knock on the door for quite a long time

before Bart heard her above the decibel level of his CD player. He did an exaggerated double-take when he finally opened the door.

'What are you doing here?' he asked. 'I thought you had a hot date in Belfast?'

'You know what they say,' she answered, wandering through into Bart's hall and dumping her bags on the floor. 'If you can't stand the heat, get out of the kitchen.'

'Belfast was the kitchen?'

'Yeah. Or rather, a hotel room in Belfast was the kitchen.'

'I thought you'd have been wined and dined and tucked up in bed by now.' He raised an eyebrow at her. 'French men are meant to be experts in the art of seduction, aren't they?'

'You clocked who he was, then?' asked Deirdre.

Bart nodded. 'Have no fear. I'll keep my lip zipped. Poor baby. Did you get badly burnt?'

'A little singed is all.' She yawned, and then looked in the direction of Bart's kitchen. 'Talking about kitchens, I'm famished. What is that wonderful smell?'

'My own home-made French Peasant Soup.'

'I'd die for some. They had nothing left on the train except tuna sandwiches.' Suddenly the image of Jean-Claude Valentin stranded in a hotel bedroom with a plate of chicken sandwiches and a box full of tacky underwear flashed across her mind's eye. She started to laugh. 'Oh Bart – you wouldn't *believe* what a disastrous day I've had!'

He gave her a sceptical look. 'Somehow, knowing you, Deirdre, I expect I actually *might* believe it. Come into the kitchen and tell me all about it.'

'Are you on your own tonight?'

'I am. Birgitta's gone to a Grieg concert in the NCH. I couldn't hack it. That troll dance gives me a headache.'

'And Radiohead doesn't?' She followed him through and nearly fainted when he lifted the lid from the pot on the cooker and the aroma of the soup intensified.

'Sit down. Pour yourself some wine.' He plonked an oversized wine glass down on the kitchen table.

She sat down on a bentwood chair, helped herself to a generous measure of red and then topped up Bart's half-empty glass. Bart ladled a small ocean of soup into a bowl and fetched bread from a shelf. 'Here,' he said. 'Get that into you.'

'Thanks,' she said, breaking off a chunk of bread and spreading it thickly with butter. 'Oh, you've no idea how *comforting* this is! You make the best soup of anyone I know. You could be a chef if you gave up the acting game, Bart.'

'I know. I sometimes don't think you realize how lucky you are to live across a landing from a man who's capable of making more than just beans on toast. Now. Tell me your troubles.'

Deirdre laid into the soup and simultaneously launched into her story, feeding Bart snippets of the narrative between mouthfuls. By the time the bowl was empty, both of them were helpless with laughter.

When they eventually sobered, Bart set them off again.

'Scandalous Scanties!' he said. The mere mention of the sad underwear made them both crease up. Betty Grable wandered into the room, sat down carefully on a tiny scrap of paper on the floor and looked at them both with disapproval.

'Oh, lighten up, Betty,' said Bart. 'Take her off that bloody "lite" cat food, will you Deirdre? She's become totally challenged in the humour department since you started her on that diet. Anyway, she's cuddlier when she's fat. So are you, come to think of it. Have another bowl of soup.'

'A small one. That last helping was enormous. Thanks, Bart. What a chum you are.' Deirdre knocked back the wine in her glass and emptied the bottle into Bart's.

'I'd better open another,' he said.

'You will not. It's my throw. I'll get some from next door.' She stood up. 'Back in a tick.'

She nipped across the landing to her own flat and examined her sadly depleted wine rack. There was only some home-made elderberry wine that her mother had given her and a bottle of rather embarrassing white hock in evidence. Somebody had brought it to a brunch she'd given. She rarely gave parties because her culinary skills were so deficient, but brunch had been manageable. She'd just thrown bagels and smoked salmon onto plates and made sure everybody had had too much to drink.

Then she remembered the claret Rory had

brought her. He always put wine away in a dark cupboard, while she liked to display the bottles on her groovy Habitat rack. 'You are pathetic,' he'd told her. 'Wine should be stored in a cool, dry place, not in a rack on the wall hung directly above a radiator.'

'It's the only place on the wall where the rack will fit properly, Rory,' she'd explained.

'What a load of crap. You mean it's the only place on the wall where your bottles can be displayed to their full advantage, Deirdre, so that visitors will come into your kitchen and think: "Oooh. Bit of an oenophile is Deirdre O'Dare." You'd better make sure they don't get a chance to examine the labels and find that their initial impressions weren't that accurate after all. That's my advice to you, sweetie-pie.' He'd plonked a kiss on the back of her neck. 'My claret remains in the cupboard, OK?'

'OK, OK.' And she'd shot him a snooty look as she slid a bottle of mediocre Chardonnay into the rack, making a mental note to herself to stick ice-bags in the ice-box. She often forgot, and it meant that she sometimes found herself drinking white wine that was distastefully luke-warm.

Rory's claret was still in the cupboard. She grabbed a bottle, and then her eyes fell on a stack of Betty Grable's gourmet cat food which she used to give her as a treat from time to time in the days before she'd been put on a diet. Hell – she'd relent and give the cat a surprise. She selected a tin of Scottish salmon in jelly, and then crossed back over the landing to Bart's flat.

'Excellent claret,' he said, examining the label while he peeled the foil off. 'How did you manage to get it so right?' He glanced at her and she looked away. 'Oh. A legacy of McDonagh's, is it?'

'Yeah.' Deirdre started to open Betty Grable's Scottish salmon in jelly. The cat copped on instantly that her régime was over at last. She got up and trotted over to Deirdre, purring loudly and snaking herself round her mistress's ankles, acting as sinuously as an overweight feline is capable of acting.

'I suppose you'd better fill me in on that side of your life too, hadn't you?'

'There was another woman.' She tried not to sound terse.

'Another woman? A serious other woman?'

'He claims not.'

'In LA?'

'Yeah.'

Bart pulled the cork and poured. Then he sat down at the table, watching her as she spooned cat food into Betty Grable's bowl. He waited until she'd finished, and then he said, 'Rory's other women are never serious, Deirdre. You know that. He just finds it impossible to resist them when they come on to him. I know it can't be easy for you, but he's just not made of monogamous stuff. I thought you'd kind of reconciled yourself to that by now.'

Deirdre made a non-committal noise and set the cat's food down on the floor. Betty Grable gave an undignified, strangulated chirrup and proceeded to hoover it up.

'I mean, he could be a serial womanizer if he wanted to be,' continued Bart. 'But he's kept his indiscretions very discreet, if you follow my tortuous logic. And as far as I know, there haven't been that many of them. He does have his own idiosyncratic brand of integrity, you know. He didn't bat an eyelid that time he caught me groping you at my birthday party.' Deirdre and Bart had indulged in a drunken snog that night, and had immediately afterwards reverted to their platonic status. The snog had been an aberration. Bart was an extremely attractive man, but Deirdre simply didn't fancy him, and she knew that his *penchant* was for well-endowed blondes.

She moved to the table and sat down. Taking up her wine glass, she took an experimental sip of the claret. It tasted ripe, rich and silky. How did Rory have such a knack of knowing exactly which Bordeaux to buy? She felt despondent, suddenly.

'Oh shit, Bart. I've been really stupid.'

'What do you mean?'

Deirdre took a deep breath and filled him in on the reasons behind the split with Rory. She was completely honest with him. She told him how her ego had taken a dive after Sophie's indiscreet revelations about Rory's fling in LA, and about how her stupid pride had been responsible for ending their relationship. She told him about how she'd misguidedly embarked on the dodgy affair with Jean-Claude, and admitted to him that her chief motivation had been to get back at Rory. She told

124

him about how straight-up Rory had been when she'd confronted him about the chick from the flick, and about how near she'd been to changing her mind when any hope of *rapprochement* had been blown into orbit by Jean-Claude's incriminating message on her answering machine.

Bart sat there and listened patiently to the monologue which would have been non-stop if it hadn't been punctuated at regular intervals by gulps of claret. When she had finished, he refilled her glass.

'Why don't you write him a letter telling him what you just told me?'

'Oh, no, no, no, Bart. I couldn't. He wouldn't believe me.'

'That's immaterial. He'd forgive you. I'm certain of that.'

'No. I'd end up going into confessional mode bigtime and telling him about the hellish incident in the hotel with that odious Jean-Claude and the underwear, and he'd just crow and crow.'

Bart shrugged and leant back in his chair. 'When's he due back?'

'March some time. He's going straight down to Galway for the O'Malley film.' Deirdre took another slug of her wine. She knew it was too special to be swigging back like this, but she craved the anaesthetic effect of the alcohol. 'Oh, fuck, Bart. My life's gone hopelessly wrong. And I hate Heeney Holidays,' she added for good measure.

Bart pulled a sympathetic face. 'How much longer do you have to work on the soap? And the soup, come to think of it. You haven't touched your second helping.'

'I'm sorry. My appetite's gone, suddenly.' She pushed the bowl aside and made an apologetic face. 'Let's see. There's around eight weeks to go before the end of the season.'

'Why don't you go west?'

'To Carrowcross?'

'Yeah. There's nothing to keep you here, is there? Unless any theatre work comes up. I think you should take a break. A proper one.'

'I had thought about it,' she admitted. 'I – I have an idea for a screenplay, Bart.'

He cocked his head and raised an eyebrow in enquiry.

'Please don't ask any questions. It's still at an inchoate stage. But I'd love to work on it down there.'

'Excellent stuff! Do it, Deirdre.'

'Maybe I will. The timing'll be good then, too. I'd be too scared to go down at this time of year, even if I could. The gales coming in from the Atlantic are awesome. They'll have eased up by April.'

'Spring in the West of Ireland. You are a privileged person. Just imagine yourself strolling out after a long day slogging away at a hot screenplay, Deirdre. Your trusty cat is at your heels, the grass is still wet from the shower that fell earlier, birds are going bananas building nests, sparkling waves are dancing in the bay, there's woodsmoke in the air.'

She leant her chin on her hands and smiled at him. 'This sounds good. Go on.'

'You're not wearing the mandatory fisherman's smock or homespun gansey or hippy dippy floral-print frock. You wouldn't be so conservative as to wear a Barbour and green wellies. No – nothing so ordinary for the sartorially unpredictable Deirdre O'Dare. Nothing will do for her but her finest Scandalous Scanties!'

Deirdre had just taken a gulp of claret. It shot out of her mouth again, spraying the *Irish Times* on the table with an attractive, wine-red stippled effect. She laughed and laughed, and then she thought of poor Jean-Claude eating chicken sandwiches and watching the adult channel all by himself, and she couldn't stop herself from laughing even harder. When she eventually managed to regain control she realized she had an awful dose of hiccups. She looked down at the *Irish Times* and said rather mournfully through her hiccups, 'What a waste of good claret.'

'Look over there,' said Bart. 'Betty Grable's got fatter already. She's demolished the whole bowl.'

Deirdre looked across the room to where Betty Grable had settled down on a mat on the kitchen floor. She looked like a particularly plump hen sitting on her eggs. Her eyes were closed and she was smiling. 'The fat cat sat on the mat,' said Deirdre. 'Time to go.' She gave Bart a kiss on the cheek and then got to her feet and scooped Betty Grable off the floor. Betty's eyes opened very wide in surprise and she gave an indignant squawk. 'Shut up, you,' reprimanded Deirdre. 'Bart's not having you tonight. You're cosying up in my bed, Betty. And no snoring.'

'She snored like a pig last night,' said Bart. 'The last time I heard snoring like that was when I made the big mistake of sleeping with Sophie.'

'*What*?' Deirdre's jaw dropped so hard that it nearly cracked Betty Grable's skull open. The cat looked crosser than ever. 'You slept with *Sophie Burke*, Bart? I don't *believe* this.'

'Shit. I don't know how I managed to let that slip. Too much red wine, I suppose.' Bart looked genuinely sheepish. 'Don't tell anyone, Deirdre – promise? I've never mentioned it to another living soul, and I'm pretty sure she hasn't either. She'd never run the risk of Ben finding out.'

'How did it *happen*?' Deirdre found herself sitting down at the table again.

'I don't really know. It was that time when you were away in Manchester. A crowd of us came back here for a session one night after we'd been kicked out of Meagher's, and for some reason Sophie tagged along. Don't ask me why. She must have felt like slumming it that particular evening. Anyway, her taxi took ages to arrive and by the time it did everyone else had gone and we'd somehow ended up in a snogging situation. So we sent the taxi away.' Bart spread his hands. 'What more can I say? I'm a red-blooded male.'

'Where was Ben?'

'Off shooting some commercial in West Cork.'

Deirdre's mouth began to curve in a very slow

smile. 'You and *Sophie*? Jesus, Bart – even Rory would draw the line at Sophie!'

'I know, I know. You don't have to rub it in. It was a totally off-the-wall thing to do. But she was looking dead sexy that night in some sort of slip dress with little bra straps showing, and it seemed like a good idea at the time. I was pissed,' he added unnecessarily.

'What was she like?' Deirdre couldn't resist asking the question.

'Deirdre! I'm surprised at you.'

'OK, you don't need to answer that.' She bit her lip and looked down at the table. Then she raised her eyes to him again and gave him her best 'pretty please' look.

Bart laughed. 'Jesus, Deirdre – you are incorrigible.' He gave her a speculative look, and then relented. 'OK, then. She was kind of posy. Like she was seeing herself in a French arthouse movie – very self-consciously "sensual", if you know what I mean?'

Deirdre nodded delightedly. She had registered the inverted commas.

'Um. Let's see. How best to describe her? I know, like one of those actresses in that Antonioni–Wim Wenders collaboration. D'you know the one I mean?'

'*Beyond the Clouds*?'

'The very film.'

She hugged herself. 'And then she *snored*?'

'I'm afraid so.'

'Ha!' Deirdre laughed with undisguised glee.

'Look here, O'Dare – if this goes beyond you and me, our friendship's over for ever, right? My credibility would be blown into orbit if people knew I'd slept with Sophie.'

'I promise it won't, darling Bart.' She jumped up from the table and plonked another kiss on his head. 'Oh, you're the best friend ever! Well, apart from Maeve, but she's going away soon. You feed me with soup, allow me to get drunk and maudlin and then you tell me the best joke I've ever heard! I owe you, Bart.'

'I'll hold you to that.' He stood up and moved towards the door. 'I'll take your bags in for you, shall I? You can't manage them *and* that seriously overweight cat.'

Deirdre thought for a moment and then she thrust Betty Grable into his unprotesting arms. 'You can have her tonight,' she said with decision. 'You deserve a reward for lifting me out of what could have been a serious case of the glooms.' She retrieved her bags from where she'd dumped them in the hallway and danced through the door. 'Night, Bart. I love you.'

'Night, Deirdre. I love you too.'

Lying in bed later, Deirdre still couldn't stop smiling.

* * *

For the next eight weeks she kept her head well down. Her agent had landed her a radio series, so what with that and the soap and the horrific Heeney Holidays commercials she was kept too busy to think often about Rory. Neither she nor Sophie Burke had succeeded in landing the part of the young Grace O'Malley, so at least she knew she wouldn't be working with him on the film. She'd done some detective work about who *had* got it, but no-one seemed to know. It hadn't gone to the little redhead Deirdre had seen coming out of the studio the day she'd screen-tested. It still pained her to remember how the actress had gone all swoony when she'd talked about the way Rory had kissed her. Shooting was due to begin in Galway in March. If she was to take Bart's advice and hole up in Carrowcross for a while she'd be fewer than fifty miles away.

She found herself having coffee in the canteen with Sophie and some of the *Ardmore Grove* cast members one morning. Sophie had been griping on about how unfair it was that someone else had got the part of the young Grace O'Malley when *she'd* been offered it first time round three years earlier.

'I'm only twenty-five, for goodness' sake. And that makes me too old? I most certainly have the edge in terms of experience.' She examined her French-polished nails petulantly. 'Who else is in it?'

'Well, there's Rory, of course,' Cressida responded. Everybody at the table was careful to avoid looking at Deirdre, which really pissed her off. It was obviously common knowledge by now that they'd split up irretrievably. She sent poisonous thoughts in Sophie's direction, wondering if the actress guessed that she'd been instrumental in the destruction of the relationship.

'And Maeve Kirwan's got a lovely cameo.' Deirdre was glad to be able to let this slip. There was no love lost between Maeve and Sophie.

Sophie looked startled and cross at the same time. 'Maeve? I thought she was tied up with the RSC for the next year?'

'The show's in rep,' explained Deirdre smugly. 'Apparently she's been able to juggle dates so that she can fit in a couple of days on the film as well. Bart ran into Jacqueline the other day and she filled him in.' Jacqueline was Maeve Kirwan's partner.

'Bart? Bart Walsh?'

'Yes. He's a very good friend of mine. In fact, he's my next-door neighbour.' Deirdre looked directly at Sophie with an inscrutable expression on her face. She was delighted that Sophie had the good grace to look rather pink and alarmed. Maybe she'd be more discreet about badmouthing her in future.

*   *   *

Around the beginning of April Deirdre's assignments started to wind to a close, and she finally got round to approaching her mother about taking the cottage for a couple of months.

Rosaleen had sounded surprised when Deirdre had mooted it. '*Months,* Deirdre? Are you sure you'd be able to hack it? Carrowcross isn't the social centre of the universe, as you well know. Don't you think you might get awfully lonely?'

'Well, Galway's just a bus journey away if I miss being in the thick of things. And Eleanor's round the corner for when I crave human company.' Eleanor had been a close friend of Deirdre's grandmother. She was a painter – an elegant woman in her seventies whose attitude to life was that of a much younger person, and who possessed a wicked sense of humour. She and Deirdre had always hit it off.

'How will you manage financially?'

'Bart's found someone I can sub-let the flat to, so I won't be forking out rent money. And jolly old Heeney Holidays own me until the autumn – I'll have to commute up to Dublin for a few gigs. I don't have a whole lot of dosh, but I should be able to manage. I've been putting money away since I first came up with the idea – it's had a nasty knock-on effect on my social life, I can tell you. That's been non-existent for the past couple of months.'

'Well, Deirdre. You're developing real life skills at last.' She could hear the smile in her mother's voice. 'If you're really stuck you can hit me for a loan.'

'Thanks, Mum. I hope I won't have to. I've kind of got used to living frugally.'

'Will you take your bike down on the train?'

'Yeah. I'll get seriously fit cycling in and out of town. And any time I need to do a big shop I'm sure Eleanor will oblige with a lift.'

'What's your screenplay about?'

'Um. It's a love story. And a comedy. Bit inchoate

at the moment. But I'm hoping for more inspiration when I get down there.'

'It all sounds a bit vague, Deirdre. Are you sure you're doing the right thing? Don't you think it would be a better idea to stay here and put out feelers for acting work?'

'There's nothing happening, Mum. And anyway, my agent will do that. If something comes up she'll let me know. I might as well spend my free time profitably messing around on a screenplay in Carrowcross. I'll just get side-tracked if I stay here.'

'Well. I hope it works out, my love.'

Deirdre could tell that her mother's tone lacked conviction. Maybe she was right – maybe her rosy idea of escaping to the West of Ireland was totally off the wall. Maybe Bart had just been humouring her when he'd encouraged her the evening that she had been down.

'By the way,' added Rosaleen. 'I'm trying to organize some work to be done on the place. Part of the boundary wall has got damaged, and I asked Eleanor if she could recommend somebody to repair it. She said she'd do some detective work, but I don't expect to hear from her for a while. Dry-stone walling isn't the kind of skill you come across every day. You might remind her when you're down there.'

'I'll do that.'

'If you do decide to go to Galway you might ask around. Someone there's bound to know.'

'OK.'

There was a fractional pause, and then Rosaleen said, 'Did I read somewhere that Rory's starring in a movie being filmed there?'

'Yeah.'

'It might be an opportunity to look him up?'

'Mum, I told you that Rory and I have split up.'

Rosaleen gave a little sigh of resignation. 'I know. But I thought you might have given the matter some – oh, how shall I put it? Some mature reflection?'

'No.'

'That's a shame,' said Rosaleen. 'I always liked Rory. So did your father. He was asking about him just the other day, and was very put out when I told him you'd called it off.'

'I didn't call it off, Mum. It was a mutual decision.'

'I don't imagine much thought went into this "mutual" decision, did it?'

'Yes, it did. We'd been thinking about it for ages,' lied Deirdre.

She put the phone down feeling a bit uncertain, suddenly. Her mother had been sensible to remind her of how isolated Carrowcross was. Maybe she wouldn't be able to hack it? Her father often spent weeks at a time at the cottage, but he was the most self-sufficient person she knew. He didn't even need a radio for company. He was quite happy with his boat and his dog and his fishing rod and his books. He'd adamantly refused to install a television when Deirdre had suggested it, and when she had told him she could get her hands on a play-station at a really good bargain price he'd given her one of his extremely rare black looks. Rosaleen had just laughed.

Hell – if it didn't work out, it didn't work out. At least she would have tried.

* * *

She was all set. Packed and ready to go.

'Christ,' said Bart when he saw the state of her luggage. 'Your street-cred is seriously compromised now, Deirdre. You're like some sick-makingly fit tourist on a cycling holiday.'

'You can say what you like, Bart. It's the only way I can manage it.' She did up a zip on one of her bicycle panniers, in which she'd safely stowed her laptop. 'Anyway, you don't need street-cred in the country. And somehow I don't think mine was ever that convincing.' She shrugged her shoulders. 'Street-cred's too much like hard work.'

'Jean-Claude thought you had street-cred.' Bart grinned at her.

'No, he didn't. He thought I was *sophisticated*, Bart. That's different again.'

Bart was helping her hang the panniers on the bicycle carrier. 'Why don't you invest in an old banger? That would make life a lot easier for you.'

'I'm an actress, remember? I can't afford the insurance. The lowest quote I got when I did some asking around nearly made me hyperventilate. Anyway, knowing my luck a banger would die on me on my first week there. I'll enjoy cycling.'

Bart looked dubious. 'Deirdre, I think you have some crazy notion that you'll have nothing but Mediterranean skies while you're there. Cycling in the West of Ireland is no joke.'

'Oh, pooh, Bart. Don't be such a pessimist. The long-range weather forecast is brilliant.' Deirdre picked up Betty Grable and gave her a farewell kiss. 'Look after Betty. Don't let her get too fat.' She had toyed with the idea of bringing Betty with her until Bart had pointed out to her that balancing the cat basket on her bicycle carrier would be out of the question. 'I'll miss you, Bart. And thanks again for sorting the tenant for me. You'll iron out any problems, won't you?'

'Sure. But I'm not mending that shagging kettle if it goes on the blink one more time. I'll just get you a new one.'

'OK. You won't forget to forward my mail? I'm expecting Heeney Holidays cheques any day now, and I'll need to get them into the bank ASAP.'

'Heeney Holidays? Is that the gig you do with the client who rewrites all the commercials?'

'Yeah. Janine Heeney, director and writer *manqué*. Do you know what she said to me when I stupidly let slip to her that I wanted to go west to work on a screenplay?'

'What?'

'She gave me this totally condescending smile and said, 'Don't we all, dear.''

'Ouch,' said Bart.

    *   *   *

Five and a half hours later, Deirdre O'Dare had
retrieved her bicycle from the conductor's van at the
front of the train and was merrily cycling along the
narrow winding roads of County Mayo with a warm
breeze in her hair and a very happy heart.

Chapter Six

The small townland known as Carrowcross lay about six miles outside of Westport town, way off the beaten track. To begin with Deirdre enjoyed the cycling. The countryside was just as Bart had predicted in his bucolic fantasy. The grass was wet from the shower that had fallen earlier, birds were going bananas building nests, sparkling waves were dancing in the bay, there was woodsmoke in the air. And it was that wonderful, heady West of Ireland air that makes you feel as if you've drunk a pint of Guinness, and puts you to sleep with a smile on your face at night. She always slept better here than in Dublin.

However, after a couple of miles the journey became more tough-going. It was uphill most of the rest of the way, and Deirdre soon started to feel hot and a bit cross. The prospect of cycling back from town laden with groceries every other day filled her with dread. She'd have to make immediate contact with Eleanor and find out how often she made the trip in her little Volkswagen Polo. Maybe Eleanor's insurance would cover her and she could borrow the car from time to time.

As she cycled she noticed that there were more

and more brand-new houses springing up along the sides of the country roads – the majority of them holiday homes for rich city-dwellers, she reckoned. Most of them were ugly constructions, erring on the ostentatious side, and Deirdre felt even crosser. She considered this to be her exclusive territory; it was the place she loved most in the world. She'd spent every summer as a child at the cottage where her grandmother had lived, in the days before the West of Ireland became a trendy holiday destination. She hoped the secret peninsula where the cottage was situated hadn't been discovered yet, and wondered bleakly how long it would be before it was.

As the gradient stiffened even more she was forced to get off the bike and push. She was extremely sweaty now, and the breeze that had sprung up did little to cool her down. She muttered to herself occasionally as she went along, and the cows in the fields on either side of the road eyed her with bovine suspicion.

At last the turn-off to the cottage came into view, and her heart lightened a little, only to sink again when she saw the figure of a man rounding the bend. There were only two dwellings down that particular laneway – hers and Eleanor's. People rarely bothered to investigate it because it was so obviously a cul-de-sac. The main road – if it could be called that – led to a white-sand beach two miles away, and that was where the holiday-makers tended to head.

The man was moving in her direction. He had a dog with him, and he was swinging a stick, lashing out occasionally at nettles in the hedgerow which bordered the narrow road. As he drew nearer, Deirdre could see that he was wearing workman's overalls and heavy-duty boots. There was a navy woollen hat pulled down over his forehead. She felt a flash of fear. What was a strange man doing coming out of her laneway?

For the first time she realized how vulnerable she was going to be, stuck in her cottage on a remote peninsula with only an elderly woman to run to for help if something went wrong. She'd never spent much time there on her own. In fact, there had only been one occasion she had visited the cottage by herself, when she'd gone to open it up after a long winter. Rory hadn't been able to join her for a couple of days because he'd been tied up with an Abbey production of *A Streetcar Named Desire*, but as soon as the run had ended he'd driven down. Somehow the knowledge that his arrival was imminent had coloured the two days she'd spent by herself, and she hadn't felt remotely unsafe. But now she felt uncomfortably aware of what potential there was for danger down the road.

Hell, Deirdre – cop yourself on, she told herself. If you're going to spook yourself on day one of your rural idyll, you might as well turn around and go straight back to Dublin now. Think of Eleanor. She's been living on her own down that lane for years and years without anybody hassling her.

She succeeded in reassuring herself. Momentarily. As the man advanced he looked at her, and her complacency crumpled when she met his eyes. They were the blackest eyes she had ever seen, and they wore a slightly guarded expression, which immediately made her even more wary of him. Long black hair spilled from under his knitted cap, he had two days' growth on his jaw, and there was a scar where his cheekbone jutted. A curious earring hung from his left earlobe, and his overalls were worn and filthy.

He gave her an impenetrable look as he passed her. 'Good evening,' he said. Then he cleared his throat the way people do when they haven't spoken for some time, and added, 'It's a soft one.' *It's a soft one* was the rural Irish way of saying *Thank God it's not blowing a storm and raining from the heavens*. Deirdre knew that it was common courtesy to exchange greetings in the country, but she really had no desire to encourage this man.

Then she had a sudden brainwave. '*Guten Abend!*' she found herself saying. If she pretended to be a foreigner there'd be no necessity for further pleasantries. After all, hadn't Bart told her she looked like a tourist on a cycling holiday?

But as she trundled the bicycle past him she wondered if she had done the right thing. He could be a local with a grudge. A lot of the locals resented the wealthy foreigners, who had settled in fine big houses in the area and who went around looking more Irish than the Irish themselves, dressed in Aran jumpers and bawneen trousers held up with *crios*. Most of them were expert tin-whistle players. When she successfully reached the corner of the laneway

142

that led down to her cottage with no abuse or daggers being flung after her, she glanced back over her shoulder. The rough-looking geezer was lying back on his elbows in the long grass of the ditch beneath the hedgerow, watching her. His dog was sitting between his master's sprawled legs watching her too, with its pink tongue hanging out.

Deirdre began to sweat even more. She didn't want to turn the corner while this man was observing her. If he saw her disappear in the direction of her cottage he would more than likely deduce – and deduce correctly – that she was staying there alone. She would be a sitting target for, at worst, rape and murder; at best, a brick through the window. Her pace slowed as she flailed around mentally for a way out of her predicament, and then her pace quickened again as she walked straight past the turn-off, ignoring it ostentatiously. She was just another tourist on her way to the white-sand beach.

After a couple of hundred metres the road levelled out and became a manageable cycle. She paused before hoisting herself back onto the bike, checking over her shoulder to see if the man was still there. He was, and although he didn't seem to be interested in her any more, she knew she couldn't turn around and cycle back until the coast was well and truly clear. She ploughed on, cursing the ignorant black-eyed bastard. Every turn of the pedal was becoming increasingly tough; she was seriously knackered now. After five more minutes of torture she snuck another backward look. He was finally, thankfully, gone.

Deirdre effected a clumsy U-turn and started back down the road, still steaming. At least the gradient was downward this time. She freewheeled round the corner and managed one final spurt before the cottage came into view round a bend in the laneway – and then she stopped dead.

This was a sight that never failed to make her heart sing. There was Carrowcross Cottage nestled in its green hollow at the foot of a long driveway, surrounded by blossoming pink weigela and ancient pines so windswept they were bent almost double. The tide was in, and the surface of the water was covered in giddy white horses which were being soundly whipped by the stiff breeze coming in from beyond the rocky headland. White clouds scudded over an impossibly blue sky towards the most dominant feature in the vista: there, on the other side of the bay with its three hundred and sixty-five islands – one for every day of the year – stood Croagh Patrick, the most mystical mountain in Ireland.

Deirdre had climbed it with Rory once, on a day when thick cloud cover had suddenly shrouded the mountain, so that it had felt as if they were climbing through a dream. At the top she'd stood leaning against her lover, tired but very, very happy in spite of the fact that the view of the bay below had been obliterated by clouds. Sitting in a small pub afterwards over pints of Guinness they had resolved that they would do it again on a bright, blue-sky day so that they could treat themselves to the vista which had inspired Thackeray to write: *It forms an event in one's life to have seen that place, so beautiful is it and so unlike all other beauties that I know of.* Now Deirdre wondered suddenly if she would ever see it – if it would be worth the gargantuan effort of climbing to the top again with someone who wasn't Rory.

She got off the bike and opened the gate that would take her down the steep slope to the cottage. She hadn't ridden a bike down this slope since she was nine years old when she had skidded and come off on the gravel, causing her to bite her tongue hard. It had pumped so much blood she'd passed out. She proceeded with caution now, keeping her left hand firmly wrapped round the back brake handle.

The driveway led between fields on either side to another gate at the very bottom of the slope, which was there to prevent cattle from trampling the lawns around the cottage. The lawns had grown wild – nobody had been there to take care of the garden for some time – and the luxuriant, sappy green grass was cheerfully polka-dotted with daisies and dandelions.

As Deirdre opened the gate into the garden she noticed that the boundary wall her mother had mentioned to her had been mended in places. There were piles of stones lying at intervals along the foot of the wall, and a plumb line hung from a fork in the tiny chestnut tree which her father had planted two summers earlier, and which was struggling against the odds to grow in the face of the east wind which hurled itself in off the Atlantic in the cold months. Eleanor must have found someone to do the drystone walling.

She leant her bike up against the back door and strolled around to the front of the house to let herself in.

The front of the cottage looked out over the bay. It had a glassed-in verandah where Deirdre's grandmother had liked to sit for hours at a time, drinking in the view which she had described as being in 'perpetual motion' because it was never the same from minute to minute. She paused before slipping the key into the lock, and turned her face to the sea. Then she stood quite still. There was a robin perched on one of the weigela bushes, watching her at quite close quarters with its head cocked on one side. It looked disapprovingly at her, as if she was a trespasser. She supposed she was. She hadn't set foot in this garden for nearly two years.

'Hello,' she whispered.

The robin cocked its head to the other side and gave her the once-over for a few more seconds before taking off and bobbing to the safety of the sally bush that grew in the middle of the lawn. It landed on a branch and scolded her until she disappeared through the front door of the house. Once inside she wandered from room to room, pulling up blinds and opening windows. The place had the slightly fusty smell that creeps into houses that haven't been lived in for a while.

The cottage was timber-clad on both the outside and the inside. It wasn't really a cottage, although that's how the family always referred to it. It was more of a bungalow, but since the advent of

Bungalow Blitz in the West of Ireland in the past couple of decades there was a reluctance to describe it as such. It certainly didn't conform to the stereotypical notion of a bungalow. It was a quirky building, built by Deirdre's grandfather for her grandmother as a wedding present years before, and intended as a holiday home. After Deirdre's grandfather had died, her grandmother had retired to Carrowcross to live.

There were six rooms in the little house. Leading off the main sitting room was a kitchen, a bathroom and a bedroom to the rear, with two more bedrooms to the front. Each room had two windows, and that and the cream-washed walls lent the house a blissfully airy feel. It was comfortably furnished with Deirdre's grandmother's old furniture, and was utterly unpretentious. Deirdre sometimes dreamt about doing it up along the lines of something she'd seen in a trendy magazine, but her mother had refused point-blank when she'd suggested it, and Deirdre secretly knew she was dead right.

She retrieved her bags from outside the kitchen door and deposited them in the cream-painted bedroom at the front of the house. She wanted to fall asleep at night lulled by the sound of the sea. The first item she unpacked was her precious laptop. Which room should she use as her work room? She wandered onto the verandah. The idea of setting up her laptop on the table there was enormously seductive. She set it down and gazed out the window.

To her delight, there was an otter doing the back-stroke down by the little stone jetty, which she noticed was seriously overgrown with seaweed. She'd have to clear it if she wanted to swim. A heron made a lumbering landing on the shore directly below her and then took off again across the bay. She could hear the sound of its wings as it flapped off towards the island known as Mad-eyed Maura's island. Maura had lived there in splendid isolation for decades, rowing to the mainland only when she needed supplies. The haunting cry of a curlew came floating across the water.

She couldn't work here. There were so many distractions that she knew she'd never be able to concentrate. Reluctantly she picked up her laptop and headed towards the bedroom at the back of the house.

* * *

Later that evening she curled up in the old chintz armchair on the verandah and watched perpetual motion over Clew Bay as the sun sank over the headland and an orange moon rose like a celestial pumpkin in the east. She'd dined on Heinz cream of tomato, tinned tuna and some stale oatcakes. She'd have to get into town tomorrow to stock up on supplies. There had been wine in the rack in the pantry, and she'd helped herself to the one with the least impressive label, resolving to replace it tomorrow. She didn't want her parents subsidizing her oenomania. Before she went to bed she phoned her mother to let them know she'd arrived safely.

'Hi, Mum. I tried phoning earlier but you were out.'

'We were at Eithne's exhibition opening. Her new stuff's more glorious than ever. What's it like down there?'

'Heaven. Like being in one of Eithne's paintings.'

'I'm jealous. You're not nervous on your own, are you?'

'No, funnily enough. I thought I might be, but I'm as serene as a pig.'

'Are pigs serene?'

'Definitely. The dry-stone walling's underway, you'll be happy to hear.'

'Good. Who's doing it?'

Deirdre suddenly made the connection between the plumb line left swinging from the baby chestnut tree and the man in overalls she'd passed on the road. 'I'm not sure. Somebody local, by the look of things. He'd left before I arrived. I'll ask Eleanor about him tomorrow.'

'Find out how much he's charging, will you? You'll have to pay him. I'll reimburse you.'

'I don't mind covering some of the cost, Mum. I owe you. You're a real chum to let me have the run of this place.'

'You're more than welcome, my love. I hope you get loads of work done. Blow kisses all over Carrowcross for me, won't you? And send my love to Eleanor.'

'I'll do that. Night, Mum.'

It was only after she'd put the phone down to Rosaleen that a thought hit her which made her go hot with embarrassment. If the overalled bloke *was* the person responsible for the dry-stone walling, how was she to explain away her bizarre behaviour of this afternoon? Her stupid attempt to disguise herself as a German tourist was going to seem pretty damn batty. Hell – maybe she wouldn't have to talk to him. She'd make it very plain that she was down there to lock herself away and do some serious work, not to be sociable. She didn't have to explain herself to anyone.

But the prospect of the black-eyed man hanging around the place made her feel uncomfortable, suddenly. She made sure all the doors and windows were securely locked before she went to bed that night.

* * *

The next morning she rang Eleanor.

'Deirdre! How lovely to hear your voice!'

'You might get fed up of it sooner than you think, Eleanor. I'm down for a while, and I'm going to be pestering you for lifts in and out of town.'

'Any time. I'm going in this evening. I've a doctor's appointment at six o'clock. Is that any help to you?'

'That would be cool. I'll do a big shop while you're at the doctor and then take you off for a pint.'

'I've got a better idea. I got a big cheque from an insurance company yesterday. Let me take you out to dinner to celebrate. Then you can tell me all your news.'

'Excellent idea. Where'll we go?'

'Quay Cottage. Where else?'

* * *

Deirdre didn't get much work done that day. She pottered around the place, doing bits and pieces of housework and making endless excuses to wander onto the verandah to admire the view.

One new feature on the landscape gave her very little pleasure. A barn had been constructed on Mad-eyed Maura's island. It was a ramshackle affair comprising corrugated iron, breeze-blocks and rough timber. On inspecting it through the binoculars, Deirdre saw that it housed the remains of last autumn's bales of hay. Lengths of black plastic hung from the makeshift rafters, flapping drearily in the wind like a scarecrow's coat-tails.

Deirdre knew that a local farmer had grazing rights on the island, but she doubted very much whether he also had planning permission for such a dismal example of construction work. Still, she didn't think she'd bother about looking into that side of things. If a blow-in like her started making noises about planning permission she'd be asking for a brick through the window. It just wasn't worth it.

At around five o'clock she set aside Syd Field's

book on the foundations of screenwriting. Her afternoon had been spent revising – or at least that's what she'd persuaded herself she was doing. If she were to be honest with herself, she knew she was just procrastinating. Sooner or later she was going to have to open her laptop and get started.

She went into the bedroom and stood studying the clothes she'd brought with her, which were now hanging in the wardrobe. She'd been as economical with her packing as possible because there simply wasn't room to carry much in a backpack and a pair of panniers. However, she had included one decent frock, just in case. It was a pretty, eau de nil slip trimmed with silk flowers. She opted for that. Quay Cottage wasn't screamingly posh, but Eleanor always made an effort when she went out anywhere, and Deirdre wasn't going to let her down. She had left the little matching cardigan that she usually wore with her slip dress behind in Dublin. Pity. She'd just have to make do with her denim jacket.

She slapped on some lipstick and went into the pantry to choose a bottle of good wine as a present for Eleanor. It was the least she could do if her elderly friend was going to foot the bill for dinner. Flowers would be a nice idea, too. As she slipped out of the back door with secateurs and proceeded to attack the weigela, she noticed that the plumb line she'd spotted the previous day was still hanging from the fork of the little chestnut tree, and that the piles of stones remained undisturbed. The dry-stone walling geezer hadn't bothered turning up today.

She realized with some relief that she hadn't thought about him since last night. Good. She didn't want to allow him the power to faze her.

*   *   *

Eleanor was waiting for her, looking elegant in a pale turquoise coat-dress. She accepted the wine gladly and the weigela with effusive thank yous, which Deirdre knew were completely genuine. Eleanor was a gardening fanatic, and she and Rosaleen could spend hours swopping gardening stories. Eleanor's chief regret now that she was getting on was that she wasn't able to do much for herself in the garden any more.

The journey into town took about ten minutes by car. Deirdre calculated glumly that it would probably take thirty by bike, and forty or more to negotiate the uphill cycle home. Eleanor deposited her at the supermarket before continuing on to the doctor's surgery, arranging to come back for her in half an hour's time. The table at the restaurant was booked for seven o'clock.

Deirdre did a massive shop, stocking up on as much tinned food as she could. She didn't want to waste any time cooking while she was here. She hoped Eleanor wouldn't get a load of how many carrier bags contained wine bottles. The off-licence in the supermarket carried an impressive range. Deirdre had opted mostly for her usual moderately priced Chardonnay, but for some reason she also found herself including a couple of bottles of rather pricey claret in her selection. Just in case anyone visits, she reasoned to herself as she scribbled the cheque. After all, people from Dublin were always descending on Westport for weekend breaks.

She was standing in the supermarket car park guarding a trolley stacked high with bags by the time Eleanor appeared.

'Goodness, Deirdre – you must be planning to stay a long time. You look as if you're preparing for a siege.'

'I'm determined not to waste time cycling in and out of town, Eleanor. I'm here to work.'

As they negotiated the winding road that would take them to the restaurant, Deirdre filled Eleanor in on her intention to write a screenplay.

'I think it's an excellent idea. All actresses should have another string to their bow. I wish you every success with it.' The car rounded the bend onto the quay where the restaurant was situated, and Eleanor pulled over beside the hulking, half-rotten prow of a long-abandoned boat. 'I just hope you don't get too lonely. You're a gregarious animal at heart, aren't you?'

'I'll take you as my role-model, Eleanor. I've always admired your self-sufficiency.'

'I wouldn't go so far as to describe myself as self-sufficient. I'm just an insufferably anti-social old bag at heart.' They got out of the Polo and Deirdre linked Eleanor's arm as they strolled towards the restaurant. 'The only person I have time for is your mother,' the elderly lady continued with feeling. 'And you, of course.'

'Why's that, I wonder? You'd think with the big discrepancy in our ages that we wouldn't get on at all.'

'You make me laugh, Deirdre,' said Eleanor, simply. 'You make me feel young again.'

Deirdre smiled at her as she held the door open and gestured for Eleanor to precede her into the restaurant.

They were shown to a table next to the window by a smiling waitress, and as Deirdre ran her eyes down the menu she realized she was seriously hungry. She'd had tuna and stale oatcakes again today, and tinned minestrone soup instead of tomato.

She ordered mussels to start, and lemon sole as a main course. Eleanor ordered chowder, lamb cutlets, and a bottle of Burgundy.

'What a good start to my holiday,' said Deirdre. 'Except I shouldn't be describing it as a holiday, should I?'

'You should take time to enjoy yourself, too, Deirdre. Take things easy. I imagine you work punishingly hard in the city.'

The waitress returned with the wine, uncorked it expertly and poured. They raised their glasses at each other.

'Here's to you, Eleanor. Thanks for dinner.'

'Here's to you, Deirdre. Good luck with your new project.'

As the glasses chimed together with a pleasing

resonance, the door to the restaurant opened and a stunningly beautiful woman walked in. She had an exquisite pre-Raphaelite face, her sleek dark hair was coiled in a chignon at the nape of her neck, and she was casually but expensively dressed in jeans and a soft, toffee-coloured suede shirt. Deirdre couldn't help but stare. This woman looked like Italian aristocracy.

Suddenly Deirdre's gaze swooped to her lap. The man who was following the *principessa* through the door was the man she had passed on the road yesterday. As he stood in the doorway surveying the room Deirdre panicked. She knocked her napkin onto the floor and dived under the table, taking her time to retrieve it. When she eventually summoned the nerve to show her face again, the *principessa* and her dining companion were being escorted to a table on the other side of the room. The woman sat down in a seat facing the room, the man took the seat opposite her, with his back to Deirdre.

Eleanor was observing her with a perplexed expression.

'What on earth's the matter, Deirdre? You've gone bright red in the face.'

Deirdre took a swig of her wine and wiped her mouth with her napkin. 'Eleanor? Do me a favour, will you? Pretend you're looking at that piece of driftwood that's hanging on the wall on the other side of the room, and take a sneaky look at the couple who've just come in.'

'Why?'

'I need to know if you know them.'

Eleanor did as she'd been asked, casually turning her head as if studying the surrounding décor. Then she turned back to Deirdre. 'I don't know her,' she said. 'But I know him. His name's Gabriel Considine.'

Deirdre's eyes returned to the man Eleanor had called Gabriel. He was in profile to her now, pushing his black hair back from his forehead so that he could study the menu. His face would have been as aristocratic as his partner's if it hadn't been for the scar on his cheekbone. He wore a floppy moleskin shirt, loose linen trousers and Timberlands. He had shaved today, Deirdre noticed. In fact, he cleaned up extremely well. He certainly looked nowhere near as dangerous as he'd done yesterday. She could hardly believe that this was the same rough-looking individual she'd seen on the road, swinging at nettles with a stick.

'Why are you so interested, Deirdre?' There was a hint of amusement in Eleanor's voice.

'I saw him coming out of our laneway yesterday. I wondered what he'd been doing along there.'

'Your mother asked me to find someone to mend your boundary wall. My gardener recommended Gabriel.'

Deirdre was puzzled. 'He doesn't *look* like a labourer. I mean, he did yesterday when I saw him in working clothes, but he's completely different today.'

'He's not a labourer. He's an architect.'

Deirdre made a sceptical face. 'He must be a pretty inept architect if he's reduced to doing odd-jobs like mending walls.'

Eleanor laughed. 'On the contrary. He's an exceptionally talented architect, apparently, and very much in demand. The dry-stone walling is his private passion. It's how he unwinds. I had a chat with him when he called round last week to ask me where your cottage was. He's a thoroughly charming, well-educated young man.'

Deirdre slid an oblique glance at Gabriel Considine and his beautiful dining companion. They had about them an aura of composed self-assurance – yet there was nothing remotely self-conscious about them. The woman was asking the waitress a question. With a smile, she thanked her and then rose to her feet, obviously on her way to pay a visit to the loo. Deirdre thought with a sudden rush of anxiety about how she'd avoid this Gabriel geezer clocking her if he decided to go to the loo. She couldn't keep diving under the table all night. She'd just have to make herself as inconspicuous as possible, and with a bit of luck, she'd avoid any kind of embarrassing encounter this evening.

As his partner passed their table, Deirdre caught the faint trace of some expensive scent. The woman's eyes met hers briefly, and Deirdre looked away, but not before she'd registered the discreet Vuitton logo on the leather satchel which hung from her shoulder.

She looked across the table at Eleanor. 'They're *rich*,' she said, in an awed undertone.

Eleanor smiled back at her. 'His father's a British peer. Lord Considine. That makes Gabriel an hon. And a Lord-in-waiting.'

'Wow.' Deirdre was impressed. 'Where did you get all this info, Eleanor?'

'Carrowcross is a small place. And my gardener's a great source of gossip. Locals have been speculating about Mr Considine ever since he took possession of Carrowcross House.'

'He's living in *Carrowcross House*?'

'Yes.'

'Since when?'

'Oh, about a year now. He inherited it from some obscure uncle, and he's been living in the gate lodge while he does it up.'

'Oh.' Deirdre had fantasized about living in Carrowcross House since childhood, when she'd used to explore the grounds. She'd dreamt about one day being wealthy enough to buy it and restore it to its former glory. It was a big house, built in the early nineteenth century and abandoned in the 1920s when the country had been gripped by political unrest. It had been pillaged by locals and had languished uninhabited ever since. It was amazing that the place was still standing – most of the big houses belonging to landed gentry at that time had been razed to the ground by irate arsonists.

'I'm surprised your mother didn't mention him to you,' continued Eleanor.

'Mum never bothers with gossip,' said Deirdre ruefully. 'It's her one major shortcoming.'

'I never used to bother with it,' said Eleanor with a sigh. 'But I've little else to distract me these days. Getting old is such a curse.'

'You're not old in here, Eleanor.' Deirdre smiled and tapped her temple as the waitress arrived with their starters.

As she dug into her mussels, her eyes kept being drawn back to Gabriel Considine. 'What else do you know about him? What kind of architecture does he do?'

'He's been commissioned to design some civic building in Castlebar. And I heard a rumour that he's going to be responsible for redeveloping the old grain store off the Louisburg Road. It's being converted into apartments.'

'Oh *no*!' Deirdre's tone was indignant. 'Not *more* bloody holiday apartments!'

'I have a friend in the planning department who tells me it was the most sympathetic and eco-friendly of all the designs they considered. There was serious competition for that particular project. Of course, there was lots of muttering about the job going to a blow-in. I think he may have had a contact there.'

A blow-in. A blow-in who'd staked claim to Carrowcross House. Deirdre felt absurdly resentful suddenly that her cherished childhood dream had been snatched away from her. She wouldn't even be able to go for walks in the grounds now. That had always been the place she'd made a beeline for on the first day of her summer holidays. Although the gardens were overgrown and choked with weed, the original lay-out was still faintly discernible under its cloak of tangled growth. If you stood on the crumbling terrace that stretched the length of the back of the house you could just make out the geography of the centuries-old garden – the buried paths that had led round and between flowerbeds, carving the landscape into Lutyens-inspired symmetry. The fountain which had been its centrepiece was parched and clogged with detritus now, and the delicately wrought sundial was filigreed with rust. The walls of the disintegrating summer house were covered in graffiti.

One of Deirdre's favourite things as a child had been to peer through gaps in the boarded-up windows of the house, imagining how the rooms had looked in the past, when the owners had held weekend parties and shooting parties and balls. She'd pictured the women drifting through the rooms in gowns of sprigged muslin, the gentlemen in breeches, lolling against the enormous fireplaces with pointers at their heels, the children pushing open the French windows to tumble through into the garden, laughing and shouting.

She had dreamt of reconstructing that halcyon time one day. Either she would become an incredibly wealthy film star who could command millions of dollars per picture, or (and this was the more likely of the two scenarios) she'd win the lottery. Then, thanks to Deirdre O'Dare, Carrowcross House would rise like a phoenix from the ashes of its past splendour. She'd even fantasized once about converting the stables into a theatre so that she and her friends could put on all the luscious costume dramas she'd ever wanted to do, with herself in all her favourite roles: Rosalind, Viola, Miranda.

'Why are you looking so pensive all of a sudden?' Eleanor's voice woke her from her reverie.

Deirdre looked up. 'Oh, no reason!' she replied, making an effort to sound breezy. She couldn't admit – even to Eleanor – that she was pissed off with Gabriel Considine for thwarting her in her juvenile ambition. And *juvenile* was the right word, she admitted resignedly to herself. When would she ever cop on to real life and stop living in a fantasy world? Maeve had once told her that she had grown up overnight, but that had been over three years ago. She must have regressed since then.

The waitress came and took their starter plates away, and made to refill their glasses.

'No more for me, thank you,' said Eleanor, putting her hand over her wine glass. 'I'm driving. You can have the rest, Deirdre.'

'Are you sure? It's awfully good.'

'I'm absolutely sure. I don't have much of a head for it any more. I used to be able to swig it back when I was younger – just like you.'

Deirdre looked guilty. 'Oh. Am I swigging?'

'No, no – I didn't mean it like that. You just enjoy yourself.' Eleanor gave a little sigh of contentment. 'It's nice to be sociable for a change. I see so few amusing people these days. Of course, when you get to my age all your friends start popping their clogs all over the place. My favourite cousin died last month.'

Deirdre didn't want Eleanor to get depressed. She started to work hard at keeping her friend entertained. By the time they'd finished eating, Eleanor was in excellent form again.

'We'll do this again, Deirdre.'

'My throw next time.'

'No, I wouldn't dream of allowing an out-of-work actress to foot the bill.'

'It's sweet of you, Eleanor, but I couldn't allow you to treat me more than once. When I sell the rights to my screenplay I'll take you somewhere dead glamorous. Like Ashford Castle.'

Ashford Castle was a seriously posh country house hotel about twenty miles from Westport, and a million miles out of Deirdre's league.

A sudden thought struck her. 'Eleanor? D'you think that the Considine bloke means to turn Carrowcross House into one of those country house hotels?'

Eleanor looked speculative. 'I suppose he might. I never thought of that. I must ask my friend in the planning department if she knows anything.'

Deirdre gave a big huffy sigh and then drained the last of her wine. 'God!' she said dismissively. 'That would be the last straw, wouldn't it? Imagine Carrowcross being overrun with people in Beamers and Mercs.'

Just then the waitress arrived with two glasses of brandy.

'I didn't order brandy,' said Eleanor. 'You've got the wrong table, my dear.'

'No,' returned the waitress with a smile. 'Mr Considine asked me to bring two Remy Martin VSOPs to you, ladies.'

'How very kind of him.' Eleanor looked over her shoulder and raised her glass to Gabriel Considine.

Biting her lip, Deirdre followed suit. Here goes, she thought, as he got up from his table and moved towards them.

'How did you enjoy your meal, Mrs Devereux?' he asked. His voice was low, his accent educated, but not unduly posh.

'Excellent as usual, Mr Considine,' Eleanor replied.

'Gabriel.' He corrected her with a smile.

'Gabriel,' echoed Eleanor. Deirdre noticed that she was dimpling. 'Well, many thanks for the brandy.'

'My pleasure,' he said. Then he turned his disconcertingly black eyes on Deirdre and said, '*Guten Abend, Fräulein. Habe ich Sie nicht gestern Abend durch Carrowcross Fahrad fahren gesehen?*'

Deirdre was struck dumb. Across the table from her she was aware that Eleanor was looking at the pair of them as if they were both bonkers. There was no way out.

'Actually, I'm not German,' she blurted.

Gabriel Considine looked puzzled. 'Oh? I could have sworn you wished me *Guten Abend* when we passed each other on the road.'

'Did I?' said Deirdre, foolishly. 'No – it was, um – I think I said something like, "Good weather we're havin'."' She deliberately distorted her voice so that the sentence sounded ambiguous.

'Ah.' He gave her a look in which scepticism was plainly written.

'Gabriel.' Eleanor smiled up at him. 'This is Deirdre O'Dare. Deirdre – Gabriel Considine.'

Gabriel took her hand and she assessed his grip. It was perfect. She hoped her palm didn't feel too hot.

'Deirdre is staying at the cottage just down the road from me. It's her wall you're working on,' continued Eleanor.

Gabriel looked at her again.

'Well, it's my parents' wall really,' explained Deirdre. 'I'm borrowing the cottage from them for a while.'

'You just arrived yesterday?'

'Yes.'

'You're not very familiar with the locality, are you? You missed your turn-off. How did you manage to find the cottage in the end?'

'Oh, I – um, I didn't miss it, actually. I – um – felt like cycling on to Carrowhead beach.'

'Carrowhead beach?' queried Eleanor. 'I thought you never went near that beach, Deirdre.'

'Well – I just thought it was worth checking out, you know. To see if it was crowded yet at this time of year.'

'And was it?' Eleanor asked.

'Was it what?'

'Crowded.'

'Uh. So-so, you know. Not too crowded really. But actually too crowded for my taste. And too cold for swimming.'

'But you never swim there. You always swim from the jetty, down from the cottage,' insisted Eleanor.

'Yeah. I know. I just thought it was worth a look. It's a long time since I've been there.'

She was uncomfortably aware of Gabriel Considine's fathomless black gaze.

'A long way to cycle when you're laden with luggage,' he remarked.

Eleanor was astonished now. 'You mean you cycled all the way to Carrowhead beach yesterday evening without leaving off your luggage first, Deirdre? What on earth possessed you to do that?'

Deirdre shrugged her shoulders in what she hoped was a nonchalant fashion. 'Oh, you know me, Eleanor. I'm an impulsive kind of gal.'

Eleanor looked at her dubiously. 'I know you're impulsive Deirdre, but I didn't think you were a glutton for punishment. That cycle to Carrowhead must have been frightfully hard work.'

'Yeah. It was,' she said, giving another casual shrug. She took a sip of the velvety brandy, desperate to change the subject. 'Thank you for the nightcap, um – Gabriel,' she managed.

He inclined his head and she looked away. She didn't want to see the expression on his face. He must think her a raving lunatic. Then he turned to Eleanor. 'A pleasure to meet you again, Mrs Devereux.'

'Likewise. Good evening, Gabriel.'

He turned and strolled back across the restaurant to the table where the pre-Raphaelite looker was waiting for him. She smiled up at him as he advanced towards her. Then he stopped suddenly and looked back at Deirdre. 'I'll probably see you tomorrow, Deirdre,' he said. 'I'd like to do some work on that boundary wall.'

'Oh, sure. Sure. Whenever you like.'

He nodded at her before resuming his seat. Deirdre noticed that his partner laid an elegant hand on his as he reached across the table for the cheese board.

Across the table Eleanor was sitting up very straight, looking at her with an expression of indulgent amusement. 'Isn't he simply gorgeous?' she said.

This time Deirdre's shrug was non-committal. 'Not my type,' she said. She helped herself to the cream jug and poured a thin stream into her coffee.

'You mean you don't go for the tall, dark and handsome type?' Eleanor sounded surprised.

'He's not that handsome,' lied Deirdre. 'And any dealings I've ever had with tall, dark, handsome men have been unmitigated disasters.'

Those were the first true words she'd spoken since she'd been introduced to Gabriel Considine.

Chapter Seven

The next day she got down to work. Her own self-discipline took her by surprise. After a quick breakfast spent admiring the view from the verandah she took her cafetière of coffee into the back bedroom where she'd set up her laptop on a table underneath the window, and allowed herself no further procrastinations. She worked fast until lunchtime, when she made herself some cheese on toast and admired her view again. She'd reward herself this evening by opening a bottle of wine and chilling on the verandah with her book. She was re-reading *Wuthering Heights*, and was gloriously caught up in the flaring passion that consumed the pair of lovers. What must it be like to love someone as Cathy loved Heathcliff, she wondered – with such singularly selfish, voracious intensity? Then she realized that *she* had once loved someone like that. The memory of Rory made her want to weep.

She distracted herself by taking her empty plate into the kitchen and getting back to work.

Late in the afternoon, she typed in the words 'DISSOLVE TO', and then sat back, feeling pleased with herself. She'd made pretty good progress. Five scenes had been completed on this, her very first day of serious application to her pet project. As she scrolled through the pages she paused from time to time, making small adjustments, and being careful to click on *Save* each time.

A sudden noise made her stop in her perusal of the text. It was the faint grating sound of a bolt being drawn on the top gate. Then came the sound of boots on gravel. Someone was coming down her driveway. Deirdre froze as she heard another bolt sliding against its iron sheath. This time it was the garden gate. She got up from her chair and backed a little way into the room, keeping her eyes fixed on the garden beyond the window. A black Labrador moved into the frame, followed by the figure of a man. She edged to her left, anxious to keep out of sight. It was Gabriel Considine.

He approached one of the small sandstone mountains that littered the grass and looked down at it meditatively. He remained perfectly motionless for some minutes with his head bent and his hands in the pockets of his overalls. His long black hair lifted a little in the breeze coming in off the sea, but otherwise Gabriel Considine could have been carved from the very stone he was contemplating. Then he took a band out of his pocket, drew his hair back into a loose ponytail, and squatted down to sort through the pile of stones. Deirdre watched as he hefted the big rocks between his hands, picking them up and running his palms over them, examining the shape before deftly fitting one into place in the body of the wall. Occasionally he would reject one in favour of another, but some instinct seemed to tell him which were the ones that would merge most seamlessly into the rocky geometry.

The Labrador ran in and out of the picture, following a million criss-crossing rabbit trails. On one occasion he presented his master with a stick. Gabriel laid a hand on the dog's head and rubbed its ears abstractedly. 'Later, boy,' Deirdre heard him say in a low voice, and the dog deposited the stick at his feet and bounded off obediently.

She remained still for some minutes, observing him with interest. She could tell that he was completely absorbed in what he was doing. There was something relaxed about his demeanour which was at complete variance with the hard physical nature of the work. Although relaxed was too casual a word to describe how he looked; Zen was a better choice.

The robin – presumably the same one that had scolded her yesterday evening – alit on the branch of a tree above Gabriel's head, looking down at him curiously. Then it hopped onto the wall not far from where he was working and studied him with cheeky insouciance.

Gabriel paused in his work to push a strand of hair back from his face and wipe his forehead with his sleeve. Then he slid the zip of his overalls down as far as it would go, and stepped out of them. Underneath he was wearing jeans and a faded indigo T-shirt. He rested for a while, looking up the hill with one hand on his hips, the other shading his eyes against the sun. The hair on his tanned forearms was as black as the hair on his head. He was in great shape physically, Deirdre noticed – lean and lightly muscular. She checked herself almost immediately. What was she doing, behaving like one of the sad women in the Diet Coke ad?

She turned away from the window and went into the sitting room. She wanted to go into the kitchen to get her treat – a chilled bottle of Chardonnay – out of the fridge, but she knew if she did, she'd have to acknowledge Gabriel Considine. There was no way she could potter around her kitchen without him seeing her. Maybe she should just resign herself to languishing on the verandah minus her glass of wine? Hell, that wasn't her idea of fun after a hard day's work. She wouldn't allow Mr Considine to foul up her plans.

In the kitchen she opened a cupboard and took out a wine glass. After a moment's consideration, she took out a second one. Then she turned to the kitchen window and opened it. 'Hi!' she called brightly. 'Fancy a glass of wine?'

Gabriel was crouching over a pile of stones. He had a rock in either hand, assessing their comparative weight and shape. He set them down when he heard Deirdre's voice and rose slowly to his feet.

'Hi. Cider or beer would go down better. It's thirsty work.' He rubbed his hands clean on his denim-clad hips.

'Sorry,' she said. 'There's an old bottle of alcohol-free stuff in the pantry for some reason, but otherwise wine is all I have.'

'Wine is fine.' He smiled at her, and Deirdre wondered how she could ever have thought he looked dangerous. Right now he oozed serenity.

'Come round to the verandah,' she said.

As she passed through the sitting room on her way to the front of the house, she squinted at her reflection in the mirror on the old dresser. She fluffed out her hair, noticing that she looked a bit peaky. It was too late to do anything about that, unfortunately. She'd have to resign herself to the fact that she was going to look like a pasty-faced city-dweller plonked down in Arcadia.

He arrived as she was pulling the cork. 'Will we sit in here, or on the step?' she asked.

'The step. It's a beautiful evening.' He lowered himself onto the wooden step of the verandah and stretched his long legs out in front of him. 'I'm slacking,' he said.

'It's very good of you to spare the time to do this for us,' said Deirdre, sploshing Chardonnay into the glasses.

'I enjoy it,' he replied. Deirdre handed him his glass and he raised it to hers before drinking from it.

'Cheers,' said Deirdre. She fetched two cushions from the couch on the verandah and rejoined him on the step. 'Most people would look on that kind of work as the chore from hell,' she remarked. 'What makes it different for you?'

'It's my therapy,' he said.

'What do you mean?' Deirdre plonked herself down on her cushion beside him.

He frowned a little. 'It's hard to explain. I suppose it's like doing a jigsaw puzzle in stone – the ultimate combination of the physical and the cerebral.'

'Satisfying for the mind, gratifying for the body? Oh, hang on – isn't that an ad for something? Some kind of aromatherapy beauty treatment?'

He smiled at her. 'I wouldn't know,' he said. 'I'm hardly a specialist on that side of life.' He stretched his hands to show her the evidence of his hard manual work. They were long and elegant – the hands of a man who spent his working days behind a drawing board – but they looked strong, too. The black hair on the backs was filigreed with fine dust from the stones he'd been handling, and there was earth under his nails. 'Anyway,' he continued, 'when I heard that your mother was looking for someone to repair her wall I was glad of the opportunity to get my hands dirty again.' He let his hands relax between his thighs and smiled at her again. For some reason she found herself looking away. 'What do you do for a living, Deirdre?' he asked.

'I'm an actress,' she said. 'But I'm not working at the moment.'

'Oh. You're resting?'

Actors considered this euphemism for being out of work rather coy and hardly ever used it, but Deirdre was too polite to point this out to him. 'Well, no, not really. I'm writing a screenplay. That's why

173

I came here, out of the way of urban distractions.' She took a gulp of Chardonnay and looked out at the bay. 'Unfortunately, there are quite a lot of rural distractions, too,' she said. 'I had to make the back bedroom my study because I knew I'd never get any work done if I had that view in front of me.'

'I thought I saw you in there earlier.'

Shit. She'd assumed she'd been unobserved. She hoped he hadn't thought she'd been spying on him. That was, when you came to think of it, exactly what she *had* been doing. The old adage flitted across her mind: *You can fool some of the people some of the time, but you can't fool all of the people all of the time.* Shit again. Why couldn't she, Deirdre O'Dare, fool any of the people *any* of the time?

They sat in silence for a minute or two, watching the bay. There was a bank of clouds like whipped cream on the horizon. Half a mile overhead a skylark sang dizzily. It was the only sound to be heard. A sudden splash made them both look to the right. About forty metres out she just caught the dark shape of an otter as it disappeared beneath the waves.

'Oh!' exclaimed Deirdre, leaping to her feet. 'My otter!' She grabbed the binoculars where they lay on the table just inside the door of the verandah, and focused on the patch of water where the otter had dived. He re-emerged almost immediately, and Deirdre exclaimed again as another small head broke the surface of the water. 'There are two!' she said in an awed tone, lowering the binoculars momentarily and gazing at Gabriel in astonishment.

'I've never seen a *pair* in the bay before!' As she focused again on the sleek couple she couldn't prevent herself from articulating her excitement. 'Oh – look, Gabriel! They're *playing*.'

The otters were leaping and twisting and kissing the faces off one another. One minute they'd fly at each other, sending showers of iridescent droplets up into the air, the next they'd plunge back below the waves, slapping the water with their tails before swerving upwards again. They'd cling together, then they'd separate and play hide-and-seek in the tangled seaweed which lay strewn over the rocks at the foot of the little island they'd gravitated towards.

'They're beautiful,' breathed Deirdre. Then she dropped the binoculars and made an apologetic face. 'Oh, how selfish of me,' she said. 'I've been hogging them. Take a look, Gabriel.'

She handed him the binoculars, and he scanned the surface of the sea until he located the otters. His mouth curved in a smile. 'They're smitten,' he observed. 'They can't keep their paws off each other.' He watched until they dived again. This time they didn't reappear for some minutes. When they did, it was Deirdre who spotted them.

'There they go – round the headland. See?' She indicated the two elegant heads gliding through the deep water beyond Maura's island. They were barely discernible now that they were so far out to sea.

Gabriel set down the binoculars, but continued to

gaze at the horizon. 'I feel privileged to have seen them,' he said.

Deirdre sank down onto the cushion, hugging herself. She was still smiling. 'I love this place more than any other place on earth,' she announced. 'It's strange to think that when I was a sulky adolescent I used to throw a wobbly any time my parents dragged me down here. Now I wish I could live here all year round.'

'Why don't you?' He leant up against the doorjamb of the verandah and looked down at her.

'There's no work for actors in Mayo. Dublin's the hub as far as employment's concerned.' She gave a big sigh and raised her face to the sun, shutting her eyes against its glare. When she opened them again, Gabriel was still leaning against the doorjamb, looking down at her. She felt uncomfortable under the scrutiny of his black eyes, and looked away from him again, out over the bay.

'The blot on the horizon,' she said to change the subject, indicating the eyesore of a barn on Maura's island. 'There always is one, isn't there?'

He followed the line of her gaze. 'It's pretty hideous, all right,' he agreed, sitting down beside her again.

'I bet he doesn't even have planning permission for it. More wine?'

'Thanks.'

She reached for the bottle of Chardonnay and topped up both their glasses. 'I wish somebody would burn it down.'

'Maybe it'll spontaneously combust.'

'Like Granny Godkin in *Birchwood*.'

'*Birchwood*?'

'Yes.' She could see he hadn't made the connection with the Banville novel. Rory had insisted that she read it after she'd given him a guided tour of the grounds of the then-empty Carrowcross House during one of their breaks away in Mayo. 'It's a novel set in a big rambling mansion and the grandmother explodes in the summer house.' She cringed. She had made one of the finest works of contemporary Irish fiction sound like a tale told by an idiot.

'I don't have time to do much reading any more. Things have taken off for me work-wise since I came here. I'd like to be able to slow down, but I seem to spend all my time either slaving over a hot slide-rule or trudging around building sites in a hard hat.'

She couldn't help looking at him again, this time with a new spark of interest. She somehow found the idea of Gabriel Considine wearing a hard hat rather appealing. He had turned away from her, and was reaching out an easy hand for the binoculars. The fabric of his T-shirt was stretched across his back, and she could make out the lines of the muscles on his shoulders. Somewhere inside her, something went slightly taut. She identified the sensation immediately as sexual tension, and while part of her was telling herself to wise up, another part of her was wondering if it might be reciprocated. Probably not, she reckoned, remembering the *principessa* of the previous evening. But maybe it was worthwhile checking out.

She stood up and wandered over to the sea wall, keeping her back turned to him. She wasn't wearing anything madly provocative – just combats and a T-shirt which had the advantage of being too tight – but she knew what could be achieved through body language. She stretched herself languorously, and then bent over the waist-high stone wall and leant her elbows on it, resting her chin on cupped hands. After a couple of minutes spent ostensibly admiring the view, she turned round to him, leaning back against her elbows.

She knew immediately that there was no point in sending him the smile she'd been preparing. Gabriel was looking through the binoculars which were angled way to the left of her. Her attempt to size up the sexual status quo had proven futile.

Feeling a bit miffed, she sat up on the sea wall and started swinging her legs. A tractor was rumbling somewhere in the distance. She scanned the islands, and then caught sight of it hoving into view over the hill on Mad-eyed Maura's island. 'How did that get there?' she asked, turning back to Gabriel.

'He must have accessed it at low tide, over the causeway on the other side.'

'I didn't know there was a causeway. There never used to be, in Maura's day. That island was only accessible by boat in those days.'

'Who's Maura?'

She filled him in on the story of the old woman who'd lived there.

'The causeway's been there since I've been

178

living here,' said Gabriel. 'The farmer must have built it when he acquired the grazing rights.'

'I bet he didn't bother about planning permission for that, either,' said Deirdre. 'God, how I hate that barn. Burn, barn, burn.'

'You obviously suffer from pyromania, Ms O'Dare,' remarked Gabriel, getting to his feet and checking out his watch. 'Thanks for the wine.'

'Have some more,' she offered.

'I'm afraid I have to go. I didn't realize it was so late. I got completely distracted by that courting couple.'

'What courting couple?' Deirdre was momentarily baffled.

Gabriel laughed at her puzzled expression. 'Your otters,' he said. Just then the mobile clipped to his belt chirruped. He sent her a look of apology as he reached for it. 'Excuse me.'

Deirdre rediverted her attention to the panorama of the bay as he spoke into the phone.

'Little Rosa?' he said. 'How bad is she? OK. You managed to get a flight? Leaving from Knock? Sure. I'm on my way.' He clipped the phone back on his belt. 'My sister,' he said, by way of explanation. 'She has to go back to England. Her youngest child's been taken sick.'

'Oh. Nothing serious, I hope?'

'An ear infection. Poor Rosa. My favourite niece has always had problems with her ears.' He frowned to himself and then looked at his watch again. 'Bad timing. Sarah's had to cut her holiday short. I'd better

179

get moving if I'm to get her to the airport on time.'

'Who's Sarah?'

'My sister. She was with me in the restaurant last night.' Gabriel picked up his overalls and slung them over his shoulder. 'Thanks again for the wine, Deirdre.' He gave her that smile again, that smile that didn't make him look dangerous any more, and then he was gone. She heard the sound of the bolt being slid on the garden gate, and then there came a piercing whistle. A second later a black shape went speeding past her and round the corner of the house, nearly upsetting her wine glass as it rushed to find its master.

Deirdre refilled her glass and moved to the sea wall. She remained sitting on its smooth stone surface for many more minutes, looking out to sea with a very pensive expression on her face.

*   *   *

The next day Eleanor phoned to say that she was going into town, and would Deirdre like a lift? In fact, Deirdre didn't really need anything from town, but she thought it might be pleasant to go in for an hour and wander around. She hadn't taken a stroll through Westport for a long time, and she knew there were lots of new shops to investigate. Maybe she'd stock up on some beer or cider. It would be nice to have a glass of beer with her lunch from time to time.

Eleanor left her off on the Mall, and she crossed

the bridge and headed up the main shopping street of the pretty little town. Being a weekday meant that the footpaths weren't crowded, but the streets were bumper to bumper. The town hadn't been designed with twenty-first century traffic in mind, and holiday-makers escaping the stress and road rage of Dublin were astonished to find it was equally rampant in some parts of the West of Ireland.

It was another sunny day. Spring had arrived so unexpectedly this year that there was even some sunburnt flesh around. In the chemist shop window displays on Bridge Street sun-related products featured heavily, and the dress shop dummies were all decked out in summer clothes. Deirdre was seduced by the centrepiece in the display window of a small boutique. It was an old-fashioned sunhat swathed in metres of gauze – a beekeepery thing. She wandered in and took a look at the price tag. Too expensive. She didn't need another hat, anyway. She had dozens of hats back in Dublin, all of which she had bought on impulse and never worn, because some wise little voice inside her head warned her that she actually looked stupid in them.

It was a curious shop, crammed with bric-à-brac and small antique artefacts as well as clothes. She rummaged through the rails without much hope of finding anything she both liked and could afford. Most of the stuff was good quality retro, dating from the thirties and forties right up to the seventies, but there was some second-hand contemporary stuff on sale as well. She finally, and more realistically, turned her attention to the bargain section. A silk blouse, a skirt in last season's awful grey, a pair of hipsters in the season-before-last's awful brown, and an aquamarine Nicole Farhi number. She could hardly believe it. She'd seen it in Brown Thomas a couple of seasons ago, and had laughed at the price. Even though it was *her* frock and assuredly nobody else's, she hadn't even bothered trying it on. There simply wasn't any point, at that price. Biting her lip, she reached for the tag. It had been marked down not once, not twice, but three times. She could afford it. Just. She made a beeline for the tiny, curtained-off changing cubicle at the back of the shop, where she slid out of her combats and into the blue silk. It felt perfect, but she needed to check out whether it looked as good as it felt. She emerged from the changing cubicle to inspect herself in the full-length mirror on the wall just outside.

'It looks great,' said the smartly dressed woman behind the counter. Deirdre could tell by her tone that she wasn't just saying it to flatter her. The evidence of her own eyes confirmed that. The dress fitted her like a sheath to just above her hips, but the ankle-length skirt was cut on the bias, so that when she moved it moved with her, and when she turned it lifted, revealing a satisfactory expanse of leg. 'You've an excellent eye,' continued the woman, leaning her elbows on the counter and looking at Deirdre appraisingly. 'You wouldn't believe the number of customers who've picked that frock off the rail and put it straight back again without bothering to check out its potential. That's why it's been marked down so many times. It's one of those dresses that looks totally shapeless on the hanger, but amazing on – if you've got the figure for it. I'd have snapped it up ages ago if it was in my size. I'd need to diet for a month to get into it.'

'It's a pity about the pantyline,' remarked Deirdre, moving into the light which came in through the shop window. The dress was very slightly diaphanous, and the demarcation line of her pants was visible.

'Leave 'em off,' said the elegant woman matter-of-factly. 'In weather like this you don't need underwear – especially not under something that skims your ankles.'

Deirdre smiled at her. From her demeanour she could tell that this woman owned the joint. 'You're right. It's too amazing a bargain to let go.' She took another look at her reflection. 'In fact, I think I'll keep it on,' she declared. 'It's too gorgeous to take off.'

She dived into the cubicle and gathered up her discarded clothes. 'D'you mind bunging these in a bag for me?'

'Not at all.'

As Deirdre scribbled the cheque, her eyes fell on a neat stack of receipts by the side of the cash register, held down by a curious ornament. It was in the form of a sleeping lion, carved from alabaster. 'I love your paperweight,' she said.

'Beautiful, isn't it? I got it at an auction a year or

183

so ago, when I was fitting up the shop. Most of the stuff you see around you was picked up in auction rooms. I'm like a magpie. I love old things, especially old things with a history.'

'What's the history behind this?' asked Deirdre, picking up the paperweight and taking a closer look at it.

'They say it came from Carrowcross House. Do you know it?'

Deirdre looked at the woman with sudden interest. 'Yes,' she said.

'I imagine a lot of the stuff in here came from there. The locals must have had a field day when they looted that place. Half the cottages in Mayo are probably furnished courtesy of the Considines, and their owners don't know that they're sitting on shithot antiques. Literally. A pair of Hepplewhite dining chairs was found in some farmer's outbuilding last month.'

'It's kind of sad, when you think about it.'

'Sad for the Considines. Not for people like me. I suppose Gabriel Considine will try to track down a lot of stuff now that he's come back to claim his inheritance.'

'Gabriel Considine? The architect? Do you know him?' Deirdre asked with as much disingenuousness as she could muster. For some reason she was interested in finding out what impression this woman had formed of Gabriel.

'I know someone who approached him about designing a summer house on a site near Doo

Lough,' said the woman, clearly delighted to have an opportunity of passing on gossip about the enigmatic proprietor of Carrowcross House. 'He's a very private individual, apparently, but my friend said she found him very charming.'

'Oh?'

'Mm. *Quietly charismatic* was how she described him. She pointed him out to me when we were having dinner in Quay Cottage one night last week. He's madly aristocratic-looking. Sexy with it.' The woman smiled, and then she made a rueful face. 'Needless to say, he was with a very beautiful girl.'

'Dark-haired? In her thirties? That's his sister.' Deirdre was pleased to be able to contribute a nugget of information of her own.

'Oh no,' came the unexpected response. 'This girl wasn't dark. She was a Gwyneth Paltrow lookalike.'

*　*　*

When she finished work later that day, Deirdre checked her watch. It was twenty past five. Gabriel would be arriving soon, she calculated, if her previous encounters with him were anything to go by. It seemed to suit him to slot his 'therapy sessions' with the boundary wall into the late afternoons. She hadn't bothered to change out of her new dress because it felt so blissfully cool in the unseasonably warm weather. As she wandered towards the kitchen she debated whether to have a glass of Chardonnay or a can of beer. She'd stocked the fridge with Bud

185

earlier in the afternoon, when Eleanor had dropped her home. On second thoughts, it was still a bit early to start swigging alcohol. She'd wait until Gabriel got here.

She had a long wait. Gabriel didn't turn up that afternoon, nor the next, nor the next, nor the next. She didn't have a phone number for him, and though she could have got it from Eleanor, she chose not to. What would she say to him? Please come and finish the repairs you started on my boundary wall? It wasn't as if he was some odd-job man who was doing the work to make a few extra bob. He was a respected professional who was doing her a favour.

He showed up late on Friday afternoon, when she'd almost given up hope. She'd washed her hair every single day that week, just in case, but because there didn't seem much point in making *too* much of an effort, she was just wearing her usual combats and T-shirt. At least her skin wasn't as winter-white as it had been the last time he'd seen her. She'd managed to acquire the beginnings of a tan from sitting out of doors at lunchtimes and after she finished work in the evenings. As soon as she heard his footsteps on the drive she grabbed her Diorissimo and gave herself a quick spray before positioning herself casually at her laptop by the open back bedroom window.

'Hello, Deirdre.'

She gave a little jump, hoping that her rather startled smile managed to convey the impression that she'd been taken off guard. 'Oh – hi, Gabriel.' A glance at her watch. 'Goodness! Is that the time?'

'You've obviously been working too hard,' he remarked. His Labrador was leaping up at him, trying to distract him.

'Yes. I've been concentrating so hard that I haven't a clue what time it is.'

'Don't let me disturb you.' He smiled at her and inclined his head before turning away and getting on with his work.

Dammit, thought Deirdre. She'd have to wait until he'd put in an hour at least before she could offer him a drink. Her own work had been so sporadic over the past few days that it wouldn't do her any harm to put in an extra hour, too. But it was difficult to concentrate on the screen of her laptop. Gabriel had stripped to the waist, and she was feeling more and more like one of the women in the Diet Coke ad. The dog continued to pester him for attention, but as his master became more absorbed in the serious business of his stone jigsaw, it gave up and wandered away.

Fifteen minutes of extremely desultory writing later (she actually found herself at one stage typing in 'Pat-a-cake, pat-a-cake, baker's man,' over and over again because she couldn't think of anything to say) she gave up and transferred from her word-processing programme to her games programme. It would still look as if she was working away. Gabriel couldn't know that she was actually playing game after game of Solitaire.

After what she estimated to be a decent enough

interval, she yawned and stretched and said, 'Right. I'm going to call it a day. I'm all done in. Fancy a beer?'

Gabriel looked up. 'You got some in? Not specially for me, I hope.'

'No, no,' she replied carelessly. 'I was expecting some people, but they had to cry off at the last minute.'

'I'd love one.'

She fetched beer and wine from the fridge and went and sat on the verandah steps, waiting for him to join her. After a few minutes, when there was still no sign of him, she picked his can of Bud up off the step and walked round the back. He was still working away. She didn't know whether to offer him the can or ask him if he was going to join her round the front.

Gabriel resolved the issue by taking the can from her. 'Thanks,' he said. He pulled the tab and took a long drink. Then he smiled at her and returned to his work.

Deirdre retraced her steps, feeling foolish. She sat down on the verandah and sipped her wine, pausing now and again to sweep the bay with the binoculars. She'd bought some olives in town the day she'd gone in with Eleanor, and was busily eating them and spitting the pips into the hydrangea bush when Gabriel reappeared. He took her by surprise. Bored with not discovering anything majorly exciting in her view this evening, she was amusing herself by looking at things through the wrong end of the binoculars, and humming the theme from a particularly naff ad for some kind of disinfectant that she'd heard on the radio earlier that morning – one that she hadn't been able to get out of her head. She was on her second glass of wine, and her mouth was stuffed with olives.

'Thanks for the beer,' said Gabriel. The can was scrunched in his hand.

Deirdre jumped to her feet. 'Have another one,' she mumbled as brightly as she could through the olives.

He looked uncertain. 'I can't go drinking all your liquor,' he said.

'There's plenty. I was expecting a whole gang of friends from Dublin to descend on me,' she said.

'What happened to make them change their minds?'

'Oh, they all had to go to auditions.' Yikes! As a distraction, she conjured up an imaginary wren in the sally bush. 'Oh, um – look at the wren!' she exclaimed.

He looked in the direction she was pointing. 'Where?'

'You missed it. It just sort of barged into that bush.'

He took a seat on the step. 'I'd love to help you drink your friends' Bud,' he said.

Deirdre waltzed into the kitchen, spat a shower of pips into the pedal-bin, and was back in a flash with another cold can.

He was surveying the bay through the binoculars. He looked up as she came through the verandah doors. 'No sign of your otters this evening,' he remarked, taking the can she was holding out to him.

She felt a little *frisson* as his bare arm brushed hers.

'No,' she replied. 'I haven't seen them since. There's a stoat living in the sea wall, though. I catch a glimpse of him from time to time.'

'I had a family of stoats living in the old stableyard for a while. I think Tinkerbell finally did for them all.'

'Who's Tinkerbell?'

'My cat.'

'Oh! You have a cat! For some reason I thought you'd be a strictly dog person.'

'Tinkerbell never really belonged to me. She belonged to my wife.'

Deirdre was so taken aback that she didn't register his use of the past tense. She turned astonished eyes on him. 'You're married?'

Gabriel bowed his head. A curtain of black hair fell across his profile, obscuring his face. He took a breath, and then he raised his head and fixed his eyes unseeingly on the blue beauty of the bay. 'My wife died three years ago.'

'Oh, God. Oh, God – I'm so sorry.'

'I know you are.' He remained sitting very still, staring at the point on the horizon where the otters had disappeared the evening they'd performed their courtship ritual.

'How – how did it happen, Gabriel?' Deirdre never knew what to say in situations like this. Nothing ever seemed adequate. But she knew a stiff silence would be worse.

'A car accident,' he said.

'Oh, God. Oh, God – how hellish.'

'Yes. It was. Unutterably hellish. We'd only just found out that she was expecting our child.'

'Oh!' It hit her like a physical blow. She almost found it difficult to draw breath again. 'Oh, that's fucking awful!' She could feel tears of anger rising. 'That's so fucking unfair.'

He nodded. Then he picked a stem of grass and wound it abstractedly around a finger. 'Daisy wanted that baby so badly. That's all she really wanted out of life. To have babies. Endearingly old-fashioned notion, isn't it?' He turned to her and, registering her tears, wiped one away with the pad of his thumb. 'No tears for Daisy. Or for me. I never, ever saw her cry. She laughed her way through life. She always said she wanted her funeral to be a celebration. We played her favourite Gershwin piece.'

Deirdre could find no words. For a while they sat without speaking, listening to the water lapping over the shingle below. A curlew broke the silence. Its fluting call came to them, gliding across the water like the song of a ghost.

Gabriel shook his head, as if to wake himself out of a dream. His hair smelt of some kind of herb. Rosemary? For remembrance. Ophelia's lines from *Hamlet* came back to her: *There's rosemary – that's for remembrance* . . . More than three years had gone by since she'd played the part. Rory had played her brother. Rory McDonagh. She hadn't thought of him for at least two hours. How strange life was sometimes – how unpredictable. If she and Rory hadn't split up maybe she would never have come here to write. She'd be stuck in the city, living on the dole, scrabbling around for work. Now here she was, sitting in the middle of one of the most beautiful views in the world, listening to one of the saddest stories she'd ever heard.

'It's strange, sometimes, how things turn out – isn't it?'

She gave him a startled look, slightly unnerved that they'd been thinking the same thoughts.

'If Daisy hadn't died I would never have come here. I'd have sold Carrowcross House sight unseen. I couldn't have been bothered with it. Now it's my *raison d'être*.' He took a swig from his can.

Oh, God. Poor Gabriel. It was all too searingly sad. Deirdre couldn't bear the expression in his eyes as he gazed across the bay. She wanted to help. She wanted to banish the sadness, restore the laughter. She leant back with a faint smile playing around her lips. 'I've a confession to make,' she said. 'When I was a little girl I used to fantasize about buying that house and doing it up.'

'Did you really?' he smiled back at her.

She thought she could detect a new spark of interest in his eyes. A tiny spark, but enough to encourage her. It was working.

'I'm sorry to be the one responsible for thwarting your childhood ambition,' he said in a lighter tone. 'What did you fantasize about chiefly?'

'Oh – the usual kind of stuff, you know? House parties with beautiful people drifting in and out of

192

rooms, afternoon tea, cocktails at six, children playing in the garden . . .' She wished she hadn't mentioned children. She took a sip of wine to hide her confusion. Shit. How could she have been so clumsy? There was a splash in the bay.

'There they are.'

She looked up to see Gabriel pointing out to sea.

'The otters. Do you see them?'

'No,' she said, suddenly animated. 'Where?'

'Follow the angle of my arm,' he said. He laid his left hand on her shoulder, and kept his right arm pointing towards an expanse of water directly ahead. Deirdre craned in towards him, trying to pinpoint the spot where he'd seen the otters. 'They've gone,' he said. 'No – there they are again! Have you got them?'

A spangled shower of droplets told her where they were. They leapt into the air simultaneously, coiling their sinuous bodies around one another and gnawing hungrily at each other's faces, before falling back into the water with a joyous splash. Deirdre and Gabriel remained motionless, waiting for them to re-emerge, but as the ripples made by their spectacular dive spread further out across the bay and gradually melted away into the calm surface of the water, they realized that they'd witnessed the final curtain call of the evening.

Deirdre was the first to move. 'They've gone,' she said, turning to him. His face was very close. Again she felt that sensation of tautness inside. He turned his head to the left. Their mouths were almost

193

touching. Then he leant towards her and took her bottom lip between his teeth, very, very gently. Deirdre didn't breathe. He drew back and looked at her and she felt as if she was drowning in his black, black eyes. Then he took her in his arms and laid his black head on her shoulder. He stayed that way for a long time. Deirdre remained motionless. She badly wanted to stroke his hair, but she had a suspicion that if she caressed him she would not be able to stop herself from taking his head between her hands and initiating a seriously sexy kiss. And instinct warned her that that wasn't what he was looking for from her.

Gabriel slowly disengaged himself, planting an almost imperceptible kiss in the hollow of her collarbone as he did so. She wanted to swoon. When he finally removed his hand from her shoulder and stood up, the place where it had been felt empty.

'It's time to go,' he said.

'When will you come again?' She couldn't stop herself.

'Tomorrow. I'm not making as much progress on your wall as I'd like. Real life tends to get in the way. I was in London for the past few days, on business.'

'Oh.'

'There's no hurry, though, is there?'

'No, no – none. Take all the time you like.' She gave him her best smile.

'Once I'm finished I'll have to find some other project to occupy my evenings. I might have a go

194

at the garden at Carrowcross House. It's a daunting task, but it needs to be done.'

'I could help you.'

'Do you know anything about gardening?' He looked dubious.

'No. But I could learn.'

He gave her a curious smile.

'I could! I bet I could even master a dry-stone wall if you could spare the time to teach me.' Even as she said the words she could imagine the reaction of her friends to such a pronouncement. Deirdre O'Dare build a dry-stone wall! She'd find building a wall out of Lego something of a challenge.

Gabriel's smile had gone. He was looking at her strangely, as if he'd met her once before and was trying to remember who she was. 'Daisy was just like that,' he said. 'Always wanting to learn new things.'

The mention of Daisy's name made Deirdre want to break contact with his eyes, but she found that she couldn't. They looked at each other in silence for a long minute. Then she said, 'I haven't trespassed in your garden for years. I'd love to see it without feeling that some gamekeeper's going to descend on me and put me in the stocks. That was something else I used to spook myself out with when I was little.'

'All right.' He smiled at her again. 'I'll give you a guided tour. You'd probably like to see the house too, wouldn't you?'

'Oh, yes – I'd love to! I've never been inside.'

'I hope you won't be disappointed. It's very spare.

195

But it's time for me to move in. There's a tenant arriving to take over the gate lodge soon.' He drained his can and put it down on the step. 'Thanks for the beer. Again. I'll make sure there's wine in the fridge when you visit. Goodbye, Deirdre.'

'Goodbye, Gabriel,' she said.

Oh shit, she thought as she watched his retreating figure. She was in love again.

Chapter Eight

They fell into a kind of routine. Gabriel would show up at around six o'clock most days, invariably accompanied by his dog, whose name, she found out, was Inigo Jones. Occasionally he would bring her a present of a bottle of really good wine, to repay her for all the Bud he was getting through. After he'd worked on the wall for an hour or so, he'd join her at the front of the house, and they'd watch the bay and talk.

Deirdre was intrigued by Gabriel's family, and plagued him with questions about what it had been like, growing up in the big house in Buckinghamshire. It all seemed so madly romantic, and fascinatingly complex too, in terms of lineage. She found out that he was the second son of a baron. He had had an older brother with a drug habit who had hanged himself on his twenty-first birthday, and a younger brother, Hugo, who had run away from home to become a Franciscan monk. Gabriel's father claimed that his eldest son's suicide had led to the decline and premature death of his wife, and he had destroyed all existing photographs of him. When Hugo had announced his intention of entering a monastery, an apoplectic Lord Considine had banned him from ever setting foot inside the house again. Gabriel was the only one of his boys who had done the right thing by him. He doted on his second son.

'My childhood was so ordinary and happy,' said Deirdre apologetically. 'Yours is like something out of a Gothic novel.' She was sitting on the step with her arms wrapped around her legs. There was a light dusting of goosebumps on her arms. The weather today had been a little chillier, but it hadn't discouraged her from wearing her Nicole Farhi dress.

'It didn't feel like being in a novel when I was living it,' said Gabriel. 'It felt all too real. The day I realized I was to inherit the title which should have been my brother's, I grew up fast.'

'All that responsibility!' said Deirdre, curling a strand of hair around her index finger. 'I suppose being the second son, you never thought you'd inherit?'

'No. I was totally unprepared for it.'

'Well, I'm impressed. Here I am, a base peasant, talking to a real nobleman!' She released the hair around her finger so that it sprang back into a curl in the middle of her forehead.

Gabriel smiled at her. 'Don't be too impressed,' he said. 'There's not that much to inherit. Just a hell of a lot of furniture and some bits and pieces of jewellery.'

'What about the house in England?'

'That's falling down. We can't afford to maintain it properly, and the old man is always having to sell parcels of land to keep the place going. I'll probably sell up when he dies. He won't mind that, as long as the title lives on. That's important to him. That's his badge of honour.'

'It's so *English*,' said Deirdre. 'All that stuff about hereditary peers. Does he sit in the House of Lords?'

'Absolutely. He's a staunch defender of the monarchy, too.'

'Are you?'

'No. But I humour my father. It costs nothing to keep him happy, and he went through a tough time after my mother died.'

'How old were you when she died?'

'Sixteen. I was sent back to boarding school the day after the funeral.'

'Oh my God!' Deirdre's jaw dropped. 'That's barbaric!'

'It's how my father wanted it. He wanted me to develop backbone.'

'Did you?'

There was a pause while Gabriel studied his knuckles. 'I don't know about backbone. I developed a talent for survival, I think. The school I went to was into mind-games big-time. Sometimes I think it helps.'

'How? Have some more olives.' The olives were in a bowl between them on the step.

'Thanks.' He took one and chewed thoughtfully. 'How do mind-games help? Well, I suppose I never thought that I would have so much truck with other people in the profession I chose. I'd always considered architecture to be a solitary business, and that rather appealed to me. It was a bit of an eye-opener when I discovered just how much of my time and energy I'd have to invest in ego-massage.'

'You mean you don't just sit at a desk and draw all day?' Deirdre took aim at a weigela blossom and spat an olive pip at it. 'Shit. Missed.'

Gabriel followed suit. He hit his target, and the pink blossom shuddered. 'Sadly, no,' he said. 'There's a lot of hands-on stuff involved.'

'Such as?'

'Well, people tend to have very different ideas about what they want from a project, and some of their ideas are just plain silly. I'm the expert. I have to convince them that my way is best, and sometimes that means being incredibly diplomatic. You have to do a lot of schmoozing in this game. I hate it, but if I'm going to be successful in the longterm, it's absolutely necessary.'

'Are you very ambitious, Gabriel?'

He thought for a moment. 'Yes. I suppose I am,' he said. 'I'm passionate about my work – I'm passionate about beautiful buildings. That's why I've poured so much money into Carrowcross House.'

'It must have been horrifically expensive. It was practically falling down the last time I saw it.'

'The great-uncle who bequeathed me the house bequeathed me a decent sum of money as well. It's just as well he did – I'd never have been able to haul the place out of the ashes without it. I feel so privileged that the house ended up in my hands. It was fated, in a way. I'd have felt suffocated if

I'd had to carry on living in England.'

'Where were you living before you came here?'

'London.'

'Oh.' Deirdre gave a little shudder. 'I can understand why you felt you had to get out.' She stretched her legs out in front of her and wriggled her toes. The silk slid between her legs in an undulating fold, and the line of her thighs, the soft mound of her mons veneris, and the curve of her belly were clearly outlined. She knew he was looking at her hard before she raised her eyes to his.

'You have goosebumps.' Gabriel ran a finger gently down her arm. They gazed at each other, their eyes suddenly reflecting the heat of unconcealed desire. 'I'd like to take you to bed, Deirdre O'Dare,' he said, in what was almost a whisper. 'Will you allow me?'

Oh, God. She dropped her eyes to her lap. She couldn't allow herself to look at him any more. 'Yes,' she said, in an equally insubstantial voice.

He put a finger under her chin and raised it so that she had to face him. He was looking at her with such intensity that she felt as though she was melting. When he spoke again she knew by the tone of his voice that what he was saying to her was of the utmost importance. 'Listen to me, Deirdre,' he said. 'I haven't made *love* to a woman since Daisy died. I've fucked around, I'll admit it, but I haven't slept with anyone for whom I had real feelings.'

Oh, God, oh, God. She could hardly believe what she was hearing.

'I don't want to fuck any more. I want to make love again.'

She swallowed hard. She was aching with sexual tension.

He leant in to her and brushed her earlobe with his lips. 'You're beautiful,' he said. She almost flinched at the sound of his voice in her ear. If he didn't touch more of her she'd die. He raised the curtain of hair where it fell over her shoulders, exposing her collarbone. Deirdre felt his breath warm against her skin, and then came the light rasp of his tongue. She reached out her hand and took his, guiding it towards her breast. A light breeze lifted the silk of her dress a little. She felt it move against her legs like a caress in a dream.

Suddenly an ear-piercing shriek of rage came from the bay. They both looked up automatically.

A pair of black-headed gulls were dive-bombing something in the water. They saw a splash and a flurry of wet fur as an otter hauled itself out of the water and onto a rocky ledge on the island opposite. It had in its mouth a shining silver salmon, almost as big as itself. The salmon was thrashing from side to side as the animal dragged it towards a grassy overhang where he would be safe from the marauding birds. The gulls continued to wheel and scream in the blue sky above, and then a heron joined in, taking flight from the island and lumbering away towards the mainland. Its distinctive honking cry added to the cacophony. It was impossible to ignore the din.

The moment was broken. The mood was shattered.

She cursed the otter as Gabriel rose to his feet and scanned the horizon.

'Where's his partner?' he asked. 'Where's she got to?' There was no sign of the female. He regarded the horizon steadily for a minute more. The expression in his eyes was unreadable. Then he looked down at the ground. Deirdre was reminded of the way he'd stood in her garden, the evening they'd first become friends, when she'd imagined him carved out of stone. When Gabriel finally turned to Deirdre there was something eloquent about the look they exchanged. It was full of mutual understanding. Then: 'May I come tomorrow?' he asked.

She nodded.

Gabriel moved towards where she had remained sitting on the step of the verandah. He bent down and kissed her lightly on the forehead. Then he raised his hand and let a finger slowly trail down the curve of her neck, studying her expression as he did so. He ran two fingers down further, tracing the valley between her breasts, and then, ignoring her unspoken plea for him to continue, he withdrew his touch. 'I'll see you tomorrow,' he said. And Gabriel Considine turned and walked out of her garden.

Many minutes later she stood up, retracing his touch with her own fingers as she moved like a sleep-walker towards the sea wall. The sudden rise to her feet made the blood rush to her head, and she leant her hands against the mossy surface, glad of its support.

Against the sea wall, Deirdre O'Dare went limp,

the moss gratifyingly cool where it cushioned the burning skin of her cheek.

* * *

The next day she wrote as if driven by demons. She didn't dare look at her watch. She knew that if she did, she'd spend the entire day calculating how many more minutes were due to go by before she could see Gabriel again, and her work would suffer as a result.

When the shadow of the little chestnut tree had doubled in length, she knew it was almost time. She quickly scrolled through what she'd written, surprised by how much she'd accomplished. As she clicked on *Shut Down*, the phone went.

She went to grab the receiver, and then forced herself to hold back. She waited until the fourth ring before answering. It was Gabriel.

'Deirdre? I'm sorry – I won't be able to make it this evening.'

She went stiff with disappointment. 'Oh. That's OK.' It was patently obvious from her tone that it wasn't OK.

'I'll miss my can of Bud. I'd much rather be sitting on the steps of your verandah watching otters flirting in Clew Bay than taking clients out to dinner.'

'Oh! Is that what you're doing this evening?' She was absurdly relieved that it was business rather than pleasure that had put paid to their tryst.

'Yes.'

'Where are you taking them?'

'Newport House.'

'Oh – cool! I've always wanted to eat there. I've never been able to afford it.'

'I'll take you some time.'

Yes! Deirdre stood on tiptoe in her bare feet and performed little dance steps. 'Will you come tomorrow?' she asked.

'Definitely.' There was something about the way he said it – something so significant – that her heart looped the loop. There was a beat, and then he said, 'Tell me what you're wearing, Deirdre.'

She sucked in her breath a little. 'My combats.' She hadn't yet changed into the dress she would wear to seduce him, the dress she had worn last night.

'Take them off. Don't worry, I'm not going to start heavy breathing down the phone. I've never understood the appeal of telephone sex. I just want to visualize your long bare legs.'

She believed him. She did as she was asked, tucking the phone into the crook of her shoulder and fumbling with the buttons on her fly before shucking her combats to the floor and stepping out of them. 'I've done it.'

'Are you wearing your white T-shirt?'

'Yes.' The response was a whisper.

'A bra?'

'No.'

'Put your hand on your breast.' Again, she complied. 'Does this feel OK, Deirdre? If it doesn't, I don't want you to do it.'

'It feels OK.' It actually felt more than OK. It felt right. And it felt kind of sexy.

'Good. I've taken a mental photograph of you. I'll file it away in my mind and take it out when my clients drone on too long about the minutiae of planning regulations.'

She laughed. 'Delighted to have been of service,' she said. Suddenly she was feeling thrillingly happy.

'I'll see you tomorrow,' he said.

'I'll ask Eleanor if she's going into town. I'll need to stock up on more Bud.'

'Don't bother,' he said. 'I'll bring champagne.'

Deirdre put down the phone and burst into song as she skipped into the kitchen. It was only as she was uncorking her Chardonnay that she realized the song she was singing was the naff theme from that awful disinfectant ad.

*   *   *

It was later than she'd realized. *Wuthering Heights* had gripped her and not let go. It was definitely time for bed. As she got up from her favourite cosy chair on the verandah and stretched herself luxuriously, she became aware of the acrid smell of something burning. She parted the curtains and scanned the horizon, pin-pointing the source of the fire immediately. A thick plume of smoke was streaming into the sky above the bay. The barn on Maura's island was ablaze.

She let *Wuthering Heights* fall to the floor and took a step forward with an expression on her face which was half awed, half incredulous. The fire was magnificent. Deirdre picked up the binoculars and went out into the garden, moving straight for the best vantage point on the sea wall. As she watched, the blaze increased in intensity. Even at this distance she could hear the crackling noise of burning hay and timber. The breeze was whipping the flames into a frenzy, and the fire responded as if to a bellows. When a great tongue of scarlet flame leapt into the night sky and lapped at the Milky Way, she suddenly realized that it was monstrously neglectful of her to be sitting watching the barn burn as though she were watching a particularly lavish fireworks display. She should phone the fire brigade. She ran back into the house, grabbed the phone and punched in 999, continuing to watch the conflagration from the open doorway as she waited for the connection. She was put through at once.

'Thanks for calling, madam,' said the man at the other end when she reported the blaze. 'It's being investigated – we've had several reports in already. The island's uninhabited, so we don't think there's much cause for alarm. But there's an appliance on its way to check it out, just as a matter of routine.'

She replaced the receiver and curled up in an armchair, happy to enjoy the spectacle now that she had done her civic duty. As she focused the binoculars on Maura's island, the words she'd uttered the other night came back to her: *Burn, barn, burn.* What an extraordinary coincidence that her wish had come true, less than a week after she'd expressed her loathing of the barn so vehemently to Gabriel! A thought crept into her brain and rooted itself there subtly. Was it possible that *Gabriel* had stage-managed this incident? She'd articulated her intense antipathy for the hideous structure on more than one occasion since they'd become friends, and she knew that he felt the same way about it. The haphazard pile of concrete blocks, rough timber and corrugated iron couldn't help but offend his architect's eye.

Don't be stupid, Deirdre, she told herself. When the blaze started Gabriel would have been sitting in Newport House, working on his schmoozing skills. The notion of him dousing bales of hay with petrol and scattering matches around the place like some crazed arsonist made her want to laugh out loud. But the idea persisted. The fire really was too coincidental for words. Maybe he'd paid someone to do it? She knew that invidious stuff like that went on all the time: rural politics could be as sleazy as its urban cousin. There'd be any number of people willing to set fire to a barn for a few quid, no questions asked.

There was something rather thrillingly romantic about the notion of Gabriel masterminding the annihilation of her pet hate. She pictured him behind the desk in the library – there was sure to be a library in Carrowcross House – handing over an envelope full of cash to a forelock-tugging type, shaking his hand manfully and telling him to make sure no-one got hurt. 'Don't worry, sir,' the forelock-tugging individual would say. 'That barn has got to go.

There's been too reckless a disregard for planning permission in this area. We locals are mightily sick of it.'

Deirdre was looking very thoughtful as she reached out a hand for the wine bottle and poured the remains of its contents into her glass. Not that there was much to pour, she acknowledged. She'd really gone overboard on the Chardonnay tonight. She gulped it back and, getting to her feet with her head full of dreams, she took one last look at the burning barn. The blaze had subsided now, and the barn was a glowing shell silhouetted against the black canvas of the sky. It wouldn't be long before the wild gales from the Atlantic would topple whatever was left standing, and then nature would take its course. By this time next year the site would be overgrown. The blot on her landscape would have disappeared for ever. Deirdre teetered towards the bathroom, smiling.

*　　*　　*

The next day the mild hangover she was nursing didn't prevent her from being busy. She phoned Eleanor to see if there was any chance of a lift into town, but there was no answer. She'd have to cycle. She didn't mind, really. It was another fine spring day, she was feeling happy, and she could do with the exercise. She'd been sitting at a hot laptop for so long, her bum was bound to have got bigger.

The cycle ride in was fun. Carrowcross was in top

form, obliging her by observing all the usual clichés about the countryside in spring. The fields were at least thirty-nine shades of green, blossom dripped from blackthorn, and woolly white lambs gambolled and frisked on liquorice-stick legs. She passed a pair of white calves so tiny that she couldn't refrain from going 'aaah' when they batted their big baby eyes at her. She said hello to everyone she passed, which was precisely twice.

In town she bought a pricey Chablis, a loaf of crusty brown bread, a slab of country butter, smoked salmon and lemons, and the sexiest food she could find in the supermarket: figs, blush-pink peaches, a melon, grapes. She would have loved to have bought fresh lobster – lobster was seriously sexy food – but the idea of flinging the poor things into a pan of boiling water made her shudder. What if they tried to climb out?

In the newsagent's she treated herself to a holiday blockbuster and picked up a copy of the *Irish Times* when she saw that there was a big feature on Eva Lavery and the Grace O'Malley film, which had been shooting in Galway for some weeks now. Deirdre went into a coffee shop for cappuccino and a doughnut, and read the article. There was a big photograph of Eva in costume as the older Grace O'Malley.

Looking at the picture of her friend in the paper made Deirdre feel terribly nostalgic. Eva was such an important part of her history. She still felt a rush of pride when she remembered how instrumental she'd been in restoring the film star's lost happiness to her, almost four years ago when they'd both appeared in a season of Shakespeare plays at the Phoenix theatre. What a turbulent time that had been! She hadn't seen Eva for nearly a year now. That last time they'd met, Eva had been heavily pregnant, and incandescent with happiness. She had finally been blessed with the baby she'd been yearning for since the day she had been reunited with her lover, David Lawless. She smiled as she gazed at the photograph. The story of that passionate, poignant love affair between the beautiful leading lady and the drop-dead gorgeous theatre director still had the power to make her heart go all mushy.

The *Irish Times* feature carried another photograph, this time of Eva sitting on a canvas director's chair – obviously on location – with her baby at her breast. She noticed that the empty chair on her right bore the legend 'Caít Murray' – an unfamiliar name which Deirdre assumed must belong to the actress playing young Grace – and that the one on her left read 'Rory McDonagh'. Trying to ignore the uncomfortable feeling the name produced in her, Deirdre squinted more closely at the picture. Eva's little baby! She'd sent her a present after she'd been born, but she hadn't had an opportunity to meet her yet. Eva spent most of her time in London these days. Maybe she should get the bus to Galway for a day-trip? She'd love to see Eva again before shooting finished and she disappeared back to London with little Dorcas.

She checked her watch and stuffed the last of the doughnut into her mouth. It was nearly four o'clock. She'd better make tracks. She was going to need a shower after the uphill cycle home, and she had a lot of preparation ahead for this evening's assignation with Gabriel Considine.

*   *   *

She was showered and scented. She was sitting on the sea wall admiring the view and trying to ignore the flutterings of anticipation in the pit of her stomach. She had put the Chablis in the fridge, and arranged slices of bread and smoked salmon on the prettiest plate she could find. The fruit in the bowl was suitably seductive-looking, and there was a jug crammed with bluebells sitting in the middle of the table on the verandah. She'd stopped to pick them on the way home. She was, of course, wearing her Nicole Farhi number and absolutely nothing else.

He took her by surprise. She'd been expecting Inigo Jones to come racing into the garden, announcing their arrival with excited barks the way he usually did. Nothing prepared her for the intensity of the *frisson* she experienced when Gabriel came up behind her and gently parted the mass of her hair, kissing her neck in exactly the same way he had done the last evening she'd seen him.

She turned to him with a beatific smile, raising her face to his the way a flower raises its face to the sun, basking in the warmth of his gaze.

'God, you look glorious. I stood by the gate and watched you for ages before making a move.'

'I didn't hear the gate open.'

'I vaulted it. Soundlessly. Like a cat-burglar.'

She laughed, and he produced a bottle of champagne from behind his back.

'Beats Bud,' she remarked.

'I dunno. I've spent some very pleasurable evenings drinking you out of Budweiser.' He held the bottle against the lightly tanned skin of her arm and she gasped.

'Well chilled,' he said. 'Exactly where I want to be. A couple of glasses of this should do the trick.'

'I'll get them,' she said, making a move to slide down from her perch on the wall.

'Don't stir,' he said. 'You're perfect there. Part of the landscape. I want to sit back and drink champagne and look at you, Deirdre O'Dare.' He smiled at her and disappeared into the house, leaving her inchoate with desire.

When he returned she had arranged the folds of her dress around her as artlessly as possible. It looked as if she was sitting in a pool of silk. The left strap had 'slipped' down her arm, and she drew it slowly back up over her shoulder as Gabriel descended the steps of the verandah with the champagne bottle in one hand and two wine glasses in the other.

'Sorry I don't run to flutes,' she said, accepting a glass from him and holding it out so that he could pour.

He poured a glass for himself and then he stood back and raised it, looking at her with serious black eyes. 'To the otters,' he said.

'The otters,' she echoed.

To her intense disappointment he didn't sit down on the wall beside her, but moved to his habitual vantage point on the verandah steps. He studied her in silence until she felt she had to say something. Deirdre had always found too much silence unnerving.

'How did your dinner go last night?' she asked.

'The food was excellent,' he replied. 'The company was decidedly dull. I was glad I had a mental photograph of you to look at from time to time.' He smiled at her, and Deirdre felt herself colour. She took an unwisely hefty gulp of champagne, and then another one, and felt it go straight to her head.

'It's amazing the way champagne has such an instantaneous effect, isn't it?' she said, shaking her head a little in an attempt to diffuse the sudden wooziness. 'It's almost as if it's intravenous, it kicks in so fast.'

'It's the fizz.'

'Oh?'

'The bubbles help it to enter the bloodstream faster.'

He was looking at her in a way that made her want to stagger over to him and lay herself at his feet. Instead she wrenched her eyes away from his and let them meander over Clew Bay. Croagh Patrick was wearing a wreath of flimsy white cloud. 'Oh, look at

214

the mountain!' she cried. 'It looks as if it's wearing a perruque!'

Gabriel smiled. 'Perruque?' he said. 'What an endearingly old-fashioned word.'

Deirdre's gaze continued to slide over the bay until Maura's island came into view. The blackened remains of the burnt-out barn sprawled like a drunk on a green velvet cushion.

'Oh, I forgot to tell you!' she exclaimed. 'The barn went on fire last night!'

'What barn?' Gabriel got to his feet and strolled lazily across to join her. She thought there was something rather too casual about his demeanour. Was he being disingenuous?

'You know – my hate object. The barn on Maura's island. It's toast.' She took another swig of her champagne, sneaking a look at him over the edge of her glass to see if there was anything incriminating in his expression, but it remained unreadable.

He raised the binoculars and let out a low whistle. 'Wow,' he said. 'It's toast, all right. Did you see it?'

'Yeah. It was pretty spectacular.' She took another sip of champagne and then started pleating the hem of her dress. 'Gabriel?' she ventured after a beat or two.

'Mm-hm?'

'It wasn't you, was it?'

'What wasn't me?' He continued to study the burnt-out remains through the binoculars. Deirdre got the impression that he was reluctant to meet her eyes.

'It wasn't you who – you know . . .' She was uncertain, suddenly. 'Who torched it?'

'Torched it?' Gabriel lowered the binoculars and looked at her strangely.

'Yeah. You know – because you knew I – we – hated it so much.'

'I'm sorry, Deirdre,' said Gabriel slowly. 'I'm having a bit of a problem here. Are you asking me if I burnt down that barn?' He was looking at her in a speculative way, as if trying to work her out.

'Well – yes. Or maybe not you precisely. I mean – did you maybe *ask* someone to do it for you?'

He set the binoculars down on the sea wall and leant against it, folding his arms. 'Why would I do that?'

'Because – well, because you might have thought that I was dropping big hints about it being a good idea. You know, the way I kept going on about how I'd love to see it razed to the ground because it was spoiling my view?' A slight note of desperation had crept into her voice. Gabriel was looking at her with disbelief scrawled all over his face. Then he started to laugh.

'Why are you laughing?' she asked uncertainly.

'Oh, Deirdre! Where are you coming from? You don't really believe that I would do such a thing, do you?'

'You mean, it wasn't you?'

He shook his black head. He was still laughing. 'No, Deirdre. It wasn't me.'

She felt totally ridiculous. 'But you hated it too!' she protested.

'Yes, I did. I thought it was unsightly in the extreme. But that doesn't mean it fired me to act like some crazed pyromaniac, if you'll excuse the pun.'

She was so fazed by her own foolishness that it took her some time to work out the pun.

'You really do live in a parallel universe, don't you, Deirdre?' Gabriel was regarding her with a kind of tender amusement. 'I rather envy you. It must be fun to escape the way you can, into fantasy land. I suppose that's why you became an actress? Don't actors get off on fantasy, instead of getting real?'

Getting real. Get real, Deirdre. How many times in her life had she heard those words? You'd have thought by now that they'd have sunk in, that she'd have learnt something about real life. She bit down on her lip. She'd have to start working overtime on proving to Gabriel Considine that she wasn't a complete klutz. 'I'm an eejit,' she said, giving him the kind of smile that most men couldn't help returning. 'Please ignore my bizarre ramblings in future. I get so caught up in a fantasy life that sometimes I find myself believing all kinds of daft things.'

'Give me an example.'

'Well. Let's see.' She thought for a moment. 'Oh, yes! Here's a good one. I was convinced for ages that a man in a flat on the opposite side of the square to me was a spy. He was dead scary. I was on the verge of reporting him to the Department of Defence until my neighbour told me what he really was.'

'What was he?' Gabriel was looking at her with an inscrutable expression.

217

'A voyeur. He had his binoculars trained on the house next door to mine. A prostitute entertained her clients there.'

This time she found his laugh gratifying. 'No wonder you've taken up screenplay writing,' he said. 'You've the kind of mind that would launch a thousand scenarios.'

'I'd rather have the kind of face that would launch a thousand ships.'

'You have that, too.'

They smiled at each other, and the look in Gabriel's eye reminded her of why he'd come this evening. It was time for her gorgeous feast of aphrodisiacs. 'Wait there,' she instructed him. She gathered up her dress and jumped down from the sea wall. 'Have some more,' she said, pouring champagne into his glass. 'I've food in the kitchen. I hope you like smoked salmon?'

Gabriel nodded at her as she disappeared into the house. 'Yes,' he said. 'I like smoked salmon.'

In the kitchen she started to panic a bit. That was always the effect kitchens had on her. She blundered around ineffectually for a minute or two, picking things up and putting them down again. Then she gave herself a mental slap across the wrist. Stay calm, Deirdre, she told herself. There's nothing less seductive than a het-up gal who's trying too hard. What had Gabriel said earlier? That he wanted the evening to be like the champagne – chilled to perfection. She had to somehow conjure a mellow vibe. How?

Music. Of course! Music would set the mood quicker than anything.

She stood up and fetched an ancient radio from the top of the cupboard. There was no CD player in the cottage, and no cassette player. She'd have to trust that there'd be something suitably mellow on the radio. She turned it on. Björk blared out. Deirdre shut her up with panicky fingers. Björk would never do. She twisted the dial, keeping an ear pressed to the front of the radio. She wanted Classic FM or Radio Three.

There were a lot of hissing-between-stations noises before she hit on the right sound. Something jazzily joyous jumped out. Joyous wasn't really what she had in mind, but it was better than Björk. She slowly raised the volume and the music swelled correspondingly. As she fetched the smoked salmon from the fridge and started to peel the cling-film away from the plate, she found herself humming along to the melody. She must have heard it before somewhere and filed it away in her subconscious. Her father probably had it. He was a classical music enthusiast, and had hundreds of CDs.

She cut the lemons into wedges and arranged them artistically on the plate of smoked salmon. As she stood back to admire how pretty the plate looked she noticed that the jazzy music had slid from joyous to sexy mode. This was more like it! She tucked the radio under her arm and made her way out to the garden, wondering as she examined the plate of pale-pink fish if she should have bought capers to sprinkle over, the way they sometimes did in restaurants. Nah, it wasn't important, she told herself. Anyway, she hated capers.

She emerged into bright sunlight. Gabriel was sitting on the sea wall with his back to the view, his head between his hands. She hesitated before setting the plate and the radio down. 'Gabriel?' she queried as she took a tentative step towards him. 'Are you all right?'

The look on his face when he raised his head made her catch her breath. 'Turn the radio off, Deirdre.' he said. 'Do it now. Please.'

There was something about the way he said it that made her know that it was important. She hit the 'off' button on the radio hard. The silence that descended felt like a ton-weight. She turned to look at him. He had moved towards the garden gate.

'I'm sorry,' he said. 'I have to go.'

'What's wrong?' she asked. 'What have I done?'

'The music,' he said. 'It's the *Rhapsody in Blue*. I'm sorry.'

Rhapsody in Blue. Gershwin. Daisy's funeral music. It was Deirdre's turn to bury her face in her hands. When she eventually raised it, Gabriel Considine was gone.

Chapter Nine

Days passed with no sign of Gabriel. The dry-stone wall remained unfinished.

Deirdre attacked her screenplay with a vengeance. It was the only way she could stop herself from thinking about Gabriel Considine, and it was the only way she could escape her own self-loathing. She got up early every morning to work, and carried on until the evening – sometimes as late as nine o'clock. She finished it and revised it and polished it, and then she redrafted it and polished it again. It had taken her a week of working flat out.

As she read it through she projected it onto a screen before her mind's eye. It looked pretty good, she thought. Jean-Claude Valentin had been right when he'd said that all the best love stories were set in the West of Ireland. She laughed at her own jokes, hoping that she wouldn't be the only person in the world who would find them funny, and she cried at all the sad bits. It could best be described as bitter-sweet, she supposed. The only thing she was uncertain about was whether the ending should be sad or happy. Her instinct told her to give it a happy ending, but a rational voice somewhere in her head told her that logistically speaking, things shouldn't work out for her hero and heroine. They hardly ever did in real life, and she wanted to keep her script grounded in real life, no matter how tempting it was to escape into the realms of fantasy. She hedged her bets by writing two endings – one happy, one sad.

The evening she finished, she sat back, dazed and exhausted. What to do now? She stretched her sluggish, sedentary limbs and shut down her laptop. It felt weird to be finished, and weirder still to have no physical manifestation of her hard work. She was at a stage now where she needed to see the stuff printed out, to see how it looked on paper rather than on the screen of her laptop. That was the one drawback of working away from Dublin. There was nowhere in Westport that had the facility to print from floppy. She had made enquiries the very first day Eleanor had driven her into town, and had been told that she'd have to go to Galway for that particular service. Hell. She wasn't going to worry about that now. She'd postpone that problem till tomorrow – her brain would burst if she started trying to work out the dynamics of compatability and translating documents and all that computer shit this evening.

She stood up, stiff and yawning, and wandered out through the kitchen to the back of the house where the piles of stones still flanked the boundary wall. The robin was singing in the sally bush, the sun was casting long, mysterious shadows, and the landscape was inviting her to take a walk.

She started up the lane, and then veered off along a sheeptrack which would take her up to the headland. Sheep scattered at her approach, dainty hooves drumming on the turf. The only other sound was the skylark, which had been singing rhapsodically overhead all day.

It was a tough climb, but worth it. The sea breeze blowing in from the Atlantic was sweeping her mind free of the self-doubt and self-loathing and all the other débris that had been accumulating there for the past week. As she cleared the brow of the hill, she felt better than she had felt in days.

Clew Bay and its islands lay stretched at her feet, bathed in that strange, amber, evening light which is peculiar to the West of Ireland. She could see the roof of her cottage below to her left; to her right, the roof of Eleanor's little house. On the other side of the narrow landbridge that connected the peninsula to the mainland, she could just make out the chimneys of Carrowcross House poking up above the trees that surrounded it.

Her descent was easy. Her feet ran away with her, tumbling over themselves and putting rabbits to flight. By the time she reached the foot of the hill she was breathless and dizzy. She stood holding her side for a minute, attempting to recover. Through the trees on the other side of the inlet she could see the glint of glass. Carrowcross House had windows at last. She pulled a yellow iris from where a rash of them grew on a patch of marshland, and stuck it in her hair. Then she set out with a purposeful stride towards the landbridge that would take her across to the other side of the inlet, where Gabriel's house was.

It took ten minutes of energetic walking to get there. The gates were shut. Through the elaborate wrought iron Deirdre could see the front of the gate lodge, where Eleanor had told her Gabriel was staying. She tried the gates, but they were locked. A thick chain with a padlock attached was wrapped around the rusty bolt that held them together. There was another way in, though, she knew. A way that she had always used when she was a little girl.

The wall had become so overgrown that it took her some time to find the place where it had crumbled away, allowing easy access into the grounds of the big house. When she finally located the spot, her hands were sore from pulling back whip-like branches and tough strands of tangled ivy. She climbed through, grazing her bare arm against a rough stone which protruded through the thick canopy of green foliage and practically tearing the side pocket off her combats.

Inside was cool and verdant. The decibel level of the birdsong was unreal. She pushed her way through banks of violent pink rhododendrons and emerged on what had once been a driveway and was now more of an overgrown laneway. To her left the path curved up to the big house; to her right it curved down to the gate lodge. She turned right and set off down the path with a hammering heart.

There was no bell. An ancient, unpolished brass knocker in the shape of a lion *couchant* was screwed onto the door. She knocked. She knew even as the knocker made contact with wood that there would be no answer, but it didn't stop her knocking again, harder. After a minute or two she stepped back a few paces and looked up.

The house had an uninhabited air about it. Some blinds were drawn in the first-storey windows, others were half drawn. Feeling furtive, she went round the corner to the back of the house and looked cautiously through a window into what was obviously the kitchen. She was a bit taken aback by how untidy it was. There were breakfast dishes left unwashed on the kitchen table alongside a half-empty cafetière. A tin of dog food with a spoon stuck in it sat on the draining board next to an open carton of milk. There were clothes spewing from the open mouth of the washing machine into a laundry basket on the floor. Mail was scattered on a counter under a bulletin board that bristled with documents. He must have been running seriously late for work, Deirdre reckoned. She backed away from the kitchen window and worked her way round to the front of the house, peering briefly into windows as she went, and not much liking the snoopy feeling it gave her.

The rooms were spartanly furnished with basics – a couch, a table, a few very elegant ladder-backed chairs. In the little sitting room at the front of the house there was nothing but a chaise-longue, a grandfather clock, and a Turkish rug on the floor. On the rug was a copy of the *Irish Times*, its pages scattered about rather haphazardly as if someone had been looking for something in a hurry, an open bottle of red wine, some glossy books on architecture, a pair of scissors and a glass. Deirdre's eyes scanned the room for a second glass, and she felt absurdly relieved when she couldn't find one.

She focused in on the newspaper that had been left lying on the floor, wondering if it was today's or yesterday's, and not feeling overly optimistic that she'd able to gauge. She hadn't paid much attention to the news over the past week. Still, there was something oddly familiar about the page lay-out. Then she made the connection. It was the *Irish Times* she had bought a week ago: she recognized the photograph of Eva that had dominated the Arts section. Deirdre hadn't bothered to read any of the rest of the paper that day – she'd had too many other things on her mind – but she obviously should have. On one of the pages a bold headline queried: 'End of the Line for Ardmore Grove?'

Holy shit! That was the first she'd heard of it. Since last year, anyway. Every time the soap reached the end of its seasonal run there was speculation in the press as to whether it had reached the end of its shelf-life. What rumours had been flying around Dublin since she'd left? She'd have to check this out when she got back to the cottage – she knew that that copy of the *Times* was still lying around somewhere. Well. If the soap was for the chop, she'd be out of a job. She frowned a little and considered. For some reason the realization didn't bother her that much. Amber was washed up, anyway.

Deirdre went to move away from the window, and

then something made her stop. Underneath the headline, a square had been cut from the paper. She wondered what interest Gabriel Considine could possibly have in the politics of soap opera, and then told herself to cop on. There had obviously been an article on the reverse of the page that he had wanted to clip.

She moved away from the gate lodge in the direction of the big house, still feeling like an intruder. As the house came into view around the curve of the driveway she stopped dead.

This was Carrowcross House the way it should be – the way she'd envisioned it since childhood. Brickwork had been cleaned up and replaced, a new roof had been grafted on, and Georgian windows had been inserted into what had once been gaping holes in the graceful double bays. The low walls flanking the steps leading up to the house had been repaired, and ivy was being trained along the pillars on either side of the great front door. Chimneys which had once been broken and crumbling now stood proud, their pale terracotta chimney-pots turning rosy in the light of a sun which was disappearing behind the high, sloping roof. The symmetrical beauty of the house made Deirdre almost want to weep. She started to move forward again, hoping to discover what lay behind the dark panes until she realized that further exploration was fruitless. All the windows were shuttered. She paused, undecided whether to continue round to the rear, where the terrace led down to the old formal gardens, and then she decided against it. The shadows had lengthened considerably, and it was cold under the overhanging trees that lined the driveway. If any ghosts were hanging around, they'd be starting to wake up now. She shivered, hugged herself briefly for warmth, and then turned and walked back down the overgrown driveway, imagining the noise of the carriage wheels that had once echoed on its gravelled sweep.

*　　*　　*

It was dusk by the time she got back to the cottage. As she let herself in the kitchen door, the phone was ringing. She made a lunge for it too late. Whoever it was had hung up. Deirdre felt seriously pissed off. She would have loved to have had a long chat with someone. How about Maeve in Stratford? No. She'd be on stage right now. Maybe she would ring Bart later. She thought about calling round to see Eleanor, and then decided against it. Her torch was out of batteries and she didn't fancy the idea of stumbling home in the pitch dark.

She fetched her biggest, most comfortable sweater from the bedroom and shrugged into it. She'd taken to wearing it every evening now that she realized there was very little chance of Gabriel showing up. In the kitchen she opened the fridge to help herself to a glass of plonk, and noticed that the Chablis she'd bought to share with Gabriel was still waiting on a shelf. It was wasting its time, she thought.

Gabriel and she would never lounge in bed together sipping cold Chablis and eating grapes. Hell – she'd crack it now. She'd finished her screenplay – she should celebrate.

She sipped at it as she threw together a supper of pasta with a shop-bought pesto sauce, wishing that she could afford to drink expensive wines all the time. The best wine she'd ever drunk had been a Meursault which Eva Lavery had opened for her when they first became friends. It had been during that fateful production of *A Midsummer Night's Dream*, when she'd been promoted from playing First Fairy to the juve-lead role of Hermia, and her career had been launched. She'd really been thrown in at the deep end, and Eva had provided enormous moral support. She'd been so chuffed that an actress of the stature of Eva Lavery had taken her under her wing!

The thought of Eva made her recollect the feature in the *Irish Times*, and the article she wanted to read about *Ardmore Grove* going down the tubes. She stirred the sauce into the pasta and left it on the table on the verandah while she went to root it out. It was among a pile of old *Vanity Fairs* on a shelf in the sitting room. Tucking it under her arm, she fetched her wine glass from the kitchen and settled down in her favourite armchair to read while she ate.

She leafed through the paper, forking up fusilli with her free hand. When she came to the page she was looking for, her right hand froze mid-forkful. Directly under the banner headline was a photograph of her. A caption under the photograph read: 'Actress Deirdre O'Dare: her storyline was among the most contentious in the history of the long-running series.' It wasn't one of her favourite photographs. The photographer had taken her unawares – before she'd had time to give him her best look – and he'd caught her with a half-smile on slightly parted lips and a completely unguarded expression on her face. He'd taken it at the very end of the session and her lipstick had smudged a bit, making her look as if she'd just been snogging someone. The photographer had advised her to opt for that last shot, but she'd ignored his recommendation and had instead ordered half a dozen prints of her own personal favourite – one in which her cheekbones were really prominent, and one eyebrow was raised in a kind of cynical question mark. Deirdre reckoned that particular photograph had real attitude, and that her expression in it more closely mirrored the current 'ironic' *Zeitgeist*. The photographer had printed up a couple of the others all the same, and stuck them in with the ones she'd ordered at no extra charge. The publicity department in RTE had obviously run out of her favourite shot if they'd had to resort to using this one.

So: Gabriel had cut out her picture. A thrilling sensation raced through her, and she almost sighed out loud with relief. He cared enough about her to want to keep her photograph! Maybe he had it tucked away in his wallet, or pinned up on the notice-board she'd seen in his kitchen. Maybe he'd put it in a frame? She reconsidered this scenario immediately. No. The idea of Gabriel Considine sighing love-lorn sighs while gazing at her framed photograph really was stretching credibility.

She replayed in her mind's eye the image of Gabriel's sitting room as it had looked when she'd peered through the window. She remembered the newspaper scattered over the floor, and the empty square on the page where the picture had been, and the scissors – and suddenly she wasn't quite sure *how* she felt. It occurred to her that it was the kind of thing loonies sometimes did in films.

Deirdre folded the paper without bothering to read the article about *Ardmore Grove*. Her mind was too densely crowded with confused and confusing thoughts to concentrate on it. She looked down at the pasta in her bowl and thought that she'd never seen anything so unappetizing. Pushing it away, she leant back in her chair and surveyed the darkening sky with tired eyes. No wonder she was feeling paranoid and unhappy. She'd forgotten how knackered she was. She was lonely too, she realized. She missed her evening sessions with Gabriel, even though she'd tried to distract herself from the big gap he'd made in her routine by working her butt off. How strange life was. Gabriel Considine had come from nowhere and disappeared as unexpectedly as he'd turned up. He hadn't hung around for long, but he'd still managed to make a devastating impact on her. She suddenly wanted very badly to talk to somebody. She grabbed the phone and punched in Bart's number. Shit. It was engaged. She set the phone book back down on top of the *Irish Times* which lay folded on the table. Eva Lavery's smiling eyes looked up at her. That's what she'd do! She'd ring Eva.

She got to her feet and fetched her ancient Filofax from her work room. It was crammed with scraps of paper with phone numbers and memos on them, and receipts for stuff she couldn't remember buying. One of the memos read: *Could one of them have been allergic to chocolate? This would get round the fact that there were only four individual mousses.* She tossed it aside. She hadn't a clue what it meant. Obviously some inchoate idea she'd had for the plot of a screenplay at some point.

Scanning the L section, she found Eva's mobile number with a pencilled doodle of a smiley face beside it. It was a long time since Deirdre had called the actress on her mobile – the number was probably invalid now. Eva was always losing her mobile phones. Her attempt to dial it proved her right. When she punched in the number she heard the warm tones of Tara Flynn, current Queen of Irish voice-overs. *This is an Esat Digiphone announcement,* she heard. *The number you have dialled is not in service. You have not been charged for this call. This is an Esat Digiphone announcement* – Thanks, Tara, she thought, as she plonked down the receiver.

She felt absurdly disappointed. Having hit on the bright idea of calling Eva, she was determined not to be thwarted. She did some quick lateral thinking. The Grace O'Malley film was being shot in various locations in the county of Galway, but the production company would probably use somewhere in the city as their base. Where would be the most likely place for Eva to shack up if she was staying in Galway? It was obvious. The Great Southern Hotel in Eyre Square – the oldest and grandest hotel in the heart of Galway city.

Deirdre got out the telephone directory, located the number of the hotel and punched it in. As she waited for an answer, she wondered if she'd be put through even if Eva *was* there. She supposed the actress's privacy would be closely safeguarded by the hotel: after all, Eva was a hot-shit movie star even though she was chum to a minor soap opera starlet called Deirdre O'Dare. Maybe she would stand a better chance of gaining access to Eva if she gave her name. Then they wouldn't be under any misassumption that she was some ardent fan or crazed stalker trying it on.

The phone at the other end was picked up. 'Good evening – the Galway Great Southern Hotel. How may I help you?' came the courteous greeting.

Deirdre injected her voice with an assurance she was far from feeling. 'Good evening. Deirdre O'Dare here for Eva Lavery.'

'One moment, please.'

As the jingly music kicked in, Deirdre felt stupid with embarrassment. Eva probably wasn't even staying there. For all she knew she could have finished on the film and gone back to London. Maybe she should have tried the London number instead? But David Lawless might have answered, and she always felt a bit shy talking to him. She'd never forgotten the time she had made a total idiot of herself by making a pass at him at the opening night party of *A Midsummer Night's Dream.*

As the jingly music cut off, Deirdre expected the receptionist's voice to come on again, telling her that there was no Eva Lavery in residence.

Instead: 'Deirdre!' she heard in Eva's familiar throaty purr. 'What a lovely surprise!' And Deirdre found herself wreathed in smiles for the first time in what really was ages. Well – a week, anyway.

'Hello, Eva! How are things?'

'Things are just amazing – and even more amazing now I find myself talking to you. I'm thrilled you rang. Who told you where to find me?'

'I kind of worked it out for myself.'

'Of course you did, you clever creature. And your timing is as impeccable as ever – I've only just this minute got in the door from work. Now, hang on a sec, I want to put you on to someone.'

A winsome gurgle came over the phone, followed by a loud belch. 'Oh, Eva!' exclaimed Deirdre. 'Is that Dorcas?'

'Well, it certainly wasn't me. Although I have been known to sound like that after a couple of glasses of wine too many.'

'Oh, Eva – I'm dying to see her!'

'She's dying to see you. I've told her all about you, and said the nicest possible things. I'm hoping she might choose you as a godmother, you see, when she's old enough.'

Deirdre was puzzled. 'What do you mean – *choose* me? Haven't *you* chosen her godparents?'

'Good God, no. I wouldn't dream of foisting my choice on her – she might grow up hating the poor buggers. Anyway, there's been no christening – I'm not going to foist that on her either. But I certainly don't intend to deprive her of the opportunity of choosing someone immensely wise who'll guide her through life . . .'

'Eva. If that's your intention, I'm hardly the right candidate.'

'I know, darling, but you don't have to teach her nuclear physics, you know. Or domestic science or accountancy or any of that real-life nonsense. You can just tell her all the essential things she needs to know and is too embarrassed to ask her aged white-haired mother.'

'You're not aged, Eva.'

'Not yet, darling. It'll get me in the end, though. David and I will live out a blissful retirement in a suburban house with stripey lawns. He will take up golf and I will take up bridge and wear sensible shoes and behave with dignity.'

'Not,' said Deirdre.

'I suppose you're right, darling,' said Eva with a sigh. 'I wouldn't fool anyone, would I? Anyway, let's get off this painfully depressing subject.' Eva didn't sound remotely depressed. 'How are things in Dublin?'

'I'm not in Dublin. I'm in Carrowcross.'

'Where on earth is Carrowcross?'

'It's a little townland – very isolated – about six miles from Westport.'

'Westport? Then we're practically neighbours, for heaven's sake! You must come down to Galway and meet your putative godchild. When she sees you she'll know you're the one. You can dandle her on your knee and read her stories.'

'But she's only six months old, Eva! She won't understand a word!'

'Of course she will, darling. I've been reading her stories since the day she was conceived. She's incredibly intelligent – she understands everything. She's inherited David's genius, and my looks, thank goodness. It would have been a disaster if it had been the other way round.'

Deirdre laughed. 'I'm dying to meet her, Eva,' she reiterated. An idea started to take shape in her mind. 'I have to come to Galway soon anyway, to get some stuff printed out.'

'Oh? What kind of stuff?'

Deirdre still felt shy about her screenplay. She squirmed a little before saying, 'Well I've written a kind of a screenplay.' She took a hefty swig of her Chablis and bit down hard on her lip.

'A screenplay?' Eva sounded awed. 'Wow. I always knew you were a clever girl. I'm practically inarticulate with jealousy. I've always wanted to write one so that I could put brilliant parts in it for all my friends, and cast all my enemies in the boring roles. You know – second raddled whore, fat and boring cabinet minister – those kinds of characters.'

'But Eva, you don't *have* any enemies!' protested Deirdre.

'Oh, yes I do, darling – hundreds of them,' replied Eva cheerfully. 'Now, when are you coming?'

*   *   *

It was later than she wanted it to be by the time Deirdre got to bed that night. She was going to have an early start in the morning. She'd checked the timetable for buses to Galway and found that there was one leaving at nine twenty-five. She wanted to arrive as early as she could so that she could get all her printing business out of the way, and be able to spend the rest of the day with Eva and Dorcas. She wouldn't allow herself to think of Rory McDonagh. It was highly unlikely that he was staying in the Great Southern anyway. He had family in Galway, and the McDonaghs were a clannish lot.

She looked longingly at her Nicole Farhi dress floating on its hanger in the wardrobe as she laid out clothes for the morning, anxious to be organized for once. There was no way she could cycle into Westport to catch the bus wearing *that*. It would catch in the spokes and tear, or get wound up in the chain.

Her combats were torn and filthy after climbing through the undergrowth in the grounds of Carrowcross House. She had jeans, but she wanted to put some effort into her look tomorrow.

Perhaps she should wear the little slip dress she

had worn to Quay Cottage with Eleanor? It was a bit dressy, but the denim jacket added just the right touch of understatement. It would also be a bit chilly – she'd noticed that the weather was definitely taking a turn for the worse – but that had never put her off before. She slipped it off its hanger and held it up against her, studying her reflection in the mirror. Definitely. She'd have to remember to leave enough time to wash her hair, as well.

The last thing Deirdre laid out on the chair by her bed was her Agent Provocateur underwear.

Chapter Ten

The next morning she was hurtling towards Galway in a rattly bus, feeling a bit daft in her little slip dress with the silk flowers and her silver sandals. All the other passengers were wearing sensible jumpers or anoraks. She'd brought her book, but had only got through a couple of pages because it was some rather boring Nellie Deane/Lockwood stuff. So she stared out the window instead and indulged in an extremely juvenile fantasy involving herself and Joseph Fiennes receiving intelligent direction from Neil Jordan on some non-specific film set. In period costume, of course.

The countryside as she approached Galway wasn't much to look at – flat and dusty, with ubiquitous bungalows scattered over the landscape, and the occasional palatial house. One had an adobe extension to one side, a neo-Victorian conservatory to the other, Doric columns to the front and bobbly blinds at the windows. She'd love to have been able to tell Gabriel about it. By the time they hit Galway city Deirdre had left Joseph Fiennes laughing at one of her wittily trenchant observations, and was studying the view through the bus window with horror. Apart from a flying visit to see a Druid show

– when she'd come via the Dublin road – she hadn't been in Galway city for years. She was unprepared for the ugliness of the outskirts as the bus progressed at a snail-like pace along a road dense with traffic. The route was lined with industrial parks, retail parks, supermarkets, an omniplex. She couldn't believe how tacky it had become. Maybe it's because I've got so used to living in the most beautiful view in the world, she thought. Maybe as soon as I re-acclimatize myself to being in a city I won't notice stuff like that.

The bus set her down on Eyre Square and she slung her backpack over her shoulder and rounded the corner to the Great Southern, feeling a bit intimidated by its imposing entrance. She climbed the steps and negotiated the revolving doors, hoping she was looking as if she strolled into posh hotels every day of her life.

Behind the reception desk was a clerk with crinkly blue eyes and curly dark hair. He looked up at her approach. 'Hello,' she said. 'I'm here to visit Eva Lavery. She's expecting me.'

'Ah. Let me see – are you –' the crinkly-eyed clerk reached for a sheaf of envelopes and sorted through them – 'are you Deirdre O'Dare?'

'That's right.'

'Ms Lavery left this for you.' He handed her an envelope with her name scrawled on it in violet ink. Deirdre recognized Eva's swirly handwriting.

'Thanks,' she said, accepting the envelope with a slight hesitation. What did this mean? Had Eva been called away somewhere unexpectedly? She tore open the envelope and quickly scanned the note which Eva had left for her:

Hi, Deirdre! The wretched schedule's been changed again to accommodate Mr McDonagh and Mr Rea. Their scenes are to be in the can as a matter of priority. Am on location in Clarenbridge. I've organized a car so that you can come out and join me for lunch. Knowing you, you could probably do with a square meal and the catering's excellent. Just talk to Robert, who is the divine creature behind the reception desk, and tell him to give my driver a buzz. See you soon, love Eva. XXX

Deirdre looked up to see the crinkly-eyed individual looking at her with an expectant expression on his face. 'Are you Robert?' she asked.

'Yes,' came the reply. Deirdre noticed that he was smiling at her quite a lot. She smiled back.

'Um, Ms Lavery asked you to give her driver a buzz to let him know I'm here.'

'No problem. Would you like to take a seat while you're waiting?'

'Thank you.'

'May I organize tea or coffee for you?'

'No, thank you.' She gave him another smile and wandered further down the lobby, pausing to admire the landscapes of rural Ireland that hung at intervals on a backdrop of pale gold wallpaper, and feeling chuffed if she recognized the artist without having to look at the signature. There was an elderly American couple sitting on a couch in an alcove with their morning coffee, looking relaxed and at ease in the comfortable ambience of the old hotel. Deirdre sat in the alcove opposite and listened to them debate how they were going to spend the rest of the week now that a change had been forecast in the weather.

She re-read Eva's note while she was waiting. *The wretched schedule's been changed again to accommodate Mr McDonagh and Mr Rea. Their scenes are to be in the can as a matter of priority.* That could only mean one thing. Film schedules were only ever changed to accommodate actors if they were under pressure to be somewhere else in a hurry, and if there was an appropriate clause in their contract. Rory's agent must have something else lined up for him.

'Ms O'Dare?' Robert was addressing her. She looked up, surprised. People hardly ever called her Ms O'Dare. 'Your car is waiting for you at the front of the hotel.'

'Oh!' Deirdre jumped to her feet and followed Robert back down the lobby. 'That was quick.'

'Yes. The driver came straight back here after dropping Ms Lavery at Clarenbridge this morning. Enjoy your day.'

'Thanks, Robert.' She sent him a last smile, swung through the revolving door and nearly stopped dead. At the foot of the hotel steps was a seriously glamorous black stretch-limo with tinted windows.

'Ms O'Dare?'

'Um – yes.'

242

'Hop in.' The driver opened the rear passenger door for her and she slid inside, feeling madly self-conscious and wishing she could take a photograph of the interior. She'd never travelled in a limo before.

It wasn't far to Clarenbridge, and the drive was through countryside a lot prettier than the bleak terrain that lay to the north of the city. The car moved along winding roads like a sleek black beast. She knew they were travelling quite fast, but their progress was so smooth that Deirdre felt she was being transported rather than driven. What a contrast to the bumpy ride in the bus from Westport! She took off her denim jacket and sat back, resting her arms along the back of the leather seat and enjoying the feel of it against her bare skin. She couldn't help preening a little, wondering if the people she passed were speculating about the identity of the VIP behind the tinted windows. It was just as well no-one could see her. She didn't think she'd fool anyone who *did* manage to catch a glimpse of her.

About twenty minutes outside town she saw signs of location activity. Through gaps in the hedge they were passing she could see lines of cars, trucks, trailers. Her driver indicated right at the gateway to a field, and then paused to give way to a limo travelling in the opposite direction. The two vehicles came to a halt simultaneously within a couple of metres of each other, and the rear door of the other car opened at exactly the same moment as Deirdre emerged into the pallid sunlight. She gave the kind of gulp that even a pantomime performer would consider OTT.

The occupant of the other car was standing looking at her with a curious expression on his face and eyes greener than she remembered them. It was Rory McDonagh.

'Well, well,' he said in that irritating drawl she knew so well. 'If it isn't Deirdre O'Dare. Good morning, Deirdre.'

He leant down and kissed her hot cheek. She was at a complete loss for words. Then: 'You look stupid getting out of a limo, Rory,' she heard herself saying, as she took in his rather scruffy-looking jeans and T-shirt.

'I can't say the same for you, Ms O'Dare.' It was the third time she'd been called Ms O'Dare that morning. 'You look quite the little film star. Nice bra,' he added, indicating with a nod of his head the delicate lace strap that had slipped down her shoulder. 'Did I buy that for you?' He reached out a hand and started to draw the strap back up her arm.

His finger scorched her. 'Don't touch me!' she said before she could stop herself.

Rory removed his hand and spread his palms in a conciliatory gesture. 'Sorry about that. I'd forgotten that I was *persona non grata* around you.' He gave her his best narrow-eyed look. 'It's a shame, really. I always liked touching you. You're the most touchable girl I know.'

There was a beat of silence. Deirdre remained obdurately mute. Another beat went by. And another. She held his gaze. She wouldn't give him the satisfaction of seeing her eyes drop.

Rory's gaze got narrower and narrower. Finally he bowed his head at her in a courteous fashion, smiling at her from under his eyebrows. He took a couple of steps backwards. 'Well. Sayonara, sweetheart. Eva's trailer's over there, by the way,' he added, pointing to a silver trailer parked a little way down the field. 'I can only assume that it's her you've come to see, not me. Pity. You're looking good enough to eat. Literally.' Then he turned and walked away.

Deirdre unzipped her backpack and rummaged around inside for a couple of minutes. She wasn't actually looking for anything. She just wanted something to do to cover herself while her mind recuperated from the emotional battering it had received. How ironic that the very first person she should run into on location should be the person she most dreaded meeting in the whole world! The bastard couldn't have timed it better if he'd tried. She tried to erase the image that had plonked itself in front of her mind's eye of Rory's green eyes boring into hers, and the shocking sensation she'd experienced when his hand had made contact with her skin, and realized miserably that it was hopeless.

She also knew that some part of her had wanted this to happen. If she was to be perfectly honest with herself she'd have to admit that she hadn't just come to Galway to see Eva and her baby, or to get her screenplay printed out. She'd also come in the hope of seeing Rory.

Zipping up her backpack, she trudged across the field in the direction of the trailer that he had pointed out to her, ignoring the curious glances that came her way. She knew she looked very out of place among all these film people with their Timberlands and puffa jackets and belts with tools hanging off them, but she didn't care. She was dying to see Eva. Eva had always been able to cheer her up when she was feeling low. And she wasn't just feeling low right now. She was feeling positively subterranean.

'Come in!' Eva's voice rang out from inside the trailer when Deirdre knocked. She opened the door and was met by a waft of Eau d'Issey mingling with the smell of freshly made coffee. Eva was sitting on a banquette at the other end of the trailer wearing a long, cream-coloured linen smock and a matching turban. She had her feet up on a coffee table, a script on her lap, and a baby at her breast.

'Deirdre! My darling girl!' Eva stretched out her free arm so that Deirdre could be hugged. Deirdre gave her a smacking kiss on her cheek. Then: 'Look!' said Eva, indicating the baby with a proud smile. 'My best production ever!'

'Oh – Eva! You clever thing!' Deirdre peered at the tiny creature clinging to Eva's breast as her mother disengaged her nipple from the little rosebud mouth to afford her a better look. The baby gave a squawk of protest and blinked. Then she fixed curious eyes on Deirdre's face and regarded her solemnly. They were the most amazing eyes Deirdre had ever seen in a baby's face. They were the colour of amber – lustrous, slanting, and fringed with lashes that wouldn't have looked out of place in a mascara commercial. 'Oh, my! Oh, my! She's the most beautiful baby I've ever seen, Eva! It's like looking at a miniature of you with David's eyes looking out!'

'Yes – it is, isn't it? It's a rather startling combination, I think. You always expect blonde babies to have big blue eyes, don't you?' Eva smiled indulgently at the baby in her arms and then held her out to Deirdre. 'Would you like to hold her?'

'I haven't ever really held a baby, Eva. None of my friends have got round to having any yet.'

'Oh, it's easy. She's a lot more robust than she looks, you know. I sling her around all over the place.'

Eva transferred the bundle into Deirdre's awkward arms, and Deirdre gazed down at the miniature film star with her soft platinum curls and kissable cheeks. Then an amazing thing happened. The baby smiled at her. 'Oh! Eva – she's smiling!'

'Told you she'd like you,' said Eva, putting her breast away. 'No more grub for you, fatty Dorcas. She'd stay on my nipple all day if I let her.' Eva stood up and stretched, looking at herself in the full-length mirror opposite. 'The great big bonus about breast feeding is that you get the most amazing tits. David can't keep his hands off them – I have to keep slapping his wrists and reminding him that he doesn't have exclusive rights to them any more.'

Deirdre smiled at Eva and then returned her attention to Dorcas. Dorcas obliged with another smile, and Deirdre cooed at her. 'Hey, she really *does* make you want to go cootchy-coo, doesn't she? I thought that was just a baby cliché in films.' Dorcas burped and Deirdre nearly swooned. 'Wow. Even her burps are cute. D'you know something, Eva? I didn't believe that I had a maternal bone in my body until now.'

'Don't get all broody. I read somewhere that if you start to feel broody your hormones go into silly season and you're more likely to conceive.'

Deirdre made a glum face. 'Not much chance of that where I'm concerned.'

'No man in your life?'

'No.'

Eva gave her an oblique look. 'Rory told me you were seeing some Frenchman.'

'He told you we'd split up?'

Eva nodded. 'He got very drunk and maudlin one night in Neachtain's. Said you'd both been unfaithful to each other.'

Deirdre looked at Eva with stricken eyes. 'He got it all wrong, Eva. We were talking crossed lines, big-time.'

'He's going soon, Deirdre.'

Oh God. Deirdre suddenly felt unreal, as if she was in a film and ominous music had just been cued. 'What do you mean? He's going where?'

'To LA. He's got a major contract with Amblin.'

'The Spielberg outfit?'

'Yes. That's why all his scenes have been brought forward. We're running way behind schedule on this epic, and he needs to be released as soon as possible. He's leaving at the end of the week.'

'Oh.' Deirdre looked down at the baby in her

arms. Dorcas's eyes were closing. A tiny snore escaped her pink pout.

Just then they heard a knock at the door. On Eva's invitation to enter, a smiling girl came into the trailer. She had a freckled face and a mass of red hair tied back with a hank of bright wool. 'Eva? Jamie asked me to tell you they're ready for you.'

'I'm on my way. Your timing's impeccable, Mairead. Your charge is due a nappy change. I was just about to do it before you arrived.'

'Sure you were.' The redhead gave Eva a sceptical smile, and Deirdre couldn't blame her. Something told her that changing nappies was not the aspect of motherhood that Eva would find the most appealing.

'Deirdre – this is Mairead. She's my nanny. Or rather, she's Dorcas's nanny.'

'Sometimes I feel like I'm yours, too, Eva,' said Mairead. 'Hi, Deirdre – nice to meet you. Do you want to hand over the most brilliant, well-behaved, beautiful baby that was ever born to any woman on the face of the planet or in the history of the universe?'

'With some pleasure, actually,' replied Deirdre. 'She's beginning to pong a bit.'

Mairead took the baby from Deirdre, fetched a bag full of nappy-changing gear from a cupboard and swung it onto a table, expertly extracting various nappy-related items from the bag with one hand while balancing the baby on her left hip. Dorcas eyed the nappy-changing bag with mistrust, and her mouth went into such a pout that it looked more like a rosebud than ever.

'Oh – no, no, no, no, no, Mairead! Wait till I'm gone, please? I'll be out of here in a minute. Just let me adjust this stupid hat.' Eva was standing in front of the mirror, poking around at the turban on the top of her head. 'Isn't this the most ridiculous looking article?' she said, as she met Deirdre's eyes in the mirror. 'I'm going to get my agent to put a clause in my next contract: "Under no circumstances is Ms Lavery to wear a hat. She looks too silly in them."'

'I think you look very elegant in it, Eva.'

'Thank you, darling. I think it looks like a dishcloth. Oh, hang on – it doesn't actually look *too* bad at this angle, does it? Kind of rakish. I like that.' Eva had tweaked the head-dress so that it sat at an angle to her head. She gave her reflection a satisfied smile. 'Now, Deirdre. Come and keep me company. You couldn't be an absolute angel and run lines with me? They keep making changes to the script.'

'OK. Bye, Mairead,' said Deirdre as she followed her heroine.

'Bye, you two,' said Mairead, laying a crosslooking Dorcas on her back on the changing mat. As Deirdre closed the trailer door behind her she heard the baby give out a kind of growl.

Eva gave her a disingenuous smile. 'What unfortunate timing for Mairead,' she said, handing Deirdre a single page of dialogue. 'Now – where am I meant to be? Oh yes, underneath ye old oak tree. Or is it a chestnut?' Eva linked arms with Deirdre and began to stroll across the field, saying hello to everyone she passed. Deirdre felt privileged to be in such illustrious company.

'Who's your scene with?' she asked, scanning the page.

'Stephen Rea. I'm a lucky woman. He's playing Grace's second husband.'

'And Rory's playing number one – Dónal O'Flaherty?'

'Yup.'

'Have you any scenes with him?'

'Good God, no. I'd look like a raddled old bat beside Rory. All his scenes are with the young Grace.'

Deirdre bit her lip and looked back down at the page. 'So, how come you're working on a scene that doesn't include Rory if his stuff's meant to be priority?'

'Stephen's stuff's priority too. They need this in the can today – he's buggering off to some exotic location tomorrow. There he is now.' Eva waved at Stephen Rea, who was leaning against a tree trunk talking to one of the crew. He was in full period costume, which made the sunglasses he was wearing look extremely anachronistic. Deirdre wondered if she'd get the chance to meet him. 'It's astonishing to be working with all these actors who are in such demand,' continued Eva. 'They're practically on a movie production line. *I've* nothing coming up at all, except an extremely badly paid radio play.' She didn't sound remotely concerned.

'That's unusual for you, Eva.'

'I'll let you into a secret, darling. It's through choice. I want to spend more time playing at being mumsie with my beloved Dorcas.'

They were drawing close to the spot where the crew had set up. Deirdre stopped and turned to her friend. There was a question she wanted to ask that had been burning a hole in her brain for some time. 'Eva?'

'Mm?' The actress stopped too, regarding the location with a gloomy expression. 'There's Deborah from wardrobe. She'll spend the next ten minutes poking around at my horrible hat, trying to make it sit straight.'

'Eva,' said Deirdre again. 'What's Caít Murray like as young Grace?'

Eva grimaced. 'I hate to have to tell you this, darling, but she's actually rather good.'

'I thought she might be.' She attempted a stoical smile. 'Do you know something that's really puzzled me? *I* tested for that part, and I haven't a clue why. I'm too old, for starters – Grace was only fifteen or sixteen when she married Dónal O'Flaherty, wasn't she? And I bear absolutely no resemblance to you. I'd have been lousy match-up material.'

Eva didn't answer for some time. Deirdre was so unused to seeing Eva wearing such a serious expression that she almost took a pratfall. 'Deirdre?' she said in a solemn voice. 'If I let you into a secret will you promise not to tell Rory?'

Deirdre was puzzled. 'What on earth has Rory to do with any of this?'

'I won't tell you if you don't promise.'

Deirdre bit her lip. 'OK,' she said. 'I promise I'll never let Rory know what you're about to tell me.'

'He engineered that screen test. He persuaded the casting people to see you. He said he'd known it was a wrong thing for him to do, in case it got your hopes up about getting a part in the movie, but he just couldn't resist it. He thought it might be a way for the two of you to get back together again.'

Deirdre stopped dead, staring at Eva in disbelief.

Eva nodded. 'It's true. It was the same night he told me about your split. He said the most sublime thing about you, darling – and you know what they say about *in vino veritas*. He said that when he kissed you during the test, he knew how it must feel to be a drug addict getting a fix. He said that for the entire time you'd been apart he'd been suffering from withdrawal symptoms. Arranging that test was the only way he could get to kiss you again.'

'Rory said that? You're sure?'

'I couldn't dream up a line like that, darling. A word of warning, though. Watch out for Caít. Since shooting started she's been behaving as if Rory's her private property.'

'Oh.' Deirdre took a deep breath and then she gave Eva a level look. 'Has she shagged him?'

The other actress made a little *moue*. 'I suspect so. She did kind of offer herself to him on a plate, and you know how difficult Rory finds it to refuse to oblige a woman. And how easy it is to let a screen romance develop into something off screen. Rory's always had a *penchant* for his leading ladies. You should know, darling. You were his leading light for a long time after all, off stage as well as on.'

His leading light. Not any more. He was like quicksilver. She had let him slip through her fingers once too often.

* * *

She didn't see him until lunchtime. Due to some technical hitch it had taken longer than anticipated to get through the short scene involving Eva and Stephen Rea, and Deirdre had spent the morning sitting on the sidelines observing the proceedings and glancing over her shoulder from time to time, on tenterhooks that Rory might take her unawares any minute. Mairead rolled up at one point, with a belligerent Dorcas looking for lunch, and Eva had sat down under the tree and obliged the baby while lights were tweaked and a make-up lady powdered her nose. Eva borrowed a blusher brush from her and tickled the baby's cheeks while she fed. Deirdre thought she had never seen the actress look so happy.

Shortly after one o'clock the scene was in the can. The First Assistant announced that Mr Rea was leaving the set, and cast and crew applauded – traditional procedure when an actor's through on a film. Eva invited Deirdre to join her at the top of the queue for lunch, and Deirdre was disappointed when she learnt that she wouldn't have the chance to meet her co-star – he was being driven directly to Knock International airport.

The pair of actresses bypassed the hot food and made for the cold buffet instead. Deirdre piled a selection of salad dishes on top of the nest of lettuce leaves she'd made on her plate. There was smoked chicken, mixed beans, artichoke hearts, and mozzarella with cherry tomatoes. There was bulgar with apricots, baby potatoes, and something Eva called *chouchouka*. There was *Tarte Tatin* for later.

They made their way to one of the trestle tables that had been set out in a corner of the field under the leaf-green canopy of a beech tree. As Deirdre laid into the best meal she'd had in ages, a familiar voice came from behind her. She didn't need to turn round to know who it was – in fact, she kept her back firmly fixed to the speaker.

'Do you ladies mind if I join you?' asked Rory.

Deirdre could feel Eva's eyes on her. It was obvious that the leading lady was uncertain as to how welcome Rory really was, but Deirdre wouldn't look back at her. She kept her eyes firmly fixed on her plate.

'Please, do,' said Eva after a beat or two of rather embarrassing silence.

Rory strolled around to the other side of the table and set down his tray. Deirdre dared to steal a look at him. He was dressed in an outfit similar to the one Stephen Rea had been wearing – the regalia of a sixteenth-century Irish chieftain. He lifted a heavy woollen cloak from his shoulders and threw it over the back of a folding chair. Underneath he was wearing tight worsted leggings, a wide-sleeved, saffron-coloured linen shirt, and a jerkin of studded leather. A dagger was slung low on his hip.

Eva looked at him admiringly. 'I'll never get over how edible you look in that rig-out, Rory,' she said.

'Don't you think the shirt's a bit Michael Flatley?' asked Rory, digging into his pasta.

'Not on you, darling. Anyway, linen's much sexier than satin. It's so kind of coarse and *rugged*. I much prefer linen sheets to satin ones. Satin's tacky.' She speared a cherry tomato. 'What have they lined up for you this afternoon?'

'I'm galloping through the wood with my trusty wolfhound at my trusty horse's heels. Then I'm galloping through the wood with my girl on the saddle in front of me. Then I'm galloping through the wood with my falcon on my wrist.'

'Not the same one that nipped you last week?'

'The very one. He's an evil bastard, that bird.'

Eva popped the cherry tomato into her mouth. 'Any dialogue?'

'Some rather soppy stuff later.'

'On top of it?'

'I will be.'

Deirdre felt a twinge of jealousy as the actors talked film-talk.

'So. How's my gorgeous babe?' asked Rory finally.

Deirdre shot him a look, but he wasn't looking at her. He was concentrating on his pasta.

'Oh – she's fine.' Eva answered the question. 'She's sleeping off her lunch in the trailer.' He'd been referring to Dorcas. Absurdly, the realization made her heart lurch.

'I'll miss that baby. She has a wicked sense of humour. I can't wait to see how she turns out sixteen years down the line.'

'You'll be far too old for her, Rory, and an extremely bad influence. Anyway, David would break your face if you laid a finger on her. He's already thinking about sending her to a convent school.'

'Convent schoolgirls can get up to the most unexpected things, Eva,' said Rory knowledgeably. 'You were a convent schoolgirl, weren't you, Deirdre?'

'No – I wasn't, actually.' She gave him a look which she hoped might be interpreted as withering, and then found that she couldn't look away from him. He was giving her his great smile.

'How's the screenplay going?' he asked.

'How did you know I'd started it?'

'I rang your flat the other night.' What! Why? 'I got straight onto Bart when some geezer answered. Bart told me you'd become a scribe and a hermit in Carrowcross. Who was the geezer?'

'Oh – nobody,' she answered quickly. 'Just somebody who's taken my flat for as long as I'm happy being a scribe and a hermit in Carrowcross.' She looked at him carefully, and then returned his smile. 'He's gay.'

'His sexual persuasion doesn't interest me, Deirdre.' But he was *really* smiling at her now.

Eva suddenly pushed her plate away. 'Well,' she said brightly. 'I'm off to make-up to wipe off my screen face.'

'But, Eva – you've hardly eaten any of your lunch!'

'I had the most enormous fry-up for breakfast, darling. I don't have room for any more.' She got up from the table and looked at Rory. 'Anyway,' she said, 'my tits are bursting. Dorcas is due another feed.'

'Jesus, Lavery,' groaned Rory. 'I sometimes think you have no idea what you can do to a man.'

'On the contrary, darling,' she replied, giving him a feline smile. 'I generally have a very *good* idea. See you later.' With a little wave of her fingers, she was gone.

Deirdre and Rory were left facing each other. Deirdre resumed eating, even though she wasn't very hungry any more.

'How's Carrowcross?' Rory asked.

'Beautiful.'

'Have you been getting much work done?'

'Yes. I've finished it.'

'Clever girl.' Rory looked at her with admiration. 'I'd love to have a look.'

'That's one of the reasons I came to Galway. To print it out.'

'You have it on floppy?'

'Yes.' She pronged a wedge of potato and stuck it in her mouth.

258

'You have it on you now?'

She nodded and swallowed potato without tasting it.

'Give it to me. I'll get it printed out for you.'

'How?'

'Trish in the production office owes me a favour.'

'Maybe.' She looked at him, and then looked down at her plate again. 'But you don't owe *me* any favours, Rory. I'll get it done somewhere in town.'

'Don't be a pillock, O'Dare. You'll spend half the afternoon trying to locate a printer's, and then more time hanging around while they print it out. Trish can run off a couple of copies for you no problem, and it'll cost you nothing.'

She pronged another potato and considered. 'OK. Thanks.' She was still a bit reluctant to accept his offer, and she knew why. 'You won't look at it, Rory, will you?'

'Not if you don't want me to,' he said, surveying her with interested eyes. 'But don't you think it's time you got feedback from someone?'

She knew he was right. She'd have to show it to someone sooner or later. And Rory had been in on her idea since its inception. If she had to show it to anyone, it really should be him. 'You won't laugh at it, will you?'

'I thought it was meant to be a comedy?'

'Yeah – I know – but I mean . . . You won't laugh at it in a sneery way, will you?'

'I never sneer at people who are brave enough to try something new, Deirdre. Give me the floppy.'

She took it from where she'd safely stowed it in a pocket of her backpack, and slid it across the table. As he went to take it, she hesitated suddenly. He put out his other hand and gently released her grip. 'Don't worry, sweetheart, I'll guard it with my life. You know I will.' His right hand slid the floppy disk into a pouch on his thick leather belt. His left hand remained resting on top of hers. She turned her hand so that her palm was upwards. Rory traced the contours with a finger and she shivered involuntarily. Then they looked at each other and exchanged a smile.

'Rory!' A tiny blonde was weaving her way through the network of trestle tables towards them. She was wearing flowery-printed shorts and a little cotton top with a beaded trim. A sweater was slung round her shoulders and her feet were bare. Deirdre whipped her hand out from under Rory's and flashed him a look.

'Shit!' he muttered under his breath. Then he took a visible breath and stood up. 'Hi, Caít – how's–'

The greeting remained unfinished. Caít Murray flung herself at Rory like a playful puppy before pulling his head down to her face and snogging him in full view of the entire film crew. There was laughter, and one or two ribald remarks. When she finally let go of him, she curtseyed to her audience with a radiant smile.

Deirdre's eyes met those of her erstwhile lover, and they stared at each other in mutual helplessness for a moment before she got up from the table. 'Gotta

260

go,' she said. 'Nice seeing you again, Rory. Good luck in LA.'

'Aren't you going to introduce me?' Caít was looking at Deirdre with eyes the colour of bluebells. She had no make-up on, her mane of unbleached golden hair was pulled back off her perfectly heart-shaped face, and her full, sensuous mouth was curved in what was – indubitably – a genuinely candid smile. Caít Murray was exquisite.

Rory made a perfunctory gesture with a slack hand. 'Deirdre O'Dare – this is Caít Murray. Caít – Deirdre.'

Caít held out her hand. 'Hi, Deirdre. It is so cool to meet you! I've been a fan of yours for years.'

'Hi. Thanks.' Deirdre returned the handshake, wondering exactly how many years Caít Murray could have been a fan. Not many. She was the most vibrantly youthful actress Deirdre had ever met. She wore the bloom of a fruit that was just ripe to be plucked. No wonder Rory had been tempted to pluck her. He'd described Deirdre as looking good enough to eat earlier on that morning. This girl was positively toothsome.

Deirdre knew when to acknowledge defeat. 'Um. Sorry – I don't mean to be rude, but I've got to dash. Bye.'

'Deirdre – wait!' Rory stepped forward and laid a hand on her arm. She shook it off, registering Caít's blue blink. 'How will I get your manuscript to you?'

'Send it to the cottage in Carrowcross,' said Deirdre. Then she turned and walked blindly across the field to where Eva's trailer was, hoping she wouldn't stumble.

Eva was zipping up blue jeans when Deirdre rounded the door of her trailer. Her discarded costume was suspended from a plastic hanger.

'Deirdre! What's wrong?'

Deirdre sat down on the banquette and buried her head in her hands. 'Oh, Eva!' she sobbed. 'I don't think I can bear it. I don't think I can bear the thought of Rory going away without sorting things out between us. I love him so much, Eva. I can't stand it.'

She felt Eva's arms go round her.

'It's like a physical pain. I can't bear not knowing if I'll ever see him again. I can't bear the thought of there being no Rory in my life. I can't bear the thought of him and that totally gorgeous young thing . . .' She couldn't continue. She laid her head in Eva's lap and wept and wept, while Eva stroked her hair and murmured to her. She wept at full throttle for some minutes, and when she felt Eva coaxing a wad of tissues into her clenched hand, she realized that her sobs were subsiding. She shuddered and blew her nose and then cried a little more. She was just beginning to wonder how she would ever stop weeping when an ear-splitting yell came from the other side of the room. She sat up abruptly, looking around with a disoriented expression.

'It's Dorcas,' explained Eva, getting to her feet with an apologetic expression on her face. 'Sorry – I'll only be a tick.' Dorcas's decibel level was mounting steadily. 'It never ceases to amaze me how such a tiny creature can produce such a deafening racket,' Eva said, unbuttoning her shirt with deft fingers as she crossed the floor. She lifted the baby from her crib and held her to her breast. 'Shut up, you,' she said. Dorcas latched on, and the crying stopped as if by magic. 'Well. That's worked for one of you, but it sure as hell won't work for both of you.'

Despite herself, Deirdre gave a weak laugh.

'I know what might work for you, though, Deirdre.'

Deirdre raised tearful eyes to where Eva stood on the other side of the trailer, swaying to the rhythm of the baby's sucking. 'Oh? What?'

'Come back to my hotel and we'll treat ourselves to a night in with room service. You can raid the mini-bar. I'd help, but I have to be careful. Dorcas with a hangover is worse than the kraken with a migraine.'

Deirdre's crying jag had dulled her wits. 'Dorcas with a hangover?' she asked stupidly. 'How could Dorcas get a hangover?'

'The alcohol passes through into my milk,' explained Eva. 'I have to be careful. It's the only disadvantage of breast-feeding. The day this baby's weaned I'm going to crack open a magnum of champagne. Scratch that. Let's make it a Nebuchadnezzar.' She gave Deirdre a complicitous smile, and Deirdre knew that the actress was working overtime to make her feel better. 'Sometimes I indulge in a couple of glasses of port before the last feed of the night. That puts her to sleep with a smile on her face. Well?'

'Well what?' Deirdre was still feeling a bit dopey and very sniffly.

'Let's do girly shit.'

'I'd love to, Eva – I honestly couldn't think of a nicer way of spending the evening – but I have to get the last bus back to Westport. It leaves at five-thirty.'

'What have you got to get back for?'

She thought of her finished screenplay. She thought of her unfinished dry-stone wall. She thought of Gabriel Considine. She wouldn't let herself think of Rory. 'Nothing,' she said.

*   *   *

Later that night she and Eva and Dorcas were lounging on Eva's king-size bed in the Great Southern Hotel, painting each other's toenails and watching MTV on a wide screen. Dorcas couldn't join in the nail-painting, but she submitted to having hers painted, and gurgled every time Ronan Keating appeared on the screen. 'She's crazy about him,' explained Eva. 'I don't blame her. The only other person she goes all coy for is Rory. And her dad, of course.'

'When is Rory off?' asked Deirdre, pleased that she could finally ask the question without behaving like the Niagara Falls.

'Mm. Let's see,' said Eva, sticking out her tongue a little as she concentrated on painting Deirdre's middle toenail palest pink. 'What day's today? Tuesday?'

'Mm-hm.' Deirdre was perusing the room service menu and swigging mini-bar wine.

'Well, he's working all day tomorrow, according to the schedule. I'm free – hah! And then he's got a pick-up shot to do on Thursday morning, and then he's finished. He's flying to the States the next day.'

'Friday.'

'Yeah.' Eva glanced up at her and gave a little shrug, as if to say: *Bear up, darling – c'est la vie.* Then she deftly changed the subject. 'What are we having to eat?' she asked.

Deirdre dragged her attention back to the menu. 'What would you recommend? You probably know this menu off by heart by now.'

'Crab claws are good. So's the club sandwich.'

'OK. I'll have those. What about you?'

'Rack of ribs, please. And cannelloni. Death-by-chocolate goes without saying. Will you order? I'm on a crucial bit of your pinky.'

Just as Deirdre reached out a hand for the phone on the bedside table, it rang.

'Hello – Ms Lavery's room,' said Deirdre into the phone.

'That's not Ms Lavery, is it?'

'Er – no.' The people at reception had obviously got used to Eva's honey tones.

'Would you be so kind as to tell Ms Lavery that Mr Lawless is on the phone for her?' said the voice at the other end.

265

'Certainly.' Deirdre covered the receiver with her hand. 'Eva? It's David,' she said.

It was as if someone had thrown a switch behind Eva's face. She was luminous, suddenly. 'Thank you darling,' she said, letting varnish drip onto Deirdre's toe as she held brush and bottle towards her. 'Will you stick the top back on?' Then she took the phone from Deirdre and launched into a stream of endearments.

Deirdre put the nail varnish back into Eva's rather chaotic cosmetics case and then looked around for something to occupy herself with while the actress was on the phone. She wandered over and curled up on one of the yellow upholstered sofas that faced each other across the glass-topped table in the middle of the big room, glancing back at Eva, who was lying on her tummy on the blue-and-yellow counterpane. She was stroking Dorcas's blonde curls with an enraptured expression on her face and Dorcas was still gazing at Ronan Keating on the telly with an equally enraptured expression on hers. The room had been chosen with the baby in mind, Eva had told her. She'd been shown a couple of grander, more traditional suites before opting for this one with its bright décor and airy feel.

There was a bowl of fruit and a pile of magazines on the table in front of her. Deirdre helped herself to some grapes and looked through the magazines without much interest – until she came upon a spiral-bound, A4 document. It was Eva's script. She gave the actress a little wave to attract her attention. 'Can

I have a look?' she mouthed. Eva smiled and nodded, and then returned her attention to the phone. Deirdre leafed slowly through the manuscript, examining the format to see how hers compared. It was something that was of extreme interest to her now. She'd read as many scripts as she could get her hands on before starting work on her own screenplay in order to familiarize herself with the structure.

One page made her suck in her breath. It was the scene that she had played with Rory the day she'd tested for the film. *What shall we do now?* she read. It was Dónal's line to Grace.

What's customary behaviour for newly weds after the ceremony?

They spend a lot of time making love. Or so I'm told.

Deirdre swallowed hard and turned the page.

What do you feel now? were the next words she read.

I feel strange.

Warm?

Yes.

Ardent?

That too.

Is there a better word to describe how you feel?

Yes. I feel aflame.

You are as brazen as you look, Grace. I think I'm going to enjoy being married to you.

They kiss. Fade to . . .

Deirdre stopped reading. She couldn't visualize that scene now without seeing Caít Murray winding

267

her beautiful arms around Rory's neck and kissing him deeply the way she had done on location today.

She put the script back on the table and moved to one of the windows which overlooked Eyre Square and the city. It was teeming with people on their way to pubs and clubs and cinemas. The sky was darkening, but instead of that rich, dark velvety blue she saw most nights as the sun slid down behind her western headland, a jaundiced night sky was suspended slackly over the city. Any stars that might have hung there had been bleached out by the harsh glare of streetlamps.

Behind her Eva laughed into the phone – a low, throaty, sexy laugh – and suddenly Deirdre felt unbearably, heart-wrenchingly lonely.

Chapter Eleven

Deirdre spent the following day and the following night being molly-coddled by Eva and flirting with Dorcas. They all three had a leisurely breakfast in bed and then Deirdre took Dorcas up to the swimming pool at the top of the hotel and swam with her while Eva sat at one of the tables by the side of the pool, sorting through a heap of scripts that had arrived that morning. Her mobile phone rang so incessantly that the actress turned it off with an exasperated, 'Oh, shut up, you horrible thing!' Dorcas looked more like a miniature filmstar than ever as she reclined – supported by armbands – in the water, her curly hair floating around her head like a golden halo.

Eva suggested that they go out to eat that evening, but Deirdre asked rather piteously if they couldn't go for the room service option again. The club sandwich last night had been so good she'd love to try it again, she'd added rather unconvincingly. In fact the real reason she didn't want to venture onto the streets of Galway was that she simply couldn't run the risk of bumping into Rory and Caít Murray.

The next morning, Eva's driver dropped Deirdre at the bus station before taking the actress to location.

She felt a tad ridiculous getting out of the limo and boarding the single-decker. Passengers stared as the film star emerged from the back seat so that they could exchange goodbyes. Dorcas put out a fat fist and grabbed a hank of Deirdre's hair, as if resolved not to let go of her new friend.

'That clinches it,' said Eva. 'You are now official godmother to Dorcas Daíre Lavery-Lawless.'

'Daíre?' said Deirdre. 'I didn't know Dorcas had a middle name.'

'Didn't you? I thought I told you I'd named her after you?' replied Eva.

'Daíre?'

'Mm. For O'Dare. I didn't want to call her Deirdre – I hope you don't mind. I'm superstitious about names, you see. I know Deirdre was a legendary Irish beauty, but I couldn't find a way round the fact that her full title was "Deirdre of the Sorrows".'

'Ha! I certainly was that the other day, wasn't I? I'm sorry, Eva.'

Eva smiled. 'I cried myself out on your shoulder once, remember? I'm glad I was able to reciprocate when you needed it. Anyway, I know you well enough to know you'll bounce back. You're made of resilient stuff, Deirdre.'

'What does Dorcas mean, by the way?' asked Deirdre, stroking the baby's plump cheek with one hand and trying to prise Dorcas's fist open with the other.

'Gazelle. David chose it. Dorcas is an obscure character in *A Winter's Tale*. A shepherdess.'

Deirdre had managed to back up the steps of the bus, having disentangled her hair from Dorcas's tenacious grip, and now the baby was casting round for something else to amuse her. She had started to pull at the gauzy fabric of the dress over Eva's breasts. 'Sometimes I think Porcas would have been more suitable,' sighed Eva, resignedly undoing buttons.

'Send David my love.'

'I will. I do hope things work out, darling. Every which way.' Eva stood on tiptoe and kissed her cheek. 'Keep in touch.'

The engine shuddered into life and Deirdre jumped up the final step. 'Bye, Dorcas. Bye, Eva. Thanks for everything.' She waved from the window until the bus rounded the corner, and then she slumped down in her seat, wrapping her denim jacket tightly round her, for comfort as much as for warmth.

As the bus negotiated Eyre Square it passed by another of the black stretch-limos that were being used for transport on the Grace O'Malley movie. Deirdre looked down at the black-tinted passenger window, and then looked away again immediately. She had the distinctly uncomfortable impression that whoever was sitting in the rear seat of the car was looking straight back at her.

*   *   *

The bus got into Westport ten minutes late. As Deirdre unchained her bike from the fence where she'd left it two mornings ago, the sky was darkening with the storm clouds that had been forecast earlier in the week. She cycled down Main Street and out onto the Newport road as fast as she could, anxious to get home before the rain started. There was nobody else on the road. The cattle in the surrounding fields were all lying down, and gulls were wheeling their way inland – both sure signs of bad weather. It was ominously still and silent – until a storm thrush started to sing its melancholy song from the wood at the brow of the hill.

Deirdre's legs were cold, but she could feel sweat on her upper lip and under her arms. She cycled on until the gradient became unmanageable, and then she dismounted. As she swung her leg over the saddlebar, she felt the first drop land on her thigh. It landed with a distinct splat. She looked up at the bruised sky overhead and another drop hit her on the cheek, making her blink. There was nothing tentative about this rain; there would be no soft, gradual drizzle to announce the advent of the bad weather. It was going to descend from the heavens in torrents. Thunder growled somewhere over the bay, and then lightning snapped as the rain started to drum heavily on the canopy of leaves over her head.

It took less than a minute for her to become completely soaked to the skin. She looked as if she had just emerged fully clothed from the sea. Her hair was plastered over her face like damp weed, and her denim jacket felt heavy with rain on her back and on her shoulders. Her thin dress clung to her thighs, and walking was made even more difficult by the fact that her bare feet kept slipping on the leather of her silver sandals. Rivulets were streaming down her face and into her open, gasping mouth. She looked around at the sodden countryside, pushing wet tendrils out of her eyes. There was nowhere nearby where she could shelter. There was no point in doing so, anyway. She would never dry out. The only thing to do was to press on.

The Land-Rover took her by surprise. It passed her with a swooshing sound of wet wheels, and she practically fell into the hedge. A little way ahead of her the vehicle pulled up, then rear lights illuminated the wet road and the reverse gear whined, and suddenly it was beside her. The passenger door swung open. 'Get in,' said Gabriel Considine.

'My bike . . .' she said. 'I can't—'

He was beside her on the road, taking the handlebars and pushing her gently in the direction of the passenger door. 'It'll go in the back,' he said.

Deirdre climbed up into the Land-Rover and landed heavily on the passenger seat. The windscreen wipers were on full tilt. Behind her she could hear Gabriel stowing her bike. When he resumed the driver's seat he was nearly as wet as she was. He looked at her before putting the Land-Rover into gear. 'What on earth possessed you, Deirdre O'Dare, to go cycling in a storm in a little party frock? You look like the Lady of the Lake.'

'Oh,' she said tiredly. 'There's no point in trying to explain.'

'Is this another example of the impulsive behaviour that sent you careering off on your bike to Carrowhead beach the first day you arrived? The day you were inspired to address me – for reasons best known to yourself – in the Teutonic tongue?'

She laughed suddenly. The whole situation was too ridiculous for words. 'Oh, Gabriel! I land myself in the most absurd situations. Thank you for rescuing me.'

The Land-Rover slid away from the verge of the road and moved smoothly in the direction of Carrowcross. She sat back in the passenger seat feeling safe, now, and comfortable despite her wet clothes. The heating was on, something light and classical was playing on the CD player, and there was that faint smell of rosemary in the air from whatever soap or shampoo Gabriel used.

A car travelling in the opposite direction peeped its horn at them in a friendly fashion, and Gabriel raised a hand in salute.

'Who's that?' asked Deirdre.

'That's Gladys,' he said. 'My housekeeper. She's been cleaning up the gate lodge for the new tenant.'

Deirdre turned round to look at the car, but could see nothing. 'Your rear window's all fugged up,' she remarked. 'Your de-mistifier mustn't be working, Gabriel.'

He flicked a switch on the dashboard and gave her an amused look. 'You mean my de-mister,' he said.

'Oh, yeah. Of course. A de-mystifier's what I need

for real life. Oh, God,' she said, stretching herself and yawning. 'I can't wait to get back to my little cottage.'

'I'm not taking you back there. I'm taking you to Carrowcross House.'

She looked at him, perplexed. 'But why?' she asked.

'Think about it. You haven't been home in a while. Will there be any hot water?'

'No.'

'There's plenty at the house. You need to get into a warm bath as soon as possible, Deirdre.' She looked away from him out of the window at the drowned landscape. He was right. The cottage would be cold and miserable. 'Anyway,' he continued, easing the Land-Rover through a flash-flood which had claimed several metres of road, 'it's about time you saw Carrowcross House in all its restored grandeur, isn't it?'

'But I thought you were living in the gate lodge?'

'Not any more. My tenant's arriving today. I've moved into the main house.'

She suddenly felt as though there was a humming-bird held hostage in her heart. 'Oh,' she said. A silence fell, and then a thought occurred to Deirdre. 'How did you know that I hadn't been staying at the cottage, Gabriel?'

'I wandered down there last night. I waited for ages before giving up and going back to my ancestral home. You didn't come, but the otters did.'

'Oh!'

'Where were you?'

'Painting my godchild's toenails in Galway. Where were you?'

'Ministering to Rosa.'

'Rosa?'

'My niece in England. She got very sick.'

Deirdre shot him an alarmed look. 'What happened?'

'Nobody really knows, but when the word "meningitis" was mentioned I had to get over there straight away. She took a serious down-turn, and then suddenly rallied. She's fine now.'

'When did you go over?'

'The day after I last saw you. I didn't get back until late on Monday night.'

So that was why he hadn't come near her since the evening of her aborted seduction attempt! She felt flooded with relief that his visits had been discontinued not because of the unholy gaffe she'd committed in playing Daisy's funeral music, but by circumstances beyond his control. Her mind went back to the evening she'd peered through the gate lodge windows, and the abandoned air the rooms had worn. He'd obviously dropped everything and left in a hurry several days earlier. He would have arrived back shortly afterwards that same evening. Perhaps that had been him who'd been trying to get through on the phone?

'I tried phoning you from England on a couple of occasions,' he said, as if reading her mind. 'And again on the night I got back. But there was no answer.' The Land-Rover was now running parallel to the boundary wall of the grounds of Carrowcross House. They travelled in silence for some minutes before the gate lodge came into view. Gabriel indicated right and turned into the driveway. The gates were lying wide open, as if expecting him. They bumped up the long driveway and came to a stop outside the front door. Gabriel shrugged out of his long waxed coat and wrapped it around her shoulders, and then he opened the driver's door and got out. Before she had finished disengaging herself from her seatbelt he had swung open the passenger door. 'Run for it,' he said.

They raced up the steps and Deirdre kept running on the spot at the top as Gabriel unhooked a bunch of heavy iron keys from his belt. He turned one in the lock, pushed open the door and they were inside.

'Oh!' was all she could say. She took a couple of steps across the tiled floor of the hall, and the slap of her sandals echoed under vaulted ceilings veined with intricate plasterwork. She stopped and gazed upwards, executing a slow, three-hundred-and-fifty degree turn as she did so. 'Oh!' she said again.

'Stop saying "oh",' said Gabriel matter-of-factly. 'You'll have lots of time to admire the place later. Right now I want you to stop dripping all over my floor and get into a bath before you catch pneumonia. Follow me.'

He took the stairs two at a time and then led the way along a gallery that flanked the main hall. A corridor leading off the gallery took them past a pair of mahogany doors. He opened the second one and showed her into a high-ceilinged room which had bare wooden floors, white-washed walls and a tall, white-curtained window set into the far wall. A Victorian lavatory stood like a throne on a podium at one end of the room, and a huge, cast-iron bathtub stood proudly on claw-and-ball feet in the middle of the floor. A couple of bentwood chairs provided the only furnishing.

Gabriel moved to the bath and turned on the taps, sending water pumping into the tub and steam rising into the air. 'There are towels in the airing cupboard,' he said. 'I'll root out something for you to wear and leave it outside the door.' He turned and walked towards the door. 'Come on down to the library when you've finished.' She knew there'd be a library! 'I'll get a fire going. Are you hungry?'

She was. There'd been no time that morning for a leisurely breakfast in bed. 'Yes,' she said.

'Good. Gladys made some kind of casserole. There's bath stuff in the cupboard,' he added, as he pulled the door to behind him.

Deirdre moved to where he'd indicated the airing cupboard was housed, behind a panelled door on one side of an elegant, cast iron fireplace. The mantelpiece was covered in candlesticks, and lying ready was an unopened box of plain white candles and a big box of long-stemmed matches.

She opened the door of the airing cupboard and was assailed by the comforting smell of warm towels and some kind of herb. Rosemary. There was a big bottle of Badedas on a shelf beside a basket full of heavy-duty French bath-soaps, and a cardboard box on the floor of the cupboard crammed with bottles of Jif and Dettol and bleach.

Gabriel Considine seemed very together for a man living on his own. This Gladys person must look after him very well indeed. Cleaning products, a cupboard stocked with toiletries, and masses of clean towels and sheets. Linen sheets. The image flashed across her mind's eye of Rory, and the way he had looked at Eva yesterday when she'd mentioned her predilection for linen sheets. Deirdre put out her hand and rubbed the nubbly fabric experimentally between finger and thumb. Eva had got the right idea. Then she helped herself to the bottle of Badedas and turned back towards the bath. A good dollop of the gloopy green liquid clouded the water and scented the steam.

She untied the thongs on her sandals and peeled off her dress and underwear. Then, holding on gingerly to the cast iron scroll-work, she arched her leg over the side of the high, ancient bath and tested the temperature with a toe. It was perfect. As she slid luxuriously into the warm, silken water she wondered what Gabriel would find for her to wear. A bathrobe? One of his own shirts? She knew that whatever it was she was going to feel vulnerable. The rain had literally drenched her to the skin – even her underwear was saturated. There was no way she could put it back on. What if Gabriel had come up with something like a sweatshirt or baggy T-shirt? She'd be madly self-conscious – she knew she wouldn't be able to stop pulling at the hem and making sure to keep her legs crossed.

She could hear his footsteps echoing down the corridor. Then his voice came from outside the door. 'Deirdre?'

She caught her breath. 'Yes?' she called, trying to sound urbane.

'I hope you don't mind getting into something rather exotic. I don't have a great line in women's clothing, as I'm sure you can imagine.'

'Oh – anything'll do, Gabriel. Thanks.'

The footsteps disappeared back in the direction of the gallery. Deirdre started to feel a bit panicky. *I hope you don't mind getting into something rather exotic.* Oh God, oh God. What did he mean by exotic? Was it possible that he was just another sad bastard like Jean-Claude Valentin, with a penchant for tacky underwear? She was suddenly very anxious to find out.

She hauled herself out of the bath and scampered across the room, dripping water all over the floor. Opening the door cautiously, she looked down the corridor before stretching out a hand for the glossy carrier bag which lay just outside and whisking it into the bathroom. She parted the cord handles, and what she saw when she looked inside made her suck in her breath. The bag contained a dense mass of burnished silk. She drew the fabric out slowly, and then flung it over a chair in a panic when she realized she was dripping all over it. The garment that snaked over the curved back of the bentwood chair was an intricately embroidered Indian sari trimmed with sequins.

*   *   *

She spent a long time working out how to wear the sari. Rory had once brought her a length of plain saffron silk back from India, but she'd never really mastered the art, and the sari had ended up swagged around her bedroom window. Now she got very busy winding and tucking and draping until it felt reasonably secure. Nearly ten minutes passed before she padded on bare feet down the curve of the cantilevered staircase. As she hit the bottom step she checked for the half-dozenth time that the silk was securely knotted over her breasts.

The crackling sound of burning logs told her where to go. The library looked out through tall curtainless windows onto the terrace at the back of the house. The rain had eased off considerably, and beyond the windowpanes she could see overgrown lawns stretching down to the stagnant, weed-choked pond which, in another incarnation, had been an ornamental lake. The garden was a wild place, dark green with dripping foliage, and the sporadic noise of the rain spattering against the window made her shiver and wish that she was wearing a cosy dressing-gown and warm slippers. There was no sign of Gabriel.

She surveyed the room with curious eyes. The walls were lined with bookshelves from floor to ceiling, but there were no books ranked there yet. A dozen or so packing cases were stacked in one corner. There was no furniture in the room apart from a baby grand, the Turkish rug that she'd seen in the sitting room of the gate lodge, and a heap of big oriental cushions in front of the log fire that was burning in a cavernous grate. A portrait of an autocratic-looking man with sculpted cheekbones stared down at her from above the mantelpiece. A Considine ancestor, she conjectured, looking back into his unfathomable black eyes. On the floor to one side of the fire was a copper saucepan filled with ice. There was a bottle of champagne sticking out of it. Next to it, two champagne flutes. Deirdre felt her heart start its familiar race.

A noise from behind made her turn. Gabriel was standing in the doorway, leaning against the jamb and watching her with his dark eyes. He'd changed out of his wet clothes into jeans and a dark blue cotton shirt, and he was barefoot. He didn't take his eyes off her as he moved with a relaxed tread to where the champagne was waiting. 'Sorry about the saucepan,' he said. 'I haven't got round to acquiring an ice-bucket yet.'

'D'you know something, Gabriel? I could almost find that surprising. You seem to be incredibly well-supplied for a bloke who's just moved house.' The lightness of her tone belied the slight jitteriness she was feeling.

'Gladys takes care of all that side of life,' he said. Of course she did. He stretched out a hand and ran

282

a finger down the side of her face. 'You look incredibly beautiful, Deirdre O'Dare,' he said. 'I knew you'd do that sari justice. Nobody's worn it since Daisy died. It was her favourite thing. She found it in an antique shop on the Portobello Road. It belonged to a genuine Indian princess.'

Deirdre swallowed. She wasn't sure whether to feel flattered that she wore Daisy's sari well, or upset that he'd felt the need to make the comparison between her and his dead wife. She didn't really know what to say. 'Have you kept many of her clothes?' she asked, in as conversational a tone as she could muster.

'No,' he said. 'Only that. And the jewels my mother left, of course. They're family heirlooms.' He lifted the champagne from its nest of ice. 'Mm,' he said. 'Not quite chilled enough. Maybe we should eat first? How hungry are you?'

'I'm seriously ravenous,' said Deirdre with decision. 'I didn't have any breakfast today.'

'That settles it,' he said, holding out his hand. 'Come with me.'

She took his hand and he led her downstairs to the kitchen. It was a big room located on the lower ground floor of the house, looking out onto an old stableyard. There wasn't much in the room – an Aga, a massive table, the ladderback chairs she'd seen in the gate lodge. The floor was of terracotta-coloured tiles, worn smooth by the passage of a century of scullery-maids' feet. A pair of Belfast sinks had been plumbed in under a window, and cupboards and

283

shelves had been set into alcoves in the walls. There was a glorious smell coming from the Aga.

Gabriel took an oven-glove from a hook, opened the oven door and drew out a casserole dish. 'Get plates, will you? And wine glasses. They should be in one of those cupboards over there.'

Deirdre started peering into cupboards. She was mildly surprised to find that his dinner service was a half-baked reproduction of a Susie Cooper design that she'd once seen on special offer in a rather cheesy shopping catalogue. She wasn't exactly expecting Sèvres porcelain, but she'd thought that a man of wealth and taste like Gabriel Considine could run to something a bit groovier than shopping catalogue plates. At least the wine glasses were elegant.

'That casserole smells delicious,' she said, setting plates and glasses on either side of the table. 'Does Gladys cook for you every day?'

'Most days,' he said. 'I'm no great shakes in the kitchen. If Gladys isn't around I usually eat in Quay Cottage.' He fetched a second casserole dish from the oven.

'She sounds like a bit of a find.' Deirdre sat down at the table and watched Gabriel as he spooned rice onto plates.

'She is. She does most of my shopping for me as well.'

'I thought as much when I saw how well-stocked your bathroom cupboard is. Is she responsible for the shopping catalogue dinner service?'

'What?' Gabriel paused in his dishing out of the food.

'These plates with poppies on.'

'No. They're Art Deco.'

'They're the real thing?'

'Yes.'

Deirdre turned over a side plate. *Susie Cooper Production*, she read. *Crown Works, Burstem, England.* 'Hell's bells,' she said. 'They must be worth a fortune, Gabriel! Do you think it's wise to use them? I mean – shouldn't you keep them for special occasions?'

He smiled at her. 'As far as I'm concerned, this *is* a special occasion, Deirdre.' He crossed the room and disappeared through a door which led off the kitchen. When he came back he had a bottle of wine in his hand.

'What's through there?' asked Deirdre in a jokey voice. 'The wine cellar?'

'Yes.'

She gave him a sceptical look. 'Are you serious?'

'Yes I am, actually,' he said, sending her an amused smile as he pulled the cork. He poured, and then set the wine down on an antique silver coaster.

She sat down at the table, open-mouthed. 'I am *so* impressed,' she said.

He took a seat opposite her and raised his glass. 'To us,' he said.

'To us,' she echoed. Then, 'Oh! Excellent Bordeaux!'

'I'm afraid I didn't have time to *chambrer* the stuff.

I didn't expect to have to rescue a drowning young lady and then fix lunch for her.'

'I'm delighted you did, Gabriel. But how can you spare the time? Don't you have to be in the office?'

'I intend to work from here as much as I can. I've fitted out one of the spare rooms with a drawing board and a computer, and I've arranged for any calls I need to take to be diverted here. I started the routine a couple of months ago when the workmen had finished on that side of the house. I couldn't have hacked the demolition noises earlier in the year.'

Deirdre noticed that he waited for her to take her first forkful of casserole before allowing himself to do the same. She'd have to be careful to mind her manners. 'Of course there are times when I have to be in the office in town,' he continued, 'but it's a real luxury to have the option of working from home. I can do things at my own pace – start work early and finish early, or vice versa.'

The casserole was hot. Deirdre blew on each forkful before putting it in her mouth, taking extreme care not to let any of the sauce drip onto the sari. She felt slightly idiotic sitting at Gabriel's kitchen table wearing an ensemble that would be more appropriate for dinner in the Taj Mahal, although she was by now getting kind of used to wearing the wrong clothes for every social occasion. She'd done it so often recently that she could write a fashion feature entitled 'The Art of Incongruous Dressing by An Expert.'

A silence fell. Deirdre glanced up to find him

looking at her, and she turned away, aware that the look was an emphatically meaningful one.

'What were you thinking? You looked very enigmatic just now.'

She could hardly tell him that she'd been thinking about something as frivolous as frocks.

'I was just thinking,' she said, surveying the spartanly furnished kitchen with a furrowed brow, 'that you should, um—' A brainwave hit her. 'You should start visiting auction rooms, Gabriel. You can pick up some amazing things really cheaply. Someone was telling me recently that there's still a load of Considine antiquities floating around. You might find your ancestral gold-plated dinner service up for grabs. Then you could use Susie Cooper for lunch and plates with your coat-of-arms emblazoned on them for dinner.'

He laughed. 'It's a nice idea,' he said. 'But I don't have time to go gallivanting off around auction rooms trying to relocate long-lost heirlooms.'

'When are you going to get around to furnishing this place?' She forked a little hill of rice into her mouth.

'I left most of my stuff in storage in England. I'll have to arrange to have it shipped over.'

'Well, I suppose you have everything you need for the time being. And everything in the best possible taste, too.'

'All down to Daisy. Anything you see in this house that has any aesthetic value was chosen by her.'

She had done it again. She was beginning to feel

that she was wandering around a maze, and that all paths led to Daisy. Thankfully she was spared the necessity of changing the subject yet again by the sudden ringing of the phone. The irritating electronic noise bounced off the walls and vaulted ceiling of the old kitchen, sounding as incongruous as she looked.

Gabriel moved quickly to pick it up. 'Yes? Not *again*. Hell.'

Deirdre turned to him immediately, wondering if this had anything to do with little Rosa, but his rather pissed-off, resigned demeanour told her it hadn't.

'That's why I came over last time. Are you telling me that that last trip was a total waste of time? That's their responsibility. OK. OK. Yeah. Book me in somewhere, will you please? Yeah – that'll do. Yes. See you then.' He put the phone down and turned to her with a grim face. 'I've to go to London,' he said.

'Oh.' Deirdre was taken aback by how floored she felt. 'When?'

'Now.'

'When will you be back?'

'If I'm lucky, tomorrow.'

She put on a brave face. 'Come to the cottage tomorrow night. I'll do dinner,' she said recklessly.

'I'd like that.' That meaningful look again. 'Maybe we'll finally get round to cracking that champagne. It'll be *extremely* well chilled by then.' He smiled at her as he moved across the room. 'I'd better pack an overnight bag. And you finish your lunch, Deirdre.

I hate to think of Gladys going to all that trouble only to have her lovingly prepared casserole end up in the bin.' He swung through the door and Deirdre heard his footsteps disappearing up the stairs.

She looked thoughtfully at her forkful of casserole, realizing as she did so that her look was *genuinely* enigmatic this time. Why? She was picturing herself in her princess's sari reclining on the pile of cushions in front of the log fire in the library upstairs, sipping champagne from a crystal flute and sending her most seductive look to Gabriel Considine as he moved slowly towards her, studying her with his dangerous black eyes.

*   *   *

He dropped her back at the cottage, so instead of reclining against cushions she found herself reclining in her princess's sari against the passenger seat of Gabriel's Land-Rover.

The rain had stopped, and a pallid sun was trying its hardest to break through the cloud. When it finally succeeded, the sodden countryside sparkled as if someone had scattered green sequins over it, and residual raindrops glistened like diamonds on the blackthorn bushes.

As they drove along the landbridge, Gabriel saluted a girl who was walking in the opposite direction. She waved back at him, laughing. Deirdre couldn't disguise her curiosity. The girl had golden skin and hair, slanting blue eyes and a glorious figure. In fact, she bore a strong resemblance to Gwyneth Paltrow. 'Who's that?' she asked.

'That's Gladys,' he answered.

'*That*'s Gladys?' she repeated. She was gobsmacked. For some reason she'd imagined Gladys to be a dumpy, middle-aged woman.

He gave her a sideways smile. 'She's a looker, isn't she?'

Deirdre shrugged. 'She's OK.'

Now he laughed out loud. 'Oh – you look sexy when you pout like that, Deirdre!' he said. 'There's no need to be jealous. I haven't taken her to bed. I respect her too much.'

'Thanks a bunch.'

'Don't be so wilfully obtuse. You know very well why I want to take you to bed.'

'You took her out to dinner, though, didn't you?'

'Yes, I did – to Quay Cottage when I was interviewing her for the job. How did you know that?'

Now Deirdre felt really silly. 'Oh – Eleanor saw you going in,' she lied.

'I'm glad to know that my profile is high enough to merit being included in Carrowcross gossip.' He smiled again, and then continued. 'The reason I took her out to dinner,' he said, 'was to win her respect. It's a fact of life that you win respect when you treat people well, and I wanted to be sure I could trust her to be discreet. You find out a lot about people after a glass or two of decent wine. Don't you, Deirdre?'

Her mind went back to the evening he had told her he wanted to make love to her. What had he said? *I haven't made love to a woman since Daisy died. I've fucked around, I'll admit it. But I haven't slept with anyone for whom I had real feelings.*

'Yes,' she said, returning his smile. 'You do.'

They travelled on in a kind of pensive silence until they reached the gate at the top of her driveway. Gabriel pulled over and turned to her. 'I'll miss you,' he said. 'I'll have to take out my mental photograph.'

Deirdre looked blankly at him.

'Remember? The one I took of you to get me through that business dinner at Newport House? Although I have a real one, now.'

'Oh?' She looked even blanker.

'Yes. I cut your photograph out of the *Irish Times* just before I went to England. It's beautiful. Captures you perfectly. I stuck in it my wallet.'

The knowledge that Gabriel was carrying her photograph in his wallet produced an intense thrill in her. 'Oh,' she said, trying to make her voice sound light. 'Maybe you should give me one of you?'

Gabriel smiled at her. 'I'll look one out,' he said. Then he leant over to kiss her goodbye. It was a light kiss, but it held an infinity of promise.

As she climbed down from the Land-Rover he said her name. She turned to him, and when she saw the way he was looking at her, she crawled back in to be kissed again. And again. Then Gabriel finally drew away. 'I'm going to have to go. I'll miss my flight if I don't stop kissing you.'

Deirdre slid out of the passenger seat. 'Phone me later!' she called as he turned the Land-Rover.

He smiled and nodded, and then he drove back down the lane.

Deirdre ran down the driveway to the cottage humming a makey-uppy tune. What would she do with the rest of her day? She had no screenplay to work on. She'd chill – that's what she'd do. She'd lose herself between the pages of *Wuthering Heights* and then start reading the romantic blockbuster she'd bought in Westport once she'd finished the Brontë book.

A splash in the bay made her stop dead – but it wasn't an otter. It was a black-headed gull that had dived. She watched the bird swoop up from the surface of the water, a small silver fish twisting in its beak.

Chapter Twelve

She let herself in through the verandah door and
surveyed her little house. It looked a bit scruffy, and
she felt sorry for it. She'd do some housework
and maybe light a fire later. She liked the idea of
cosying up in her cottage with no work to be done,
and the prospect of a new man in her life. And what
a man! Aristocratic, *genuinely* sophisticated – unlike
that impostor Jean-Claude Valentin – and sexy. And
rich. Of course, that wasn't really important. The fact
that he was rich was immaterial. Well, maybe it was
just a tiny bit of a bonus. It would be nice to be taken
out to decent restaurants, wined and dined and
bought presents from time to time. But all that stuff
didn't *really* make a difference.

She wandered out onto the verandah and leant
against the doorjamb, allowing herself to project a
fantasy scenario before her mind's eye. What if . . .
What if the relationship blossomed into something
meaningful? He'd already confessed to her that he
had – well, *warm* feelings towards her. He'd told her
that he hadn't felt like that about another woman
since Daisy died. What if – outrageous thought – he
asked her to marry him? She almost blushed at the
arrogance of the idea. But it was such a beautiful

fantasy she had to allow herself to indulge in it. Mistress of Carrowcross House! House parties with beautiful people drifting in and out of rooms, afternoon tea, cocktails at six, children playing in the garden . . .

Wise up, wise up, get real, get real, get real. Things like that don't happen in the real world, Deirdre. With a sigh, she straightened up and eased her limbs into a long, luxurious stretch, revelling in the sensation of silk on her shoulder and thinking abstractedly that she ought to change into something a little more appropriate for a quiet night in.

As she moved towards the bedroom she started to fiddle with the intricate knot she'd devised to hold the sari in place. Then something suddenly made her stop. It was the sound of the top gate opening. She froze, and then turned back towards the verandah. Footsteps were coming down the driveway. Gabriel? Maybe his plans had changed. She put a tentative foot on the top step. There came the clunk of the bolt on the bottom gate as it slid home. Her left foot joined the right on the verandah step, and she crossed her arms over her breasts, craning a little to one side, as if by doing so she would be better able to establish the identity of who would appear around the corner. It was Rory.

He stopped when he saw her. 'Hi,' he said. He took off his sunglasses and put them in the breast pocket of his jacket. It was a Hugo Boss jacket, and he'd only worn it once before, when he'd had to pick up his award for best actor at the annual theatre awards ceremony in Dublin. There was an unknotted tie around his neck, and he was carrying a bottle of champagne.

'What are you doing here?' she asked. She didn't move and neither did he.

'I've come to say goodbye,' he said. 'It's my last night in the Emerald Isle before I hit the fleshpots of LA, and I thought it would be churlish of me not to say farewell in person.'

'Why are you wearing a jacket?' She couldn't think of anything else to say.

'I'm taking you out to dinner. Why are you wearing a sari?'

'I'm researching my next screenplay. It's set in India.'

'Ask a stupid question . . .' said Rory.

She still stood there motionless, as if immobilized. 'You don't need to get dressed up in a jacket and tie to go to Quay Cottage, Rory.'

'I'm not taking you to Quay Cottage, Deirdre. I'm taking you to Ashford Castle.'

'That's bananas. That's the most exclusive joint in the county. How did you manage to get a reservation?' Each question she asked sounded stupider than the one before.

'The assistant manager is an old friend of mine,' he said. 'We were at school together.'

'Oh.' She was finally able to move. She sat down very slowly on the step.

'Well? Do you want to come?'

'Of course I do. It's Ashford Castle, isn't it?'

'I'd hoped the company might form part of the rationale, Deirdre – not just the venue.' He moved towards her and smiled. 'That sari is very sexy, darling, but I would hope you've got something a little less outré to wear.'

'Yes,' she said. 'I have.'

'What about that little number you were wearing the other day?'

'It got wet.' It was actually hanging up in Gabriel Considine's airing cupboard. But her silk Nicole Farhi was languishing in the wardrobe.

'Shame. Still, I'm confident that you'll be able to conjure up something else sartorially suitable.'

'I'll need twenty minutes.'

'Fair enough. Do you want some of this?' He indicated the champagne.

'No. Yes. Please. I'll get glasses.' She got to her feet and stumbled inside. As she fetched glasses from the cupboard in the kitchen, the phone on the verandah rang. She ran back outside, thrust the glasses unceremoniously into Rory's hands and picked it up. 'Yes?' She knew she sounded breathless.

It was Gabriel. 'Hi, darling,' he said. It was the first time he'd used the endearment. 'How are things?'

'Fine.'

'How are you spending your afternoon?'

'Um, reading.'

Rory had moved away from her and was standing by the sea wall, scanning the view and peeling the foil away from the neck of the champagne bottle.

'Lucky girl. I'm in for a very dull time. I've a

296

feeling I'll be taking out my mental photograph of you rather a lot.'

She laughed rather raggedly. There was a hiatus. Then: 'I've bad news, I'm afraid,' said Gabriel.

'Oh?'

'I'm going to be stuck in London until Saturday.'

'Oh.'

'Can I take a raincheck on that dinner?'

'Yes.'

'I'll drop over Saturday evening, then?'

'Yes.'

'Deirdre?'

'Yes?'

'I'd like you to keep that sari.'

'Oh! I couldn't possibly—'

'Of course you could. Are you still wearing it?'

'Yes.'

'Are you naked underneath?'

'Er – yes.'

'Do it again for me, will you darling?'

'Um – what, exactly?'

'Remember the time I phoned you before and took a mental photograph?'

'Yes?'

'Well, let the sari drop.'

'Oh. All right.'

There was a pause. Then Gabriel said 'You're naked?'

'Yes.'

'Wow. You're beautiful. I can't wait until I can see the real thing, though.'

Deirdre managed another unconvincing laugh.

'I'll talk to you on Saturday, OK?'

'Yes please.'

'Goodbye, darling.'

'Goodbye. Thank you.'

As she put the phone down, the cork popped. Rory was pouring the champagne into the glasses he'd set down on the sea wall. 'Come and get it,' he said over his shoulder.

She moved across to join him and took the proffered glass.

'That has to be one of the most monosyllabic telephone calls I've ever had to listen to,' he remarked. 'Did the person on the other end hang up or just fall asleep with boredom?'

She sighed. 'Jejune as ever, Rory,' she said.

'I hope your repartee is going to be a little more sparkling by the time we hit the castle, darling. You're going to earn this dinner – every exclusive mouthful of it – by ensuring that your companion is rivetted by your sophistry, dazzled by your éclat and wowed by your élan. Remember that for the foreseeable future much of my social intercourse will be with Tinseltown bimbettes. I want to spend my last evening in my native land being spoonfed the wit and wisdom of a genuine Irish colleen before I face the pop music.'

For some reason his words hit her with a kind of devastating finality. *His last evening in his native land.* She bit down hard on her lip. She could feel her eyes beginning to well up with tears. A distraction was needed. She conjured up her very useful imaginary wren again. 'Oh, um – look at the wren!' she exclaimed.

He looked in the direction she was pointing. 'Where?'

'You missed it. It just barged into that bush.'

'Oh, God,' said Rory.

'What's wrong?'

'I can see it's going to be a long evening,' he said.

* * *

She was showered and scented. She took one last look at herself in the wardrobe mirror, then she took a deep breath and walked out into the garden.

'Holy shit.' Rory's eyes travelled down her body and then back up again. 'Where did that come from?'

'I got it in a second-hand shop in Westport,' she said.

'Well, you get ten out of ten for éclat. Sadly, sophistry gets *nul points* so far.'

'Just because of my "barging" wren?'

'I seem to remember you told me once that your school reports always said, "Could do better." Even a Tinseltown bimbette could do better than a "barging wren", Deirdre. Wrens alight. Daintily.' He got to his feet and swigged back the champagne in his glass. 'Drink up. We should go.'

She set down her glass and moved towards the gate.

'Aren't you going to lock up?' he asked as he followed her.

She turned to him, surprised. 'Don't you remember? We never bother about that down here.'

'Dear God in heaven, what am I doing?'

'What do you mean?'

'Why am I exchanging the kind of life where people never need to bother to lock up for the kind of life where people are probably wired with their own personalized security systems?'

'You're selling out, that's what you're doing.'

'No I'm not. I'll never compromise. You know I don't play those kinds of games. If I can't hack it I'll come home.'

'You know what it's like, Rory. They're all going to want a piece of you, over there. You're *happening*. They're not going to let someone who's happening go that easily. You won't get away without a fight.'

They walked up the drive in silence for a while. Then: 'Where's the limo?' asked Deirdre as they approached the top gate.

'What limo?'

'The limo to take us to the castle?'

Rory gave her a pitying smile. 'There's no limo, O'Dare. I'm driving myself.'

'Not in that awful Saab?'

'The very roadster.' He unbolted the gate and held it open for her.

'Oh, God, Rory – I can't roll up outside Ashford Castle in a '74-reg car!' Deirdre rounded the corner and looked at the battered orange Saab in dismay.

'It's all right, darling. I'll drop you off in the

driveway before anyone clocks you and you can walk the rest of the way. Get in.'

* * *

They drove south into Connemara. The landscape changed as they travelled along the winding roads, becoming rockier and more barren. The fields were criss-crossed with mile after mile of dry-stone walls.

'Farmers here must be much worse off than their cousins down the road,' remarked Rory. 'Get a load of how tiny some of those fields are.'

'They're not necessarily boundaries,' said Deirdre knowledgeably. 'The land in this part of the country is so rocky that when they break it up they pile the stones into walls. If they didn't do that the ground would be littered with rock, and that would make farming it untenable.'

Rory gave her a curious look. 'Well, well, well. Maybe I am going to learn something of the wit and wisdom of an Irish colleen this evening after all. Where does all this rural savvy come from?'

'You forget that I've been coming here for years, Rory. I know a lot about the Mayo countryside. I've always loved it.'

'Not when I first met you, you didn't. I had to practically drag you down here, little Ms City Clogs. You told me it was tedious, wet and insular.'

'Well, maybe I thought so for a while, but I soon wised up, didn't I? D'you know, if my job didn't keep me in Dublin I think I'd like to downshift and move here.'

Rory gave her an incredulous look. 'Don't make me laugh, O'Dare. What the fuck would you do? Swan around, like Marie Antoinette did at Versailles, in your shepherdess frock, carrying a golden milking pail?'

'Don't be facile, Rory.'

'OK – I'll modify the scenario a bit. Laura Ashley?'

She made a face. 'Absolutely not. Voyage. Or Romeo Gigli.'

'OK. So you're wandering around your garden in a straw hat with secateurs, pruning the flowers. What happens when it rains?'

'I retreat indoors with my cat and bake bread.'

'Uh-huh. And how do you subsidize this rosy future? Working the lobster pots? Rearing cattle?'

'I'd think of something. Maybe I could open a restaurant. Look what happened with Quay Cottage. They started up as a tiny concern, and just took off. It's an amazing success story.'

Rory's incredulity peaked. 'I'm sorry, Deirdre. Run that by me again. Did you say something about opening a restaurant?'

'I wouldn't do the cooking, of course – that goes without saying – but I could find someone like Maeve's Jacqueline. Loads of people want to move to the West of Ireland and start up a business.'

'Do you know what I think you'd be better off doing, darling?'

'What?'

'Marrying the local squire.'

Deirdre shot him a look, but he was concentrating on the road ahead.

'There it is now,' he said.

'The castle?'

'Yup.'

She craned forward in her seat. She could just discern the battlements of towers emerging from the tree-tops. 'Oh,' she said, sounding disappointed. 'It's not really that big, is it?'

Rory crowed.

'What's wrong?' she asked.

'The evening's looking up,' he said.

'What do you mean?'

'That's not the castle, you pillock. It's the gate.'

'Thank goodness for that,' said Deirdre, smiling at him as they drove through the elaborate, tower-flanked gates. 'I'd have hated to have thought I was slumming it.'

The car travelled along the curving driveway for half a mile, the castle appearing and disappearing from view as they rounded its serpentine bends. Deirdre clapped her hands and laughed every time she saw it. 'Oh – it *is* a real castle!' she exclaimed. 'It's beautiful, Rory – just like one in a fairytale!'

'Knew you'd be impressed, O'Dare,' he returned laconically.

As they approached the courtyard at the front of the castle, Deirdre suddenly turned to him and grabbed his arm. 'Stop! Stop now!' she said.

'What's the problem?'

'Let me out here, please Rory. Did you get a load of the cars that are parked in there? They're all Mercs and Daimlers and they've all got this year's regs . . .'

Rory pulled over. 'You are the biggest snob I have ever met,' he said.

'I know,' she said without a trace of apology as she got out of the car. 'We can't all espouse that *liberté, égalité, fraternité* ethic, Rory. Think how dull life would be if we did.'

'Ten out of ten for élan, O'Dare,' he muttered darkly. But as the Saab jolted its way through the archway into the car park, Deirdre could see that he was smiling.

She joined him on the steps and they passed through a front door which was flanked by two suits of armour. Deirdre looked around trying to appear nonchalant, while Rory approached the reception desk. The walls and ceilings of the lobby were of elaborately carved wooden panels. There were chandeliers everywhere, and serious antiques. Portraits and gilt mirrors hung on the walls, and flowers in Chinese porcelain vases were banked on highly polished side-tables. This place was *stately*.

'Deirdre?' Rory beckoned for her to join him at the desk. 'This is my friend, Martin. He helps run the joint.'

'Nice to meet you, Martin.' He was an urbane-looking man in his early thirties with short, dark hair and a wonderful smile. They shook hands. 'Are you the one who used influence to earmark a table for us?'

'That's right,' said Martin. 'I owe Rory a favour – going way back.' The two men shared what could only be described as a knowing smile. 'I was glad to be able to oblige. Can I offer you a drink in the drawing room before dinner?'

Deirdre looked at Rory, who looked at her.

'Champagne for the lady, I think, Martin,' he said. 'Follow me.'

On their way to the drawing room they passed a small table where a chessboard had been set up. 'Oh, Rory!' Deirdre tugged at his sleeve. 'Let's play!'

'You play chess? I wouldn't have imagined that the left hemisphere of your brain was well developed enough for that, O'Dare.'

'My father could have been a grand master if he'd wanted to,' she retorted snootily.

'OK,' said Rory equably. 'Martin? Can we have our champagne out here?'

'Certainly, Mr McDonagh.'

'And you can cut the "Mr" crap, buddy.'

Martin smiled. 'Certainly, sir,' he said, with a wicked glint in his eye before continuing towards the bar at the end of the long drawing room.

Deirdre sat down on a damask upholstered chair and surveyed the chessboard. 'I'll be white,' she said. 'That means I make the first move.'

Rory took the seat opposite her. 'Fools rush in . . .' he said.

'Check,' said Deirdre smugly. Over an hour had gone by since they'd sat down.

'Checkmate.' Rory moved his knight.

'How?' exclaimed Deirdre.

'My bishop to your king.'

'Shit. That's so *obvious*! How did I miss it?'

'Too much champagne,' said Rory matter-of-factly. He rose to his feet and extended a hand. 'May I escort you into the dining room?' he asked, with exaggerated courtesy.

She took his hand and he helped her up. They regarded each other appraisingly over the chessboard for a moment or two, and then Rory said, 'D'you think they might run to a Vindaloo?'

'Batter burger and chips is what I fancy.' Deirdre took his arm and together they moved in the direction of the dining room. 'Crikey,' she said, as they crossed the threshold into a high-ceilinged room dominated by an immense, carved mahogany fireplace. The walls were covered in eau de Nil shot silk, the tall windows draped with gold damask. The caryatid heads of angels supported the carved wooden beams of the ceiling, from which was suspended a magnificent crystal chandelier. The restrained sumptuousness of the room was reflected in a vast rococo mirror which hung on the wall at the opposite end, above an antique sideboard. Candles shimmered in candelabra, glass gleamed and linen prinked.

'You're going to have to mind your manners,

O'Dare,' said Rory in an undertone, as the waiter held out her chair for her. 'This joint is so exclusive they only have seven tables.'

'I'll dance on them all,' said Deirdre. 'And swing from the chandelier as my *pièce de résistance*. Holy shomoly – look at the view!'

The room overlooked an expanse of formal garden with a fountain playing in the centre. The lawns ran down to a lake, which stretched to the horizon.

'Wow, they even have their own lake,' breathed Deirdre. 'With loads and loads of islands. Wouldn't it be fun to take a picnic out on a boat one day?' As soon as she said it she wished she hadn't. She was feeling choked, suddenly. She knew that she and Rory would never, ever do it. She cast around for a way of changing the subject. 'Maybe Gabriel's garden will look like that one day,' she said.

'Who's Gabriel?' asked Rory.

'Oh, just a neighbour in Carrowcross.'

'A neighbour of yours in Carrowcross has a garden worthy of inclusion in the Chelsea flower show? You surprise me.'

'No. Well, I mean – the garden's been lying derelict for years. But with a bit of work it could be amazing.'

'Not that garden you took me to once? The one with the crumbling mansion?'

'Yeah.' Deirdre didn't want to be having this conversation. She reached for the menu, but Rory was dogged about it.

'You mean someone's doing it up?'

'Well – he's done it up. The house, that is. The garden's still a mess.'

'Who is this bloke? Some wealthy international corporate type?'

'No. He's Gabriel Considine. He's actually related to the people who once owned the house.'

'No shit.' Rory leant back in his chair and gave her a long, interested look. 'The local squire.'

Her eyes dropped back to the menu. 'What are you having to start, Rory?'

He glanced at the printed sheet. 'Mussels,' he said briefly.

'"Cleggan mussels removed from the shell and tossed in smoked bacon and brie sauce served in a filo basket,"' she read out loud. 'Mm. Sounds good. I think I'll go for the bouquet of hand-picked organic leaves and herbs drizzled in buttermilk dressing and presented in a regatto cheese basket.'

'You mean lettuce,' said Rory.

* * *

She'd been hungry earlier, she remembered. Now her appetite had vanished into the ether. The food was exquisite, but she barely tasted it. The service was meticulous, but she barely registered it. The gorgeous palace that was the dining room could have been the RTE canteen for all the awareness she evinced of her surroundings.

'I got two copies of your screenplay printed out,

by the way,' said Rory, as he stirred cream into his coffee. 'I put one in the post to you, and I kept the other to read. I finished it last night.'

'Oh? What did you think?' she said with outward casualness, avoiding his eyes.

'I thought it was bloody good, Deirdre.'

She started to make a disparaging noise, but he cut her off.

'I mean it,' he said. 'It made me laugh out loud.'

'Honestly?' She allowed herself to look at him.

'Honestly.'

'Which bits?' she asked with sudden enthusiasm. 'Did you like the bit where they get stuck in the *curragh*?'

'Yes,' he said. 'And I liked the bit where she pretends to be fishing. And the scene in the pub in the middle of nowhere. That was inspired.'

'That happened to us once,' she said. 'I based it on that bananas joint in Queensland. Remember?'

'I remember,' he said. Simultaneously they reached for their coffee cups and smiled at each other over the rims.

'Can I make you a proposition?'

Her smile was inviting. 'Of course.'

'I'd like to take a copy with me to LA and tout it around. I've some very useful contacts.'

'Oh.' She bit her lip and pretended to be examining the pattern on the delicate china cup. She knew she'd gone a bit pink.

'What do you think, Deirdre? Will you let me? It's important to have contacts, you know, otherwise you'll send out that screenplay and it will languish in some sub-editor's slushpile for months before being unceremoniously dumped. Unread, more than likely.'

'OK,' she said doubtfully. 'If you really think it's good enough, Rory.'

'I do. And I think you should get cracking on another one right away. It's always useful to have a follow-up. Even if they don't go for the first one – for whatever reason – they might be interested in seeing anything else you have to offer.'

'It's a long shot,' she said. 'But go ahead if you think it's worth it. And if it's not too much trouble.'

'You know it's not.'

'You always were a real pal, Rory,' she said, smiling at him again. This time there was nothing arch about the smile. It was as sincere as the one he sent her.

Then: 'Which ending are you opting for?' he asked. 'The happy or the sad?'

'I don't know yet,' she said.

As she bit into a jewel-like petit-four, Martin approached them.

'How was your meal?' he asked.

'Excellent,' said Rory, draining his cognac.

'Mm. Excellent,' repeated Deirdre, with a vague smile.

'How about a guided tour of the castle before you go?'

Deirdre brightened. 'Oh – I'd love that!' she said.

Martin led them upstairs to a gallery of memorabilia, and downstairs to the dungeon bar. He led them through a maze of corridors so elaborate it would be easy to get lost. Every time Deirdre turned a corner she would give an 'ooh' at a flower arrangement or an 'aah' at a portrait.

'Wow!' said Rory as they passed a massive canvas depicting a bodacious blonde with wings. 'Get a load of the *überbabe*. That's what I call an angel with attitude.'

They stopped outside a panelled mahogany door at the end of a corridor, and Martin produced a key. 'What's through here?' asked Deirdre.

'It's the presidential suite,' said Martin. 'I can let you have a privileged look around. There's no-one staying here tonight.'

He held the door open for them and then backed out of the room. 'Give me a shout. I'll be at reception.'

Deirdre turned to survey the room. Martin had showed them into a sitting room which served as an ante-room to the main bedroom. There was a couch with a marble-topped table in front of it, a little ladies' writing desk, a splendid gilt mirror over the fireplace, all antiques. An ormolu clock here, an elegant candelabra there. As if in a dream she moved up steps and through a door into the bedroom. The walls were pale gold, the carpet the colour of Bailey's Irish Cream. The soft-focus lens of her eye registered a glass-fronted bookcase, a pair of armchairs, another low table with a decanter and glasses. A box of chocolates. 'Oh, Rory, look!' The writing paper in

311

the folder on the side-table bore the Ashford Castle coat-of-arms with 'In Residence' in discreet type at the top. 'Maybe I should drop Sophie a line!'

He gave her an indulgent smile and sat down in one of the armchairs, crossing one leg over the other. Deirdre veered through a doorway to the right and gave a little shriek. 'I don't believe it! A walk-in wardrobe! Oh – *bliss!*' She caught sight of her reflection in the full-length mirror and gave herself a quick once-over.

Rory sent her an amused look as she emerged. 'What is it about women and walk-in wardrobes?' he asked in a tone of total incomprehension.

Deirdre gave him a pitying look as she crossed the room to the bathroom. 'There's no point in trying to explain,' she said as she checked out the quality of the towelling robes hanging on the door. They passed more than muster. 'Excellent!' she said as she continued through. 'Double basins, bidet, classy fittings, pot-pourri – oh! Lovely curtains!' White lace billowed at the open window. 'Hey – Rory!' she called over her shoulder. 'There's even a phone by the loo!'

'They've thought of everything,' he remarked.

Deirdre came out of the bathroom with a radiant smile on her face, and turned towards the bed. It was king-sized, with fabric swathed and swagged and pleated around the head. The mattress responded beautifully when she tested it with her bum. It yielded neither too much nor too little. She looked towards the big windows, which overlooked the garden. She could vaguely discern the plashing of the fountain. 'It's the same view as the dining room,' she remarked, 'of the ornamental lake.'

Rory was sitting opposite her, watching her. 'That's not an ornamental lake, you daft bitch,' he said in a dead pan tone. 'It's Lough Corrib.'

They sat in silence for some minutes, observing each other. Then: 'Well?' said Rory.

'Well, what?' she responded after a fractional pause.

'What do you want to do? You can either stay in the hotel tonight or I'll ask Martin to organize a car to take you home.'

For some reason she felt hesitation in her heart. 'I thought you were taking me home,' she said in a small voice.

'What? You expect me to drive you all the way back to Carrowcross before setting off on the one hundred and fifty-odd mile journey back to Dublin? I wouldn't dream of it, O'Dare. The plus-side to going home on your own is that you get to ride back in a Daimler with a chauffeur. The downside to staying overnight here is that you either sleep on the couch in the ante-room or you share the bed with me.'

'I thought you said you were driving back to Dublin?' The words sounded as if they'd been spoken by a ghost.

'After a feed of champagne, Margaux and cognac? How irresponsible do you think I am?'

He moved to the phone by the bed and picked up

the receiver. 'Well? What do you want me to tell Martin? Will I ask him to round up the car now, or in the morning?' He looked down at her. His demeanour was relaxed, but there was a watchfulness about the expression around his eyes.

Deirdre looked down at her hands. The knuckles were white. 'Ask him to wait till the morning,' she said.

She heard Rory release his breath in a rather shuddery sigh, and then she felt his finger under her chin. He tilted her face so that she had to look at him. 'I'm so glad you said that, Deirdre,' he said.

She stood up and moved towards the door. 'Where are you going?' he asked.

'I'm going to make up the couch in the sitting room,' she said, giving him a disingenuous look. Then she smiled and ran back across the room to him, launching herself into his arms. 'Oh God, oh God – I've missed you so much,' she said into his mouth as Rory McDonagh stretched her out across the presidential bed.

*   *   *

The next morning – very early – a porter came to their room, moving about on quiet feet as he set out breakfast things. She heard Rory thank him and tip him. Deirdre didn't move. She just lay on her tummy on the bed with the sheet pulled up over her head and her face buried in the pillow.

'Have some breakfast, darling.'

'No,' she said in a muffled voice.

She could hear pouring noises, and the sound of a stirring spoon, and then he was sitting on the bed. He slid the sheet down and pushed the damp hair back from her face. 'Have some tea,' he said, stroking her forehead.

'No.' She wished her eyes could stop raining tears.

'You've got to get up, baby. We've got to go. Your car will be waiting for you.' He helped her sit up, and then he held the cup to her lips.

She took a sip and managed a feeble thank you. Then she scrawled the tears from her cheeks and inched out of the bed, abstractedly noticing as she did so that the pillow was saturated. Rory picked up her dress from where it lay like a pool of silk on the floor. 'Here,' he said. 'Arms up.' He slid her dress over her upraised arms, and kissed her face when it emerged from the folds. Then he fetched her sandals and made her sit on the side of the bed. He got to his knees and wound the silver thongs round her ankles. When he had finished, he wrapped his arms around her waist and laid his head in her lap. They stayed that way for a long time. Then Rory stood up. 'Time to go,' he said.

They negotiated the corridors without meeting anyone. It was too early for many people to be up and about. They walked in silence, hand in hand. As they emerged into the main lobby area, Deirdre started to cry again. Rory slung an arm around her shoulders. 'Sh, baby. Sh,' he said.

She leant her head on his shoulder and wept

openly, not caring who might see. On the steps of the castle Rory took her face in his hands and kissed her gently. Then he steered her towards the Daimler that was waiting, and opened the back door. She practically fell onto the seat. 'Don't go,' she begged. 'Please don't go, Rory.'

He leant in, gave her one last kiss, and then he shut the door. It sounded to her ears like the lid of a coffin closing.

As the car pulled away from the front of the castle, Deirdre's swollen eyes became vaguely aware of someone leaning out of an upstairs window, waving at her with a mouth working frantically in a grinning face. It looked spookily like Sophie Burke.

Chapter Thirteen

It was still early when she got back to Carrowcross. She wandered into the kitchen and put the kettle on. In the sitting room she slid out of her silk frock and left it lying on the floor. She moved into the bedroom and got under the duvet. She heard the kettle boil and then switch itself off, but she made no move to get out of bed and make tea. She lay there with eyes so dry they hurt, watching the pool of sunlight on the floor move slowly across the room.

Then the shivering started. She curled herself into a ball, wrapping her arms around herself to keep warm. The shivering was uncontrollable. She felt as if she'd been seized by a giant hand that was shaking her remorselessly. Her eyes were on fire, her legs felt as if she'd just finished a marathon and there was a stabbing pain in her chest. She crawled out of bed and pulled on a pair of pants, a T-shirt and a jumper, and then she got back into bed. But the shivering just got worse. She could hear herself whimpering from a long way away and she knew that she should get out of bed and fetch some paracetamol from the bathroom, but she couldn't summon the energy. Instead she slid into an unpleasant, heavy sleep that was thick with dreams.

She was wandering around the corridors of Ashford Castle, looking for someone. Except it wasn't Ashford Castle – it was Gabriel's house, and Inigo Jones, his black Labrador was walking in front of her, carrying something in a bundle in his mouth. She was appalled to see that the bundle contained baby Dorcas; but the baby seemed perfectly content. She just gurgled at Deirdre and smiled. Deirdre stretched out a hand to try to extricate Dorcas from the dog's mouth, but Inigo Jones backed away from her, and then ran off down the corridor towards the library. Someone in there was playing the piano, but when she went into the room there was no baby grand there, just a big bed with fabric swathed and swagged and pleated around the head. She moved towards the bed with heavy feet, saying somebody's name over and over – she couldn't hear whose. There was a figure sitting on the counterpane, back turned to her, and her heart slid into her stomach when she realized that this wasn't the person she was looking for. 'Who are you?' she asked. The person on the bed turned round. 'You can't have forgotten already. I'm Sophie Burke,' she said, with an ominous smile.

Deirdre woke up to find herself writhing from side to side on the mattress. The sheet was drenched with sweat, and she felt as if someone had rubbed a cheese-grater across the back of her throat. She was burning up. She tore the bedclothes off the bed and plucked at the sleeves of her jumper with fumbling fingers. Oh, God – it would be easier to free herself from a straitjacket than from this mass of suffocating wool. Then cold air hit her skin and she could feel the sweat start to dry instantly. It was pitch dark.

She staggered naked into the bathroom and drank directly from the tap, feeling sweat spring from every pore as she gulped at the water. She drank so much that she could feel her belly start to distend. When she could drink no more she took a towel from the rail and held it under the cold tap. Then she wrung it out and held it to her burning forehead, her cheeks, the back of her neck. She wrung it out again and sponged herself all over, shivering as the damp fabric made contact with her skin. There was paracetamol in a drawer. She knocked back two and then moved with the gait of an old lady to the airing cupboard to locate clean sheets.

In the bedroom she laboriously changed the linen. Every movement was an effort. When she had finished she left the old sheets lying on the floor. Then she crawled into the kitchen, poured water into a carafe and fetched a glass from a cupboard. It slipped from her hand and shattered on the floor. She didn't bother to clear it up – just fetched another and crept back into the bedroom. Every nerve-ending on her body felt exposed. She set the carafe on the table by her bed, lay down and pulled the clean sheet over herself. When she started to shiver again she reached for the duvet and wrapped herself up in it. She fell asleep with the sound of the sea on the shingle below washing over her.

She slept fitfully, not really sure what was dream

and what was real. On several occasions she awoke to the echo of a phone that had been ringing and ringing. Once she picked it up in time to hear an operator's voice asking her if she would accept a reverse-charge call from LA. 'Yes,' she answered, weeping with relief. 'Yes, please.' Then someone gave an unpleasant rasp of a laugh, the phone melted in her hand and she emerged from the dream with her face wet with tears.

Night noises came from the darkness beyond her window: the sounds of nature red in tooth and claw. Snuffling, screams, the beating of wings – fitting sound-effects for her continuing nightmares.

Then there came the distant barking of a dog. She woke up, surprised by how weightless her limbs felt and by the sunlight that was flooding the room, and realized that the barking was real. She turned her head on the pillow, tentatively. There was no pain, only a little stiffness. The clock on her bedside table read three thirty-five. She'd been in bed for a day and a half.

Her mouth was so parched it felt rictus. Deirdre raised herself on an elbow, poured water into the glass by her bed and sipped at it until it was all gone. Then, wrapping herself in her sheet, she slid gingerly off the bed and moved to the door like someone just learning to walk. She fetched her toothbrush from the bathroom – narrowly avoiding her reflection in the mirror above the basin – and then she trailed out onto the verandah, scrubbing her teeth with as much energy as she could muster.

She sat down on the step and blinked at the sunshine bouncing off the bay. She tried stretching and winced. She'd heard of twenty-four-hour flu, but had never experienced it. It had made her feel as if she'd just done a round with Chris Eubank.

Inigo Jones raced past the verandah at exactly the same moment she heard the sound of the bolt on the gate. She made a move to get up – she wanted to run into the house and hide. She couldn't allow herself to be caught looking as she knew she must, like some wrung-out, tangle-haired hag. But she knew the sudden effort of standing up would send her reeling. She just sat there with her toothbrush sticking out of her mouth, waiting for Gabriel to find her.

He rounded the corner and stopped dead when he saw her. 'Christ – you look wretched,' he said, moving towards her with concern in his eyes.

'I've been sick,' she said, through the bristles of her toothbrush.

'Oh, hell, Deirdre – you poor thing!' He sat down beside her and took her face in his hands. Then he took the toothbrush out of her mouth and kissed her lightly. 'You taste of mint,' he said. 'What happened to you?'

'I dunno. Some awful twenty-four-hour thing. I must have caught cold that morning I got rained on.'

'You must learn to take better care of yourself, Deirdre O'Dare.' He pulled the sheet up higher over her shoulder and then wrapped an arm round her and kissed her forehead. 'You're coming home with me. I'm going to put you to bed and

321

spoon-feed you chicken broth until you're better.'

'But I hate chicken broth. Can't I have chowder instead?'

'Sure. I'll put in a call to Quay Cottage and see if they'll put some in a flask for us.' He got to his feet and put out a hand to help her up. 'You look like something out of the Greek myths,' he remarked, slinging an arm around her as they ascended the verandah steps. Deirdre's sheet was trailing along behind her like a train.

'Athene, Goddess of Wisdom?'

He dropped a kiss on her bare shoulder. 'No. Aphrodite, Goddess of Love.'

'Can I have pudding as well as chowder?' she asked. 'I'm starving.'

'You're a resilient creature,' he said, smiling down at her.

'Yeah. I know.' She gave him a tired smile in return. 'Someone said that to me just the other day. I'm good at bouncing back.'

*   *   *

Barely an hour later she found herself back in Gabriel Considine's bath. This time he left a big towelling robe outside the door for her. She wrapped herself in it and descended towards the library on cotton-wool legs. The cushions were still piled in front of the blazing fire, but instead of champagne in a saucepan full of ice there was a flask of soup.

'Quay Cottage chowder,' said Gabriel. He was

322

sitting at the piano, idly picking out a tune. 'That outfit certainly knows how to deliver the goods.' He got to his feet and moved across to where she was standing in the doorway.

'So do you,' said Deirdre. 'Thank you for looking after me.'

He offered her his arm, and she leant on it as he escorted her to the pile of cushions. 'I thought you'd be more comfortable in here,' he said. 'There's a problem with the Aga and the kitchen's a bit parky.'

She lowered herself gingerly onto the cushions. 'Won't you have some?' she said, watching him pour chowder into a big mug.

'I had lunch on the plane,' he said. 'They booked me onto an earlier flight. I tried ringing you to let you know.'

'When did you ring?'

'Around ten o'clock on Thursday night. I've tried ringing on and off since then. Of course I didn't get any answer. You were burning up with fever.'

Oh, God. At ten o'clock on Thursday night she'd been making feverish love with Rory McDonagh in the presidential suite in Ashford Castle. And at eleven, and at midnight, and right through until the early hours of yesterday morning, when Rory had had to leave for Dublin and his flight to LA.

'So I just decided to come straight to the cottage from the airport with my duty-free champagne.'

'Oh, dear. And here I am drinking chowder instead.' She made an apologetic face at him.

'How are you feeling now?' he asked.

'Better after the bath, thanks. A bit weak, still.'

'Tired?'

'Not really. I slept until half past three this afternoon. What time is it now?'

He looked at his watch. 'Nearly five o'clock,' he said. He sat down beside her. 'You look awfully sweet in that bathrobe, Deirdre. Like a lost little girl.' He took her face between his hands and looked at her for what seemed an age before leaning down, breathing between her parted lips and running his tongue along the lower one so gently that she might have thought a ghost was kissing her. Then he sat back up. 'Finish your chowder,' he said.

She drank down what remained of the soup, and when she finished Gabriel took the mug from her unprotesting fingers and set it down on the floor. 'Good girl,' he said, pushing her hair back from her face and letting his hands glide down onto her shoulders. Then he took hold of the towelling fabric and slid it down over her arms so that her breasts were exposed. 'Dear God,' he said, looking at her with awe in his eyes. He drew her left arm out of its sleeve, then the right. Then he laid her back against the cushions before putting his mouth to her breast. He kissed her left breast, and then her right, and then he kissed her mouth. She allowed her tongue to meet his – a butterfly touch – and for a long moment they remained barely moving, lip lightly brushing lip, raggedly breathing in each other's breath. Deirdre was intensely aware of his black eyes boring into hers, and of his hands moving slowly down her body.

When his tongue began to follow the course initiated by his hands she felt herself automatically responding, each zone of her body blossoming at the physical contact. She arched her back, stretched her limbs and allowed him full access. His lips and tongue were satin-soft, and most irresistibly persistent. She felt so delicious that it seemed as if she was dissolving under his touch like finely spun sugar. A little cry escaped her, and then the familiar surge started – and suddenly she wanted to stop. It didn't seem right, somehow, that she should be revelling in love-making so soon after having made such exquisite love with another man. 'No,' she murmured, pressing her palms up against the silk of his black hair. 'No, Gabriel. Not yet.' But he ignored her. He continued to coax her to her climax until she felt sweeter than chocolate melting in his mouth. When he finally trailed his tongue back up her body she was limp-limbed as a rag-doll.

The condom was in his hip pocket. He was gorgeous. He was expert, he was thorough, he was imaginative. He was the second-best lover she'd ever had. When he finally allowed himself to climax inside her she was wearing the unique, blissed-out smile that only ever manifests itself after indulging in truly excellent love-making or truly excellent hash.

'Well. That was worth waiting for,' said Gabriel eventually. 'I now truly understand the appeal of delayed gratification.' Deirdre gave a little shudder. It was actually a sexually induced *frisson*, but Gabriel misinterpreted it. He pulled the robe back up over her shoulders and then wrapped her in his arms. 'I'm sorry,' he said. 'I should have waited until you were in the full of your health before making love to you, Ms O'Dare. But we've been thwarted in our attempts to get each other into bed so often at this stage that I just couldn't resist you.' He kissed her lightly on the forehead, got to his feet and then held out a hand to her. 'Come on. I'm going to tuck you up in bed.'

'But it's not even six o'clock yet!'

'I don't care. I don't want to be responsible for you relapsing. All that activity can't have improved the state of your health.' He smiled down at her. 'Invalids should be cosseted, not ravished.'

'I feel cosseted,' she said, allowing herself to be pulled up and kissed. 'Oh Gabriel – you kiss beautifully. Will you come to bed with me?' She suddenly found she couldn't stifle a vast yawn. 'We could just cuddle?'

'No,' he said. 'I want you to get some rest. Look at you – yawning your head off.' He led her through the hall and up the stairs.

'When can I have a guided tour?' she asked.

'Let's see how you're feeling tomorrow. I'll bring you breakfast in bed and if you eat all your healthy porridge like a good girl I might allow you to get up for a while.'

'But I hate porridge!'

'All right. How about bagels and cream cheese? And there's some excellent smoked salmon in the fridge.'

'Haven't you any Pop Tarts?' She felt like comfort food.

'Pop Tarts? I've never heard of them.'

Deirdre yawned again. 'They're dead handy.' They had reached a doorway a little further down the gallery from the corridor that led to the bathroom. Gabriel held the door open for her. 'Oh – cool!' she said. 'A four-poster!'

'Take off your robe,' said Gabriel. 'Get into bed.' He pulled back nubbly linen sheets and she slid between them, smiling. Gabriel stroked her hair. 'Sleep well, Deirdre. I'll see you in the morning.' Then he kissed her briefly on the lips and left the room.

Her smile faded shortly after the door closed behind him. For a long, long time she just lay there staring with unseeing eyes at the canopy of the four-poster bed above her. Then she clamped her eyelids shut and tried to do as Gabriel had instructed.

* * *

The next morning she woke to the smell of Pop Tarts. 'How did you manage Pop Tarts?' she asked sleepily, as Gabriel plumped up pillows behind her back.

'I spotted them when I was buying the Sunday papers,' he said. 'They're pretty disgusting, if you don't mind me saying so.'

'I know,' she admitted. 'But they're kind of addictive. What time is it?'

'Half past nine.'

'Wow. I really conked out, didn't I?' She took a bite of Pop Tart. He'd even got the flavour right: her favourite, strawberry.

'Your eyes are still sleepy.' Gabriel removed a smear of icing from her mouth with a thumb. 'Hell, you look sexy, Deirdre. All tousled and swollen-lipped.'

She looked back at him. Then: 'I'm sorry, Gabriel,' she said, pushing away the tray. 'You shouldn't have gone to the trouble of buying Pop Tarts. I don't feel like them any more.'

He lifted the tray and set it down on the floor by the bed. 'What do you feel like?' he asked.

'You,' she said. She reached up a hand and undid a button on his shirt. Another. And another. Her fingers slid under the clean-smelling cotton and traced a line down the muscles of his stomach. When she allowed her palms to make contact with his skin just above his hipbone she slid her thumb underneath the waistband of his jeans and deftly undid the metal button.

'What are you doing?' asked Gabriel, lying down on the bed beside her.

'I'm learning your physical geography,' she said. She pushed his jeans down over his thighs and calves, trailing a finger over the curve of his instep as the denim crumpled to the floor. His shirt followed in what seemed like slow motion. His black hair had fallen back from his face, exposing its every contour. With the index finger of her right hand she traced the clean line of his patrician jaw; with the index finger of her left hand she traced the crooked line of the scar on his cheekbone.

'How did you get the scar?' she asked. She'd always wanted to know.

'A cricketing accident.'

'Oh.' For some reason she felt a bit disappointed. She'd secretly hoped there'd be a more romantic explanation.

He regarded her unwaveringly as she continued her exploration of his physique. She gathered up the dark waterfall of his hair and wound it between her fingers. She ran a thumb along the curve of his mouth. She smoothed the black lines of his eyebrows. She took his right earlobe between her teeth and bit gently. She avoided the left. She didn't want to hear the story behind the earring that hung there. It was some kind of hieroglyph, and she was certain it had some special significance. She didn't want to risk hearing the D-word again.

She drew the heel of one hand along his collarbone and across his sternum, and slid the other over his ribcage and down the incline of his belly, allowing it to come to rest on his pubis. Then she began to explore the thick black tangle of his pubic hair with her fingers, her eyes fixed on his. She saw them narrow over dilated pupils, making them look blacker than ever.

'How edifying is your geography lesson?' he asked.

'It's extremely edifying,' she said, smiling into his eyes.

'Well. It might interest you to know that while you may find your geography lesson extremely edifying, Deirdre, *I* am finding it extremely stimulating.'

She looked down, raised an intrigued eyebrow and smiled again. 'Oh! So you are!' she said.

* * *

'How many times have we made love now?' she asked at around four o'clock.

'I've lost count,' said Gabriel. He watched her as she knelt up and unhooked the tassels that held back the swagged curtains on the four-poster.

'It's like playing house when you were a kid,' she said, smiling at him as she drew the curtains round the bed. 'Did you ever do that? Take all the counterpanes off the beds and drape them over a load of joined-together tables? I used to line up all my dolls underneath and give out to them if they didn't eat the vile food I served up.'

'Sorry, I hate to be so stereotypical, but I was more into Meccano.'

'I'd love to do this on a stormy night,' she said. 'Get in here with you and snuggle down with a racy book and a box of chocolates and listen to the sound of the rain outside.'

He gave her a sceptical look. 'Forget the book bit, Deirdre,' he said. 'I don't think you and Stephen King would make compatible bed fellows.'

'When I say racy I don't mean Stephen King kind of racy. Have you read any Anaïs Nin?'

'No. I've heard her journals are pretty tough-going, though.'

'Forget the journals. I'll introduce you to her short stories. With pleasure.'

'I'll take that on trust.' He licked her mouth. 'Chocolate's not such a bad idea. Maybe we should do it tonight?'

'Oh – yes, please! We could get Godivas.' Deirdre slid out from between the sheets and wandered over to the window. 'We'll have to forget the rain bit as well,' she said. 'There isn't a cloud in the sky.' A hazy sunshine was filtering its way through the windows. 'Your windows need washing, Gabriel.'

'I'll mention it to Gladys.'

Deirdre looked down at the garden below. The rain had washed it with a green as green as – as what? Emeralds? Jade? Rory McDonagh's eyes? *Go away, Rory. How dare you intrude on me here!* 'There's a cat in the garden,' she remarked.

'Tinkerbell,' said Gabriel. 'I'm glad she's come home. I haven't seen her since before I went to London.'

Tinkerbell. Daisy's cat.

'Daisy would never forgive me if anything had happened to her.' Gabriel came over and joined her by the window.

Deirdre bit her lip. 'Oh – shit, Gabriel. I'm sorry to remind you of Daisy again. I seem to–'

'Look at me, Deirdre.' She had her back to him and he put his hands on her shoulders and turned her to face him. 'Look at me,' he repeated. With

331

considerable difficulty she raised her eyes to meet his. 'What have we spent most of the day doing?'

'What do you mean?'

'What have we been doing in bed? What did we do in the library yesterday afternoon?'

'We made love.'

'Say it again.'

'We made love.'

'Yes. We did, didn't we? We didn't just fuck. Not then in the library, not today in bed. *We made love.*'

She made the connection. What had Gabriel said to her the evening they had acknowledged their mutual sexual attraction? *I haven't made love to a woman since Daisy died. I've fucked around, I'll admit it. But I haven't slept with anyone for whom I had real feelings.*

She looked at him with grave eyes. 'It was real?'

'It was real.'

Then Deirdre put her arms around him and laid her head on his shoulder. 'Oh, Gabriel,' she said. 'I'm so glad.'

*   *   *

After supper that evening he gave her a guided tour of the house. As well as the big kitchen and the wine cellar the lower ground floor housed a laundry room and a warren of pantries. There was another big unfurnished room on this level which as yet served no specific purpose. 'I don't know what this will be,' said Gabriel. 'I could stick a gym in it, I suppose. It's one of those undefined spaces that estate agents call "family rooms".'

On the next floor five reception rooms led off the vast entrance hall. The library she had already visited. The four remaining rooms he escorted her through were dining room, drawing room, morning room and – she almost swooned at this one – billiard room.

'There is,' said Gabriel, 'you'll be glad to know, an actual Considine heirloom in this room.'

'Oh? Let me guess!' She surveyed the room. 'Is it the chandelier?'

'No.'

'The love seat?'

'No.'

'The bust of that lady showing most of her bosoms?'

'No.'

'The billiard table?'

'Yes.'

'Oh, Gabriel! Really? You mean your ancestors used to play billiards on this very table?'

'Yes. It was discovered in a barber's shop of all places, in North Mayo. It cost a small fortune to have it restored.' They moved to the table, and Gabriel took hold of a corner of the white dust sheet that shrouded it and pulled it away. The sheet slid to the floor, revealing an expanse of pristine green baize.

Deirdre let her hand glide over the soft felt surface of the table and along the polished mahogany sides.

333

She lifted a cue and tried a few practice shots on an imaginary billiard ball.

'Can you play?' asked Gabriel.

'Badly.' she said. Rory had once tried to teach her, but had given up in disgust at her deficiency in hand-eye co-ordination. 'Do you want a game?'

'I think I'll file that particular pleasure under "delayed gratification".' He bent down and kissed her, and then he gathered her up in his arms.

'Oh! I love being gathered up in men's arms,' she said. 'It makes me feel kind of itsy and feminine.'

'*Men's* arms?' He raised an eyebrow at her and then set her down on the baize surface.

'Well. *Your* arms,' she amended.

'Do you like being made love to on the top of billiard tables?' he asked.

'Oh – yes! It's my totally favourite thing. Last time it was a bit embarrassing because I was wearing a rayon dress and the static that was generated was scary. But the time before that was fun. And the time before *that . . .*'

'Do you know something, Deirdre? I've a suspicion that what I am hearing emerge from your extremely sexy lips is a concoction of fairy tales.' He slid himself alongside her on the top of the table and leant over her. 'Come here,' he said. 'I can listen to your fairy tales another time. Right now I can think of something a lot more useful you can do with those lips.'

'Well?' she said. 'What?'

'Kiss me,' he said.

'Is that *all*?' Deirdre O'Dare took his head between her hands and looked at him with laughing eyes.

'That'll do for starters,' said Gabriel.

'Sometimes I like to go straight to the main course.'

'You,' he said, trailing a finger up her spine, 'are a glutton.'

'I know,' she said happily. 'And I've never felt so satisfied.'

* * *

She spent the next few days at Gabriel's house, 'convalescing'. She felt a bit tired still, and slept a lot, but other than that there was patently very little wrong with her. Gladys came in every other day and cooked for them, and some evenings Gabriel would drive down to Quay Cottage and bring back food. Deirdre developed a craving for their smoked salmon and cream cheese fritters.

Gladys was a revelation. As well as being stunning to look at, she was incredibly efficient and incredibly down-to-earth. She cooked, cleaned, and organized Gabriel's laundry. Sometimes she'd visit Deirdre in the bedroom with mugs of tea and slices of barmbrack.

'How did you get to be so enviably together?' asked Deirdre one afternoon. She was sitting up in bed against a mound of pillows, and Gladys was sitting cross-legged at the other end of the massive four-poster.

335

'I inherited it from my mother. She's an organiz-ational wizard. She's even written a book about it.'

'Oh? What's it called? Maybe I should buy it.'

'*Cut the Clutter*. I'll lend you a copy, if you like. You can't buy it here, it's only available in Australia.'

'Why Australia?'

'That's where my parents live. They moved there five years ago.'

'I thought it was practically impossible to get a visa?'

'My Dad was sponsored by his company. He does offshore exploration for Esso.' Gladys knocked back her tea and started stacking used mugs and plates on a tray. 'Right,' she said. 'Enough of this slacking. I'd better get back to work. Hell – look at those windows, they're filthy! I must do a job on them.' She wandered over to the big bay window that looked out over the garden and ran a finger down the glass. 'I'm starting to get behind with things. I've a list of chores as long as your arm.'

'You really work hard, don't you, Gladys?'

'I enjoy it. I like to keep busy. And Gabriel's a generous employer. He's suggested that I come in every day once the painters and decorators are here and the furniture's arrived from England.'

'So you'd be a full-time housekeeper?'

'He needs someone to keep an eye on his diary and organize that side of his life as well as looking after the house. He's getting busier all the time.'

'Have you secretarial training?'

'No. But I could learn.'

'God. You make me feel so inadequate, Gladys.'

'Don't be daft. It's just that we're skilled in completely different areas. I couldn't learn lines the way you have to, and I couldn't write a screenplay if someone offered me a million dollars for it.'

'No-one's offered me a million dollars for mine.'

'Not yet they haven't,' said Gladys.

* * *

While she was convalescing, Gabriel worked from his office at home every day, and every day Deirdre said she would get up and do something to make herself useful. But he insisted on her taking things easy. 'I know exactly the kind of person you are,' he said. 'You're the type who gets so bored of being in bed that you get up and potter around unnecessarily and then you end up flat on your back with a relapse.' He was right. Being stuck in bed bored her rigid, unless Gabriel was there beside her. He certainly didn't seem to mind her indulging in the strenuous physical exertion of love-making.

He brought her stacks of expensive magazines and volume after volume of light summer reading that she'd whizz through in a few hours. He knew that she was getting seriously bored when he walked into the bedroom one day and found her drawing a moustache and glasses on a picture of Claudia Schiffer. 'Bring me my laptop,' she said, looking up at him with beseeching eyes. 'I've an idea for a screenplay coming on, and I can work on it in bed. I'll go out of my mind if I've to spend one more day looking at supermodels smirking up at me from the pages of glossy magazines.'

'All right,' he said. 'I'll fetch it from the cottage this afternoon.'

When he came back he sat down on the edge of the bed and handed her the phone. 'Someone's been trying to contact you. Urgently,' he said.

'Oh?' She felt something lurch in the pit of her stomach. 'Who?'

'Your agent,' he replied. 'The phone rang just as I was leaving. She says she's been trying to reach you since Monday morning.'

'Oh.' She looked down at the phone on her lap.

'Well, aren't you going to ring her back?'

'Yeah.' Deirdre punched in the number with unenthusiastic fingers.

'Cheer up, darling. Maybe Mr Spielberg wants you.' Gabriel lobbed a smile at her as he disappeared through the door.

'Hi, Deirdre. At last,' said Sally when the secretary put her through. 'I hear you haven't been well?'

'I'm more or less OK now. But I had a nasty bout of twenty-four-hour flu.'

'Maybe this will gladden your heart. The BBC is interested in you.'

'Oh? For what?'

'They're casting a two-hour drama: *Clarissa d'Arcy*. A period piece, and a peach of a part. Can you get yourself up here to see them?'

'Sure.'

338

'Your – er – friend – the one who picked up the phone at the cottage – says you're under doctor's orders to stay in bed?'

Deirdre was surprised. 'I'm not that bad, Sally. Really.' Trust Gabriel to exaggerate. There was something rather touching about this over-protective streak in him. 'I'll be fine to come up to Dublin as long as I don't overdo things. When are they seeing people?'

'Beginning of next week. Monday or Tuesday.'

'How about Tuesday? I'll get the train up on Monday evening. It'll be less crowded than the Sunday train.'

'Perfect. I'll put you down for twelve-thirty, Tuesday. Oh – and Deirdre?'

'Yeah?'

'You might have to beg a bed from a friend for a few days before you go back to your rural idyll.'

'Oh? Why?'

'Someone else has been looking for you.'

'Who?'

'Heeney Holidays,' said Sally.

'Oh, shit,' said Deirdre.

* * *

'I heard that advertisement on the radio today,' said Gabriel when she told him why she had to head back to Dublin. 'I hope you don't mind me saying this, but it really is bloody awful.'

'I know,' she said with a sigh.

339

'Do you really need to go back for that?'

'Janine Heeney'll go apeshit if I don't turn up. Then there's the incentive of the BBC interview. It's not often they come calling.'

They were sitting in front of the fire in the library with a bottle of champagne and a picnic of smoked salmon and nutty brown bread. Gladys had managed to find a proper ice-bucket at last.

'And Heeney Holidays pays the bills, Gabriel. Well, some of them, anyway.' She sighed again. 'Hell. Acting is so bloody insecure. Maybe I should give it all up and find some regular, pensionable work. Sometimes I think I crave security more than anything. It's frightening not to know where the next job's coming from.'

'You've got the soap opera,' he pointed out. 'Although I read somewhere that it was in trouble. Wasn't there a question mark over whether it would be back at all next season?'

'Oh – that happens every year,' she said. 'Sometimes I think they stage manage it deliberately so that the actors feel insecure and don't dare ask for an increase in salary.'

'Well. That's a reasonably secure number for you, isn't it?'

'For the next year, anyway.' Sally had told her that her contract for next season had come through. She had been offered marginally fewer episodes than usual, which Deirdre found unnerving. 'They might decide to push me under a steam-roller.'

He refilled her glass, and then: 'Eat up,' he said.

340

'We have to build up your strength for your trip to Dublin. You can't go into an audition for a costume drama looking like someone who's stuck in a heroin-chic time warp.'

'Do I?'

'You look a bit peaky, all right.'

She did as she was told with pleasure.

As the evening wore on and it got dark outside, the weather began to change again. Light rain spattered on the windows and the sound of branches soughing in the wind came from the garden. Gabriel went to the window and looked out. 'I'll have to get Gladys to organize curtains for these windows,' he said. 'Bloody bore. Maybe I can wait till the rest of the stuff arrives from England. Gladys has enough on her plate.' Then he turned and looked at her where she reclined on her cushions. 'You look like an odalisque,' he said.

'An odalisque? Isn't that some kind of monolithic, phallic-shaped stone thing?'

He laughed. 'No, Deirdre. That's an obelisk. An odalisque is a sex-slave in a sultan's harem.'

She smiled. 'And I suppose you look a bit like a sultan,' she said. 'Dark and mysterious. You know, the first time I ever saw you I thought you were dead scary.'

'That time we passed each other on the road?'

'Yes.'

'Is that why you pretended to be a German tourist and cycled miles past your turn-off?'

'Yes,' she confessed.

He laughed again. 'I thought as much when I met you that night in Quay Cottage. You never opt for the simple route, do you Deirdre?'

She turned her face away as though she'd been slapped. Rory had once levelled the very same accusation at her, using those very same words. *Bastard.*

'Are you all right?' Gabriel had moved towards her and was looking at her closely.

'Yes.' She managed a wan smile. 'I just got a sudden twinge, that's all.' It wasn't a lie.

'Maybe you're in for a relapse,' he said, joining her on the cushions.

'Oh, no, Gabriel – I'm fine. Honestly I am. I just can't seem to shake off the feeling of fatigue, that's all.' Then she leant over and gave him a lingering kiss. 'But I think I should go back to bed now.'

'Are you that exhausted?'

'On the contrary. I find I feel a sudden surge of energy.'

'Then why go back to bed?'

'I want you to make love to me again,' she said.

*   *   *

They indulged in the sweetest foreplay imaginable under the canopy of the four-poster before lust hit them both simultaneously as an irresistible force. Deirdre's hands travelled in a hard sweep up Gabriel's back to the nape of his neck. She pulled his head close and kissed him deeply. He returned the kiss with a passion so intense it was almost brutal. His hands were on her breasts, her belly, her buttocks, between her thighs.

She took the condom from him and slid it on, and then she snaked her hips over his and mounted him. She started slowly, matching her rhythm to his, knowing intuitively when to quicken and when to hold back. When he climaxed inside her she allowed herself the orgasm she'd been denying since they'd started making love and they came together, still gazing fiercely into each other's eyes.

They lay back, exhausted. Gabriel's orgasm had been almost shocking in its intensity. He was still breathing hard, studying her face through half-closed eyes. Then suddenly he got out of the bed and moved across the room to a chest of drawers. He opened one and took something out, pausing fractionally before strolling back to the bed and gazing down at her. He stooped to kiss her, and she felt his fingers caress the lobes of her ears. She caught her breath. When he stood back, her earlobes were heavy with the jewels that he'd hung there. She put up a hand, uncertainly, and fingered the earrings.

'What are these?' she asked.

'They were my mother's. Look at yourself.'

The only mirror in the room was a long cheval glass. Deirdre got out of bed and moved across to it on rather wobbly legs. Gabriel followed her and lifted the curtain of her hair to reveal the miniature green chandeliers that were hanging from her ears.

'Emeralds?' she asked in a strange voice.

'Emeralds,' he affirmed.

343

'Real ones?'

'Real ones.'

'Hang on, Gabriel.' Her bewildered eyes met his in the mirror. 'You're not *giving* me these earrings, are you?'

'No,' he said. 'I'm *presenting* them to you. That's infinitely more meaningful.'

'You mean for me to keep them?'

'I do,' he said, trailing a kiss over the nape of her neck and a hand over her right breast. 'I can't think of a more beautiful setting for those jewels, my darling. Unless you get your nipples pierced.'

Smiling incredulously, Deirdre reached up her arm and pulled Gabriel Considine's mouth down hard against hers.

* * *

He put her on the train on Monday evening, kissing her goodbye with such thoroughness she wanted to wilt. 'Good luck with your interview,' he said. 'Wear your emeralds. My mother always claimed they brought her amazingly good luck. Phone me when you're ready to come back and I'll pick you up at the station. Look after yourself, and keep taking those vitamins.'

'Yes, yes, yes,' she replied meekly to all his admonishments.

As the train started to draw out of the station he walked alongside it until he had to stride to keep up, and then he stopped and watched her as she was carried off up the tracks.

Deirdre waved until he was out of sight, and then she sat back and studied the pages of the *Clarissa d'Arcy* script which Sally had faxed through to Gabriel's machine. Her agent had been right – it really was a peach of a part. She was lucky to have the enforced idleness of the train journey ahead of her – she'd easily have the dialogue down by the time she hit Dublin. She fingered the lucky emeralds which hung from her ears, hoping that Gabriel's mother was right about them. She should have asked him if they were insured. It would be a bit irresponsible of her to wear them if they weren't.

* * *

On Tuesday, after her interview, Sally rang Deirdre at Bart's flat, where she'd stayed overnight, and told her there were call-backs. They wanted to see her again on Friday. She also told her that she'd lost the Heeney Holidays gig.

'Sorry about that, Deirdre. They rang yesterday to say that Janine Heeney was in a state because they hadn't been able to get hold of you. They've gone with another voice.'

'Shit. That was a nice earner, Sally. Still, I can't say I'm sorry. I really hated those recording sessions.'

'If the BBC want you, you won't have to worry about losing Heeney Holidays. You'll be well covered financially until the soap starts back in August. How's your health, by the way?'

'OK. I'm still feeling tired, though. That bout really knocked the stuffing out of me.'

'You take care of yourself. There's a nasty virus going round and if you're at a low ebb you'll be a walking target for it.'

'Don't worry, Sally. Gabriel got me a load of vitamins.'

'Gabriel. The person who looked after you?'

'Yes.'

'He was perfectly charming to me on the phone. Where did he come from?'

'I don't know. Heaven.'

Sally laughed. 'Looks like you've landed yourself a guardian angel, Deirdre.'

'What do you mean?'

'Angel Gabriel.'

As soon as she put the phone down to Sally, she picked it up again and dialled his number.

'I'm not sure when I'll be down again,' she said. 'I've been called back to see them again on Friday.'

'When are you likely to hear?'

'Pretty soon. They need the part cast in a hurry, apparently. They'd been let down.'

'And when will you start if you land it?'

'In three weeks' time. I'll need my flat back.'

'That soon? Well. It looks like the earrings might be working,' he said.

'Looks like it. By the way, Gabriel – they are insured, aren't they?'

346

'Jesus, yes,' he said. From his tone she inferred that he wouldn't have let them out of the house if they hadn't been insured. It made her feel slightly uncomfortable to speculate how much they might be worth.

*　　*　　*

On Friday evening, Deirdre waltzed into Bart's flat brandishing a bottle of champagne.

'Hi,' he said. 'Are we celebrating?'

'Absolutely. I got the BBC gig.'

'Hey! Well done! When did you hear?'

'Just this afternoon.' She followed him through to the kitchen and sat down at the table, hugging herself. 'I called in to see Sally on my way back from town.'

'What's the money like? The BBC's not renowned for their princely munificence.'

'I'm happy with what I'm getting. And they're a class act. My credibility will go spiralling upwards.' The champagne cork popped and Betty Grable jumped up with an indignant squawk from where she'd been snoozing in her basket. 'Hurray!' shouted Deirdre. 'The best sound in the world! I'm getting kind of used to it,' she added, in a rather perplexed tone.

'Oh? Who have you been swigging champagne with lately?'

'Well, there was that disastrous episode with Jean-Claude Valentin—'

'Of Scandalous Scanties fame.'

'The very one. And then I stole a snipe from Eva's mini-bar—'

'La Lavery? You went to Galway?'

'Mm-hm.'

'How is my favourite goddess?'

'Divine as ever. And then there was—' She stopped herself from pronouncing Rory's name just in time. 'There was Gabriel,' she said. For some reason she'd put off telling Bart about Gabriel. She felt a bit shy about it.

'Who's Gabriel?'

She filled him in.

'He gave you *those*?' Bart said when she'd finished, unhooking one of the emeralds from her ears. 'Are they real?'

Deirdre nodded. 'They belonged to his mother.'

'Holy shit! I assumed they were huckster-stall replicas. They must be worth a fortune!'

'Do you really think so?'

'Well, I'm not an expert, but you're definitely talking four figures. This Gabriel geezer must be loaded.'

'I suppose he is. I've never really thought about it.' In fact, she had thought about it. On more than one occasion.

'And you've moved in with him?'

'Well – not really. I mean – you couldn't call it *moving in*. I just went there to recuperate.'

'But you'll see him again?'

'Yes.' She considered for a minute. 'I don't know

when, though. This BBC thing's going to keep me busy until August. I suppose I'll get down to Carrowcross at weekends. And I know he comes to Dublin on business sometimes.'

'Business,' said Bart. 'Wow. A real life person. What makes him so interested in a crazed fantasist like you?'

'I don't really know,' said Deirdre. 'I do good sex.'

'So I inferred from McDonagh.'

She sat bolt upright and looked at Bart with blazing eyes. 'What? How *dare* he talk about our sex life!'

'You weren't listening, Deirdre. I used the word *inferred*. I'm talking about the expression that used to cross his face when he looked at you.'

'What do you mean?'

'Well, to put it plainly, it was very clear indeed from the look on his face that the beast with two backs you made together had a serious pedigree. He didn't have to *talk* about it. He's not that kind of a bloke.'

Deirdre felt herself blush. She looked at her watch. 'Oh, turn on the radio!' she said.

'What? Why?'

'There's a programme about dry-stone walls in the Gaeltacht.'

'Why the fuck do you want to listen to a programme about dry-stone walls?'

'It's Gabriel's hobby.'

'Holy shit,' said Bart again, reaching out a hand and flicking the switch on the radio.

'Here comes the sun!' A bright, enthusiastic voice came shouting at them from the radio. 'Yes! You're ready at last for that longed-for holiday! You know you deserve it, your boss knows you've earned it – and we at *Heeney* Holidays know *just* where to take you!' Bart and Deirdre looked at each other. Their mouths had fallen open in stupefaction.

'It's Sophie,' said Bart.

Deirdre nodded, and put a finger to her lips. A slow smile spread itself across her face as she listened to the commercial.

'Open our *amazing* colour brochure and get lost in the country of your choice – in the nicest possible way, of course! Our continental deals will confound you! Fascinating France, sensational Spain, interesting Italy – they're all there between the covers of our *fabulous* brochure! You'll think you're *dreaming* when you see the special summer offers we have lined up for you! Whether it's night-life, shopping and *craic* you're after, adventure or sporting activities, or simply sun, sea and sand – whatever you want, you'll find it – between the covers of a *Heeney* Holidays brochure! Happy holidays! Happy *Heeney* Holidays!' The French accordion music that was playing in the background came to a zingy, upbeat end and Sophie shut up at last.

'Lo! The new voice of Heeney Holidays has spoken!' said Bart.

Deirdre shook her head in dumbfounded admiration. 'Wow,' she said. 'Sophie's gone way up in my estimation. What an amazing performance! She sounded so enthusiastic she made me want to run straight out and get a copy of their amazing brochure!'

'Your *bête noir* Janine Heeney excelled herself on that one, Deirdre,' said Bart. 'I have a sudden overwhelming compulsion to visit – how did Sophie describe it? – *interesting* Italy. And dig that new endline! "Happy holidays! Happy *Heeney* Holidays!"'

'Crikey! It must have taken Janine a whole day of creative angst to come up with that.'

Bart poured more champagne. 'Here's to a wonderful new partnership. Janine Heeney and Sophie Burke,' he said.

'Maybe they should go on a Heeney holiday together. They'd have a ball.' Deirdre took a swig of champagne and Bart did likewise.

'Heeney Holidays would be a bit naff for Sophie,' he said, settling back in his chair. 'She's spending a fortnight doing a grand tour of Ireland with her dad. Apparently they're visiting all the poshest country house hotels and staying one night in each, just so they can say they've done it.'

'Oh? Who told you this?'

'I ran into Cressida last week.'

Deirdre gave him a thoughtful look. 'Why do people like Sophie get to have such a good time?' she said. 'Why can't we be rich, Bart, and go swanning around on expensive holidays and drink vintage champagne and go to the races and have Daddy buy us little runabout Renaults?'

'You're sounding very bitter and twisted.'

'I know. But it must be nice to be rich.'

'I dunno. We poor people appreciate good times all the more when they happen. Rich people get blasé about all that shit.'

'Do they?'

'Yeah. They sit around drinking champagne, quite oblivious to the fact that they're decked out in Chanel or that they're sitting on a Louis Quinze chair, or that there's a Fragonard hanging on the wall above their head. Or that they've got thousands of pounds' worth of emeralds hanging out of their ears.'

Deirdre laughed. '*Touché*,' she said. Then: 'Oh! Here it comes!' She reached out and turned up the volume on the radio.'

'Didn't know you were so partial to diddle-ee-i-di music, Deirdre.'

'I'm not,' she said. 'It's the introduction to my programme.'

'Dry-stone walls have had a long and fascinating tradition in this country,' began the narrator.

'Oh, fuck,' said Bart, reaching for the bottle. 'Do you know what you are, Deirdre?'

'What?'

'An enigma.'

'Oh, good. That's much more romantic than calling me a crazed fantasist like you did earlier. Now shut up and listen.'

'The dry-stone walls of the Aran islands have a particularly interesting history,' droned the voice on the radio.

Bart sighed. 'And you're off them,' he said.

'What do you mean?'

'You're not only an enigmatic fantasist, Deirdre. You're off the dry-stone wall.'

He refilled his glass and disappeared through the kitchen door. Within seconds Radiohead was blasting out of the sitting room.

Chapter Fourteen

Deirdre didn't go back to Carrowcross. There really was very little point. The project Gabriel was involved in was taking him to London on a weekly basis, and she didn't want to spend too much time on her own now that she had finished her screenplay. Anyway, the tenant she'd let her flat to had moved on and she no longer had income from that source. Her finances would be a bit dodgy until the BBC money came through.

It seemed absurd that she should be making obsequious phone calls to the bank when she was wearing thousands of pounds' worth of emeralds in her ears. She'd taken to wearing the emeralds on a regular basis. They weren't so madly ostentatious that they couldn't be worn every day, and she knew that no-one who saw them would believe they were real. It felt kind of cool to be wearing faded combats and T-shirts and real emeralds.

On the days when Gabriel had to go to London he'd make a point of travelling up and staying with her the night before. He brought her her laptop and the other few belongings that she'd left in Carrowcross, and took her out to dinner in restaurants she couldn't afford. She loved the way women watched him when he walked into a room.

Bart had been dreading meeting him. 'I feel uncomfortable around rich people,' he said when Deirdre invited him in for a drink one night. Gabriel had showed up with a bottle of champagne and Deirdre had suggested they share it with her neighbour.

'Oh, please, Bart. You'll really like him. He's not like a rich person at all, you know. He's really nice.'

'OK,' said Bart with a sigh. 'I suppose we'll be listening to Baroque music all night long. I've noticed you've started playing a load of classical shite lately.'

Much later, after the champagne had been finished and many Buds had been produced from the fridge, Gabriel turned to Deirdre. 'Do you mind if we listen to something else?' he asked. 'That harpsichord music is starting to get on my nerves.'

'Thank fuck I'm not the only one,' said Bart. 'It was doing my head in too.'

'Philistines,' said Deirdre snootily. 'What'll I put on instead? Mozart?'

'Got any Radiohead?' asked Gabriel.

'*I* have!' Bart jumped up, grinning. 'Give me two minutes.'

'What have you got?'

'Everything,' said Bart, making for the door.

'Did you get to the gig at the Point?'

'Totally fucking amazing, wasn't it?'

355

Gabriel spread his hands in an attitude of regret. 'I couldn't make it.'

'I have a bootleg recording of it. I'll let you have a listen.' Bart disappeared through the door. They could hear him singing in his best Radiohead drone as he crossed the landing.

Deirdre gave Gabriel an aggrieved look. 'I *hate* Radiohead,' she said.

'Sorry about that. We'll listen to Mozart later, I promise,' said Gabriel.

'Those sexy arias?'

'Sure.'

'Will you make love to me as they play?'

'With extreme pleasure.' Gabriel's black gaze was so meaningful that her aggrieved look turned into a smile of anticipation.

From the next-door flat they could hear Bart rummaging around in his CD rack. He was singing the only Radiohead song that Deirdre had ever bothered to listen to properly. She cocked her head at one of the lyrics. 'Listen,' she said, joining in with Bart's doleful singing. 'That's what you've got, Gabriel. A pretty house.'

'Pretty's hardly the right word for Carrowcross House, Deirdre.'

'All right, magnificent. *Such a magnificent house. And such a magnificent garden,*' she sang. 'Except the garden's not really magnificent yet, is it?'

'It will be,' said Gabriel.

*　　　*　　　*

356

The week before she was due to start filming was a busy one. She had costume fittings, a photo call and a medical. The medical was standard procedure for anyone who landed a substantial role in a movie or television drama. Deirdre was quite glad to have an opportunity to see a doctor. She was still feeling a bit run down after her illness, in spite of all the vitamins she was shovelling into herself.

The doctor did all the usual things like banging her knees for reflexes, measuring her blood pressure and taking a urine sample. When he'd finished examining her he sat back and surveyed her with a grave expression. 'Well,' he said. 'The BBC are going to have to fork out a lot more insurance money for you than they might have expected.'

Deirdre felt a twinge of anxiety. 'What's wrong?' she asked. 'Has it got anything to do with that horrible twenty-four-hour thing I told you about?'

'No, no,' said the doctor. 'You're not ill, Ms O'Dare. You're pregnant.'

She sat there in silence.

'There's no question but that I'm right. You've missed a period, haven't you?'

Deirdre couldn't think. Her mind was completely numb.

'When was your last period, Ms O'Dare?'

She wished he'd stop calling her Ms O'Dare. 'Oh God,' she said. 'Oh God. I don't know. My periods are always all over the place. Oh God.'

'Have you been careful about contraception?'

357

'Oh, yes!' she said with relief. The doctor had to be wrong. She couldn't be pregnant. Gabriel always used a condom. And Rory had too – more than one, actually – the night she'd spent with him in Ashford. 'Oh, yes – I've always been careful. Always.'

'What method of contraception have you been using?'

'Condoms.'

'In conjunction with a spermicide?'

'A spermicide?' She didn't know anyone who bothered with a spermicide. The idea was too totally gross. 'No.'

'Then you haven't been careful enough. No contraceptive can guarantee one hundred per cent protection. Condoms without spermicide have around a ninety-five per cent reliability. It's a tiny risk, but a real one.'

'I see.' She bit her lip and looked down at her hands lying white-knuckled in her lap. 'How – how pregnant am I?'

'Around five weeks.' He rose to his feet. It was her cue to leave. 'I suggest you consult your own GP,' he said. 'He or she will advise you on hospitals, obstetricians and the changes you can expect your body to undergo. Congratulations, Ms O'Dare.' He spoke into an intercom. 'Next patient, please. A Ms –' he glanced at the list on his desk '– Burke.'

Deirdre left the surgery with her mind reeling. She was around five weeks pregnant. Five weeks ago, she had slept with Gabriel for the first time. And not even two nights earlier she had slept with Rory. She had no idea who had fathered the child she was carrying.

She made her way to the bus stop like a sleep-walker. How could this have happened? How could such a grotesque scenario have arisen? How would her parents react? Who could she ask for help? Who knew about these things? Who could she ask to accompany her to England for an abortion?

An abortion. Oh, God. She couldn't ask the doctor she'd just seen about an abortion. He hadn't even mooted that it might be an option – he'd just told her to consult her own GP. She felt a sudden surge of panic and then told herself to calm down. She didn't have to do that right away. She could do it next month. The month after . . .

She had breathing space, after all. Hang on, hang on. Take things a little slower, Deirdre, she told herself. Why had she automatically arrived at the conclusion that an abortion was the only solution to her quandary? She forced herself to think harder. Did she really want one? The thought of aborting Gabriel's child was anathema to her. He had already lost one unborn baby. But what if the child wasn't Gabriel's? What if it was Rory's?

She began to cry. Oh, God, oh, God. She couldn't abort Rory's child either. Rory and she had never discussed the possibility of having children – she didn't even know how he felt about them – but she knew she couldn't abort the baby they could have made so beautifully in Ashford Castle.

Maybe that's why she'd dreamt about babies recently – more than once. She'd put it down to the fact that she'd spent time with Dorcas, but now she realized that her subconscious must have been trying to tell her something – warn her. It had tried to warn her about something else, she knew. What? There had been that dream where she'd been following Gabriel's dog along a corridor. There'd been someone else in that dream – not just Dorcas.

The thought of Dorcas reminded her how much Eva had longed for her baby. She remembered the look on Eva's face the day she'd told her she was pregnant. She'd wished and wished and wished for that baby! She and David had tried so hard to conceive a child together. And Deirdre bloody O'Dare had conceived without ever even taking the time to wonder whether she could do it or not.

A bus was coming. She dashed aside her tears. She'd ask Maeve for advice. Then she remembered that Maeve wasn't around any more. Bart? No, no – she couldn't. She couldn't let anyone know that the most frightening worm in the can she'd opened was the identity of the baby's father. Bart would just assume it was Gabriel's. Gabriel would, too. Nobody would ever guess that there was a question mark over the paternity of the child. Except Rory, of course. And—

Just then a red Renault Clio pulled up alongside the bus stop. Andrew Lloyd-Webber was spilling out of it. 'Hi, Deirdre,' said Sophie Burke. 'I haven't seen you for ages. Not since that morning I spotted you leaving Ashford Castle with Rory McDonagh.'

Oh, God, oh God, oh God. Sophie. It had been *Sophie* in the dream! Another nightmarish image came back to her now with blinding clarity – the image of the actress hanging out of an upper storey window in Ashford Castle, grinning down at her like a gargoyle. She'd consigned that image to her subconscious, too – blotted it out of her mind. Any time it had floated in front of her mind's eye she'd assumed it had just been part of her hallucinations that time she was ill.

'Let me give you a lift,' said Sophie. Sophie loved giving people lifts in her nifty little car. 'Where are you going?'

Deirdre thought fast. The idea of sitting beside Sophie while she showed off her driving and sang along to Andrew Lloyd-Webber had about as much appeal as having her teeth drilled without an anaesthetic, but she knew she had to bring all her diplomacy to bear in the scary situation that was unravelling in front of her. She slid through the passenger door that Sophie had pushed open, feeling like the snake in the garden of good and evil. The only thing to do was to manipulate this situation to her advantage as best as she could.

'Thanks, Sophie. I'm heading home. Just drop me anywhere near the centre of town.'

'OK. I'm going to Grafton Street. I've an invitation to the Brown Thomas sale preview. Want to come?'

'No thanks. I'm not feeling great. I couldn't face the crowds.'

Sophie shot her a pleasant look. 'Mm. You do look a bit peaky, all right. I've just come from the doctor myself. He says I'm in perfect physical shape. Lah lah . . . la la la la la lah lah . . .' she trilled as she negotiated the traffic.

Now, Deirdre. Don't do anything you're going to regret, she warned herself. Deirdre forced a smile. 'I heard you on the radio the other day, on the Heeney Holidays ad?'

'Oh, yes,' replied Sophie carelessly. 'You used to do those ads, didn't you?'

'Yes, but I can understand why they decided to go with you. You're so much better than I was. You've managed to combine the hard sell that Janine was after with a beautifully relaxed delivery. Janine used to say that I sounded as if I was going on my holidays on an express train!' She actually managed a little laugh.

She noticed that Sophie was looking at her rather suspiciously. Maybe she was overdoing things a bit?

'Well, Janine and I have a great rapport.'

'That doesn't surprise me,' said Deirdre, as disingenuously as she could.

'I find her direction really helpful. And she's a genius in other areas as well. She writes half of those commercials herself, you know. I sometimes wonder why she bothers with a copy-writer at all.'

'Ha ha ha,' went Deirdre, obligingly.

'Although,' Sophie adopted a confiding tone, 'I

have to say that I can't imagine anything worse than going on one of those holidays. Magaluf, Benidorm – yuck! Even parts of the Riviera have become tacky now.'

'I hear you went on a tour of the great Irish country house hotels recently?'

'Yes. With my dad. We were just starting out that morning I saw you and Rory. It's a beautiful hotel, isn't it? We stayed in deluxe rooms, of course. I don't suppose the standard rooms are quite as impressive.'

Deirdre couldn't resist it. 'Actually, we stayed in the Presidential Suite.' She deliberately used block capitals.

'Oh?' Sophie sounded squeaky. 'Lah lah . . . la la la la la lah lah. Of course – Rory's heading for the big league now, isn't he? He can afford to splash out a bit.'

'Yes. He's in LA at the moment.'

'Well, it's nice that you two managed to get back together before he had to leave again.'

It was time. Deirdre sucked in her breath and then said, 'Actually, Sophie – we didn't.'

'What do you mean?'

'We didn't get back together.'

'You don't expect me to believe that you spent the night in the Presidential Suite in separate beds?'

'Well – no. Of course not. We just spent the night together for – well, let's say we did it for old times' sake, if you know what I mean.' Oh, Christ. What a spectacularly bad line! 'You see, I'm in another

363

relationship now and . . .' Her voice trailed away.

Sophie looked at her shrewdly. 'So. Basically what you're trying to tell me is that you'd rather nobody knew about your little liaison in Ashford?'

'Yes,' said Deirdre meekly.

'All right.' Deirdre looked at Sophie in amazement. What had made her acquiesce so easily? 'I don't want there to be any acrimony between us since we're going to be working together again soon.'

'Soon? But *Ardmore Grove*'s not back until August.'

'I'm not talking about *Ardmore Grove*, Deirdre. I'm talking about *Clarissa d'Arcy*.'

'The BBC gig? Are you on that?'

'Yes. I've just come from my medical. Did nobody tell you? I'm playing your best friend. Oh – I love this song. Lah la lah la, la la la la la lah la . . .'

*   *   *

The next few weeks were hell. Deirdre spent day after day wandering around parkland and gracious mansions with Sophie, sharing secrets with her 'best friend'. In the script they referred to each other constantly as 'sister', and the director instructed them to air-kiss each other a lot, giggle girlishly, and link arms. She had never had to work so hard in her life.

Deirdre had told no-one about her pregnancy. She nursed the knowledge to herself, fluctuating violently between indecision and certainty. In the middle of the night she would wake up and vow that she would seek advice about a termination the very next day; the following morning she'd defer it yet again. Then she'd think about how nightmarish single parenthood would be – her cousin Nuala was a single parent and had a seriously grim life in a tiny flat in Clapham. How would she manage a baby in her own flat? She didn't even have a washing machine.

She was also suffering badly from morning sickness. The early morning calls on location were especially gruesome. The crew would help themselves to big fry-ups from the catering truck, and the smell made Deirdre even more nauseous. 'Hangover,' she said to Sophie one morning when she caught the other actress looking at her curiously.

Gabriel still visited her nearly every week. They had become closer and closer, and each time she saw him she was tempted to confess, to spill out her secret to him. But some circumspect voice inside her head warned her against it. If she told Gabriel about the baby she knew that a termination would no longer be an option for her.

He arrived to pick her up from location one day while in Dublin on a flying visit. He was driving the Aston he used in town, and Deirdre noticed that Sophie's expression went stiff with the effort of trying to look unimpressed. 'Is that your new significant other?' she asked with a little yawn, as if it was really of very little interest to her. They were waiting for the all clear from the assistant director.

'Yes. His name's Gabriel Considine.'

'Considine? I don't suppose he's connected to the Buckinghamshire Considines?'

'Yes. He is.'

Sophie couldn't not sound interested any more. 'Where did you meet him?' she asked.

'Carrowcross. Not far from Westport. He has a house there.'

'Oh?' Sophie was studying her nails carefully. 'A big house?'

'Yes. He's restored it.'

'Well, Deirdre,' said Sophie with a catlike smile. 'I can understand why you don't want Gabriel Considine to find out about your liaison with your ex.'

Deirdre very nearly told her to fuck off. Instead she said, 'Thanks for keeping schtum, Sophie. I appreciate it.'

'It's a wrap,' the AD announced.

Deirdre gave Gabriel the thumbs up. 'Five minutes,' she mouthed at him as she and Sophie headed in the direction of wardrobe to divest themselves of their constricting Victorian costumes.

'What a relief.' Deirdre let her corset drop to the floor and stepped out of it. 'It's just as well we've only two more weeks on this film. This corset won't go near me soon.'

'Why? Have you put on weight?' Sophie smirked a little and raked her eyes over Deirdre's semi-clothed body.

Too late Deirdre realized what she'd said. Sophie clocked her expression. 'You're not pregnant, are you?' she said in a jokey voice. Then the smile slowly vanished from her face. 'Oh. You're pregnant.' There was no question mark, and Deirdre knew there was absolutely no point in denying it. If she did, Sophie would simply start the jungle drums beating within hours, and before the day was out there would be speculation rife in every actors' pub in town. 'You're pregnant,' repeated Sophie. 'No wonder you've been looking so awful. Whose . . . ?' Even Sophie Burke didn't have the neck to continue the obvious question that came to mind.

Deirdre looked at her. 'Listen, Sophie. I am going to have to do something deeply unpleasant.' She took a long breath and folded her arms, looking directly into the other actress's eyes. 'I will not have word of this getting out until I am ready to handle it, all right? So this is the deal: if you refrain from speculating about the paternity of my baby, I will refrain from letting slip to Ben that you went to bed with Bart Walsh.' Sophie blanched and started to stammer something. 'There's no point in denying it, Sophie, any more than there's any point in me denying that I spent a night with Rory in Ashford Castle. We're up to our necks in it, and the only way either of us can emerge from this hellish situation with any dignity is by pretending that we don't know what we know about each other.' Deirdre was shaking. 'This really isn't my style, Sophie. I don't like myself very much for doing this to you, but you've landed me in an extremely awkward position, and I don't really see that I've any choice. What do you say?'

There was silence. Deirdre noticed that Sophie was shaking, too. She was looking down at where she was shuffling her foot in and out of her Victorian slipper. Then she looked back up at Deirdre. 'OK,' she said. 'OK. It's a deal.' She bit her lip. 'Ben and I have decided it's about time we got engaged,' she added. 'We were going to make an announcement at the weekend.'

For the first time in their lives the actresses smiled at each with a rather tentative amity.

'I swear I will never breathe a word to a living soul,' said Deirdre. 'You can trust me. I keep my promises, Sophie.'

'I swear *I* will never breathe a word to a living soul,' said Sophie. 'I know we've had our run-ins, and that you don't have very much reason to like me. I'll be perfectly honest and say that I've never much liked you. But I will keep my word on this. There's too much at stake for both of us, isn't there?' Sophie stuck out her hand and Deirdre took it. Then they kissed each other's cheeks, rather awkwardly.

'Good luck with your engagement party,' said Deirdre.

'Thanks,' said Sophie. 'Good luck with your baby. Um, when are you going to tell him?'

Deirdre knew she had made her decision. She was almost grateful to Sophie for forcing her hand. 'Soon,' she said. 'It's about time he knew. I've a couple of days off next week. I'll go down to Carrowcross and tell him then.'

'What'll you do about *Ardmore Grove*? *I'm* meant to be the one who's pregnant in that, not you!'

Deirdre shrugged. 'I don't know. To tell you the truth, I haven't given very much thought to this situation. I've been winging it wildly until now.' She gave a rather rueful laugh. 'In a way it's maybe not such a bad thing that you copped on to me. It means I have to face up to things at last. I'll phone my agent once I've told Gabriel and ask her advice.'

'Are you happy, Deirdre?'

Deirdre gave Sophie Burke a thoughtful look. 'Yes,' she said. 'Yes, Sophie, I am.'

Just then there was a knock at the door. 'Sophie?' came a runner's voice. 'Ben's here for you.'

'Thanks,' Sophie replied. 'Will you tell him I'm on my way?' She kicked off her satin slippers and slid her feet into elegant Jimmy Choo mules. 'See you tomorrow,' she said, laying a hand lightly on Deirdre's shoulder as she headed for the door. 'Take care of yourself, Deirdre.'

She actually sounded as if she had meant it.

*   *   *

A few days later Deirdre rang Gabriel. 'Can I come down and visit this weekend? I'm getting withdrawal symptoms.'

'From me or from Carrowcross?'

'Both. I've two days off at the beginning of the week. I don't have to be back in town until Tuesday evening. That means four whole days. We can spend all our time in bed.'

'I could do with some exercise. I've been poring over computer-generated graphics all week.'

'You'll get all the exercise you need in bed with me, Gabriel.'

'I know that, darling,' he said. 'But I crave fresh air. Pack your walking boots. We'll climb Croagh Patrick.'

'Oh.'

'What's wrong? Don't you fancy the idea?'

'Oh, yes – I do. It's just that –' Like an image from a dream the memory came back to her, of Rory and her climbing through cloud. 'It's just that – I've never done it before.'

'Never?' Gabriel sounded incredulous. 'Then you're in for a treat. It's one of the most remarkable views you'll ever see.'

'So I've heard.'

'Just keep your fingers crossed that the weather holds out. There's not a lot of point in climbing the mountain if there's cloud cover.'

When they finished talking, Deirdre put the phone down, buried her face in her hands, and wept.

*   *   *

On Saturday night she and Gabriel drew the curtains on the four-poster bed, ate chocolate and made love while rain lashed against the window. Deirdre read Anaïs Nin out loud to him, but she said nothing about the baby. On Sunday night they heaped cushions up in front of the fire in the library, drank wine and made love while a storm raged outside. Still Deirdre said nothing about the baby. On Monday night they lit candles in the bathroom, ran a deep bath, and watched rivulets of rain drizzle down the big, muslin-draped window before making love in the scented water. Deirdre promised herself she'd tell him about the baby the next day.

On Tuesday morning they awoke to blue skies; they were a kind of ominous, baby-blue. Deirdre ran to the bedroom window to count the number of clouds. There were two, and they were both sliding serenely over the horizon.

'Get your walking boots on,' said Gabriel.

Deirdre gave him a doubtful look. 'Will we have time to get all the way to the top and back down again before six o'clock? I've a train to catch this evening, remember?'

'Come on, darling. Where's your pioneering spirit? It's not Everest we're climbing. We'll be up and down within three hours.'

Gabriel packed a rucksack with fruit and water and his camera, and they set out in the Land-Rover. 'You're very quiet today,' he remarked as they drove.

'I know.' She gave him a rueful look. 'I'm kind of dreading going back to town. I know there's less than a fortnight to go on *Clarissa d'Arcy*, but as soon as

371

that's wrapped I'm back on the soap. I won't have breathing space.' The thought of going back to *Ardmore Grove* produced an unpleasant flutter of alarm in the pit of her stomach. She'd *have* to let them know soon that she was pregnant. The storylines for next season would be well advanced by now, and she'd be starting to show in a couple of months. They'd need to find some way of writing her pregnancy into the series. Or they'd need to find some way of writing her out before her condition became too obvious.

They had reached the foot of the mountain. Gabriel parked the car in the visitors' car park. There weren't too many other cars around.

'Unusual at this time of the year, isn't it?' observed Deirdre. 'I thought there'd be hordes of tourists hauling themselves up the slopes.'

'They've probably been put off by the bad weather. The good weather's taken them by surprise. There'll be more people around later in the day. We're lucky. We'll practically have the mountain to ourselves.' He smiled at her and stretched out a hand. 'Let's get started.'

The first stage of the climb wasn't too difficult. A kind of pathway had been worn by thousands upon thousands of the footsteps of pilgrims who made the journey to the top of the holy mountain on the last Sunday of July every year. Some of them climbed barefoot so that their penance was tougher: their feet would be torn and bleeding after the climb. She'd heard that some people even did it on their knees.

She had never understood this compulsion for self-flagellation. She knew the climb was difficult enough in walking boots.

As they progressed, the mountain became mutinous. It was as if it was determined to make sure that nobody would reach the top. The comparatively smooth path gave way to shingly rubble that dislodged underfoot, sending stones spilling. Deirdre's heart stopped when she saw a boulder bouncing its way down the mountainside.

Sometimes it was easier to climb sideways like a crab rather than straight up. The gradient had become so steep that she felt as if she was clinging onto a cliff, and she had a nasty suspicion that just one ill-judged step could send her spiralling into thin air. She stopped looking down. Gabriel was ahead of her. She wanted to call to him, to ask him how much further they had to go, but she hadn't enough breath. She looked up to gauge how much was left to climb. The mountain was like a sphere of rock: it was impossible to calculate distance. Deirdre climbed and climbed until it seemed certain that the end of the journey must be within yards. But every time she looked up the horizon was no nearer. Now she knew how travellers in the desert must feel when confronted by a mirage. There is no top to this mountain, she found herself thinking.

Just as she thought she could climb no further, she found herself emerging onto the top of the world. Clew Bay shimmered below her, blue silk splashed with green. Each jewel-like island was rimmed with golden sand, giving the impression of rich emeralds in twenty-four-carat settings. Gabriel was waiting for her. He slung an arm around her shoulders and they shambled towards the edge of the mountain. Deirdre was still too exhausted to speak. Gabriel shook his rucksack off his back, opened it and handed her a big bottle of Volvic. She drank thirstily and then handed it back to him with a smile.

'Well, that was a bloody nightmare,' she managed.

He smiled back at her. 'I know,' he said. 'But you can't say it's not worth it.'

They sat down at the foot of the small white church that perched on the summit. From the cottage in Carrowcross this church looked no bigger than a pimple. She swept her gaze over the bay and finally managed to locate her house on the coastline far below: a tiny pinprick of white against all that green. Beyond it a slash of darker green in the landscape showed her where Gabriel's house lay in its nest of tall trees. Directly below them Bartra Strand trailed out into the ocean. It looked as if someone had carelessly dragged a length of gold velvet through the turquoise water and left it lying there. For a long, long time they sat in silence. Deirdre reminded herself of the words Thackeray had used, and she felt a lump come into her throat: *It forms an event in one's life to have seen that place, so beautiful is it and so unlike all other beauties that I know of.*

She knew it was time to tell Gabriel. She turned to him and took a deep breath. 'Gabriel,' she said. 'I'm pregnant.'

He looked at her hard, and his eyes seemed very black. She wanted to look away, walk away, but she wouldn't allow herself to, couldn't allow herself to. 'How could that be?' he said, finally.

'An accident. I'm totally accidentally pregnant. I never thought it could happen.'

'Neither did I,' he replied in a strange voice. He looked away from her and she saw his chest rise, then fall as he let out a sigh.

'They're only ninety-five per cent reliable, you see, according to the doctor.'

He turned back to her with an expression of total confusion. 'Sorry? What are only ninety-five per cent reliable?'

'Condoms. The doctor said they should always be used in conjunction with a spermicide.'

'Oh.'

'The thing is, Gabriel – I don't really know how to say this – but there is a chance . . . oh, shit.' She couldn't look at him any more. She buried her face in her hands. 'There's a chance that the baby's not yours.'

There was a pause. The pause stretched into a silence. Then: 'Explain,' he said.

'Oh, I'm sorry. I'm so, so sorry. It happened before we really established where our relationship was going, Gabriel. I – I – *went* with somebody – from my past. It was a one-off.'

'A one-night stand?'

How could she describe what had happened between her and Rory that night as a one-night

375

stand? It diminished it so. To her mind it was like describing the relationship between Cathy and Heathcliff as a mild flirtation. But she couldn't tell Gabriel this. Instead: 'Yes,' she said. She still couldn't look at him.

'Did you have unprotected sex?'

'No.'

'A dodgy condom?'

'Yes. Except it might have been *your* condom that was the dodgy one, Gabriel. There's no way of telling. Oh, God – I feel so *cheap* . . .'

'Don't say that.' Gabriel put out a hand and took hers. 'There's nothing cheap about you, Deirdre O'Dare. I won't have you say that about yourself.'

She looked at him for the first time since she'd told him he might not be the father of the baby. He was looking back at her with an unreadable expression in his eyes. Then: 'Deirdre?' he said.

'Yes?' Her hair was being moved by a light breeze. Gabriel pushed a tendril back from her cheek. 'Will you marry me?' he asked.

She looked once more at his face, then down at his hands where they hung between his thighs. There was a small cut on his thumb. She looked down at his dusty boots, and at the grey ground. Her eyes travelled further, sweeping down, down to where the grey ground became purple and then green and then slid away into the smooth blue water of Clew Bay.

'I can't marry you, Gabriel,' she said eventually. There was a huge lump in her throat.

'Oh?' His tone sounded reasonable. 'Why's that?'

She felt the lump in her throat grow until it seemed to her that she would never be able to utter another word. Tears were prickling the backs of her eyes. Gabriel held her against him and stroked her hair. A long time went by. Then: 'Why did you say you couldn't marry me, Deirdre?' he asked again.

She looked up at him, despair in her eyes. 'Well, because of the baby,' she said.

'I would have thought,' he said, 'that most women would consider that a very good reason to get married. Anyway, what if it's my baby?'

A big tear slid down her cheek. 'Oh – Gabriel. What if it isn't?'

'It doesn't matter. Believe me. It will be my baby in my eyes. And if it's my baby in my eyes, then it will be my baby in the eyes of the world.'

'Are you telling me that you don't mind being father to a child that might not be your own?'

'No,' he said. 'No. I don't mind.'

'But I thought – I mean – I thought that most men wouldn't be able to tolerate the idea of–'

'I'm not like most men.' Of course he wasn't. 'And you're not like most women. Most women wouldn't have been as upfront as you if they happened to find themselves in a similar predicament.'

'A similar predicament? How could there *be* a similar predicament to this? It's the most bizarre predicament I've ever been in!' Deirdre was dashing tears away from her eyes.

'I imagine it's a lot less unusual than you might

377

think. Remember that old truism? It's a wise man that knows his own father.'

'Or a wise woman.' She gazed down at the bay below. There was another long pause. Then she turned back to him. '*I* will know, though, Gabriel.'

'Will you know? If the baby looks like a miniature you, you might not be able to guess with any great degree of certainty.'

'I suppose I won't.' She looked at him with thoughtful eyes. 'And if it looks like you, then we'll know . . .'

'Deirdre. Understand this. I don't care who the child looks like. I don't care whose the child is. I'm not going to ask for a DNA test. All I ask is that, if you suspect that it isn't mine, you will never tell anyone the identity of the father.'

'Including you?'

'Including me.'

She sat there, feeling the wind in her hair. There was a faint smell of rosemary in the air. Rosemary? she thought, stupidly. No rosemary grew in this barren place. And then she realized it was Gabriel's scent. A gull wheeled silently past, yards below them. She remembered what Sophie had said to her a week ago. A week! It seemed as if centuries had passed since that incident in wardrobe. *Are you happy?* Sophie had asked. And Deirdre had answered, *Yes.* 'I suppose we could make another baby, Gabriel?' she said. 'After this one's born.'

He stood up and looked out over the bay. She couldn't see his face. 'All that matters now is that the child you're carrying is one hundred per cent healthy,' he said. He picked up his rucksack and took an apple from it. 'Here,' he said. 'Eat this immediately. You should be eating lots of fruit. You're going to have to do something about your execrable diet, darling. You're eating for two now.'

'Yes, I am, aren't I?' She looked up at him with shining eyes. 'Do you know something, Gabriel? I feel very happy.'

'I'm glad to hear it,' he said. 'I could be happier.'

'Oh! What's wrong?'

'You still haven't answered my question.'

'What question?'

'You mean you don't remember? I thought it was a pretty significant question myself. I asked you to marry me about five minutes ago.'

'Oh! Oh, yes!'

'Do you mean, "Oh yes, you remember," or, "Oh yes, you will marry me?"'

'Both. Both!' She flung herself at him and covered his face with kisses.

Gabriel stood up and held out his hand to her. 'You take the climb down at a snail's pace, Ms Considine-to-be. Or will you keep your own name?'

'Oh. I think I'd better keep my own name if you don't mind,' she said, taking his hand and getting to her feet. 'Deirdre Considine sounds even more stupider than Deirdre O'Dare. More grown-up, anyway. People might think they'd have to start treating me like the sort of person who's good at real life.'

'I think you handled real life exceptionally well this morning,' he said. 'Careful! You nearly tripped on that stone. Now – inch your way down the slope.' He took an elbow to support her. 'Dear Jesus, Deirdre. How could you do this to me?'

'Do what?'

'Allow me to suggest climbing Croagh Patrick and then inform me at the top that you're pregnant. When's he due, by the way?'

'Beginning of February,' she said.

'So he'll be an Aquarius. The dawning of a new age.'

'How do you know it'll be a boy?'

'Intuition,' he said. 'Mind that rock.'

She grabbed his hand and held on tight. 'I love you, Gabriel,' she said.

'I love you too,' he said, kissing her neck before gesturing to her to go forward.

As Gabriel Considine allowed his wife-to-be to precede him down the rocky slope, she turned back to see that he had taken his camera out of his bag.

'Oh, don't take a photograph of me now, Gabriel,' she pleaded. 'I must look awful – all tear-stained and mucky.'

'I'm not taking a photograph of you,' he said.

'Oh?' She looked around to see if there was anything of interest that he might be taking a photograph of. There wasn't, really – just the stony landscape.

'I'm taking the first photograph of our baby.'

There was a click and a whirr, and then Gabriel Considine lowered the camera. He was smiling.

*   *   *

When he took her to the train that evening she was as skittish as an excited pony. She felt so euphoric when she jumped down from the Land-Rover that she found herself doing dance steps in the car park, not caring that people were staring at her. She took Gabriel's arm just as he was taking something out of his pocket. 'Easy on,' he said. 'You nearly made me drop this.' He took her left hand in his. Then he was slipping a ring on the third finger. She looked down. It was a cabochon emerald. A big one. 'My father bought it for my mother to complement the earrings,' he said. 'Emeralds were my mother's jewels. I'm glad they're yours, too.'

She stared down at it through a film of tears. 'Bloody hell,' she said. 'I'll never, ever be able to say I feel cheap again, will I? Nobody could feel cheap wearing a ring like this. I feel like a million dollars.'

'You are,' he said, 'more precious than a million dollars. Infinitely more precious.'

On the station platform Gabriel Considine took Deirdre O'Dare's face between his hands and kissed her speechless.

381

Chapter Fifteen

The next day, before heading off to work, she phoned her mother.

'Oh my God,' said Rosaleen. 'I'm going to be a grandmother.'

'And I'm head over heels in love, mum,' Deirdre sang down the phone. 'I'm doing the right thing. Believe me.'

Her mother was having trouble taking it all in. 'And you're going to live in Carrowcross House?'

'Yes. You should see it! It's stunning. We'll probably have the reception there.'

'Is this going to be a big wedding, Deirdre?'

'No. We want to keep it dead simple. Just family and a few friends.'

'Have you met Gabriel's family?'

'Not yet. I'm dying for you to meet *him*, mum. He wants to take you and dad out for dinner next time he's in Dublin.'

'We'd better foot the bill.'

'He won't allow you to. I know him.'

'We'll have to, Deirdre. We still owe him for all that work he did on the boundary wall.'

*   *   *

Later Deirdre arrived on set to find an admiring group of film people clustering around Sophie, who was showing off a diamond engagement ring. They were all going 'ooh' and 'aah' and congratulating her like mad. This was awkward. The entente cordiale between the two actresses was still at a delicate stage. Deirdre wasn't sure that by announcing her own engagement she wouldn't be upstaging her erstwhile enemy. Perhaps it would be sensible to keep schtum, take off the ring – which still felt strange on her finger – and stash it in her wallet?

But the matter was decided for her. 'Deirdre!' said the Second Assistant, catching sight of her as she hovered on the periphery of the group. 'These arrived for you!' He ran up the steps of a trailer and reappeared with a huge bunch of white roses. They were Vendellas.

'Wow!' Attention was suddenly diverted away from Sophie *en masse*. 'You must be someone's brown-eyed girl,' came a voice from the little crowd that was gathering round her. She'd heard those words before. They were what the florist's van driver had said the day he'd delivered Rory's birthday roses. 'Who are they from?' asked another voice, as she detached the small white envelope from the cellophane that swathed the flowers. She dropped it, then stooped and picked it up again with clumsy fingers. She took out a little card covered with florist's careful blue biro, and scanned it: *PS. I love you two*, she read. Then she gave a huge sigh of relief and laughed out loud. 'They're from Gabriel,' she said.

'Who's Gabriel?' came one of the curious voices.

'He's my fiancé,' said Deirdre, taking care not to look at Sophie.

'What? Don't tell me you got engaged at the weekend as well?' someone asked incredulously.

Deirdre smiled. 'Yes. I did.'

'Give us a look at the ring!'

She held out her left hand.

'Holy shit! I've never seen such a perfect emerald!'

'Hey! It's even bigger than Sophie's!'

Deirdre finally allowed herself to meet Sophie's hostile green stare. She gave an almost imperceptible *moue* of apology before returning her attention to the gobsmacked group of people admiring her ring. But Sophie couldn't conceal her curiosity for long. Within thirty seconds she had insinuated herself through the crowd that surrounded Deirdre. She waited until all of them had drifted away before voicing an opinion. 'Mm. Not bad,' she said.

'Wait till you see the earrings,' Deirdre almost said, but didn't. She didn't want this uneasy truce to explode in her face.

'Did you tell him?' asked Sophie directly, without a trace of coyness.

'Yes.'

'What did he say?'

Deirdre showed Sophie the florist's card, and the other actress allowed herself a smirk. 'Sweet. You're a lucky girl, Deirdre.' Deirdre knew that Sophie was sincere simply because she normally went to such extreme lengths to affect an attitude of complete indifference towards Deirdre O'Dare. Once upon a time she wouldn't have been able to bring herself to look at the ring, or to show any interest at all in Deirdre's affairs.

It felt very strange to be on open terms with Sophie. There had been so little candour in their relationship to date that it was almost as if they'd divested themselves of suits of armour and were going around naked. It wasn't a particularly nice feeling, but the suits of armour had been getting so heavy that it was quite a relief to be rid of them.

'They've changed the schedule, by the way,' said Sophie, turning her attention away from Deirdre's ring back to her own. Deirdre gushed on cue. It was her turn to do the admiring, and she did it – she hoped – with gratifying effusiveness.

'What are we doing instead?' asked Deirdre when she felt she'd done sufficient 'dazzled by the brilliance of Sophie's engagement ring' acting. 'We were meant to be doing that scene on horseback today, weren't we? I hope that one's gone. I climbed Croagh Patrick yesterday, and I don't think I'd have the strength to kick a cat, let alone a great brute of a horse.'

'It's been cancelled. The horse got colic or something. We're doing the scene where we're picking flowers in the garden and sticking them in each other's hair instead.'

'The one where I confide in you that I'm with child by the local squire?'

'Yes. And I tell you I'm affianced to my long-term love.'

They exchanged looks. 'Well, you know what they say, Sophie, don't you?'

'What do they say?'

'Truth is stranger than fiction,' said Deirdre.

And the two actresses turned as one and made their way towards make-up.

* * *

Later that day she rang Sally Ruane. 'Sally? I've got news for you. I'm getting married.'

There was a slight hesitation at the other end of the phone. 'Married? Let me guess. To Angel Gabriel?'

'Yes.'

Sally breathed a little sigh of relief. 'Phew. Glad I got that right. Congratulations, Deirdre.'

'Thanks, Sally. I'm wildly happy.'

She could hear the smile in Sally's voice. 'Good.'

'I'm expecting a baby.'

There was another pause. Then: 'Wow!' said Sally. 'This is all happening very fast. I'm having trouble taking it in. First things first. Does the BBC know you're pregnant?'

'The money men must know. The doctor who did my medical told me they'd have to fork out for extra insurance. I kept it under wraps for a while, but it'll be common knowledge soon.'

'When are you due?'

'Beginning of February.'

'When's the wedding?'

'Well, we have to give the State three months' notice, so it'll be October some time. The sooner the better. I want an outdoor ceremony, and the weather might be dodgy around then.'

'Or stunningly beautiful. Remember the Indian Summer we had last year? Where are you planning on holding it?'

'The civil ceremony will be in the registry office in Castlebar. The blessing will be by Gabriel's brother in Murrisk Abbey on Clew Bay. Do you know it? It's a beautiful ruin.'

'It was built by the O'Malleys, wasn't it?'

'Yes. They say that Grace got married there.'

'Why is Gabriel's brother doing the blessing?'

'He's a Franciscan friar.'

'You are an incurable romantic, Deirdre.'

'I know.' She hugged herself and laughed down the phone. 'Now. Down to business. What am I going to do about the soap?'

'They're not going to be wild about the fact that you're pregnant. When will you start to show?'

'Around the beginning of October.'

'Have I your go-ahead to phone them right away and advise them of this?'

'Absolutely.'

'Good. They'll need a couple of months to re-jig storylines. How do you feel about continuing?'

'I'm happy to accommodate them, Sally, whatever way I can, but come October I'm going to be living in the wilds of Mayo, so commuting is going to be a

387

problem. They might want to write me out.'

'Have you a problem with that?'

'No. No problem whatsoever. I was getting a bit sick of Amber, to tell you the truth. If they can dream up an exciting death for her I'd be very happy.'

'You're absolutely sure about this, Deirdre? Do you want twenty-four hours to think about it?'

'No, no, no. I'm absolutely sure. I'm a very happy bunny.'

'You certainly sound it,' said Sally.

* * *

That night she told Bart. For a fraction of a second she thought he looked unsure. Then he gave her a great smacking kiss on the lips. 'He's a sound geezer,' he said. 'Anyone who's into Radiohead is OK by me. I hope you'll be very happy.'

She phoned round all her friends, including Eleanor, and Maeve in Stratford. Everyone was initially stunned by the news that Deirdre O'Dare was marrying landed gentry, but her wild enthusiasm soon reassured them. However, it didn't reassure her father, who had been quite staggered by the news. In order to prove to him that Gabriel was honourable, dependable and a totally brilliant catch, Deirdre booked a table for four in a Malaysian restaurant in Temple Bar. Deirdre could tell that Rosaleen was smitten instantly. She went into flirtatious mode bigtime, but Deirdre didn't mind. Rory and her mother had flirted with each other incessantly, so she was used to it. She spend the best part of the evening talking to her father – something she hadn't done for a long time. He wasn't the most expansive individual on the face of the planet, but he made it clear that he was going to miss her.

'But I've been living away from home for years now, dad. It's hardly going to make much difference whether I'm living in Dublin or in Mayo.'

'I know, Deirdre. But at least when you're in Dublin you can hop on the DART and be out to us in forty minutes any time you need mollycoddling. Westport's a long haul. There'll be no chance of running home to Mummy and Daddy when things go wrong the way you used to.'

'When things go wrong? There's no chance of that. Anyway, Gabriel's brilliant at mollycoddling.'

'Still. I'd like to think that your boring old fart of a father might get a look in from time to time. *I'll* miss mollycoddling you even if you don't. And so will your mother. You're our only little girl, remember.'

'I know. But there's the cottage in Carrowcross. Any time you come west we'll practically be neighbours! You mustn't worry, Dad. And just think – you'll be able to babysit!'

Jack smiled. 'I'm a bit out of practice.' The waiter was clearing plates, and Jack smiled again when he saw the way the youth looked at his daughter. 'Hell. I just called you a little girl. Bit of a misnomer. You've grown up beautifully, Deirdre.'

She leant over and kissed his cheek, and Jack looked embarrassed, as he always did when he was choked up. He cleared his throat, and then he said, 'You've no worries about the baby, Deirdre? Everything's OK?'

'Everything's hunky-dory. Gabriel's setting me up with a first-class obstetrician. I suppose I'll start to worry when it's born, though. And then there's toddlerhood and adolescence to get through. Aagh, Dad! When do you *stop* worrying about them?'

'Never,' said Jack.

*   *   *

The next few months were crazy.

The BBC series wrapped, and Deirdre went straight back into *Ardmore Grove*. The executive producer had agreed to write her out, and the script editor came up with a brilliant death scene for her. It was her swan song as an actress, she realized, for a couple of years, anyway. Her mother had warned her that she might miss her career, but Deirdre had pooh-poohed the notion.

'I want to devote at least two years to the baby,' she said. 'I might think about going back to work then, but in the meantime I've a load of screenplay ideas to be getting on with. I can't imagine a more idyllic existence – living in the West of Ireland with a gorgeous husband and a brand-new baby and a little laptop to work on when I feel inspired to do some writing.'

Deirdre divided her time between Dublin and Mayo. She travelled the route so often that she got to know the ticket inspectors on the train by name. On her last day on the soap the cast congregated in the pub to buy her a farewell drink. She allowed herself two glasses of Guinness, and then stuck to water. It was the end of September, and she was beginning to show. She loved the way her belly had swollen, and she loved the little fluttering movements she could feel inside. Her morning sickness had stopped and she knew she looked wonderful. She had that pregnant glow that she'd so often read about – and occasionally seen – on other women.

Jean-Claude Valentin stopped by her table. She had had very few dealings with him since the soap resumed – in fact, they had ignored each other studiously. 'I hope you will not mind if I make a personal remark, Deirdre. You look very, very beautiful. Your fiancé is a very lucky man.'

She smiled at him. She was feeling too good to be snotty with him, and anyway, the incident in the hotel room had become even funnier in retrospect. She thought she might write it into one of her screenplays. 'Thank you, Jean-Claude,' she said.

'For you.' He set a gift-wrapped parcel down on the table in front of her. 'For your wedding night.'

'Oh. Um. Thanks very much. Shall I open it now?'

'Why not?'

She untied the ribbon from the gift-wrap, suddenly feeling a bit apprehensive. She remembered the last time she'd unwrapped a present from Jean-Claude Valentin. What if it was that tacky 'Wedding Night' outfit that had been featured in the

Scandalous Scanties catalogue – the one with the flimsy nylon bridal skirt that was split to the crotch? Surely Jean-Claude would have enough cop-on not to embarrass her like that in front of her friends?

When she removed the gift-wrap she could see a stray wisp of white lace sticking out of tissue paper. She raised horrified eyes to his. He made the connection instantly. 'No, no! Do not fear, Deirdre,' he stammered, looking as appalled as she was. 'Please – allow me.' Jean-Claude leant down and pulled away the layers of tissue paper. Underneath was a pillow sheathed in an exquisite white lace pillow-case with pale pink embroidered roses. 'Victorian,' said Jean-Claude, with evident pride at his good taste. 'And the pillow is of finest goose-down.'

'Thank you, Jean-Claude. It's beautiful. I'm really touched that you should give me such a thoughtful present.' She *was* genuinely touched. He had obviously made a huge effort to find something for her that would counterbalance the tackiness of his earlier gift. She stood up and kissed his cheek.

He smiled down at her. 'I cannot put my hand on my heart and say *je ne regrette rien*, but I can try a little to make up for past mistakes. I wish you all the best, Deirdre.'

'Thank you, Jean-Claude. It's a lovely present.' And she kissed his cheek again before sitting back down between Sophie and Cressida. Sophie was leafing through some glossy bridal magazine which displayed a beaming dame wearing a white meringue on the front.

'Mm,' she said. 'This'll be useful.'

'What are you reading about?' asked Deirdre idly.

'It's a wedding planner. Look, it counts you down. "Six to eight months,"' she read. '"Now's the time for you and your fiancé to sit down and work out a budget, draw up a guest list, decide on a menu, book your honeymoon and think about the décor for your new house." Of course, you don't have time to do all that, Deirdre.' She turned the page. 'Let's see – five months, four, three, two, one month – ah, here's your bit. "A *fortnight* ahead: arrange the seating plan; book your make-up session and talk to the make-up artist about what you'll be wearing; have a trial run with your hairdresser; make sure your *trousseau* is complete . . ."'

What *trousseau*? thought Deirdre.

Sophie droned on. '"And have you remembered to plan accommodation for your out-of-town guests?"'

Oh, fuck, thought Deirdre. She hadn't, but she hoped Gladys had.

'This is really useful,' said Sophie. 'There's a special feature on Your Wedding Day Seating. Would you like to borrow it, Deirdre?'

'No thanks. We're not having a sit-down meal.'

'Oh? Just a buffet, is it?'

Just a buffet! 'Actually, Maeve's partner Jacqueline is doing the catering, so I imagine it will be pretty sumptuous.'

'Oh, look! What a gorgeous dress,' remarked Sophie, studying another of the meringue-wearing individuals that swarmed over the glossy pages.

'Although I'm not sure about the neckline. And she should keep her upper arms covered,' she added for good measure. Then she put down the magazine. 'What are you wearing, Deirdre?' she asked. It had been obvious that she'd been dying to ask Deirdre this question for weeks, and was delighted that an opportunity had arisen at last.

'Well, it's being specially made for me. By Marc O'Neill.'

'Oh?' said Sophie, trying not to sound impressed.

'Wow!' said Cressida. 'What's it like?'

'Well, you know the Botticelli painting *Primavera*?'

Sophie said, 'Mm,' in a non-committal way, and Cressida said, 'Is that the one with the three Graces and Cupid and Aphrodite and somebody flinging flowers about?'

'That's right,' said Deirdre.

'Let me guess,' said Sophie. 'You're dressing as one of the three Graces because Grace O'Malley got married in Murrisk Abbey.'

Cressida looked curiously at Sophie. 'She can't dress as one of the Graces, Sophie.'

'Why not?'

'Because they don't have any clothes on. Well, only completely transparent veils.'

'Oh, yes. I forgot,' said Sophie. 'In that case I suppose you're dressing as Aphrodite, Deirdre?'

'Yes. I went for the final fitting yesterday.'

'Oh! What's it like?' Cressida leant forward with interest while Sophie leant back and continued to leaf through her bridal magazine.

'It's beautiful. It's ivory silk – the very heavy burnished kind – and it has a coat of diaphanous silk over it. It's very simple, really, gathered at the bust with gold braid detail on the bodice, and it falls to my ankles. I've a kind of cape thing, too.'

'Same colour?'

'No. Old rose.'

'I would have thought you'd have opted for something with a drop waist,' said Sophie. 'To hide the fact that you're thickening a bit.'

'Actually we both wanted something that would emphasize my belly,' responded Deirdre. 'The silk does just that – it kind of drapes itself over the curve.'

'Like Aphrodite in the painting,' put in Cressida. 'She's pregnant, isn't she?'

'Yes.'

'What a lovely idea! Did you come up with it, or did Marc?'

'Neither of us did. It was Gabriel who suggested it.'

'Angel Gabriel,' said Cressida. 'God – I'm so jealous of you, Deirdre. And of you too, of course, Sophie,' she added quickly. 'What's your dress going to be like?'

'I don't have it yet. I'm not under as much pressure as Deirdre. I'll pay a visit to Harrods bridal department next time I'm in London and browse. I've a budget of four or five grand.'

'Holy shit. Does that include the tiara?' asked Cressida.

'Of course not.' Sophie gave her a scathing look.

'I'm borrowing the one that my sisters wore to their weddings. It's a kind of family tradition.'

'Oh? How old is the tiara?' asked Deirdre.

'Well, one of my sisters got married last year, and the other got married two years ago.'

'Yes?'

'So that makes the tiara two years old.'

Cressida and Deirdre studiously avoided looking at each other. 'Ah,' they said in unison.

* * *

It looked like the wedding was going to be more unwieldy than she'd originally planned. Gabriel had invited not just immediate family and friends, but cousins and aunts and uncles as well. Deirdre had always been crap at remembering people's names and faces, and she found this sudden descent of people on their quiet country retreat rather scary. 'Oh, I agree *absolutely*, mmbhbh,' she'd say to one cousin whose name she'd forgotten, and, 'Don't worry, I'll organize that for you straight away, mmbhbh,' to an elderly aunt who took exception to the tea Deirdre had served, and was insisting on Earl Grey.

'Do we have any?' she asked Gladys as she ransacked cupboards in the kitchen.

'Yes, I made sure to get some in. I suspected someone would be asking for it.' Deirdre thanked God for Gladys. She had been working in the house full time for the month coming up to the wedding, and she had been of incalculable help. Deirdre had only had a fortnight to get her act together – she'd been working on the soap until the last week in September, but when she'd had any time off she'd dashed down to Carrowcross to try to keep abreast of any further developments.

Any further developments! There seemed to be a million more every time she went there. There were painters and decorators in virtually every room. Gabriel had asked her to supervise that side of life, but there just hadn't been time, so he'd handed the chore over to an interior designer. The furniture that had been in storage in London had arrived. Some of the grander pieces Deirdre didn't much like, but she couldn't complain. She hadn't forked out a penny for the stuff.

'Remember how romantic it was wandering around this house in the days before we had any furniture?' she said to Gabriel one evening. She found it hard to believe that they had once lived happily in a library without books, a dining room without a dining table and a bathroom without a power shower. They were sitting listening to music in the library. The shelves were now lined with volume upon leatherbound volume, and the room was full of the kind of armchairs you would expect to see in a gentlemen's club in London.

'That was when I was an eligible widower,' he said, kissing her ear. 'I have to prove to my family that I can take good care of the mother of future generations of Considines.'

'I'm sure they know that from – you know – from the first time you were married. They know you took good care of Daisy.' She still found it difficult to say the name.

He put a finger to her mouth. 'Deirdre, please don't mention Daisy to any member of my family. *I* am over her death, you know that. I've been over it since the first time we made love.' He removed his finger and kissed her gently. 'But I'm not sure my father is. You see, he was–' he broke off, frowning. 'Oh, hell. I really didn't want to bring this up just before the wedding in case it got to you, but my father was – well, let's just say he was very fond of Daisy.'

'Oh, God. Oh, God, I'm sorry, Gabriel. I promise I won't breathe a word.' She let out a heavy sigh, immediately wishing she hadn't, and then got to her feet, twisting her cuff. 'Yikes! It's kind of weird being the second wife. What happens if I can't take Daisy's place that easily? Will there be any resentment towards me, do you think?'

'Good God – no. They're going to love you. And even if there *was* any acrimony, it's not as if we're living in each other's pockets. Once the wedding's over they'll all bugger off and leave you to get on with having your baby.'

'Gabriel?' She turned anxious eyes on him. 'They don't just see me as a walking incubator, do they? They do know that I want to be a working mother?'

'But you've given up your job, darling. You're not

planning on looking for acting work as soon as the baby's born, are you?'

'No, no – of course not. That's not an option, I know that.'

'Well, then. Where's all this "working mother" stuff coming from?'

'Well, I *am* going to start writing a new screenplay soon, and I intend to carry on working on it after the baby's born. That makes me a working mother, doesn't it?'

He shrugged. 'If you insist, darling. But it's not as if that's *real* work–'

'It *is* real work, Gabriel!' She was twisting her cuff harder now. 'I won't have you treat it as if it's just some kind of hobby that I indulge myself in, the way you indulge yourself in your dry-stone walls–'

The way he looked at her stopped her in her tracks. When he spoke his voice was very calm, very controlled. 'That's not a hobby, Deirdre, and it's not an indulgence. I think I told you once before – it's my therapy. I work very, very hard, darling. You might allow me some time out to chill the way I want to, occasionally.'

'I'm sorry! I know you do. Work hard, that is. It's just that I feel I'm entitled to some respect for the work I do, too.'

'And you'll get respect, Deirdre. Motherhood *is* hard work, I'm aware of that. You're not the only one who's been reading the parenting magazines.'

'But I'm not talking about motherhood! I'm talking about–'

'Put some more music on, will you Deirdre?'

She broke off and looked at him, appalled. They were having their first ever serious row only days away from their wedding!

'Oh my God,' she said.

'Let's stop this conversation immediately, before we start talking in ever-decreasing circles.'

'Darling, I'm sorry!' Tears welled up in Deirdre's eyes and she bit down hard on her lip. 'Oh, this is horrible!' She took his face between her hands and kissed him. 'It must be nerves, that's all. It's been a nightmarish couple of months and my hormones are all over the place.'

'Of course they are,' said Gabriel, kissing her back. 'And of course your screenplay writing is a proper job. But it's probably not a good thing to mention to my father. He thinks that anything to do with writing is rather dilettantish, unless you're writing for the *Spectator.*'

Deirdre laughed and headed towards the CD rack. 'What do you feel like listening to?' she asked. 'I tell you what – as a special treat I'll allow you to listen to Radiohead.'

'I don't have any Radiohead,' said Gabriel. 'I hate that band.'

Deirdre stopped dead. 'But you told Bart you loved them,' she said.

'I was being nice. You told me at an early point in our relationship that the only disadvantage about your flat in Dublin was that you had a neighbour who had a penchant for Radiohead. I put two and two together, and decided it must be Bart.'

'But why did you lie?'

'I wouldn't call it a lie, Deirdre. More a strategic manoeuvre. I wanted your friend to like me.'

'Oh.'

'And he did, and you liked the fact that he liked me. So I was just keeping everybody happy. Whoever said, "You can fool some of the people some of the time, but you can't fool all of the people all of the time" was way off the mark. You damn well can fool all of the people all of the time if you work hard enough at it.' He smiled at her. 'Bach,' he said. 'Then come back here and kiss me again.'

* * *

The day before the wedding was spent sorting out Gabriel's family's itinerary. Those who hadn't already arrived needed to be driven from Knock airport and given lunch before being dispatched to Newport House, where half a dozen rooms had been booked for them. Deirdre had suggested that some of them stay at Carrowcross House and was glad when Gabriel decided against it.

'You've got enough on your plate without my family making demands on you,' he'd said. 'Anyway, none of the guest rooms has been properly furnished yet. I don't want to put you under the additional pressure of finding furniture. You'll just opt for the first thing you see and spend the rest of your life regretting it every time you walk into a spare room and confront some monstrous chiffonier that you can't stand the sight of.'

Deirdre didn't bother telling him that she already thought some of the grander pieces weren't really to her taste. It wasn't fair on him. Gabriel had made it plain from the outset that he had no real interest in painting and decorating and the cosmetic side of setting up a home. It was chiefly the exteriors of buildings that interested him.

After a day spent smiling and being charming and serving Earl Gray and gin and tonics, Deirdre needed a break. She'd found Gabriel's father particularly hard work because he was partially deaf. 'Your Irish accent doesn't make it any easier, my dear,' he'd said to her. Deirdre had tried hard to sound posher, but it didn't seem to make any difference. She was relieved to find herself at last standing on the steps of the house, waving the cortège of cars off down the driveway.

'Good girl,' Gabriel said, turning to her. 'You managed that beautifully. What did you think of my sister?'

'She's lovely.'

'She remembers you from that night in Quay Cottage. She told me she thought you had class.'

'I haven't a patch on her, Gabriel.' Deirdre sat down on the step. 'It's a pity she decided not to bring the children. They could have been bridesmaids.'

'It's not really a bridesmaids kind of wedding, is it?'

'No,' she agreed. 'Actually, I'm glad we decided

against complicating things too much. Sophie's wedding's being planned as meticulously as a military operation. She's having six bridesmaids and a matron-of-honour and two flower-girls.' Deirdre could hardly believe that Sophie Burke was coming to her wedding tomorrow.

'What's the difference between a bridesmaid and a flowergirl?'

'I haven't a clue.'

There was a pause. Then: 'What did you think of Hugo?' asked Gabriel.

Hugo was Gabriel's brother. 'Oh, he's gorgeous, Gabriel. I'm so glad he's going to perform the blessing. His soul shines out of his eyes.' Gabriel's brother, the Franciscan monk, had the kindest eyes she had ever seen. He was also devastatingly handsome, which she found rather unnerving in a holy man.

'And what did you think of my father?'

She paused. 'Well, he seems like a very, um – what's the right word? A very–'

'He's an irascible old man,' said Gabriel. 'You don't have to be polite, Deirdre. He was very charming once, but he's lost it. When my mother died he became embittered overnight. You were brilliant with him. Incredibly diplomatic. That must have been hard work.'

She smiled up at him. 'Yes, it was a bit,' she admitted. Then she stretched herself, and dug her fingers into the muscles over her buttocks. Her back sometimes gave her a bit of trouble, especially when she'd been standing a lot. 'Do you know what would do me the world of good?' she said.

'What?'

'A stroll up the headland.'

'You do that.' He looked at his watch. 'I won't join you. I have some last-minute business calls to make. I'll have to get them out of the way now, I won't get a chance for another fortnight.' They had taken a house in the South of France for their honeymoon. 'You don't mind, do you?'

'No. I don't mind.'

In fact, the notion of some time to herself after the mêlée of the afternoon was a very welcome one. She could do with some breathing space between one flurry of activity and the next. The prospect of what the next day held for her was beginning to be a little terrifying. She walked down the drive and then veered off and took the short cut, leaving the garden through the gap in the wall the way she used to do as a child. Then she crossed the landbridge and went up over the headland to sit and breathe in the heady sea air.

The baby moved inside her and she imagined it floating in its warm sac of fluid, intoxicated by the oxygen coming into her bloodstream from the Atlantic breeze. Below her lay the two cottages – her family's and Eleanor's. Eleanor was in her garden now, but she was too absorbed in whatever she was doing to see Deirdre wave. She turned and looked down at Carrowcross Cottage. She'd only been back there once since her illness, to close it up. She realized now, with a sudden rush of nostalgia, that she would probably never stay in it again.

She had to say goodbye to this little house where she had embarked on the affair with the man who was to become her husband in the morning. Imagine if he had never come to repair the boundary wall! It was unlikely she would ever have met him. She'd be back living in her flat in Dublin, cycling through filthy traffic to work every day, worrying about how many episodes of the soap opera she'd have to do to cover her overdraft, listening to Janine Heeney's mean voice telling her *exactly* how the Heeney Holidays in Hell scripts should be read.

On an impulse, she started to run down the hill, revelling in the springy feeling of the turf under her feet and the wind in her hair. Halfway down she skidded and nearly fell. She took the rest of the descent on cautious feet. Gabriel was always giving out to her about the fact that she tended to hurtle around all over the place instead of taking things at an easier pace.

She reached the gate and vaulted the top one. Gabriel was right. She should remember that she was responsible for two lives now. She'd negotiate the bottom gate more circumspectly. The bolt slid back with a bit of an effort. It was beginning to rust over. No-one had been near the place for months. The boundary wall was still unfinished. Deirdre vaguely wondered when Gabriel would get around to working on it again.

Suddenly the robin raised its warning signal,

scolding her from the sally bush. She wandered further into the garden and stood by the sea wall for several minutes, watching the bay. No otters came. Then she turned towards the cottage. It was a pity she hadn't brought the key. Her mother and father would be staying there tomorrow. She could have aired it for them.

Through the glass doors of the verandah she could see something lying on the floor. She climbed the steps and looked down at it. It was an air mail envelope with a United States stamp. It was addressed to her in Rory McDonagh's untidy handwriting. She stopped breathing and stood there staring at it, her palms pressed against the glass. She had no key. She couldn't get her letter. What was she to do?

Her breath came again then, raggedly. Feeling dizzy suddenly, she sat down on the step and put her head in her hands. Maybe he'd been trying to get through to her on the phone, as well? She remembered all the times she'd heard the strident ringing of the phone when she'd been lying in a fever, too ill to answer. Gabriel had said he'd called, but the calls couldn't *all* have been from him. Yes. It became increasingly obvious to her that Rory had been trying to contact her by phone as well. Oh, God. How could he do this to her? Write to her the night before her wedding? Had he found out about it? Was he trying to make her change her mind at the last minute?

Maybe he had decided to ask her to join him in LA! She remembered how gutted he had looked when he'd put her into the Daimler outside Ashford Castle. Maybe they really were destined to be together, like Cathy and Heathcliff. The fact that she'd followed her impulse to visit the cottage this evening was a sign. It wasn't too late. But when had the letter arrived? She squinted at it through the glass. She couldn't make out the date on the postmark. Maybe it had been lying there for months. She knew just one thing: she needed to read that letter before the morning.

A sudden brainwave struck her. She ran down to the shed at the bottom of the garden and pulled the door open with difficulty. The timber had swollen and the door was jammed against the lintel. Inside there was the usual jumble of summer house stuff – an old lilo, deckchairs, rusting tins of paint, buckets and spades that had been there since she was a child, her bike, which she hadn't bothered bringing back to Dublin. She finally found what she was looking for under a canvas windbreaker – a mouldering cardboard box of ancient tools. Deirdre rummaged through the box, selected a long screwdriver and took it back up to the verandah. Squatting down, she pushed the blade under the door and carefully tipped the corner of the envelope with it, coaxing it towards the slit between door and floor. It seemed to take for ever, but her patience was being rewarded. The envelope was slowly inching its way towards her. She was glad it was air mail. Anything thicker might not have made it through the narrow gap. A hint of pale blue paper manifested itself on her side of the door. One more gentle push with the chisel would do the trick – she'd be able to pull the letter through with her nails.

Then she heard the squeak of the rusty bolt on the garden gate. She tossed the chisel into a bush and sat up straight with her back to the verandah door.

'Thought I'd find you here,' said Gabriel, as he rounded the corner. 'Saying farewell to childhood memories?'

Deirdre nodded. She couldn't trust herself to speak. She knew she had gone bright red in the face.

'Any sign of the otters?'

She shook her head.

'Shame. It would be nice to see them on the night before our wedding. Kind of auspicious.' He leant down and kissed her. 'You taste of salt,' he said. Then he held out a hand and helped her up from the step. 'Time to go home, darling. It's getting chilly.'

Gabriel wrapped his right arm around her shoulders and escorted his bride-to-be out of the garden and through the gate. The bolt slid home with the harsh, grinding sound of rusty metal.

*　　*　　*

Later that night she lay beside him in the four-poster bed with burning eyes. She couldn't sleep. Her mind's eye kept focusing on the pale-blue envelope lying on the floor of the cottage on the other side of the peninsula. She had to know what that letter contained. She turned her head on the pillow and looked at Gabriel. He had one arm thrown back above his head and his breathing was even.

She slid out of bed and crossed the room on soundless feet, opening and closing the door with smooth fingers. Downstairs she slid into a Barbour and wellies, jammed a tweed cap onto her head for good measure, and picked up a torch. It was cold outside, and pitch black. There was no moon tonight, and no stars. She was glad there was still no gravel on the driveway. Her passage towards the big gates of the house was cushioned by weeds and moss.

Once beyond them, she switched on the torch and started to run. Night creatures called to her, and she was aware of the occasional fluttering of alarm in the ditches that bordered the road. The beam of her torch bounced off hedgerows as she ran, pallidly illuminating skeletal thorn bushes.

She vaulted both gates. The letter still lay there, one pale-blue corner sticking out from under the door. She dug a nail into the edge and drew the envelope out gingerly until she had enough purchase to pull with her fingers. She shone the torch onto the stamp and just made out the postmark. It was smudged, but it was clear that the letter had been lying there since August. She resisted the temptation to tear it open and read it there and then by torchlight. She needed to get back – dawn was beginning to inch its way over the horizon. Somewhere out on the bay a heron shrieked, making her jump. She stuffed the letter in her Barbour pocket and made the return journey to Carrowcross House on wobbly legs.

She was very out of breath when she reached the back door through which she'd left. She turned on the light, poured herself a glass of water and sat down at the kitchen table. Then she slid the letter out of the envelope:

I have a memory of you, reclining like a princess, stark naked on a bed in a castle. You really looked the part, O'Dare. I should have known you were rehearsing for the most rewarding role of your career. The lady of the house: the châteleine, no less. How astute of me to prophesy it! Maeve tells me you're marrying the local squire. Well done! I've a feeling that he will shower you with jewels and keep you in the manner to which you will – I have no doubt – become accustomed to pretty sharpish. I mean it when I wish you every joy and happiness in your new life, and trust that you will provide said squire with lots of little princes and princesses in time-honoured aristocratic tradition. Meanwhile, I treasure that memory of the girl I loved play-acting at being a princess in a fairy tale castle one thaumaturgical (look it up, airhead!) April evening.

Love, R. x

The girl I loved. Deirdre remained sitting at the kitchen table, looking at Rory's scrawl on the pale-blue page. There was no return address in the top right-hand corner, and no contact telephone number. She stood up and fetched a box of matches from a drawer, and then she moved to the sink. The first match wouldn't strike. The second burnt right down, but only a corner of the paper took. At the third attempt the blue paper flared up in flames. She held it above the sink and let it burn, watching the letter twist and turn in her fingers. Then she turned on the tap and washed the charred remains down the plughole.

Before she slid back into bed beside Gabriel she pulled the curtains back from the window. A black-bird had started to sing and pale dawn was smudging the east. The other side of the world from Rory. She remembered the stupid postcard he'd sent her on her birthday with 'Wild West' written on it. Well. He could spend the rest of his life indulging in his favourite pursuits in the wild western States of America.

She turned away from the window and noticed that the pellucid early morning light was beginning to infiltrate the corner of the bedroom where a heavy Victorian wardrobe stood. Her Renaissance wedding dress hung on the door like the ghost of a bride long dead.

Chapter Sixteen

Apart from two witnesses chosen at random, it was just the two of them in the registry office in Castlebar. The procedure was routine, the solicitor who married them friendly and positive.

Afterwards Gabriel drove to Murrisk Abbey, which lay at the foot of Croagh Patrick, to join the wedding crowd that had gathered at midday under a heavy grey sky. Dense cloud had draped itself over the mountain like a giant's duvet. Deirdre stepped down from the Land-Rover and proceeded up the nave of the ruined abbey on her new husband's arm as if in a dream. Among the relatively unfamiliar faces of the Considine family there were her own loved ones, all smiling. Her mother and father, who had travelled down that morning. Maeve, who had flown over from Stratford specially. There was Jacqueline Mercier, Maeve's partner. She had arrived at the crack of dawn, befriended Gladys and waved a magic wand over the dining table. There were Sophie Burke and Cressida, and all her old friends from college. Sally Ruane. Eleanor Devereux, elegant in grey silk. Gladys, still managing to smile, even though she'd been up since five. Bart, with headphones dangling around his neck. David Lawless, looking as sexily inscrutable as ever. Eva, with Dorcas at her breast.

When Hugo had given the couple his blessing, Eva stepped forward. Deirdre had asked her to choose something beautiful to read at the ceremony. A silence fell as the actress cleared her throat and spoke in that achingly beautiful, utterly unique voice.

> Midway, along this path of life we tread,
> I woke bewildered in a dark wood
> To find the road I knew was lost, misread:
> No shaft of sunlight pierced to where I stood.
> Old fears stir in my soul when I recall
> Those dense black trees, night's sentinels,
> That sullen, savage thicket blocking all,
> A death rung slowly upon silent bells.
> Some spiteful dreamchild must have lured me there
> For sleep hung heavy in the drowsy air.
> But I moved on, in blindness, through the maze
> Till I emerged beneath a mountain's dawn
> And looking up I saw the morning's rays:
> This traveller's foot was on the road for home.

Deirdre kept her eyes downcast. She couldn't bring herself to look at Eva, who was standing at the top of the nave looking down at the bride, her face radiant, Dorcas on her hip. Deirdre's throat felt more and more constricted as she listened, and when the actress had finished, her eyes were brimming. Then Gabriel turned to her, put a finger under her chin and lifted her face to his. She smiled at him through the great gloopy tears that were spilling down onto her cheeks, and when the couple kissed, the congregation burst into spontaneous applause just as the rain swept in from the mountain.

* * *

This was Carrowcross House as Deirdre had always pictured it should be. There were women in beautiful dresses drifting through the rooms and elegantly dressed men lolling against the enormous fireplaces. The only thing missing were the children she'd imagined, pushing open the French windows to tumble through into the garden, laughing and shouting. But there would be children in future years – her children and Gabriel's. She felt the baby flutter inside her and laid a hand on the smooth, heavy silk draped over her belly, and smiled to herself.

A passing waiter offered her a glass of champagne and she took one from him gratefully, glad to be able to celebrate at last. She was beginning to feel terribly tired, and she knew it wasn't just on account of her pregnancy. What crazy impulse had sent her careering round Carrowcross in the dead of night to retrieve a letter from a former lover? She cringed when she thought how reckless she'd been. What if Gabriel had woken to find her gone? What if he had investigated – gone out to find her running along country lanes on the eve of her wedding wearing nothing but a Barbour and wellies and a tweed cap? He would have thanked his lucky stars he'd found out in the nick of time that his bride-to-be was as loopy as the first Mrs Rochester.

'You look so beautiful.' Eva was at her side, minus the ubiquitous Dorcas, who was snoozing behind the curtains of the four-poster bed upstairs.

'Thank you.' Deirdre turned shining eyes on her friend. 'And thank you so much, Eva, for reading that beautiful piece at Murrisk. What's it from?'

'It's Dantë. From the *Divine Comedy*. Isn't it extraordinary?' Eva grabbed a quail's egg from a passing platter and bit into it. 'David was inspired to write his own version not long after we were reunited, specially for me. It's a piece which conjures up huge, life-enhancing changes of direction, and that's why I felt it was so apt for you today. Your life is going to be so *different*, Deirdre, isn't it?'

'Yes,' admitted Deirdre. 'It is. Do you think I should be scared?'

'No, no, no! Embrace change! Change is positive! Routine is the awful deadener.'

David joined them and kissed Deirdre, and she blushed as she always did when David paid her any attention. 'It's a small world,' he said. 'I know your sister-in-law.'

'Sarah?'

'Yes. She's a patron of one of the opera companies I direct for.'

'Where is she?' asked Eva, looking around the library.

'Over there.' He raised a hand at Sarah, who was

415

standing by the baby grand on the other side of the room, leafing through sheet music. She put the music back on the mahogany stand when she saw David, and started to make her way across the room. Again Deirdre was struck by her remarkable, Renaissance beauty.

'What an extraordinarily good-looking family they are,' said Eva, not bothering to lower her voice as usual. 'That monk brother is stunning. It's a shocking waste.'

'What is?' asked Deirdre, hoping that by keeping her voice down, Eva would lower hers corresponding-ly. Fat chance.

'That he's not allowed to have sex. He could have made thousands of women blissfully happy.'

* * *

As the party wore on, Deirdre's back began to get at her. She stole Dorcas from Bart, who was playing Radiohead to the child through his headphones, and sat down on a couch in the library, surveying her guests with interested eyes and telling Dorcas stories about them. Dorcas seemed to be particularly amused by Sophie, who was going around as if she was casing the joint, sliding surreptitious looks at antiques and doing loads of mental arithmetic. On a number of occasions Deirdre had observed her picking up objects and checking out hallmarks and signatures, and coming out of rooms where she really had no business to be, making feeble excuses like, 'Oh – I thought this was the bathroom! I didn't realize it was your bedroom, Deirdre.'

'It's not,' Deirdre had said. 'That's Gladys's room.'

'Who's Gladys?'

'My housekeeper. She's going to move in once the baby's born, to give me a hand. This is my room.' Deirdre couldn't resist it. She pushed open the bedroom door and let Sophie have a look.

'Oh. Very. Um. Nice.' Sophie had walked into the centre of the room with all the nonchalance of a wooden puppet. The real give-away was the more strangulated than usual timbre of her voice, the timbre she always adopted when she pretended she wasn't having a problem with something. 'I was thinking of getting a four-poster like that made for me,' she articulated with difficulty. 'Maybe you could give me a phone number?'

'Not possible, I'm afraid. The person who made it is dead.'

'Oh. Shame. What was his name?'

'Um. Chippendale.'

Sophie had gone even more stiff.

Now she was talking to Lord Considine, probably boring him to death with details of her family tree. Gabriel's father had spent the entire day studiously ignoring his youngest son. He'd even gone so far as to examine the headstones in the abbey instead of listening to Hugo as he'd delivered the blessing. Deirdre was glad that Gabriel's family lived across the water. She didn't think she'd be able to handle the intricate, diplomatic tiptoeing that would be necessary every time she encountered a family member.

Sarah wandered over and sat down beside Deirdre. 'How are you feeling?' she asked.

'Fine. A little tired.'

'I'm not surprised. I found all my pregnancies exhausting.'

'It's strange, isn't it – how women's pregnancies differ? I remember Eva was brimful of energy all the way through hers. The first three months were awful for me – I suffered from chronic morning sickness. How did Daisy feel?'

'What do you mean?'

'Well, did Daisy have morning sickness?'

'Daisy?' There was a curious expression on Sarah's face. Too late Deirdre remembered that Gabriel had expressly asked her not to mention Daisy's name to any of his family. 'Daisy never had morning sickness because Daisy was never pregnant. It was the tragedy of her life. She wanted babies more than any woman I've ever met. So did Gabriel. You've made him incredibly happy, Deirdre.'

Just then Gabriel materialized in front of them. 'Give me that baby at once,' he said, taking Dorcas from his wife. Dorcas obligingly smiled and dimpled at him. 'You,' he said to her, 'are as compulsive a flirt as your mother.' Then he looked down at Deirdre and smiled. 'Go easy on the champagne, darling, won't you?' he said.

*　　*　　*

418

Much later, the last guests left. Those who could afford it were staying in Newport House, and everyone else was staying in bed-and-breakfasts in Westport. Deirdre felt oddly comforted by the knowledge that her mother and father were staying in the cottage just over the headland.

In the bedroom, she took off her Botticelli dress and hung it in the wardrobe, wondering if she would ever wear it again. Their luggage stood by the door. Tomorrow would be a long day. The prospect of a journey usually gave Deirdre a thrill of anticipation, but she was feeling so tired that the idea of negotiating airports all day filled her with dull dread.

Gabriel was lying back against the pillows, looking at her. 'Come here,' he said, reaching out for her. She crawled onto the bed and tucked herself in the crook of his arm. They lay in silence for a while, Gabriel idly tracing circles on her round belly. 'He's sleeping,' he said. 'He's tired, too – worn out with all the excitement of his mother and father's wedding.'

She smiled. Then: 'Gabriel?' she said. 'There's something rather awkward I really need to ask you.'

'Oh? What's that?'

'I know you asked me not to mention Daisy to any of your family, but I was talking to Sarah about pregnancies and it just sort of slipped out.'

The arm around her shoulder went rigid. 'What "slipped out"?' he asked. The way he put inverted commas around the words made her feel uneasy, suddenly.

'Well, I just happened to mention Daisy's pregnancy and Sarah said something – well – strange. She told me that Daisy had never been pregnant. She said she'd wished for it more than anything, but that she'd never conceived.'

He took ages to respond. Then: 'I see,' he said, and nothing else.

'So – *was* Daisy pregnant, Gabriel?' persisted Deirdre, feeling more and more unsettled. 'I'm sorry – I know it must hurt to talk about it, but–'

'Listen to me, darling.' Gabriel straightened up slowly and looked down at her with serious eyes. 'I have to tell you something. No-one knows this. No-one in my family. No-one living in the world except a Harley Street specialist. I have a problem. I have a problem with my fertility.'

'What – what do you mean?'

'I'm infertile.'

She was feeling numb with tiredness and very confused. 'I don't understand.'

'Hell.' Gabriel buried his face in his hands and sucked in his breath. Then he uncovered his face and looked at her again. 'Will you listen to me, Deirdre? Will you try to understand what I've gone through in the last few years?'

She nodded.

'I've been through a living hell,' he said. 'I've been in torment.' He took her hands in his. His tension was palpable. 'Daisy – Daisy and I couldn't understand why she wasn't conceiving. We'd tried for a baby from the day we got married. After a year she went to a doctor and found out it wasn't her problem. It was mine. I can't make babies. I will never have a child of my own.'

She looked at him with huge, disoriented eyes. 'You mean,' she said, 'you mean that this baby is definitely—'

He leant over and touched a finger to her lips. 'This baby is mine,' he said. 'If we say it often enough we'll believe it, darling. This baby is mine.'

She felt the baby move inside her. Rory's baby. Tears began to slide down her cheeks.

'Please don't cry, Deirdre. You mustn't let this make any difference to us. I told you that day on the mountain that the baby is my baby in my eyes. And if he's my baby in my eyes, then he's my baby in the eyes of the world. No-one will ever, ever dispute it. He will inherit the Considine title. I give you my word that he will.'

The Considine title? Deirdre had so rarely given a thought to the title that she was almost surprised at the reference. 'I don't care about the title, Gabriel. It means nothing to me. It's just—'

'Don't say that. Don't ever say that about our son's inheritance.'

Deirdre was almost frightened by his intensity. He must have seen the fear in her eyes because he softened his expression immediately. 'I know it's hard for you to understand,' he said. 'It's such an English thing – the whole notion of bloodlines and inheritance. That's why the realization that I could never father a child came as such a shock to me.

Imagine how my father would feel if he knew the Considine title would die with me!'

Deirdre's mind was beginning to work again. Of course! Gabriel was the baton carrier for the next generation of Considines! It was incumbent upon him to supply the heir and the spare. Except there would never be a spare, she realized, because she and Gabriel would not be able to have another child. She stared at him in disbelief. Oh, God – what was happening?

'I had completely resigned myself to the fact that I would never have a son,' continued Gabriel. 'I wasn't going to let the family know until after my father died. I had every intention of telling them then, so that between us we could unravel all the red tape of the inheritance laws. But as long as my father is alive, I have to allow him to have hope for the future. Can you understand that?' He smiled at her, and laid a hand on her belly. 'You are that future, Deirdre. You are my father's future and mine, too.'

She was angry, suddenly. Furiously, blazingly angry. 'You bastard!' she cried. 'You total fucking bastard! You married me for the baby! You didn't marry me for *me*! You married me for the *baby*!' She swept the counterpane to one side of the bed and slid herself off the mattress. In her rush to get away from him she landed heavily, twisting her ankle. She didn't care. She hobbled to the wardrobe and started rummaging wildly for something to put on.

'What are you doing?' He was beside her.

'Getting dressed.' She pulled on a denim shirt and started doing buttons up the wrong way.

'Why?'

'I'm going. I'm leaving.' The image of Carrowcross Cottage came into her mind and she broke down, weeping. 'I want my mother!' she cried. Then her knees buckled beneath her and she dropped onto the floor, wracked with sobs.

Gabriel gathered her in his arms. 'Hush, hush, darling. There, there. Calm down.' He was stroking her hair. 'I love you. I do. How could you think that I don't? How could you think that I would marry you just for the baby? I love *you*, Deirdre O'Dare. I think I've loved you from the moment I first set eyes on you laboriously cycling through Carrowcross pretending to be a German.'

She found herself making a noise that was half-sob, half-laugh.

'That day on the mountain, when I proposed? I had already made my mind up that I was going to marry you. I collected the engagement ring from the bank the same day I gave you my mother's earrings. I didn't ask you to marry me sooner because I needed to be sure you would accept – that you wanted it as much as I did. Do you believe me?'

She looked up into his black eyes for a long time before she nodded. She believed him. 'I'm sorry I doubted you, Gabriel. It's just that it seemed such a *calculating* thing to do.'

'I can understand why you might think that. Of course I can. I just think it was destined. You and me and the baby. There's a word for that. When you find the right person by accident. What is it?'

'Serendipity,' she said tiredly.

'I knew I could count on you to come up with it.' He stood up. 'Come back to bed, darling. You're shivering.'

She allowed herself to be escorted back to the confines of the four-poster. He tucked the cashmere blankets in around her. They had been a wedding present from Sarah. There was something else niggling in the back of Deirdre's brain, one last question. Sarah had said – of course! It had been the question of Daisy's pregnancy that had opened this whole confusing can of worms!

'Gabriel?' she said. 'You never answered my first question. Why ever did you tell me Daisy was pregnant?'

'Because she *was* pregnant,' he said. 'She was pregnant by artificial insemination. Donor sperm. We had just found out that the treatment had been successful.'

'Oh, God! How awful.'

He turned his head on the pillow and she saw a single tear travel down his face. 'If there is a heaven, Deirdre,' he said, 'Daisy is there with her baby. I told you before – if you repeat anything to yourself often enough, you can make it happen. You can believe. I believe in Daisy's heaven.'

Deirdre put out her hand and wiped the tear from his cheek. 'No tears for Daisy,' she said. 'You said that to me once.'

He smiled and took her in his arms. As she lay there waiting for sleep to come she felt the baby kick.

'The baby's woken up,' she murmured. 'All that shouting and screaming.'

'We mustn't allow that to happen again,' said Gabriel. 'It can't have done his emotional health any good.'

'No,' she agreed, not looking at him. She knew there was one huge issue they were both avoiding discussing.

What if her baby was a girl?

* * *

Their honeymoon in France was lazy and uneventful – just what they both needed after the furore of the past weeks. They ate and drank and swam and made love.

It was a real luxury to make love without having to use condoms. Deirdre realized that she'd never have to bother with all that messy condom business again. It was something of a relief. Rory had insisted that she take the morning-after pill after a couple of dodgy condom experiences. It seemed wildly ironic in the light of events now.

'Why did you use them if you knew you were firing blanks?' she asked Gabriel one day after they had made love in the swimming pool of the villa they had rented. 'Firing blanks' was how he himself described his infertility. Now that it was out in the open, they were able to discuss it in an easy and relaxed way. There was no taboo attached.

He gave her an incredulous look. 'Because I'm a

responsible, nineties kind of man, Deirdre. I told you I slept with a lot of women before I met you. I'm not in the business of spreading unpleasant diseases.'

'Oh, yeah,' she said, apologetically. 'I forgot. Most women's first concern is preventing pregnancy.'

Sometimes she thought with nostalgia of the babies she would never have, and then some kind of pragmatic streak in her would take over, and she'd wonder if it wasn't for the best. She knew that some women turned into full-time mummies when they had more than one child, and something told her that she wouldn't be very good at that.

Also, Eva had been frank enough to advise her of the downside of motherhood. 'It's bloody hard work,' she'd said. 'Especially if you're holding down a job as well. Working mothers are martyrs – and I'm one of the lucky ones who can afford a nanny.'

Sometimes she wondered what would have transpired if she hadn't had that conversation with Sarah – if she'd never uncovered Gabriel's secret – and she felt uneasy. She might have gone through the rest of her life believing that her child was Gabriel's, not Rory's. As it was, Lord Considine would live the rest of his life in a fool's paradise, believing that his grandson was the continuum of his bloodline. Well, why not, if it made him happy? Gabriel had said that day he'd proposed to her that it would be his child in the eyes of the world, and she supposed it was. And then she remembered something else he'd said once: *You damn well can fool all of the people all of the time if you work hard enough at it.*

*　　*　　*

It was strange to come back to unsettled weather after the glorious fortnight in the South of France, where it was still sometimes warm enough in the evenings to eat *al fresco*. Deirdre packed away all her sexy, floaty summer dresses, and resigned herself to looking lumpen in tracksuit bottoms and baggy shirts. Sweaters, too. Temperatures had plummeted, and heating the house was problematic. There were draughts everywhere. Deirdre took to either lighting a fire in the library, or working on her laptop in the kitchen, where the Aga sent out a wonderfully comforting warmth.

The second screenplay was coming along nicely. She felt more confident, and worked fast. She ignored the indulgent little smile she would occasionally notice hovering around Gabriel's lips when he came across her labouring over her keyboard. 'Do you have to work quite so hard, darling?' he asked. 'What's the hurry?'

'I want to get it finished before the baby comes,' she said. 'It's important that I do, Gabriel – I just know that if I don't I'll stick it in a drawer and never look at it again.'

So she worked every day, worrying her script like a terrier, until she felt it was ready to be printed out. The day she finished she left it on Gabriel's desk with a note saying: *I am too embarrassed to hand this to you in person. Please read it and tell me what you think. Your loving wife, Dxxx.* Then she went out for a long walk. She trudged the entire circumference of the peninsula, and called into Eleanor's for tea, feeling guilty that she hadn't visited her for so long.

Eleanor was gloomy about the weather. 'This is it now,' she said. 'We'll have to batten down the hatches between now and April. I rarely go out after November.'

'I don't mind the wind,' said Deirdre. 'As long as I'm well wrapped up. It sweeps all the cobwebs out of my brain. It's kind of exhilarating.'

'I'm too frail to go out walking on windy days,' said Eleanor. 'But I do know what you mean. It's really the rain that I can't take. Sometimes it rains and rains without letting up for days and days on end.'

By the time Deirdre left Eleanor's cottage it was raining on the other side of the bay. She heard it before she felt it, making little plipping sounds on the sea and denting the flat pewter surface of the water. It caught up with her as she crossed the landbridge, and she was glad to see the lights of Gabriel's Land-Rover heading towards her.

He pulled over and opened the passenger door for her. 'It's becoming a habit,' he said as she climbed in. 'Rescuing you from floods.'

'Sorry,' she said, shaking drops from her hair. Then she leant over and kissed him. 'Well?'

'Well what?'

'Did you get a chance to look at my screenplay?'

There was a fractional pause, and then Gabriel said, 'Yes. I did.'

'What did you think?'

He made a non-committal noise.

'You didn't like it?'

'Well, it's not really my kind of thing.'

'What do you mean?' She knew she was starting to sound prickly.

'You don't mind if I'm completely honest with you, Deirdre?'

Of course she minded! 'No,' she said in a careless voice. 'I don't mind.'

'I thought it was a bit juvenile.'

'Mm-hm?'

'I mean – what age group was it aimed at?'

'I dunno,' she said. 'Fifteen plus, I suppose.'

'Well, you know me. I don't go to movies much. I'm not really qualified to comment. It's what you'd call a screwball film, isn't it?'

'It's meant to be, yeah.' She couldn't keep the hurt out of her voice.

Gabriel turned to her with concern in his eyes. 'Oh hell, darling, I'm sorry. I don't mean to be negative – it's just that I saw how hard you worked on it, and I'd hate to think how disappointed you'd be to find you had wasted your time.'

'It's OK,' she said in a dull voice. 'You're right. It was a stupid idea. I don't know what made me think I'd have any talent as a screenwriter. It was bloody arrogant of me.'

'No, don't say that. Lots of actors experiment with writing, don't they? It was certainly worth a try, and you've a good ear for dialogue. You mustn't be too hard on yourself.'

The rain was falling in a steady drizzle now as the Land-Rover wound its way along the curve of the drive.

'What'll I do instead?' said Deirdre, looking out at the dripping trees. 'It's going to be a long winter. I'll have to dream up *some* way of keeping myself amused.'

'Why don't you spend some time exploring auction rooms?' suggested Gabriel. 'Remember you said that, once upon a time? That you'd love to scour auction rooms for Considine heirlooms? You could take classes in antique restoration.'

It seemed as good an option as any open to her. Deirdre sighed. 'Yeah, maybe I'll do that. I'll go to the library tomorrow and see what's on offer.'

* * *

The brochure outlining which evening classes were available locally fell open at flower arranging. Deirdre gave a hollow laugh. There wasn't a bad selection on offer, though. Cookery: she felt guilty that she wasn't able to put anything decent on a plate in front of Gabriel. He never cooked, but Gladys organized most of their meals, or they ate out. There was quite a lot of schmoozing to be done with Gabriel's clients, and he encouraged her to come along. She was an asset, he claimed, being young and beautiful and something of a celebrity. Her screen death in *Ardmore Grove* earlier in the autumn had had a big impact on television viewers all over the country. One of Gabriel's clients, on being introduced to her, had said, 'It's a pleasure to meet you, Mrs Considine. Or should I call you Amber? *Ardmore Grove*'s "smouldering temptress", what? Ha, ha, ha!' He'd sat beside her at dinner and whispered innuendoes to her all evening, keeping his gaze glued to her cleavage.

'It's tiresome for you, I know, darling,' Gabriel had said later. 'But I'm really grateful for your co-operation. There's no point in antagonizing these boys.'

She continued to flick through the brochure. Antique restoration, bee-keeping, campanology, dress-making, karate . . . screenplay writing.

Without hesitation, Deirdre took out her Filofax and scribbled down two telephone numbers. Within the hour she had enrolled in two evening classes a week. 'Two?' said Gabriel. 'You must be really keen. You'll be running your own antiques business soon!'

So on Tuesday nights, Deirdre hung out with a lot of ladies in Gucci loafers learning about French polishing and inlay and hallmarks. She had been asked to bring along a couple of pieces that she could work on ('You don't mind getting your hands a bit dirty, do you?' the lady organizing the class had asked brightly when she enrolled) and she'd found a little Queen-Anne table in a junk shop that needed sanding and polishing, and a dilapidated footstool. She'd nearly passed out when the dealer had told her how much they'd knock her back. What a racket, she'd thought as she'd scribbled a cheque from the joint account. The ladies in the class tried hard to be friendly to her, because she was the new girl. They'd all been attending classes on a weekly basis from earlier on in the autumn. 'It might be fun to work your own tapestry to re-cover the little footstool,' said one. 'Maybe you should go to classes in tapestry as well? Then you'd have a charming family heirloom.'

And on Thursday nights she hung out with an eclectic bunch of people and learnt about plot points and crosscutting and constructing dialogue. 'What did you learn tonight?' Gabriel would ask her when she got home. Deirdre always had to think fast to remember to say; 'Oh – how to repair beading,' instead of, 'Oh – all about dramatic resolution.' She took to recording the *Antiques Roadshow* and programmes about furniture restoration, but she never watched them.

Deirdre O'Dare was too busy working on her laptop.

Chapter Seventeen

They spent Christmas and the New Year in the big house – just the two of them together. Gabriel's sister had suggested that they go to her – she was going to be hosting a family Christmas – but Deirdre had expressed a preference for staying in Carrowcross. 'It'll be the only chance we'll ever have to spend Christmas together as a couple,' she'd said. 'Anyway, I'd find the journey very tough-going, Gabriel.'

Deirdre was now nearly eight months' pregnant, and was feeling pretty bloody awful. Backache was a constant problem, and she'd started getting heartburn. Her impatience for the whole thing to be over made it difficult to sleep at night, and she'd lie awake beside a sleeping Gabriel wondering about the birth and the baby that she would be holding in her arms in a very few weeks.

Rory's baby. She had tried vigorously to block the thought, from the moment she'd known, but it had proven impossible. *If you repeat anything to yourself often enough, you can make it happen. You can believe.* She remembered the sincerity with which Gabriel had invested those words on their wedding night. It hadn't worked. She spent hours lying beneath the canopy of the four-poster bed imagining what the baby would look like. Would he have her hazel eyes or Rory's green ones? Would he have her chestnut colouring or Rory's fair hair?

He was big, anyway. The obstetrician had told her when she'd gone for her last check-up that her baby would probably weigh in at around eight pounds. He'd also told her at her ultrasound scan that he could tell her the sex of the foetus, if she liked. She'd declined the offer.

In mid-January Gabriel was called away to London on business. 'If anything should happen,' he said, 'anything at all, let me know immediately. I'm not going to miss the birth of my boy for anything.'

Deirdre drove him to Knock airport simply because it was something to do. She was beginning to want to scream with boredom. She'd even started watching the recordings she'd made of the *Antiques Roadshow*, which she actually found quite entertaining. She loved the way the participants tried not to look as if they were remotely interested in how much their antique might fetch, and the look of sick disappointment that they couldn't conceal when told the piece might be worth 'forty or fifty pounds' instead of the four or five thousand they'd been expecting. *Blind Date* was something else she'd rediscovered. Rory had always mocked her for watching it.

She kissed Gabriel goodbye at departures and wandered towards the magazine shop. Magazines were about the only reading material she could concentrate on these days. She treated herself to

House and Garden and *Tatler* and *Harpers* and *Hello!* and wandered up to the cash desk to pay for them. On the way, the glossy magazines slipped out of her arms and skidded onto the ground, pages flapping. She bent down to retrieve them with difficulty.

'Nice ass.'

She looked up, preparing herself to make a scathing remark to the geezer responsible for the comment. She came out with absolutely nothing. Rory McDonagh was standing there looking down at her. She took a shaky breath and then she stood up very, very slowly, watching Rory's eyes take in her condition. He sucked in his breath almost as shakily as she had done, and then let it out again in a low whistle. 'Wow,' he said. 'A princess. Or a prince?'

'A prince,' she said. 'I think.' She'd nearly said, 'I hope.'

'When's it due?'

'Beginning of February.'

'Well, well, well.'

There was a long silence. Deirdre broke it. 'What are you doing here?' she asked.

'You're always asking me that question, O'Dare. I came back for New Year. To see the folks in Galway. What are *you* doing here?'

'I was seeing my husband off on the plane.'

'The local squire.' Rory smiled at her, narrowing his eyes. 'How uxorious is he?'

She managed a smile in return. 'He's extremely uxorious.'

435

'Hey! You know what it means!'

'Of course I do,' she retorted as airily as she could. 'It means "excessive fondness of one's wife".'

'And how uxorial are you?'

'You mean how good at wifely duties?'

'Mm-hm.'

'I do some better than others.'

'I can imagine.' He smiled at her again. 'You look fan-fucking-tastic, O'Dare. Come and have a drink with me. I've loads of time on my hands and I want somebody to amuse me. I've just heard that my flight's been delayed for the third time.'

'I can't have a drink,' she said. She couldn't go for a drink with Rory.

'Why not?'

'Because – because of the baby.'

'Oh, lighten up, Deirdre. One glass of Guinness isn't going to send it spiralling into Foetal Alcohol Syndrome.' He bent down and picked up the magazines she'd dropped. 'Oh, I say,' he said. '*House and Garden*, *Tatler* and *Harpers*. Let yourself down a bit with *Hello!* didn't you, darling? Feeling a touch of *nostalgie de la boue*, were we, when we picked that one off the shelf?'

'Oh, shut up, Rory,' she said, snatching the magazines from him. 'What are you reading these days? *Variety*?'

'As a matter of fact I've been rereading your screenplay.'

'Oh?' She shot him a suspicious look. 'Why?'

'Because I passed a copy on to a scriptwriter friend

of mine. He thinks it's very good indeed.'

She could feel herself going pink as she handed over a lot of money to the cashier for the magazines. 'Honestly, Rory?'

'Honestly. He in turn has passed it on to someone else, so it's inching its way up that glittering career ladder, darling. Just be warned – the whole process takes for ever, so don't hold your breath. It could take as long as a year before you hear anything definite. But it's a very positive start.'

'Thank you, Rory. For taking it to the right person.'

'For nothing, darling.' He was steering her in the direction of the bar. Deirdre noticed that people were looking at him more than at her. She was used to getting looks from strangers on account of *Ardmore Grove*, but Rory was *really* getting looks, even though nothing about his demeanour gave any indication that he was aware of the attention. It felt kind of weird – like walking with a terrestrial star. His kudos in LA must be seriously ascending. She'd seen his photograph from time to time in gossip features, and she knew that a recent film he'd been in was doing well, but nothing had prepared her for this. The film had been shown in the multiplex in Castlebar. She hadn't been to see it. 'Guinness?' he asked as they hit the counter.

She nodded. 'A glass, please.'

They took their drinks to a corner table. Deirdre shrugged out of her coat, and then wished she hadn't. It had helped to conceal her bump.

'How's it been?' asked Rory.

'The pregnancy? Or the marriage?'

'Both.'

'Fine.' Deirdre took a sip of Guinness. She didn't want to say any more. She didn't want to talk to Rory about either of those things. She thought she might cry if she did.

Rory put out a hand as if to touch the swell of her belly, and then hesitated. 'Do you mind?' he asked.

'No,' she said, looking down at his hand. 'I don't mind.'

As soon as Rory's palm made contact with Deirdre's stomach, the baby kicked. Rory looked at her as if he'd been electrified. 'Jesus Christ,' he said. 'That's the first time I've ever felt that.' The baby moved again as Rory ran both hands over the mound of her belly. It felt shockingly erotic. 'Wow,' he said. 'This is astonishing.'

Oh, God. She *was* going to cry. She had to go. She really couldn't handle this situation. Deirdre got to her feet clumsily and then sat down again, looking back at him with a scared expression. 'Ow,' she breathed.

'What's wrong?' he asked.

'A pain.'

'A labour pain?'

'I don't know. Ow,' she said again.

'Oh, God, Deirdre. Are you all right?'

'Yes. I mean, I don't know.'

'Oh, fuck, O'Dare – don't tell me you're going to go into labour on me. I might have known something like this would happen when I ran into you.'

The expression in his eyes belied the lightness of his tone. He was on his knees beside her now, gazing at her, and she looked away. She didn't want to see what she was seeing in his eyes. She couldn't handle it. She had an awful feeling that there might be love somewhere in their green depths, as well as concern. She doubled up, wanting to howl; but this time the pain wasn't physical.

'Shit, Deirdre. What am I meant to do? I'm useless in situations like this.'

So was she, but she couldn't allow herself to lose control. She shook herself mentally, took a deep breath, straightened up, and produced a mobile from her handbag. 'I'll call my doctor,' she said, trying to appear on top of things. Then: 'Hell's bells. Low battery. Where's the pay phone?' She stood up and sat straight back down again. 'Ow, ow, ow!'

'Your doctor's not going to be able to do anything over the phone,' said Rory. 'Which hospital are you going to?'

'Castlebar General.' At one point Deirdre had mooted a home birth, but Gabriel had pointed out the risks if something were to go wrong. 'Just think, Deirdre, if you needed a Caesarean. The hospital has all the equipment necessary in the event of it not being a normal birth.' She had seen the sense of this and complied with his wishes. She was also secretly glad that she'd have the option of an epidural in hospital. She wasn't sure how high her pain threshold would be.

'Let's get you there.'

'How?'

'Taxi. Or do you think you warrant an ambulance?'

'No. Ow.'

'Are you sure?'

'Pretty sure.' The last thing she wanted was to arrive at Castlebar hospital in an ambulance with sirens blaring only to find it was a false alarm.

'OK. Let's go.' He stood up and slung his bag over his shoulder.

'But Rory – your flight!'

'It can wait. I waited long enough for *it*.'

'But – think about it, Rory. Seriously. You'll miss your connection!'

'Your concern is extremely touching, my dear, but don't waste it on me. You're the one you should be thinking about.'

'But – ow – your luggage will go astray. What–'

'This is all I've got, Deirdre,' he said, indicating the bag on his shoulder. 'You know me. I've always travelled light.'

'But – but–' Oh God, oh, God! Rory was the last person in the world who should be taking her to hospital.

'Shut up with your boring buts. Getting you to hospital is priority. Anyway, I've always fancied doing a mercy dash. Come on.'

He pulled her to her feet and together they moved towards the exit, Deirdre leaning heavily on his arm. People gave them soppy smiles or stared as they walked through the concourse. Bloody hell, thought Deirdre. They obviously thought Rory was the father. Which he was, of course. Ow. This was the stuff of nightmare. When was she going to wake up? Oh, God – Gabriel. She had to let him know what was happening. But she wouldn't be able to talk to him for ages – he would have powered off his mobile in the plane.

'Rory?' she said. 'Do you have a mobile phone?'

''Fraid so,' he said rather sheepishly.

'Hah! You said you'd never get one. Told you you'd sell out.'

'Are you inferring that because I've got myself a mobile phone I've sold out? You're a fine one to talk about selling out, O'Dare. You're the one who went and married the local squire. It wouldn't surprise me if you'd started doing flower arranging and coffee mornings and entertaining business clients and all that uxorial shit.'

'Ow,' said Deirdre. 'Shut up, Rory, and give me your phone.' He turned away in embarrassment as he handed her one of the sexiest, most hi-tech mobiles she'd ever seen. She raised a pitying eyebrow at him. 'Whatever about flower arranging, McDonagh. Looks like you've joined the boys with toys club.'

She punched in Gabriel's number and waited for the beep. Then she left her message. 'Hi, darling. You're going to have to turn round and come straight back home. Or rather, straight to the hospital. Looks like the happy event is going to be a tad premature.

The boy's on his way. I'm on a friend's mobile, so call me on this number as soon as you switch on your phone.' She put her hand over the mouthpiece and whispered, 'What's the number, Rory?'

To her horror he took the phone from her and dictated the number down the line. Then he handed it back to her with a puzzled expression, obviously wondering why she was looking so gobsmacked. 'Um. That was Rory McDonagh,' she said into the mobile. 'He's – um – he's the – friend whose phone you can contact me on. Ow. See you soon, darling. Be as quick as you can.' She switched off the phone. 'Thank you,' she said, handing it back to Rory.

'Your taxi awaits,' he said, indicating the rather shabby hackney that had just pulled up outside the sliding doors, and which was disgorging a woman and three children. 'Not really fit for a princess, is it?'

'It's better than your bloody Saab, anyway,' she said.

'You should see what I drive in LA.'

'What, Rory? Let me guess? A Porsche? An Alpha Romeo? No – a Jaguar!'

His look was as pitying as the one she'd given him when she'd seen his phone. 'How long have you known me, Deirdre? I don't do flash. I ride a classic Norton.'

'A Norton? One of those horrible old beat-up motorbikes?'

'The best ride going. Apart from you of course, O'Dare. You were always pretty special.'

She gave him a dig with her elbow. Then the baby

kicked and she got a twinge at the same time. 'Ow, ow, ow!' she said.

* * *

When they arrived at the hospital, someone called Rory 'Mr O'Dare', and Deirdre cringed. She was relieved that she'd kept her own name. It would have been even more horrific if they'd called him 'Mr Considine'.

'You don't expect me to go into the labour room with you, do you?' he said, opening the door to the waiting room.

'Good God, no. You wouldn't have a clue.'

'How's the local squire going to cope? Or did he attend ante-natal classes with you?'

'Yes he did. He knows what to expect. Oh, God – there's awful Moira. It looks like I'm going to be walking the corridors with her. She's one of the most boring people I've ever met.'

'What do you mean, walking the corridors?'

'They like you to keep on your feet for as long as possible. It makes for a more proactive birth, apparently.'

'Bollocks to all that walking proactive shit,' said Rory. 'I'd take the epidural and run if I were you.' He kissed her on the cheek. 'I'll get word to you as soon as I hear anything from Squire Considine,' he said. 'In the meantime I'll browse through *House and Garden* and *Tatler* and *Harpers* and *Hello!* Don't take too long, will you, darling? I have a pretty low boredom threshold, as you know.'

'Very droll, Rory.' She turned to follow the nurse who was taking her to obstetrics, noticing as she did so that the girl kept sneaking impressed looks at her film-star pal. Deirdre turned and looked back at him. He was leaning against the doorjamb of the waiting room, watching her. 'Goodbye, Rory. Thank you,' she said.

'Good luck, sweetheart.' He saluted her with a relaxed hand in the gesture she remembered so well.

Deirdre continued on down the corridor. 'The father?' the nurse asked.

'No,' said Deirdre. 'He's – um. He's just a friend.'

* * *

By the time Gabriel arrived her labour was well advanced, and she was hooked into an epidural. She could tell that Gabriel was a mite disappointed. He'd hoped she'd be able to have a completely natural delivery, without any medical intervention. Between contractions he filled her in on his panicky turn-around at Heathrow airport. 'I rang that mobile number immediately and spoke to your friend. Bloody decent of him to wait until I got here.'

'Has he gone?'

'Yeah. I stuck my head round the door of the waiting room to say thanks before coming on down here.'

'Ow.' Deirdre was alarmed by how gutted she felt

at the news. A massive contraction hit her. 'Oh, fuck! This is awful!'

'Don't worry, darling. You're nearly there.'

'Push now!' said the doctor.

'Push, darling! Good girl,' said Gabriel. 'Remember your breathing.'

Deirdre tried to remember the breathing she'd learned in her ante-natal classes, but couldn't.

'And again,' said the doctor. 'Rest a beat. And push again. It's coming fast now.'

She felt like a fruit that someone had split in two.

'Excellent, darling. You're doing beautifully,' said Gabriel. 'Wow, I can see his head!'

'What colour's his hair? Ow!'

'I don't know. It's too wet to tell.' Then: 'His head – his whole head is out!' shouted Gabriel. 'He's turning his head! This is the most amazing thing I've ever seen!'

'Would you like to sit up a little, Ms O'Dare?' asked the doctor. 'Take a look?'

'Oh God, no!' The prospect of looking down and seeing a human head sticking out of her filled her with horror. 'Ow, ow, ow!'

'He's out!' Gabriel cried. 'Oh, well done, darling – you clever thing!'

The doctor held the baby aloft. 'Well done, Ms O'Dare,' he said. 'You have a fine baby girl.'

Deirdre looked up at the creature he was holding. 'Oh,' she said. 'Oh, my!' Her hands flew to her face. 'Oh, my – look at my little girl! She's so beautiful!'

Deirdre's daughter was surveying the room with serene, slate-coloured eyes. Her unfocused gaze fell on her mother, and Deirdre thought she had never, ever seen an expression of such infinite wisdom on a human face before.

The doctor lay the baby on her belly, and Deirdre gazed and gazed at her for a long moment. I'm in love, she thought. I'm totally, utterly in love. Then she lifted her head to look for Gabriel, but he was gone. The door of the delivery room was swinging shut behind him.

*　　*　　*

'I'm sorry,' he said later. 'I'm so sorry, darling. Please don't hate me.'

'I don't hate you, Gabriel.' She was leaning up against a bank of pillows with her child at her breast, feeling utterly knackered. It had luckily taken very little coaxing for the baby to latch on.

'It's my own fault, I should never have projected a sex onto the foetus. I'm sorry. I was just so totally obsessed with the idea of a boy.'

'I know.'

Gabriel looked down at the little creature doggedly sucking on Deirdre's nipple. 'She's beautiful.'

'Yes. She is.'

'What shall we call her?' Their son was to have been called Henry, after Gabriel's father. 'Sarah, after my mother?'

446

'No. I want her to have an Irish name.'

She could tell by his expression that he wasn't keen on the idea. 'Deirdre?' he queried. 'Shall we call her Deirdre, after you?'

Deirdre of the Sorrows. 'No. I've always hated my name. I want to call her Aoife.'

'Come again?'

'Aoife. The Irish for Eva. It's pronounced *Oephe*, but you spell it A-O-I-F-E.'

'Oh. Aoife.' He laid a gentle hand on the baby's head. 'Well, well. How do you do? It's a pleasure to meet you, Aoife Considine.'

Aoife McDonagh. She pushed the thought away. 'Aoife was a mythological Irish princess,' she said. 'A warrior princess. And Eva gave Dorcas an Irish middle name – Daíre – after me. I'd like to call my baby after Eva.'

'Fine.' Gabriel suddenly became business-like. He starting punching buttons on his electronic organizer. 'I'd better go and make phone calls,' he said. 'Look at the length of this list! Within a couple of hours this room will be crammed with flowers.' He leant down and kissed her forehead. 'Try and get some sleep,' he said.

'I'm not sleepy, funnily enough. Just knackered.'

'Well, you've enough magazines to keep you amused till I get back.' The magazines she'd bought at the airport had been left in the room by a nurse. 'I'll phone your mother first.'

'Gabriel?' she said suddenly. 'Please don't encourage too many people to phone. I don't feel up to talking to anyone.' In fact, she was positively dreading talking to Gabriel's father.

'OK.' He kissed her again, and disappeared through the door.

Deirdre sat staring at Aoife for a long time. She had dozed off. Very carefully she disengaged her nipple from the tiny rosebud mouth and slid out of bed. She laid the baby down in the crib by the bed and stretched herself experimentally, wincing at once. As she eased herself back between the sheets she noticed that someone had folded her *Hello!* magazine back at the Cinematters page and scribbled on it. That was a bit bloody cheeky of the nurse, she thought, to deface her magazines before she'd even had a chance to read them!

She picked the magazine up and looked at the photograph that someone had drawn a circle around. It was a picture of Rory coming out of some trendy LA joint with a looker on his arm. The looker was smiling at the camera. Rory was scowling from under a Groucho Marx moustache and glasses that he'd drawn on himself. The additional graffiti read: *Thought I'd better do this before you did . . . Give me a ring on this number and let me know how mother and child are doing, will you?* The number he'd scrawled in the margin looked as though it was the same mobile number that he'd dictated onto Gabriel's voice-mail.

She studied the number. Then she looked at Aoife. Then she picked up the telephone.

It took ages for him to pick up. Then: 'Hi,' he said.

'Hi.'

'Sorry, can you speak up a bit? It's hellishly noisy here. A gaggle of nuns has just flown in and they're in serious party mode.'

She raised her voice. 'Hi, Rory – it's Deirdre.'

'Sweetheart! How are you doing?'

'OK. I got your message on *Hello!* magazine. Are you still at the airport?'

'I might have known that the first thing you'd do after spending hours in the labour ward would be to open *Hello!* magazine. Yes. I am still at the fucking airport. I've had a hell of a time trying to get on a flight. What did you pop?'

'A girl. Oh, Rory – you shouldn't have gone to all that trouble. I feel really guilty that you're still hanging around an airport when you should be halfway across the Atlantic by now.'

'Shut up, O'Dare. You know I never could stand being part of your guilt trip. What's she like?'

'My baby?'

'No. The nurse who's looking after you.'

'Oh. Well, she's very nice. She's very sexy too, Rory. You'd like her. She's called Fiona and she's—'

'Come off it O'Dare! Give me the low-down on the sprog.'

'She's beautiful.'

There was a pause. Then Rory said, 'I'm sure she is.' She could hear the smile in his voice. 'Does she look like you?'

'No.'

449

'So she takes after the squire?'

'No.'

'Who, then?'

'She doesn't really look like either me or Gabriel.'

'A changeling!'

'An extremely beautiful changeling.'

'What colour are her eyes?'

'It's too early to tell. I won't know for about six weeks. They're slate-blue now.'

'What about her hair?'

'I've a feeling she's going to be blonde.'

'No shit, O'Dare. Who in your family has blonde hair?'

'My maternal grandmother,' she lied.

'Was *she* a looker?'

'Yes.'

'Well – your girl's got good genes, Deirdre. Are you breast-feeding her?'

'Yes.'

'Wow. Ow.'

'You sound like me going into labour.'

'Was it tough?'

'Let's just say it's highly unlikely that I'll ever be doing that again.' She could have added a hollow laugh for good measure.

'You'd better take the necessary precautions then, baby.'

'Yes,' she said.

In the silence that descended between them, Deirdre could hear airport-announcement noises in the background. Then Rory finally spoke: 'Well.

That's my flight being called at last. I'd better stroll down to departures.'

She swallowed hard. 'OK.'

'Keep in touch, Deirdre.'

'Yeah.'

'And I'll let you know if anything arises from your screenplay.'

'I won't hold my breath.'

'Sensible girl. But don't give up hope.'

'I won't. Goodbye, Rory.'

'Goodbye, sweetheart. Take care of yourself.' People were always saying that to her. There was a click and then silence. Oh, God. Oh, God. Oh, God in heaven help me please, she thought, as emotion started to swell inside her. Her heart was hurting now, as well as all the other bits of her that had laboured so hard to push Rory McDonagh's baby into the world. He would have been so proud to see how hard she'd worked!

Deirdre put down the phone just as Gabriel came back into the room. 'I spoke to your mother,' he said. 'She says she'll phone you – hey! What's the matter, darling?'

Gabriel took his wife in his arms. There were tears streaming down her face. 'Nothing,' she sobbed.

'How can you say nothing's the matter?' he admonished her. 'Look at you, darling! You're deeply distressed. What is it?'

'Post partum blues,' she sobbed. 'That's what it must be. We learnt about it in the ante-natal classes, remember?'

'Oh, angel.' Gabriel rocked her in his arms. 'You are in a bad way, aren't you?'

'I'll stop soon,' she said. 'I never cry for long.' She took hold of the edge of the sheet and wiped her eyes.

'I'll run down to the hospital shop and get some paper handkerchieves,' said Gabriel. He was the only person Deirdre knew who called tissues paper handkerchieves. She looked down at the sheet. It was very wet. *Hello!* magazine was still lying on top of the counterpane. Rory looked up at her, ridiculous in his Groucho Marx disguise. She suddenly wondered what Gabriel would do if she casually indicated the photograph and said, 'By the way, that's Aoife's real father.' She started to laugh.

'Are you all right, darling?' Gabriel looked concerned.

'Yes,' she managed. 'Yes. I'm fine now, really I am.' Another gale of laughter burst out of her.

'Good God,' said Gabriel, looking perplexed. 'Talk about sunshine and showers.'

'You'd better get used to it, darling,' she said. 'My body's going to be like Pandora's box with all the hormones surging around inside.'

'Pandora! Now there's a lovely name.'

'No,' said Deirdre firmly. 'Oh, look! She's waking up. Bring her to me, Gabriel, will you? I'll try feeding her again.'

As Gabriel gently laid the baby in Deirdre's arms,

the phone next to the bed rang. It was her mother. 'How's my daughter? And how's my granddaughter?'

'She's beautiful,' said Deirdre, gazing down at Rory McDonagh's baby. 'She's Aoife.'

Chapter Eighteen

Deirdre didn't feel at all sociable after the birth. She was obliged to schmooze with Gabriel's clients on a routine basis, but she didn't get round to organizing Aoife's christening until the baby was nine months old.

Sarah came over for the event, and Gabriel's brother Hugo, but his father declined the invitation, saying that he didn't feel well enough to travel. Gabriel had suggested that Sarah act as godmother to Aoife, but he didn't seem too put out when Deirdre insisted that Maeve and Bart share the honour of being appointed godparents to Aoife Considine. She wanted to surround her baby daughter with the people she trusted most in the world. She had hoped that Eva might be joint godmother, but the actress was off working on some arthouse movie in the Sahara desert, and it had proved impossible to contact her.

'Don't worry about Daddy's non-appearance,' Sarah said, after the ceremony. They were having tea on the lawn of Carrowcross House. Gabriel had had it re-landscaped to its original specifications, and it looked stunning. Although it was the middle of autumn, it was a beautiful day. The mellow sunshine seemed to gild everything and everyone it touched. Sarah's children were running in and out of the French windows, laughing, and the guests were all standing around with Susie Cooper teacups looking elegant and happy and relaxed. It could have been straight out of a commercial for Ralph Lauren, which was Deirdre's label of choice these days. 'Daddy's terribly entrenched, you see,' continued Sarah. 'He'll soften after a while, and when you produce the son and heir he'll positively shower you with attention.'

Yikes, thought Deirdre. Maybe it was just as well she'd never be able to produce the son and heir. 'What if I don't have any more children?' she queried tentatively. Aoife was looking up at her with bright emerald eyes. She let out a sudden yell, and Deirdre obligingly presented her with a nipple.

'You'll have lots, I've no doubt of it,' said Sarah breezily, stroking Aoife's cheek. 'Just look at this healthy specimen you managed to produce. And by the way, don't believe that old wives' tale about not being able to conceive if you're breast-feeding. It happened to me. I was pregnant with my second child before I'd weaned my first.'

'Well, there's not much chance of that happening to me,' said Deirdre.

'Oh?'

'Well – I'm, um – we're being really careful about birth control. I'm not ready for another baby just yet.'

In fact, they were hardly making love at all these days. She very rarely felt the urge, and she had a suspicion that Gabriel found her physically rather unattractive since she'd given birth. She knew she should be taking more care of her appearance, but she was so busy with the baby that it was difficult to find time. Gladys was a dream, and looked after a million things for her, but Gladys couldn't feed Aoife, who seemed to have learnt on the second day of her life from Dorcas Lavery-Lawless that your mother would allow you to spend your entire waking life on her tit if you were winsome and demanding enough. Eva had visited Deirdre just two days after Aoife was born because she was flying off to LA to be a working mother again. 'Your maternity leave didn't last long, Eva,' Deirdre had said. 'I know, darling,' replied Eva with a rather guilty smile. 'To tell you the truth, I was getting a tiny bit bored, and very jealous indeed of David jetsetting off all over the place, so when I was made a film offer I couldn't refuse, I didn't refuse it. I love my darling Dorcas to bits, but a girl needs a little more in her life, sometimes, I've discovered.'

Deirdre was beginning to see the truth of this. After a massive inward struggle, she had given up her screenplay writing. It was just too difficult to concentrate on it. It was so much easier to do mindless tasks like tapestry or sanding bits and pieces of furniture in any spare time she had while Aoife was sleeping – which wasn't often. She was an exceptionally bright, watchful child, and she was developing a wicked sense of humour. She remembered how Rory had once made reference to

Dorcas's wicked sense of humour. Now he had a daughter with a mischievous streak whom he knew nothing about. It was ironic really, she thought. And then another thought struck her dully. It wasn't ironic. It was terribly, terribly sad. It was highly unlikely that Rory would ever know his daughter.

'I'd say you'd need to be. Careful about contraception, that is.' Deirdre realized that Sarah was still talking. 'I remember Daisy saying that she'd never met anyone with such a high sex drive as my brother. Oh.' She gave Deirdre an apologetic look. 'I hope you don't mind me mentioning Daisy like this, do you? I know it's always difficult for a second wife to hear the first wife's name mentioned.'

'No.' Deirdre genuinely didn't mind. She knew Gabriel had *said* that he was over the tragedy of his first wife's death, but – understandably enough – Daisy wasn't a topic of conversation that often arose between them. 'What was she like? I've never even seen a photograph of her. Gabriel's too considerate to have photographs of Daisy on display.' He didn't mind having photographs of the other members of his family on display, though. The walls of the house were covered in portraits of his ancestors, and the top of the baby grand in the library hardly ever got dusted because Gladys found it such a mammoth chore. It was covered in framed photographs of Gabriel's parents and siblings at every conceivable stage of their lives and development. Funnily enough, there weren't that many photographs of her and Aoife – just the original of the photograph he'd cut from the *Irish Times* that she had had framed for him, one formal one of the three of them together shortly after Aoife's birth, and the one he'd taken of her on Croagh Patrick the day she'd told him she was pregnant. The day he'd asked her to marry him.

'It has to be said that Daisy was pretty gorgeous,' Sarah finally said. She had obviously been debating how much information to reveal about Daisy, and how much to hold back. 'The kind of girl who's the most popular girl in the school. You'd have liked her – and she'd have loved you. She was fascinated by acting and actresses, always said that's what she would have done if she hadn't married Gabriel.'

'She never really worked at anything, did she?'

'Not really. She toyed with the idea of becoming a Montessori teacher, and she did a cordon bleu cookery course with a view to maybe starting up a restaurant one day, but it never happened. She was a very old-fashioned girl in many ways. A home-maker, I suppose you'd call her. And she had a great eye for antiques. She used to pick up really awful-looking pieces from junk shops and transform them.'

Oh, God, thought Deirdre. Daisy was all the things I could never be. No wonder Gabriel's father wouldn't come to the christening. He couldn't bear the idea of a second meeting with his total klutz of a daughter-in-law who couldn't even get a simple thing like the sex of his grandchild right.

Deirdre stood up. 'May I get you some more tea, Sarah?' she asked.

'Yes please. I'll take Aoife for you. Oh, and could

you bring me one of those little vol-au-vents?' Deirdre passed the baby over and Aoife expressed her disapproval of the transfer with a loud squawk.

'Of course,' said Deirdre.

'Actually, could you make that two? I know they'll play havoc with my figure, but they're absolutely delicious. Did you make them?'

'No,' said Deirdre miserably. 'Gladys did.'

* * *

Later on that afternoon, she dumped Aoife on Gladys and hit the library with Maeve and a bottle of vintage Veuve Cliquot. Maeve wandered around the room, checking it out.

'That secretaire is new, isn't it? Well, old-new, if you know what I mean. And that chaise-longue. Wow, Deirdre – this place is really looking the part.' Maeve turned back to Deirdre when she heard the champagne cork pop, and held out her glass. 'So are you, come to think of it. Very lady of the manor.'

Deirdre was dressed in Ralph Lauren cashmere and wool. It was an outfit she had last worn to Newport House for dinner with one of Gabriel's clients, and it made her feel very grown up. People seemed to take her more seriously when she wore it. It was also so beautifully cut that it disguised the rather lumpen contours of her hips and thighs. Now she found herself looking at Maeve's graceful form draped in loose, fluid silk with a twinge of envy. She hadn't really felt comfortable in any of the clothes she'd bought since she'd got married. She suddenly wished she'd worn her beautiful Nicole Farhi instead of this parody of a grown-up person's ensemble. She didn't even feel particularly grown-up right now, just uncomfortable, and far too hot in the unseasonably warm weather.

Maeve settled down on the chaise-longue and put her feet up on the little footstool which Deirdre had re-upholstered when she'd done her course in furniture restoration. She'd worked a tapestry to cover it, as one of the women in the class had suggested to her.

'Where did all this stuff come from?' asked Maeve. 'Has Gabriel had more furniture shipped over from England since the wedding?'

'No,' said Deirdre, sitting down in a fireside chair opposite her friend. 'I've been browsing for pieces I liked. Gabriel's things are lovely, but some of them are too monumental for my taste. I've been doing various bits of restoration, nothing major. I'm not very good at it, but it passed the time when I was pregnant. I worked the tapestry on that footstool. It's a reproduction of a design by Charles Rennie Mackintosh.'

'*You* did this?' Maeve sounded rather unflatteringly astonished.

'Yeah. Don't look too closely. You'll spot all the mistakes.'

'Well, well. You've certainly become domesticated. Where's that hoydenish streak gone, O'Dare?'

'I don't know. I've wised up a lot in the past year,

Maeve. I think I've finally got my priorities right.'

'Have you?' Maeve gave her a curious look.

'Yeah. I mean, Gabriel's work is priority, for instance. For a while I dug my heels in and insisted that my writing was as important as his architecture, and then I got real. Gabriel pays the bills, I don't. Anyway, Aoife's more or less a full-time job.' Deirdre got up and moved to the window. Outside she could see Gladys with Aoife on her hip, handing round a plate of vol-au-vents. Her mother was talking to Gabriel, laughing at something he was saying. Her father was doing the rounds of the newly restored garden with Eleanor on his arm. Bart was standing on the doorstep, deep in conversation with Hugo, who was looking rather bewildered. When Bart started doing air-guitar gestures, Deirdre could understand why. 'My screenwriting career was a non-starter, Maeve. I was a crazed fantasist to think that I could ever hack it as a writer.'

'That's not what Rory said.'

'What?' Deirdre spun round from the window.

'That's not what Rory said. He was very impressed by your writing.'

'Is he back from LA?'

'No.' Maeve was watching Deirdre carefully. 'But we keep in touch. Always have done.'

'When did he tell you about my screenplay?' Deirdre tried her hardest to sound casual, but she could tell that Maeve wasn't convinced. She sometimes wished that Maeve wasn't so very, very wise.

'About a year ago. He's been touting it round LA,

you know, trying to get people interested. He told me that the greatest drawback so far has been the fact that you're a woman. They don't believe that women can write screenplays over there, apparently. It's strictly a male preserve. They assume all female screenwriters are just actresses *manquées*.'

'Hah!' said Deirdre with hollow emphasis. 'That's exactly what I am. Actress *manquée*, screenwriter *manquée*, wife and mother *manquée*. I can't even get being a housewife right, Maeve. I'm crap at it.'

'What's all this stuff about monkeys?' asked Bart, coming into the room and heading straight for the CD rack. 'Hey – cool. All the CDs are in alphabetical order. P, Q , R. No Radiohead? I thought Gabriel was a fan.'

'No, he hates them,' replied Deirdre unthinkingly.

'Oh? He said he was really into them. We stayed up half the night listening to Radiohead that time at your gaff, remember?'

'He – um.' There was no way out of it. 'He just said that to be polite.'

Bart shot her an amazed look. 'Weird,' he said.

Maeve raised a thoughtful eyebrow. 'Weird,' she echoed. 'Or else he's incredibly well versed in people skills.'

'He is,' said Deirdre. She'd witnessed Gabriel's people skills on numerous occasions at client dinners.

'You bastards,' said Bart. 'You've snuck an entire bottle of champagne in here. Slosh some in there, Mrs Considine, will you?'

'Don't call me that, Bart!' She turned on him with flashing eyes. 'I'm Deirdre O'Dare, OK?'

'OK, OK,' he returned, spreading his hands in a conciliatory gesture. Deirdre just caught the puzzled look he shot at Maeve. 'Sorry, Deirdre.'

'Shit. I'm sorry, too, Bart. It's been a stressful kind of a day, you know?' She swigged back the champagne in her glass and reached for the bottle. 'Refills all round,' she said, recklessly sloshing fizz into the crystal flutes. 'Fuck it. Let's get slaughtered. And I'm getting out of this gear. I feel like a mummy in it.'

'An Egyptian mummy or a mumsie mummy?' asked Bart.

'Both,' she replied.

*　　*　　*

An hour later, Gabriel wandered into the library to find his wife sitting cross-legged on the floor wearing combats and a T-shirt and roaring with laughter at one of Bart's crap jokes.

'Oops,' she said, making an apologetic face at his uncertain expression. 'Come and join us for a glass of champagne, darling.' She tipped the bottle into a spare flute and looked more apologetic than ever. 'Oops,' she said again. 'It's empty.'

'Time to go,' said Bart, clocking the dark look on Gabriel's face. He grabbed Maeve's hand and the pair of them slid out of the library before the storm could erupt.

*　*　*

After the christening and the blazing row that ensued, Deirdre wasn't sure that life could get very much worse, but in fact it did. Over a mug of tea in the kitchen a week later Gladys announced that she was handing in her notice.

'But why, Gladys? Aren't you happy here?'

'Oh yes, I am, Deirdre. You and Gabriel have been fantastic – I mean that. You've treated me really well, and the salary's more than fair. It's just that I need to kick up some dust, d'you know what I mean? I've been thinking about it for ages, and then I just said to myself – stop thinking about it, girl – do it! And I'm doing it!'

'What are you doing?'

'I'm going round the world, Deirdre. I'm taking a year to visit all the places I ever wanted to visit – every single continent.'

'Oh, you lucky thing, Gladys! I did that once – well, not for a whole year, but for a few months.' She and Rory had divided a summer between South America and Australia.

'*You* did?' Gladys was looking at her curiously.

'Yeah.' Deirdre gave a little, unconvincing laugh. 'Why is that so hard to believe?'

'I dunno. It's funny. It's just that you don't look the type to go off backpacking round the world.'

Oh, God. What had happened to her? What had happened to her life?

'Well. I was once.' She heaved a huge sigh. 'Oh

464

hell, Gladys! How will I manage without you?'

'Don't worry. You'll find someone. And whatever you do, take her out to Quay Cottage when you decide on the right one. That was a brilliant thing of Gabriel to do. I liked him right away after that.'

Gladys was right. Gabriel was brilliant at getting people to like him. He was brilliant at getting people to do what he wanted them to do. He was, she realized, a brilliant manipulator. How had she not seen it till now?

A thought crossed her mind. It was so disturbing a thought that she rarely entertained it, but it had been crossing through on a more and more regular basis for the past few months. Her mind went back to the night of their wedding: the night she'd accused Gabriel of marrying her because she was conveniently pregnant, not because he loved her. He'd reassured her by reminding her that he'd taken her engagement ring out of the bank on the same day that he'd accessed the emerald earrings, weeks previously. But Deirdre now knew that he kept all the Considine heirlooms in a safe in his study. A visit to the bank would not have been necessary. Was it possible that he'd visited his study just before taking her to the train that same afternoon? That blue-sky afternoon when she'd been so happy she'd executed dance steps on the station platform just before he slipped the ring on her finger . . .

'Are you all right, Deirdre?' asked Gladys.

'Yes. Yes – I'm fine. Why do you ask?'

'You looked a bit weird for a moment, that's all,'

said Gladys. A sudden squawk came from the baby Tannoy on the kitchen dresser. 'Oh-oh. The kraken awakes.' Gladys knocked back the remains of her tea and got to her feet. 'I'll take her for a walk now, if you like. I'm going to miss her like mad. I'll be interested to see how she's turned out in a year's time, when I come back.'

* * *

It wasn't easy to find a replacement for Gladys. She had been the ultimate treasure. Because Deirdre hated the idea of sharing the house with a stranger, she interviewed half a dozen local women with a view to employing them on a nine-to-five basis, but none of them was quite right. Some weren't prepared to do child-minding, some weren't prepared to do cooking, some weren't prepared to do housework, some had untrustworthy eyes. One woman had seemed to fit the bill, but Gabriel had dismissed the idea of taking her on. 'She's too old,' he said. 'You need somebody with masses of energy to run this place.'

Carrowcross House was starting to look shabby by the time Deirdre threw up her hands in despair. '*You* find somebody, Gabriel, please? I'm crap at interviewing people. I never know what questions to ask, and I always feel like an impostor. That Mrs Tuohy rang me last week to see if I was going to take her on, and I had to lie and say we'd found someone else. It made me feel awful. Please do it for me?'

'All right,' he said. 'I'll phone a recruitment agency in the morning. They're bound to come up with some suitable candidates.'

They did. In fact, they came up with several. The only snag was that they couldn't find anyone who lived within a ten-mile radius of Carrowcross, and no-one was prepared to commute further than that.

'You must stop being so fussy, Deirdre,' said Gabriel. 'You'll just have to resign yourself to having a live-in housekeeper.'

'Oh, Gabriel – what if I don't get on with her? I couldn't bear the idea of skulking around my own home every evening, trying to avoid running into her.'

Gabriel sighed. 'You're behaving like a spoilt brat, you know.' He sounded seriously pissed off. 'Imagine how many women in the world dream about living in a beautiful house with live-in help. Get real, Deirdre, will you? It's about bloody time you got your act together.'

Get real. He was right. She was living in the house of her dreams and she was *whingeing* about it! It was time to get real. It was time to grow up.

So Deirdre O'Dare set about getting her act together.

* * *

Gladys had lent her a copy of her mother's book, *Cut the Clutter*. She read it from cover to cover, but it didn't really help. It was full of handy tips for things like storing bakeware and keeping pairs of socks together and drawing up personal property inventories. The prospect of keeping 'tickler' and colour-coded files on everything from film to be developed, to questions for insurance agents, to keeping a record of Christmas presents given and received made her practically hyperventilate. So she put the book away and tried a different way of getting her act together. She joined a gym and went on a diet for the first time in her life, she schmoozed with Gabriel's clients, she rejoined the antique furniture restoration classes (admittedly she left again after the second one) and she mastered a dozen basic recipes. She drew the line, however, when Gabriel suggested that she invite some of his clients' wives round for a coffee morning. 'Oh, please, no, Gabriel!' she begged. 'Please don't make me do that! I'll learn another recipe instead, I promise!' She made a huge effort to put some zing back into their sex life, but nothing worked. He shagged her occasionally, but she knew she could have been anybody. They never made love any more, and her attempts at seducing him were lamentable enough to make her wonder if she shouldn't have accepted Jean-Claude Valentin's gift of the Scandalous Scanties all that time ago.

At least she had somebody to help her in the house now. Gabriel had interviewed a handful of prospective housekeepers, and chosen one called Tabitha Palmer. Tabitha was twenty-three and brimful of energy. She was as efficient as Gladys had been, and as cheerful. But there was something about her, something that Deirdre didn't like. She tried to analyse her irrational antipathy for the girl from time to time, but nothing could justify it. She only knew it was instinctive, and she suspected that under Tabitha's shiny, smiling countenance, the dislike was reciprocated.

On one particularly disastrous night under the canopy of the four-poster when yet another seduction attempt had failed dismally, she had fallen asleep and dreamt about Bart and Maeve and poor Betty Grable, who had been tearfully bequeathed to her neighbour when she had moved out of the flat in Dublin. She hadn't wanted to bring Betty Grable to live in Carrowcross House. Somehow she got the impression that she and Tinkerbell wouldn't get on. And then she had dreamt about Rory. She woke up crying, and then she found herself crying even harder when she remembered that there was a dinner party to be organized that day. Gabriel was entertaining the most important and influential of his clients at Carrowcross House. They were arriving at eight for eight-thirty, and there was a lot to be done. She dragged herself out of bed and headed for the kitchen to put coffee on for Gabriel, only to find that Tabitha had already done it.

At eleven o'clock she was sitting in the morning room, going through last-minute additions to her shopping list, when the doorbell rang. She looked at her watch. The catering company – at last. They were nearly an hour late. She went through into the hall, tweaking at a flower arrangement as she passed one of her most recent purchases – a rococo console table – preparing herself to give out to the unreliable caterers. It was Gladys at the door.

'Hi!' she said. 'I tried the side door, but it was locked.'

'Gladys! Oh – it's so good to see you!' Deirdre gave her a big hug. 'Wow – you're looking wonderful! Come on in.'

Gladys was tanned and fit-looking and blonder than ever. 'When did you start locking doors around here?' she said as she stepped into the hall. 'You never used to bother.'

'Gabriel finally succeeded in drumming it into me. There have been enough recycled Considine heirlooms without me being responsible for new job-lots of them turning up in auction rooms across the county. Tabitha!' she called down the stairs. 'Would you mind awfully bringing up another cup, and maybe some biscuits?'

'No problem!' The housekeeper's voice floated cheerfully up from the basement.

'Thanks, Tabitha!'

'I take it Tabitha's my replacement?' Gladys followed Deirdre through into the morning room. 'Hey, this place is looking good!'

Deirdre acknowledged the compliment with a smile. The room did look beautiful, she supposed. She'd had it redecorated recently, even though it hadn't needed doing. Sunlight was streaming in through the tall windows, tea-things were neatly laid out on the tea-table, and expensive art books were ranged along the polished mahogany surface of the coffee table.

'It took a lot of looking to find a replacement that matched up to you,' said Deirdre, plumping a cushion.

'Well, you obviously have a lot of respect for her. You never asked me if I "minded awfully" bringing up a cup. Come to think of it, we always drank out of mugs in the kitchen.'

A smiling Tabitha came through the door, carrying a cup and saucer and a plate of biscuits, followed on wobbly legs by Aoife with a silver teaspoon.

'Aoife! Look at you, you're walking!' Gladys ran across the room and swung Aoife up into her arms. There was no way that Aoife could remember who Gladys was after all these months, but she laughed all the same.'

'Tabitha, this is Gladys.'

The two girls shook hands. 'Nice to meet you,' said Tabitha, pushing the wing of her sleek black bob behind an ear. 'I've heard a lot about you. You were a tough act to follow!'

'Thanks.' Gladys took the cup and saucer from the housekeeper and smiled at Aoife, who was tapping her on the head with the spoon.

'Have you finished the list, Mrs Considine?'

'Deirdre,' she corrected her, feeling silly that Tabitha should have called her Mrs Considine in front of Gladys.

Tabitha made an apologetic face. 'Sorry. There I

go again.' She turned to Gladys. 'I always called my last employer Mrs O'Donnell, and it's a hard habit to get out of.'

Deirdre was glad she'd explained the gaff. She really hated it when Tabitha called her Mrs Considine, but when she'd mentioned it to Gabriel he'd shrugged it off. 'It's a measure of respect. I think it's an eye-opener to be shown respect in this day and age. There's little enough of it about.'

'You don't seem to mind the fact that she *always* calls you Gabriel,' she'd returned frostily.

'If you've finished the list I'll go into town now,' Tabitha said. 'The caterers need a few basics that we're missing, and I need to get vacuum bags for the Hoover and pick up your dress from the dry cleaners. I'll take Aoife with me.'

'Oh, no! Leave Aoife here!' said Gladys. 'I haven't seen her for ages.'

Tabitha looked at Deirdre and she nodded. 'I didn't realize the caterers were here,' she said. 'I didn't hear the bell.'

'Oh yes – they've been here for nearly an hour now,' said Tabitha. 'They arrived when you were in the shower.' She took the list from Deirdre and scanned it as she headed towards the door. 'You forgot the VSOP,' she said. 'We're nearly out of it. It would never do for Gabriel to offer his important dinner guests an inferior brandy, now, would it?' she said in a mock-chiding voice, wagging an index finger. 'See you later!' she added brightly, before swinging through the door. They could hear her singing as she went back downstairs.

Deirdre's rictus smile gradually relaxed. She sat down at the table and poured tea. 'So,' she said, 'you couldn't hack a whole year of living rough, Gladys? It's only six months since you left. Why did you cut it short?'

'Well, I didn't really. I'm only back here on a flying visit to say goodbye to my friends. I'm going back to Australia for good.'

'Oh!'

'I've fallen in love with the place.'

'I don't blame you.' An image of Rory and herself on Ayer's Rock flashed across her mind's eye. 'What are you going to do there?' asked Deirdre. 'Careful, Aoife!' Aoife was pulling herself up by the starched white tablecloth.

'Wait tables until I find something permanent. I'm not particularly fussed about finding something permanent, though. I'm going to do some serious bumming round. Oh – Deirdre – you should see the Great Barrier Reef!'

She had seen it, once. 'What about a visa?'

'That's cool. Mum and Dad are citizens.'

'Oh, how I envy you, Gladys!'

'You? Envy me? I've got bugger all to be envious of. Look what you've got!' Gladys's gesture took in the expanse of the room around them in all its restored glory.

'I know. I shouldn't complain.'

There was a hiatus. Gladys took a gulp of her tea. 'How's the new girl shaping up?' she asked, observing Deirdre over the edge of her cup.

Deirdre sighed. 'She's incredibly efficient,' she said.

'So why the big sigh?'

'I don't know. There's just something about her . . .'

'Personality clash?'

'No, no. She's actually got a great personality – very friendly and all that. Stop that, Aoife.' Aoife was stuffing a corner of the tablecloth into her mouth.

'You're not very happy, Deirdre, are you?'

Deirdre looked into Gladys's candid blue eyes. 'What makes you say that?' she asked.

'You've changed.'

Aoife was reaching up for scones. 'Careful, Aoife. You'll get jam on the tablecloth,' said Deirdre. Aoife promptly knocked a scone onto the carpet where it landed jam-side down. 'Oh, you clumsy thing! What did I tell you, Aoife! Why do you never, ever do as you're told!'

Deirdre suddenly realized she was banging a fist on the table. Aoife turned astonished eyes on her mother and burst into tears.

'See what I mean?' said Gladys.

Deirdre buried her face in her hands. 'Oh, Gladys! What am I going to do? I think Gabriel's fucking Tabitha.' It was finally said. It was the reason Deirdre could never, ever like the girl, and it had been lurking like a spider in the darkest recess of her mind for weeks.

There was a pause. Then: 'Deirdre?' said Gladys.

Deirdre raised her head.

'There's something I ought to tell you. Maybe I should have been straight with you at the time, but I really didn't want to hurt you.' Gladys took a deep breath. 'One of the reasons I decided to quit my job here was because Gabriel tried to – well, he started touching me up.'

'Oh, God.'

It was true, then. Gabriel was fucking the new housekeeper. He certainly wasn't fucking her. They hadn't had sex for months.

There was a long silence, during which Aoife carefully lifted the cut crystal dish of Tabitha's home-made raspberry jam and tottered across to the coffee table with it.

'I told him where to get off on a couple of occasions, but he was pretty persistent. That's when I decided to hand in my notice. I'm really sorry.'

'Don't say that, Gladys!' Deirdre turned beseeching eyes on her friend and ex-housekeeper. 'You have nothing to be sorry for. *You* did nothing wrong.'

'I mean I'm sorry that I had to be the one to tell you.'

There was another long pause. Then: 'I'm glad you told me,' Deirdre said. 'It's no fun being a deceived wife.'

Gladys looked over at Aoife. 'Uh-oh,' she said. 'Aoife's spreading jam over the carpet.'

'I don't care,' said Deirdre, dully. 'I've always hated that carpet.'

'It's weird, isn't it?' said Gladys, looking at Deirdre

with a mystified expression. 'That Gabriel should start screwing around when he's got such a gorgeous wife? I couldn't believe it the first time he made a pass at me. He'd always seemed like such a nice guy.'

Not any more, thought Deirdre as she watched raspberry jam spread across the carpet. No more Mr Nice Guy.

* * *

Deirdre toyed with the idea of getting drunk and appearing at the dinner party wearing combats and a belly top, then rejected it. Maybe – just maybe – her suspicions about Gabriel and Tabitha were exactly that? Just suspicions. Maybe she was becoming paranoid, on top of everything else. She thought of all the books she'd read and films she'd seen where wives end up going mad in rambling houses. She didn't want to end up on a shrink's couch like a million other neurotic members of the chattering classes. Hell, she'd never dreamt she'd end up as a member of the chattering classes full-stop.

So – appealing as she found it – she trashed the idea of scuppering Gabriel's dinner party and even proffered her cheek for the perfunctory kiss he always gave her when he finished work. What a performance! she thought. What a trouper is Deirdre O'Dare!

'How are things going?' he asked in the bedroom as he fastened the clasp on her emerald necklace. It was ten minutes to eight.

'Fine,' she replied brightly. 'Tabitha has everything under control.' Tabitha came into the bedroom with Deirdre's dress in its dry cleaning bag. 'Haven't you, Tabitha?'

'I certainly have.' The housekeeper sent them both a warm smile. 'I've even remembered to time-record the Oscar highlights.'

Deirdre looked up from her jewel-case with an emerald earring halfway to her earlobe. 'The Oscar highlights? I'd completely forgotten about them.' All the panic over the dinner party had driven the Oscars out of her head – and she'd particularly wanted to watch the ceremony. Rory had been nominated for best supporting actor for *Grace*. 'Make sure you hang onto the tape, Tabitha, will you?'

'Sure. I'll label it.' She knew that she'd find the tape carefully stowed in the video rack in the family room with Tabitha's neat handwriting on it. Deirdre was always recording things and then not knowing which tape was which because she hadn't bothered with a label. She'd recorded *Blind Date* over the test match once, and Gabriel had fumed for a week. As she hooked the earring onto her earlobe she clocked Gabriel's sexy smile in the mirror. But he wasn't smiling at her. He was smiling at Tabitha.

* * *

The dinner party went swimmingly. The guests all complimented her on the catering, and on her beautiful home, and on her beautiful dress, and on her beautiful child, whom her beautiful housekeeper whisked off to bed on the dot of half past eight.

Afterwards she sat beside her beautiful husband in the library, sipping Remy Martin VSOP. She'd had quite a lot to drink, and so had he. This was unusual for Gabriel, who was normally circumspect about his alcohol consumption when there were important business contacts to be entertained. She supposed he could allow himself to indulge when he wasn't driving.

'You looked extremely elegant tonight, darling.' It was a long time since he'd bothered with the endearment. 'Very sexy, too.' He was giving her a come-to-bed look. Maybe he wanted to make love, at last!

She smiled back at him. She knew she looked seductive in her low-cut, backless sheath. And her figure was back to its pre-Aoife proportions. As she curled up her legs beneath her she saw his eyeline go to the split in her dress that exposed a discreet amount of thigh. She shifted a little so that a few more inches were exposed. This was more like it! This was more like the way things had been before Aoife had been born, before all their problems had arisen. This was the way she'd dreamt things would be when she was a little girl. Reclining on a couch in front of a log fire in the restored splendour of Carrowcross House with a beautiful husband. A handsome prince.

He looked extremely handsome tonight. Even though he'd cut his beautiful black hair quite short, it showed off the fine contours of his face to advantage.

She'd been appalled when he'd first come home with short hair, but Gabriel had told her that he'd had a vibe from clients about its length. He suspected it was too bohemian for their tastes. Deirdre hadn't commented on the fact that the earring he still wore in his left earlobe might be too bohemian for their tastes, too.

Gabriel sent her another meaningful smile. Hell, maybe her imagination had been working overtime again. What had Bart once called her? A crazed fantasist. Maybe there was no secret affair going on under her nose between her husband and her house-keeper.

'Where did you get the dress?' Gabriel asked. 'I don't remember seeing it before.'

'Harvey Nicks, when we were in London last. I've only worn it once, that night you couldn't make dinner with the Jones's.'

'Oh, yes. I remember you coming home from that. You were a bit pissed, as I recall. Laughing madly at some joke Barry had told.'

'Was I?' Deirdre couldn't remember ever having heard Barry Jones tell any kind of a joke, except some rather sexist ones, which she'd never found remotely amusing.

'Yeah. He has a terrific sense of humour, Barry.'

Had he? Maybe she'd got it wrong.

'Thank you for working so hard to make the evening such a success, darling,' continued Gabriel smoothly.

'Darling' again!

'I think everyone was suitably impressed. Especially Barry. You two really get on well together, don't you?'

Deirdre had noticed that Barry Jones had 'accidentally' made physical contact with her on more than a few occasions.

'Well, I–'

He didn't allow her to continue. 'He obviously finds you very attractive.'

Deirdre took a sip of brandy. She didn't like what she was hearing.

'You're a clever girl, Deirdre. You could have Barry Jones any time you wanted.'

'I don't want Barry Jones, Gabriel!'

'You want another baby, though, don't you? I remember you said that, the day I proposed to you on Croagh Patrick. You talked about us making another baby, after Aoife. Unfortunately, I can't oblige. But I'm sure Barry would love to. He's a good-looking man, isn't he? You'd make beautiful babies together.'

'What?'

'You heard what I said, Deirdre.'

She felt as if she'd been slapped across the face. She went bright red and then she went white. 'Oh my God,' she said, getting to her feet very shakily. 'What are you insinuating, Gabriel?'

'Just an observation, darling. It's not the first time it's crossed my mind.'

'You said something about babies. I don't quite

understand. Am I being stupid here, or . . .' She couldn't continue.

Gabriel shrugged.

Deirdre felt sick, suddenly. 'Oh – oh God, Gabriel. I've got it wrong, haven't I? Tell me I've got it wrong. I can't believe what you're suggesting!'

'I wasn't aware that I was *suggesting* anything, Deirdre. As I said, it was just an *observation*.'

Her mind started to reel. Of course she was being stupid. Had she ever been anything else? Oh God, oh God – what had she *done* to herself? Why had her fairy tale gone so wrong? Where was her happy ending?

Even as the questions barraged her brain, she knew she had the answers. She had let herself be duped, that's what she'd done. She'd been convinced she'd been loved. She'd been convinced she'd been cherished. She'd been convinced she'd been needed. And she had been, she *had* been – until the day Aoife had been born. Then Gabriel Considine had had no reason to love or cherish her, and he hadn't needed her any more. How grotesque – to think that someone should have loved her out of *necessity*! That someone needed a *reason* to love her! There was only one person in the world who had loved her unequivocally for who she was, and she'd sacrificed that love the day she'd married the man who was sitting opposite her. The man who had taken her and moulded her into something she wasn't. Why had he done it? She remembered what he'd said to her once, nearly two years earlier, when she'd asked him if he was ambitious. *Yes*, he'd said. *I'm passionate about my work – I'm passionate about beautiful buildings.* Gabriel Considine cared more for his work than he did for her. He cared more for his house than he did for her. And he certainly cared more for his heritage than he did for her.

He spoke again. 'However, I think you'll concede that it's an observation which could have extremely positive repercussions for both of us if it were acted upon.'

Her voice, when she eventually found it, sounded as though it was coming from the end of a long tunnel, but she knew she was shouting. 'You want me to *fuck* your friend, Gabriel? You want me to conceive a baby with Barry Jones? You want me to *incubate* your heir! Are you out of your fucking mind?'

'Control yourself, darling,' said Gabriel, in a voice that sounded scarily calm. 'You're overreacting to what is, after all, a purely pragmatic solution to an increasingly problematic situation. We can be grown-up about this.'

Deirdre was shaking. If this was what being a grown-up was like she'd stay inchoate for ever.

'We both know that this marriage is on the verge of collapse,' he continued. 'Things just haven't been the same between us since your daughter was born.' *Your* daughter. Not *our* daughter. 'We *need* a son. I am prepared to connive at any indiscretion you may feel tempted to indulge in if it means saving this marriage.'

'Saving this *marriage*!' Deirdre's eyes were wide with shock and pain. 'You mean if it means saving the fucking Considine title from being scratched from Burke's Peerage! You hypocrite, Gabriel! You total fucking hypocrite!'

'Deirdre, you're not looking at this from the proper perspective. If–'

She rounded on him again. 'The proper perspective? So tell me – what is the *proper* perspective? You think it's *proper* to send your wife out to whore for you? Dear Jesus! I always thought I'd married a gentleman, Gabriel. You're not a gentleman, you're a fucking lowlife pimp.'

'How *dare* you call me that,' he said. He was standing now, and his face was white. 'How *dare* you call me lowlife. How *dare* you take the high moral ground! You, whose baby was the by-product of a dodgy condom on a one-night stand!'

She felt as if she'd been knifed simultaneously in the heart and in the gut. She hurled the brandy glass straight at his head, but he ducked in time and it ricocheted off the mantelpiece and landed on the floor.

'You're behaving like a fishwife, darling,' he said, calm again. He drained his own glass and set it down. 'I'm going to bed.' He started to move towards the door.

'Whose bed?'

He stopped and turned slowly back to her. 'What did you say?' he said.

It was Deirdre's turn to say, 'You heard me.' Her voice was as calm as his, now. 'I said, whose bed?

You don't have to lie to me any more, Gabriel. I know you've been fucking Tabitha.'

'I haven't been *fucking* her, Deirdre,' he said. 'I've been making *love* to her. And do you want to know why? I've been making love to that sweet girl because she's a million times closer to my ideal than you will ever be.' He put his hand inside the front of his jacket and slid a small photograph wallet out of the inside pocket. 'Do you want to see what the ideal woman looks like, Deirdre?' he continued. He opened the wallet and held it out towards her. She didn't want to look as he twisted the knife, but some awful impulse forced her to focus on the photograph before her eyes. She took in the image of a laughing girl in her early twenties. She had been caught off guard and was turning to the camera with a carefree expression, the wind lifting the glossy black wings of her Louise Brooks bob.

'Daisy,' said Deirdre.

'Daisy,' repeated Gabriel. Then he shut the photograph case with a barely audible click and walked out of the library.

*　　*　　*

The next morning, Deirdre awoke to find herself lying on the couch in the family room with a half-empty brandy bottle by her side and the television on. What was the television doing on? She struggled to remember. Of course. She had stuck the video of the Oscar ceremony into the VCR last night after

Gabriel had gone to bed, and then she'd hit the VSOP. She ran a tongue over her parched lips. Who had won? She couldn't remember and it didn't matter. The only thing that mattered was that Rory had rolled up at the ceremony with some looker on his arm, and it wasn't the same looker who had appeared in the photograph in *Hello!* magazine.

The tape would have rewound to the beginning. She picked up the remote control from where it lay beside her discarded shoes on the floor and pressed play. Glamour erupted onto the screen. She hit the mute button and then fast-forwarded. All the glitzy Hollywood main players strutted up the red carpet, looking silly. Then she saw him. She pressed pause, and then she pressed play. Rory was strolling up the carpet with a blonde hanging out of him. The blonde was making Bambi eyes at the camera; Rory was ignoring it. Then someone must have called his name, because halfway up the carpet he turned round. The camera zoomed in close. Deirdre pressed pause again. From the screen, Rory was looking directly at her. His expression was unguarded. There was no toothpaste smile for the Tinseltown brigade. He just looked incredibly lonely. She wanted to weep for him. She wanted to weep for herself. She even wanted to weep for Gabriel.

Just then the door opened and Tabitha came in with Aoife. 'Hello, darling,' said Deirdre, stretching out her arms to her daughter. 'Come and give me my morning hug.' Aoife trundled towards her on unsteady legs and allowed herself to be hugged.

Then she turned towards the television screen. 'That's your daddy,' Deirdre whispered in her ear. 'Going to a very important ceremony for actors.' She got to her feet. Her head was reeling, her body was aching. The emeralds in her ears felt as heavy as lead pellets.

She raised a hand and unhooked the right one. Then the left. She moved to the rosewood bureau that had belonged to Daisy and set them down neatly side by side on the polished surface. Then she unclasped the necklace from around her neck and laid it beside the pair of earrings. She rubbed her neck with firm fingers, digging them into the nape. It felt as if she'd been released from chains.

There was one last thing. Deirdre took off the ring that Gabriel had slipped onto her finger on the platform of the train station in Westport, and then she took off the wedding band he'd slipped onto the same finger at Murrisk Abbey.

'Tabitha?' she asked tiredly.

'Yes, Mrs Considine? Oh, lord – sorry! I mean – yes, Deirdre.'

'Could you keep Aoife amused for fifteen minutes?'

'Certainly,' came the bright response. 'Always happy to oblige.'

You bet, thought Deirdre darkly, as she climbed the stairs.

In the bedroom, she struggled out of her designer dress and hung it in the wardrobe. Then she had a quick shower and put on her jeans and a sweater.

Her old backpack was languishing in the back of the wardrobe. She stuffed some basic items of clothing into it, and then she went to the nursery and added as many baby clothes as would fit, as well as Aoife's changing bag and her favourite books and teddy. Tabitha came into the nursery with Aoife on her hip as Deirdre was buckling the bag. The housekeeper looked at her with uncertain eyes. 'Going somewhere?' she asked.

'Yes,' came the brusque response.

Tabitha obviously knew better than to try to grill her.

Aoife was transferred from Tabitha's hip to Deirdre's, and then Deirdre left the nursery without saying another word.

As she crossed the hall Gabriel came out of the library. 'Where are you going?' he asked in a toneless voice.

'Home,' said Deirdre.

*   *   *

There was Carrowcross Cottage nestled in its green hollow at the foot of the driveway, surrounded by blossoming pink weigela and ancient pines. The tide was in, and the surface of the water was covered in giddy white horses, which were being soundly whipped by the stiff breeze coming in from beyond the rocky headland. White clouds scudded over an impossibly blue sky, racing towards the purple mass of the mountain. Deirdre's heart started to sing. She strode down the driveway with Aoife on her hip, making the baby laugh out loud at each bumpy step she took.

She hung the backpack on the gate and made for the sea wall. Gabriel had never finished mending the boundary wall. He had never been able to find the time. In the end her mother had had to organize someone else to do it.

'Look at our view, Aoife!' she said. 'Look at all that loveliness!' Aoife sneezed and Deirdre laughed. 'That air you sneezed came straight in off the Atlantic, *acushla*! Oh – look! My otters!'

She pointed towards where the creatures were necking on the rocks over by Maura's island. The skeleton of the burnt barn had collapsed back into the moss-green blanket. She stood there for a long time, rocking the baby on her hip, and thinking the same thought over and over again: What am I going to do now? What am I going to do now? Where can I go? What will I be? *Who* will I be?

She realized that Aoife was twisting uncomfortably. Deirdre set the baby down and moved towards the cottage, fishing in her jeans pocket for the key. She let herself in through the verandah door and strolled through each room, opening windows. It would have to be tinned tomato soup and stale oatcakes for lunch. She'd give Eleanor a ring and see if she could bum a ride into town later in the day so that she could stock up. *She* might be able to survive on stale oatcakes, but Aoife couldn't. She balked at the idea of explaining her predicament to Eleanor, and then she balked again. She would have to phone her parents.

* * *

They arrived the next day. Mother and daughter stayed up half the night talking. Rosaleen was astounded to learn of Gabriel's behaviour. 'I feel as if I've been conned,' she said. 'I was very fond of my son-in-law. I thought he was such a charming individual.'

'He is,' said Deirdre. 'He can charm the birds off the proverbial trees.' They were sitting in front of the fire in the cottage with a bottle of good claret. 'It's not all his fault, you know, Mum. We were never right for each other. I should have known from the start that I was in love with his glamour, with the whole idea of Carrowcross House, with all that romantic, rose-tinted stuff. And Gabriel wanted someone he could mould into a trophy wife. The fact that I'm made of much more resilient stuff than he initially thought isn't his fault.'

A silence fell, and then Deirdre broke it with a sigh. 'Poor Gabriel,' she said. 'He'll be haunted by the ghost of Daisy for the rest of his life. I almost feel as sorry for him as I do for myself.'

'You don't look very sorry for yourself.'

'No. I suppose I don't. That's because I know I've done the right thing, Mum.'

'What will you do about Aoife?' asked her mother.

'I want custody,' said Deirdre, without hesitation.

'You said that very authoritatively.'

'I mean it. I don't want anything else from him. He can keep his jewels and his money and his furniture, but I want sole custody of Aoife.'

'What if he puts up a fight, my love?'

'He won't,' said Deirdre.

*　　*　　*

She decided to stay on at the cottage for a couple of weeks. She wanted to be on her own with Aoife for a while, until she could sort out what she was going to do with the rest of her life. She fretted about the financial side of things, but when her bank statement was forwarded to the cottage from Carrowcross House she was amazed to see that it was extremely healthy. That same day she walked up the driveway to find the Land-Rover parked at the top, with a note attached to the windscreen. It was from Gabriel. *We might as well try to be civilized about this, Deirdre,* she read. *While you're staying at the cottage you can keep the Land-Rover. I have lodged funds to your bank account, and will continue to do so until we get everything legally sorted. I imagine that I will hear from your solicitor in the near future. I will not contest. We both made a mistake. I am sorry for any hurt I have caused you. I did love you once. Kiss Aoife from me. Gabriel.*

The letter tugged at her heartstrings, but she did not weep.

*　　*　　*

About ten days later, she returned from a shopping trip with Aoife to find an envelope lying on the floor of the verandah – an air mail envelope with a United States stamp, addressed to her in Rory McDonagh's untidy handwriting. She stopped dead. Then she unlocked the door with surprisingly calm fingers, sat down on the steps, and opened the letter.

Oh, sweetheart, I am so sorry. I heard about the rift from Maeve. What can I say? We all make mistakes. I've made millions, and one of them was not writing to you the minute I heard you were marrying someone else, saying: *Stop! Don't do it!*

If it's any consolation, I think I may have found you an agent. Maybe you could come to LA to meet her? She's shit-hot, and she thinks she might be able to persuade the big boys to let a lady join their ranks. But I don't know what your plans for the future are. Maybe you've got other fish to fry? Anyway, you're welcome to come and stay here until you get yourself sorted – if that's what you want, of course. And it goes without saying that your little girl is more than welcome, too.

So if you want to do some real life now that the fairy tale bubble's burst (hang about – Hollywood? Real Life? Isn't that oxymoronic, O'Dare?) come and take this town by storm. Oh – one request only. Don't start power-dressing. Some women here are *frighteningly* unsexy.

Love, Rx

Deirdre looked over to where Aoife was sitting on the grass, happily chewing daisies. 'Hey, sweetheart!' she called over to her, laughing through her tears. 'How do you feel about meeting your dad?'

Aoife smiled back at her and waved a fistful of daisies.

* * *

Five weeks later, Deirdre found herself flying somewhere over the Irish coast in a jumbo jet heading west. Aoife was strapped in beside her, licking the Rescue Remedy her mother had rubbed onto her lips and talking to herself in fluent toddlerspeak. From time to time she laughed delightedly, as if particularly amused by one of her own jokes.

Deirdre wondered what lay beneath the cloud below. For all she knew they could be passing over Carrowcross House, or Croagh Patrick or Murrisk, where she had been married just over a year and a half ago. She remembered the tears that had rained from her eyes as Gabriel had slid the ring on her finger; the tears that had been prompted by Eva's recitation of the Dantë piece. Now, as she gazed out the window at the infinite blue of the horizon, she heard again the actress's incomparable voice in her head:

Midway, along this path of life we tread,
I woke bewildered in a dark wood
To find the road I knew was lost, misread:

No shaft of sunlight pierced to where I stood.
Old fears stir in my soul when I recall
Those dense black trees, night's sentinels,
That sullen, savage thicket blocking all,
A death rung slowly upon silent bells.
Some spiteful dreamchild must have lured me there
For sleep hung heavy in the drowsy air.
But I moved on, in blindness, through the maze
Till I emerged beneath a mountain's dawn
And looking up I saw the morning's rays:
This traveller's foot was on the road for home.

She looked down at the dog-eared letter which lay in her lap, and her eyes wandered to the postcript. *I will meet you at the airport*, she read. *Please do not forget to bring Hafner's sausages and that bra with the lacy straps I bought you ages ago. It was always my favourite. It was the easiest one to get off. Love as ever, Rx.*

THE END

IT MEANS MISCHIEF
by Kate Thompson

'More than enough colour to enliven even the dreariest day' *Irish Independent*

Young Dublin actress Deirdre O'Dare has just landed her first big role and desperately wants to shine – and to impress David, the director she has fallen madly in love with.

But while Deirdre loves David, David loves leading lady Eva. Meanwhile Sebastian and Rory wait in the wings . . .

A funny, entertaining and sexy backstage tale set in Dublin's theatre world, *It Means Mischief* details the romantic adventures of a young woman who – during one long, hot summer – discovers the difference between infatuation, lust and love.

'Unputdownable!' *Irish Post*

A Bantam Paperback
0553 81245 9

A SELECTION OF FINE NOVELS
AVAILABLE FROM BANTAM BOOKS

50329 4	DANGER ZONES	*Sally Beauman*	£5.99
40727 9	LOVERS AND LIARS	*Sally Beauman*	£5.99
50630 7	DARK ANGEL	*Sally Beauman*	£6.99
50631 5	DESTINY	*Sally Beauman*	£6.99
50326 X	SEXTET	*Sally Beauman*	£5.99
40973 5	A CRACK IN FOREVER	*Jeannie Brewer*	£5.99
50556 4	TRYIN' TO SLEEP IN THE BED YOU MADE		
		De Berry Grant	£5.99
40408 3	GONE TOMORROW	*Jane Gurney*	£5.99
50486 X	MIRAGE	*Soheir Khashoggi*	£6.99
40730 9	LOVERS	*Judith Krantz*	£5.99
40731 7	SPRING COLLECTION	*Judith Krantz*	£5.99
50719 2	THE LAZARUS CHILD	*Robert Mawson*	£5.99
81287 4	APARTMENT 3B	*Patricia Scanlan*	£5.99
40943 3	CITY GIRL	*Patricia Scanlan*	£5.99
40946 8	CITY WOMAN	*Patricia Scanlan*	£5.99
81289 0	MIRROR, MIRROR	*Patricia Scanlan*	£5.99
81288 2	PROMISES, PROMISES	*Patricia Scanlan*	£5.99
81286 6	FOREIGN AFFAIRS	*Patricia Scanlan*	£4.99
81290 4	FINISHING TOUCHES	*Patricia Scanlan*	£5.99
81245 9	IT MEANS MISCHIEF	*Kate Thompson*	£5.99
81246 7	MORE MISCHIEF	*Kate Thompson*	£5.99